Face Values

By the same author:

APOLLO'S SUMMER LOOK
TOMORROW'S FORTUNE
MY FATHER'S HOUSE
A TWISTED SKEIN
A MOVE IN THE GAME
A FORGOTTEN SEASON
CONSEQUENCES
THE BEST OF FRIENDS

Face Values

KATHLEEN CONLON

HODDER AND STOUGHTON
LONDON SYDNEY AUCKLAND TORONTO

British Library Cataloguing in Publication Data
Conlon, Kathleen
　Face values.
　I. Title
　823'.914[F]　　　PS6053.O455

ISBN 0 340 37215 X

Copyright © 1985 by Kathleen Conlon. First printed 1985. All rights reserved. No part of this publication may be reproduced or transmitted in any form or by any means, electronic or mechanical, including photocopy, recording, or any information storage and retrieval system, without permission in writing from the publisher. Printed in Great Britain for Hodder and Stoughton Limited, Mill Road, Dunton Green, Sevenoaks, Kent by The Thetford Press Limited, Thetford, Norfolk. Typeset by Hewer Text Composition Services, Edinburgh.

Hodder and Stoughton Editorial Office: 47 Bedford Square, London WC1B 3DP.

This book is dedicated to my
mother, Lilian Conlon, and to the memory
of my father, Bernard Patrick Conlon

1

Situation Vacant:
Private rest-home requires reliable responsible person for general duties. Full-time post. Live-in preferred.
Employment Wanted:
Thirty-one-year-old divorcee seeks full-time post, preferably with accommodation. Nothing to offer in the way of relevant qualifications, recent experience or outstanding aptitude, therefore (almost) anything considered.

The second of these announcements existed only in Elsa's imagination, the first one was advertised in the local paper. She'd bought a copy on her way back from the Job Centre which, she'd thought, having scrutinised the pathetically few vacancies on offer, might well be a candidate for prosecution under the Trades Description Act. "Bloody waste of time," the girl standing next to her had said. "They're shutting it down, this place. Bloody might as well."

She'd also said that the only work going was the sort of skivvying where they paid you a pittance out of the petty cash and no questions asked. By the time you'd shelled out for your bus fares, you'd be better off on the Social.

Elsa reread the advertisement. "Live-in" probably meant not only a licence to pay low wages but also that one was forever on call for whatever "general duties" turned out to be. Skivvying. For a pittance. But she queued outside the nearest telephone box all the same; beggars, as they say, tending to be severely restricted in the matter of choice.

A gum-chewing youth with a bad cold vacated the call box. The telephone receiver, moist from his grasp, caused an involuntary shudder as she picked it up. Certain squeamish traits died hard; at home she'd bought medicated pads with which she'd cleansed the telephone mouthpiece weekly. But "at home" was now a phrase entirely without personal relevance; and squeamishness would have to be suppressed, for to live cheek by jowl among strangers was to be exposed to their variously revolting personal habits. Whiskered cheek by elderly jowl – if she got the job. Priory Lodge was a rest-home for the elderly: "active elderly gentlefolk" the male voice at the other end of the line informed her. "Do you have any experience of care of the elderly?" it asked.

"Oh yes," she said, surprised that anything in her experience could be considered an asset.

"Right then," the voice said (a nasal voice, the refinement of its accent marred only by the occasional suspect vowel), "Mrs Speakman can see you for an interview at ten thirty tomorrow morning, if that suits."

Ten-thirty in the morning, three o'clock in the afternoon, or midnight, she was entirely at their disposal. She sat in a tea-shop, remembering when it had not been so, when life was structured and plans were made and ten thirty and three o'clock and midnight all had their special significance.

She strung out two cups of tea and a Penguin biscuit until the town hall clock struck five and then strolled back along the Promenade to the Highview Hotel at a pace so leisurely as to be scarcely describable as motion. How time had flown when, as a child, she'd spent her holidays in this seaside town: no sooner had she bolted her breakfast and raced down to the sands to grab a front-row seat for the Punch and Judy than it was time for lunch, and the blue dusks had always descended much too soon. Now the days were unstructured, free of obligation or pleasurable pursuit, and most of her energies were directed at discovering stratagems that might speed up the slow passage of the hours that intervened between waking and sleeping.

She climbed the stairs to her room. Grasses, arranged in a vase on a window-ledge, made her sneeze. The sneezes issued with the force of small explosions in the late-afternoon hush of the hotel. Hotel, they called it – boarding-house, more like. But since she'd spent her childhood holidays here they'd installed central-heating and double-glazing and avocado-coloured bathroom suites. And raised the prices. Even with "special out-of-season rates", her limited funds were being drained at an alarming rate.

Which was why it was necessary to find a job. Any job. She took off her shoes and stretched full-length on the duvet. Years ago they'd had rose-pink ruched eiderdowns and feather pillows that made her wheeze. "You'll grow out of it," her mother had said. She had, but they'd changed the agents of irritation anyway: duck down had given way to terylene, fibrous winceyette to polyester.

Change everywhere: the lifeboat house demolished and the Empire cinema gone over to Bingo, the sea-bathing lake concreted over, the wedding-cake Palace Theatre pulled down in favour of a bar and discothèque fashioned from tinted glass and breeze blocks. And where once the one-armed man had produced sand sculptures, adorning them with brightly-coloured bottle tops, there was now a caravan park. She'd returned, running from isolation and abandonment towards a remembered familiarity, but found only strangeness.

A stranger in a strange place. From her handbag she took her building society book and a street map. The former showed a series of debits, to which she would soon need to add another – how large and solid the sum had seemed, how quickly it had dwindled. The latter showed Priory Lodge to be situated towards the west of the town, among those huge Edwardian mansions that she remembered from her childhood, with their coach-houses and croquet lawns, their turrets and crenellations, their maidservants and chauffeurs. How many of them remained, she wondered, how much Accrington brick and Portland stone still stood solid between the double-glazing and the breeze blocks?

Only those that could somehow justify their continuing existences, she discovered next morning. "Geriatrica-on-sea" the bus driver called it. She walked along Rosedale Road, past block upon block of purpose-built flats surrounded by shaved lawns and regimented flower plots, and saw that the progress of the bulldozer had been halted only by the translation of some rich merchant's proud monument into the odd preparatory school, but more frequently rest-homes and nursing-homes: the Haven, Windsor Court, Ravenswood. It had always been a town that had attracted the prosperous for their retirement years. She remembered her parents joking about it during the annual week's holiday: "How about Rosedale Road when I'm pensioned off, eh girl?" "Oh yes. I'll polish up my tiara." But the impression now was of one vast antechamber to the grave.

The proprietor of Priory Lodge (Registered) was Mrs N. Speakman SRN and terms could be arranged for either short- or long-stay residents. Lions recumbent guarded the steps at the top of which two elderly ladies equipped with walking-sticks tested the outdoor temperature before embarking upon what was obviously, for them, a slow and painful descent. Elsa paused, unsure whether or not prospective employees were meant to use the front entrance. All situations in which she now found herself lacked precedent. Was a "general duties" person meant to creep humbly around to the tradesmen's entrance or to assume the sort of status that sent one boldly towards the stout and imposing front door? She was reminded of the anomalous position of Victorian governesses, out of place as much in drawing-room as servants' hall.

As she hesitated, the old ladies negotiated their descent with little grunts of effort and triumph. They were expensive old ladies with dark fur coats and carefully-waved silver heads. One of them nodded at her and smiled, the other looked at her curiously as though wondering why she loitered. Elsa braced herself, strode up the steps and rang the bell as firmly as her flagging determination would allow.

A woman of Mediterranean origin in a pink overall and with a duster in her hand opened the door and looked at her with that disconcerting me-no-savvy lack of interest that foreigners sometimes display.

"Mrs Speakman?"

The woman jerked her head and led the way through a large parquet-floored hall, past an open lounge where two old gentlemen rustled newspapers and an old lady massaged her bandaged knees, past a public telephone and a lift, to an office door upon which she knocked and then, without waiting for a reply, pushed open, ushering Elsa inside. "Meester Rodney," she said by way of introduction.

In a corner of the room a middle-aged woman tapped at a

portable typewriter. Behind a much larger, grander electronic version sat Mister Rodney, picking out letters with one finger. He did not get up. "Marguerita," he said, as the foreign woman began to close the door behind her, "Marguerita! I've been up to the second floor this morning and I am not happy about the bowls. I am very unhappy, Marguerita. If I have to tell you again . . . *Comprendo?*"

Marguerita mumbled in a Latin tongue and left while Mister Rodney revolved through half a circle in his revolving chair, looking consecutively at Elsa's legs, her breasts and her face. He raised his forefinger and rubbed at his lower lip. "Bone idle," he said, pleasantly, confidentially. "Give them an inch . . ." His finger continued to move, smoothing the soft pink flesh that pouted from beneath the dark moustache. He looked down at a piece of paper on the desk. "Mrs? Franklin."

"Miss," she said, "or Ms, I suppose." Impossible to say it without sounding arch.

He raised an eyebrow and then turned to the typist. "Muriel, I'll have my coffee now."

Muriel lifted her large and shiny-skirted bottom from her seat, smiled pleasantly at Elsa and left the room. Mister Rodney's massaging finger sought out his upper lip and then travelled to his eyebrow where it traced a delicate curve. "Well," he said. "Sit down." His eyes flickered, from her neck to her mouth and back again.

His had been the voice on the telephone. And, unusually in her experience, the voice and the appearance matched each other precisely. He wore a blazer and a striped tie which struck her as being as spurious as his accent. His dark hair waved, matinée idol fashion, over his forehead. Too much flesh blurred what might have been considered handsomeness – in the days when the standard for good looks was set by matinée idols. He couldn't have been much older than thirty but the impression he gave was of having stepped out of some pre-war intimate revue.

She checked that irritating tendency to elaborate which over the years had developed into an automatic habit: he was merely a man about to interview her for a job. Husband presumably to Mrs Speakman SRN.

Son. "Right, thank you, Rodney," said Mrs Speakman

SRN, entering briskly. "The builder is here and I want that damp patch on the gable-end pointing out *exactly* before he starts."

No spurious refinement here, but brisk, no-nonsense Lancashire. The disparity between her accent and that of her son (for he had to be son rather than husband: it wasn't just the obvious age gap that told you, but the peremptory way she spoke to him, coupled with the fondness in her eyes; a husband would have elicited one or the other but not both) was almost as marked as that between their respective appearances. His fleshiness translated itself into her bulk, his eye was liquid, hers small and bright and shrewd; he was an almost-handsome man whose gestures betrayed a strong sensuality, she was plain and moved with the awkwardness of a woman not at home in her own body.

Mrs Speakman was also no time-waster. Within five minutes she had elicited what information she required: Mrs, Miss, Ms? Franklin, though unable to produce a work record, or any qualifications more up to date than some thirteen-year-old A-levels, was well acquainted with the needs and requirements of elderly people, having cared for her ailing father until his recent death?

Quite so. Elsa had earlier debated the advantages of fabrication: imaginary jobs, glowing – if delayed – references, but her natural disinclination, coupled with this woman's obvious acuity deterred her from attempting falsehood. She felt that the woman would know, instinctively what was true and what was not.

It was obvious, too, that she realised how much the job was needed. That was why she could be so vague regarding the nature of "general duties"; why she could quote wages that were so low as to verge upon the unlawful; why her main concern was the alacrity with which Elsa could move her belongings into one of the attics and start work. Most people, to quote the girl in the Job Centre, would do better on the Social.

Most people, but not Mrs, Miss, Ms Elsa Franklin who needed a roof, a bed, and a breathing-space. She would transfer her belongings from the Highview and start the following day. One could safely conclude that other applicants had either failed to materialise or else turned rapid tail as soon as money had been mentioned. The interview was at an end. "Have you been divorced long?" asked Mrs Speakman, rising to indicate its conclusion.

"A few months."

"No children? I always think it's such a shame for the kiddies in these cases."

"No, no children."

Strange how still, after all this time, she had to think twice before answering that question.

2

"Bloody bitch," Marguerita said. "She do it deliberate."

"I forget," said Rosa, "I told you, I forget."

"You no forget. You do it deliberate."

She went, crashing and muttering, into the stillroom to fill the teapots. The coarse black hairs sprouting at the corners of her mouth bristled with indignation. Rosa, who was young and slim and pretty and vicious, giggled and stuck out her tongue. She had neglected to collect the supper trays from the second floor the night before which meant that Marguerita, who was on morning teas, had not only to do the collecting but also the washing-up before she could start on her rounds.

They exchanged insults in their respective tongues. No one else paid any attention. It was routine. It derived from the fact that Marguerita was Spanish and Rosa Portuguese. Apparently Spanish domestics considered Portuguese domestics to be the scum of the earth, and vice versa. They even went to Mass – same time, same church – separately.

Mrs Randall, the cook, edged gently-fried eggs with frilled edges on to the waiting plates. Norman, the kitchen porter, who was simple-minded, sniffed, wiped his nose on his apron and peeled potatoes.

Elsa buttered toast and removed crusts. Few of the residents could cope with crusts. It wasn't her job to butter toast. Her job was to arrange trays and place them into Marguerita's sturdy outstretched arms with clear instructions as to each one's destination, but Mary Reilly – whose job it was – hadn't turned in. Again. Which meant that her feller must have got plastered last night and belted her one. Everyone knew this to be the case even though Mary Reilly never admitted to it and bought the sort of green-tinted make-up intended for the concealment of broken veins in order to disguise her vari-coloured bruises.

Breakfast was always chaotic. There were, at present, only twelve residents but each of them had different requirements. By comparison, lunch and dinner were a doddle: set times and set menus. Nellie Macpherson, the dining-room waitress, could have them plonked down and cleared away in no time, practically before the last denture had clicked its appreciation of the Bakewell tart.

Even after a week Elsa was not yet entirely sure who was who, let alone who ate what. She consulted the typed sheet that Mrs Speakman had handed to her on her first morning. It was a list that appeared to be arranged in hierarchical order, residents of the first floor being accorded more attention and deference than those of the second, presumably because they were better off, better bred, or simply more punctilious in the matter of paying their bills. She rehearsed each of the names again, adding rudimentary descriptions as an aide-mémoire: first floor: Colonel Pritchard (tall, clean, mottled – kippers), Mrs Cuthbert-Carew (gnarled, aristocratic – grapefruit), Miss Vyner (arthritic, ex-Ministry of Works – All-Bran), Mrs Pegler (rich vulgar – bacon and egg and tomatoes), Mrs Booth-Powell – pronounced Po-elle (rich posh – poached egg), Mrs Pendennis (lovely bones, still good-looking, must have been a stunner in her day – Ryvita); second floor: Mrs Bannerman (a grey Buddha – toast and marmalade), Mrs Crookthorne (weasel-faced – eats everything going), Miss Johns (spinster, timid – All-Bran), Mrs Grey (widow, timid – muesli), Messrs Gentile (Italian, scarcely bilingual – porridge) and Golding (eyes everywhere – and hands too – sausages).

The first-floor residents might be more prosperous than their second-floor counterparts but it was a matter of degree: all were what Elsa's dad would have called well-heeled; the terms at Priory Lodge being prohibitive of entry to those who weren't.

"Your comfort is our aim," it said in the brochure and this undertaking was largely adhered to, even if the cost of that comfort was pared in all areas where economies might go unnoticed. After all, ancient taste-buds were past discriminating between cod and whiting, were none the wiser at the substitution of well-minced neck-end for shin; and a dollop of jam could successfully disguise the fact that the scone beneath it was margarined rather than buttered.

Age, Elsa had discovered, intensified the sweet tooth. Titbits, they craved, the old dears: jams and toffees and scoops of Neapolitan ice-cream. Like the children they'd once been they skipped the bread and butter to get to the cake and here there was no one to slap their greedy liver-spotted old hands to impose restraint.

Sweetness and warmth and scoring points off each other, these were their priorities. Fierce competition was entered into and successive strategies adopted for securing the seats nearest to the mock-glowing-logs electric fire; shifting alliances were formed depending on the nature of the vendetta. Mrs Booth-Powell was irritated by Miss Johns's twittering but joined forces with her to deplore Mr Golding's unnecessarily coarse tongue; Miss Vyner and Mrs Pendennis were at daggers drawn over the matter of the volume of the television set but backed each other to the hilt when it came to complaints about Mrs Bannerman's habit; all were united in condemning Mrs Pegler's commonness. Mrs Pegler was richer than any of them but it was money from the worst sort of trade and couldn't begin to compensate for lack of breeding. It was Mrs Cuthbert-Carew (not a great deal of the former but bags of the latter: purportedly the daughter of a hereditary peer) who was the acknowledged queen of their society, who elicited everything from due respect to outright, unashamed fawning.

And it was Mrs Cuthbert-Carew who telephoned down that morning to complain about her breakfast. Not only was it the wrong breakfast: juice instead of grapefruit, eggs poached in place of scrambled, but it was also stone-cold. Things were obviously going from bad to worse. Yesterday the breakfast, though wrong, had at least been hot. The temperature of the repast was not in question; Marguerita, sulking still, had dallied too long over her deliveries, but the order served was the order that had been placed. Yesterday too. Mrs Cuthbert-Carew was losing her marbles.

The loss of one's marbles, together with incontinence and

being in a non-ambulant condition, was sufficient reason to elicit a discreet request to vacate the premises, and Mrs Cuthbert-Carew had had more licence than most. Mrs Speakman had overlooked the biscuits crumbled beneath the pillow, the table-napkins removed from the dining-room and used as handkerchiefs, even the accident on the floor of the bathroom. She had overlooked these aberrations because the daughter of a hereditary peer was a definite asset to have at the head of one's guest list.

Marguerita gesticulated, waved the paper that had the order written upon it. "Is right. Bloody woman is barmy. She call me Bessie. 'Clean it up, Bessie,' she say after she shit in bathroom."

"Language!" said Mrs Randall, wincing as the juice from the grapefruit that she was segmenting spurted into her eye. Mary Reilly it was from whom the foreigners learned "shit" and "bloody bitch" and "kiss my arse".

"I'll take it," Elsa said. Easier to do that than to try and calm Marguerita's Latin hysteria.

She carried the tray up in the lift. It was an ancient contrivance, manually controlled: getting the bottom of it to coincide exactly with the floor was quite a feat – usually one had to make a giant stride upwards or downwards – and even if one was successful the machinery came to a halt with such a jerk that tea spilled, false teeth joggled and stomachs performed swallow-dives. "When are we getting a new one, Mrs Speakman?" the residents would ask plaintively as they waited, with varying degrees of patience, for Colonel Pritchard or a member of the staff to ferry them upwards and down. And Mrs Speakman would assure them that she was merely waiting for the workmen to commence. But the workmen seemed a long time coming.

"About time, Bessie," said Mrs Cuthbert-Carew, sitting bolt upright in bed and arranging her fox-fur cape about her shoulders. "Have you got it right this time?"

She lowered her eyes to the tray. Rheum trembled at their edges. Her dewlaps quivered. The remainders of lipstick in a crude shade of magenta were smudged across the puckered skin of her upper lip. Elsa looked away. Mrs Cuthbert-Carew had probably never been pretty, but even those who obviously had – Mrs Pendennis and Mrs Grey, for example – now demonstrated such a parody of womanhood: shrivelled breasts and pouched eyelids and balding scalps, that she instinctively looked away from them when serving their breakfasts in bed.

"Don't let it happen again, Bessie," Mrs Cuthbert-Carew chided. She fumbled on her bedside table in the general direction of the glass which held an improbably large upper denture submerged in Steradent. Liquid slopped on to the polished surface as she hooked out the plate and crammed it into her mouth. It was a very beautiful table: Japanese-lacquer-ornamented with bone and ivory carvings, and matched the wardrobe and the screen and the tallboy. Residents were allowed to furnish their rooms, to a limited extent; the very old, longest-stay ones seemed to have the shabbiest furniture. Had they too arrived with Japanese lacquer and rosewood? Were there attics crammed with antiques? How soon before Mrs Cuthbert-Carew found herself surrounded with utility veneers?

Elsa closed the door behind her and remembered Dad and his *News of the World* which so often featured cases of unscrupulous nursing-home proprietors defrauding confused geriatrics of their worldly goods. "The things that go on!" Dad used to say. "You won't put me in one of those places, will you, girl?"

"No, Dad. Never."

Not that I, or you, could afford it if I wanted to, and the rate at which Robert seems to be spending lately, we'll all end up in the workhouse, she'd thought.

She paused at the window at the end of the first-floor corridor. Blossom was breaking out in all the surrounding gardens: forsythia, flowering cherry, lilac. At home she'd put Dad's bed beside the window so that he could have the benefit of the signs of spring, but he had fretted: the lilac needed pruning, the tulips should be separated, the lawn fed and he, the only one who had the interest and skill to do it, was imprisoned in a body whose function was severely impaired. Sometimes he'd cried. "Best if I was out of it, girl. Best all round."

"Don't say that, Dad. Don't ever say that."

If you weren't here, she'd thought, what earthly reason would there be for Robert to stay?

"The weather's certainly picking up, isn't it?"

He had come behind her, soundlessly, Mister Rodney. She jumped a foot. Granted that thick-pile carpet and crêpe-soled shoes did not usually combine to make a noise, but he could have cleared his throat or something.

"Settling in all right?"

He joined her at the window. Together they watched Miss Vyner making her arthritic progress down the garden path. Hail, rain or shine, Miss Vyner never missed her constitutional. She didn't believe in old age getting you down; she belonged to the Soroptimists and the Business and Professional Women and exhorted other residents, who wanted nothing more than a seat by the fire where they could nod off to a background of *Saturday Night Theatre*, to bestir themselves. She was forever organising bridge evenings or beetle drives, arranging for concerts to be given by the local Orpheus Choir. Miss Vyner was an object lesson in triumph over adversity and generally considered to be a pain in the neck.

"Getting used to us?"

She was aware of Mister Rodney's breath on the side of her face. It was moist and warm, as you would imagine his handshake to be. He smelled bracingly of aftershave but one look at him and you thought of mouldering socks and cheesy underwear.

"Yes, thank you."

Though a week was scarcely long enough for her to have found her bearings. She'd just about grasped the job specification: she worked split shifts with one day off per week. She was responsible for supervising the meals, overseeing the cleaning, dealing with the laundry, arranging the flowers, checking the menus, reordering the stores, answering the residents' bells and taking their telephone messages – and turning her hand to anything else that cropped up. General dogsbody, in fact. For which she received bed and board and thirty-seven pounds fifty per week. "Wages Council," Mary Reilly had muttered darkly, but knew that she was lucky to have a job, what with her erratic time-keeping and her last address which had been HM Prison, Styal.

"If this goes on," said Mister Rodney, edging imperceptibly closer, "we'll be on the beach in our bikinis."

"Rodney!" came the clarion call from the other end of the corridor. Rodney flushed and turned to face his mother, now approaching with stately tread. Strange how you'd noticed – even in the space of a week – that wherever Rodney was, his mother was never far behind. Nellie Macpherson said that it was nice to see a mother and son so devoted, Mrs Randall said he was a big soft jessie, spoiled to death, while Mary Reilly, ascerbic as always, claimed that he reminded her of a rapist her feller had shared a cell with while on remand at Risley.

"Rodney, I want you to check that those builders are using a proper thickness of cement for the rendering. And that guttering at the front looks very precarious to me."

Mrs Speakman consulted the little gold watch she wore, nurse-fashion, pinned to her bosom. She must have made a good nurse – in terms of efficiency, at least. Even now, pushing sixty, her stamina was remarkable: hers was the first bed to be vacated in the morning, hers the last light to be extinguished at night. She spent her time, it seemed, absorbed in the day-to-day running of the establishment, but nothing passed beneath its roof of which she was not aware. "Eyes in her bum," Nellie Macpherson said. Normally, in places like these, you could rely on a bit of knock-off: a bag of sugar, half a pound of butter, a few vacuum-sealed packs of marmalade. Not here, though. More than the job was worth. She didn't know why she stuck it. Pernickety old devils, they were, and mean! "Tight as arseholes," Mary Reilly said and Nellie Macpherson agreed. "I don't know why I stick it," she said, smoothing her starched apron over her atrophied womb, adjusting her elastic stocking.

But she did. And so did everyone else. Too old now for the big white hotels on the Front; *they* wanted bits of kids they could dress up as Nell Gwyn or Scottish dancers, nippy on their feet and nice to look at.

"Doctor's due this afternoon," said Mrs Speakman. "Perhaps you'd see to tidying the Gloucester Room."

Each of the public rooms had been christened with the name of a royal duke: lunch and dinner were taken in the Lancaster Room, the quiet lounge was the Kent; the Gloucester was where they watched television. Although many of them had their own portable sets in their rooms they still preferred to gravitate towards the Gloucester Room where they could quarrel about the choice of channel and the volume selected. Miss Johns, the rector's daughter, was avid for sex and violence, whereas Mrs Booth-Powell abhorred the merest "bloody"; Miss Vyner (deaf, but deriving benefit from a hearing-aid) would hobble across and change the position of the volume knob at which Mrs Pendennis (deaf, but unable to cope with a hearing-aid) had set it, while Mrs Pegler always chose to start a conversation at a critical moment in the twice-weekly soap opera.

Once a month, apparently, "Doctor", as Mrs Speakman called him, made his rounds and the Gloucester Room was transformed into a surgery. And so, the visit now imminent, Elsa tidied away the copies of the *TV Times*, collected up bags of knitting, the odd walking-stick and pair of reading-glasses, and the discarded *Mails* and *Telegraphs* which she carried through to the kitchen. Mrs Randall liked a scen at the *Mail* – a more refined sort of paper. Norman had abandoned his potato-peeling in order to drool over Page Three of the *Sun* that one of the workmen had left behind. Slowly he drew the newspaper towards his face and kissed each magnificent breast, then laughed his high shrieking hyena-like laugh and made a gesture with his left hand and right forearm which was a not-quite accurate copy of the gesture that the workman had made.

"Go on," Mary Reilly said. "You wouldn't know what to do with it."

He shrieked louder. Slobber dripped from his chin. Mrs Randall spoke sharply: "Stop it now, Norman, getting yourself overexcited. Or else I'll be telling your mum."

He sobered up immediately and shambled off to the swill-bins.

"And what time do you call this, Mary Reilly?"

"I call it half nine. What do you call it?"

She took off her mac and turned to face them. She sported a real shiner, purple still; it had closed her right eye.

"You want your head examining," Mrs Randall said. "No man'd do that to me more than once."

"No man'd want to," said Mary Reilly – she displayed

her bruise almost proudly, as though it was a love mark, as though for her (as Miss Johns, the rector's daughter, suspected) sex and violence were interdependent – and of course that started the second row of the morning. But that was routine too, as much a part of the day as the sizzle of eggs frying or Norman leering over Page Three or Mrs Cuthbert-Carew ringing down to complain that she had been served with the wrong breakfast.

"A common thief," Mrs Randall said. "Worse than a pro. I don't think your neck's seen soap since the midwife washed it."

"Fuckin' old cow," said Mary Reilly. "At least I've got a feller. I don't polish 'em off like you." Cruel reference to Mrs Randall's two consecutive states of widowhood.

"Why, you dirty-mouthed bitch – "

But by lunchtime they'd have forgotten all about it and Mrs Randall would be telling Mary Reilly that perhaps she ought to show that eye to Dr Rees while he was here.

Long before he was due the residents had begun to assemble in the hall. It was their monthly treat, equivalent to the visit from the chiropodist, the fortnightly shampoo and set with Tony and Jackie, the trip to the library. Of course you could call the doctor privately at any time but you had to be able to produce some convincing symptom of illness for that, whereas once a month you could trot out your aches and pains and your worries as of right. Only Miss Vyner, who despised self-indulgence in any shape or form, Mr Gentile, who was terrified that medical examination might confirm his suspicion that he had caught a venereal disease from a girl in Cairo in 1938, and Mrs Cuthbert-Carew, who paid for the attentions of the family physician, were missing. Miss Vyner passed by the queue on her way to her university extension lecture and sniffed loudly. Hypochondriacs all. The only way to deal with illness, in her opinion, was to ignore it, to prove to be such an inhospitable host that it would pack its bags and leave.

Elsa followed in her wake. She would go upstairs to her attic, change her clothes, collect her sketch-block and make for the headland. She had been advised to spend her free time away from the place or else she'd soon find that she didn't *have* any free time.

But this afternoon she wasn't quick enough. At the foot of the stairs – her escape route – Mrs Speakman stood deep in conversation with a tall grey-haired man who nodded his head rapidly and kept consulting his watch impatiently. "Oh Elsa . . ." Mrs Speakman said, turning. Her smile was wide and bright and as artificial as her teeth. "I wouldn't ask, but . . ."

Dr Rees usually brought a nurse along. This afternoon there wasn't one available, and a female presence was desirable just in case some old trout took it into her head to accuse him of interfering with her. Perhaps a couple of hours off tomorrow, in lieu?

"I'd step into the breach myself," Mrs Speakman said, "but I've an appointment to show someone round in half an hour. Of course, if any of the residents object it'll have to be postponed . . ."

Some of them did, but on the whole they preferred Elsa's presence to having to wait another week, even though Dr Rees wasn't a patch on old Dr Meredith whom he'd replaced. No *manner* with him, they said.

He certainly lacked charm, Elsa thought, as she stood beside the table that he was using as a desk, feeling very foolish indeed, praying that no one would request an intimate examination. Arthritis and arteriosclerosis were chief among the complaints; pains, vague or localised, restricted mobility, giddiness and indigestion were the symptoms most commonly described. He listened to their meanderings with what seemed scant attention, brusquely requested that they roll up their sleeves for their blood-pressure readings, pulled down their lower eyelids and released them without comment. Repeat prescriptions for Benoral, Mogadon, Gastrocote, Ferrogradumate, were issued, interviews concluded peremptorily. Miss Johns received no encouragement when reciting the vivid history of her allergies; Mrs Pendennis who had hesitantly mentioned a certain slothfulness in the region of the lower intestine was advised tersely that exercise would work wonders; Mrs Crookthorne who had wandered off the subject of health on to that of money (so closely related, anyway) was deeply offended when, having explained the problem of living on a capital sum, she was presented with the retort that should she outlive the money, she could always jump off one of the third-floor balconies.

It had been meant as a joke – but unaccompanied by an appropriate jocularity of manner, it didn't come across that way. His strong Welsh accent didn't help either: that lilt always made it seem as though you were being mocked. Mrs Crookthorne left the room. Her dudgeon had probably never been higher.

"Is that the lot?"

Elsa looked into the hall. The chairs were empty. He had seen the men first: Colonel Pritchard with his propensity to renal calculi, and Mr Golding's veins. Her presence had not been required for them; presumably they were not likely to make allegations concerning impropriety.

"There's no one else there."

He folded away his stethoscope and his blood-pressure gauge and stacked them in his case. In one fluid movement he snapped it shut and handed her a sheaf of prescriptions. "They usually have them collected," he said, "except for one or two who enjoy the outing. Are you new?"

She nodded and he grimaced: presumably to indicate that she was welcome to her job. She saw that he wasn't as old as she'd at first judged him to be – probably not more than middle to late forties, and that the angularity of his features perhaps misled one into thinking him overstern.

"God forbid," he said, lifting his case from the table, "that one should outlive one's capital."

Elsa thought of Mrs Crookthorne waking up one fine morning and saying, "Sod it! The money's all spent and I should have died last night," and she laughed out loud.

"Most of them are short of something to worry about."

His lip curled; his accent thickened. Welsh chapel, she thought, back-of-beyond, nonconformism, poverty, joylessness, never a self-indulgence to ease the long hard road to the college. No wonder he found those pampered old dears so hard to take.

"That's it then," he said. "Unless *you* need anything?"

He said it jokingly: she wasn't even registered. And, besides, what she needed you couldn't get out of a bottle. She'd already tried that.

3

On Easter Monday Norman threw the most dramatic of what Mrs Randall called his wobblers: one minute he was talking to himself quite peaceably as he scoured out the saucepans, the next he was howling and hurling crockery to the ground. Rosa and Marguerita cried out and crossed themselves while Mary Reilly ducked, quipping that in the course of answering himself back he must have said something that offended. Mrs Randall ran outside and requested the assistance of one of the workmen who was doing a foreigner and pointing the brickwork, and together they managed to pinion his arms to his sides and jam him against the wall while Mrs Speakman summoned first the doctor and then his mother. Colonel Pritchard, attracted by the commotion, poked his head around the kitchen door and commented that he'd seen a great many dos like that among the men out east; "going troppo" they had called it.

Dr Rees's locum arrived eventually and after administering a tranquillising shot, called an ambulance to take Norman to the local mental home whence his mother – who didn't turn up for about an hour, the bank holiday public transport being so irregular – was directed.

These attacks and Norman's subsequent hospitalisation were fairly regular in their occurrence, his mother – a fat woman with the flabby grey face of the heart-sufferer – confided to Elsa and the rest of the kitchen staff. Most of the time he was quite happily subnormal – hardly fratched at all – then, for no apparent reason, something would snap and he'd go temporarily berserk and need a couple of months in the Clement Attlee Ward to put him right again.

All very well, said Mrs Speakman, who had come into the

kitchen in time to catch the tail-end of this explanation, but it put her on the spot. She was understaffed as it was. And you couldn't get help easily at such short notice.

Mary Reilly shovelled up broken crockery. "I hope she doesn't think I'm putting in more hours for the same money," she said, after Mrs Speakman had left. "She can shove her job up her fat arse."

But Mary Reilly lived out and was unobtainable by telephone. If there were extra duties they fell to the resident staff and, as the only other resident staff were Rosa and Marguerita who had the advantage of being able to feign incomprehension, they usually fell to Elsa.

"She'll have to get somebody," Mary Reilly said. "She can't expect you to do the heavy work. Or else she'll have to tell that creep of a son of hers to roll his sleeves up."

But Mister Rodney did not perform manual duties. His physical exertion consisted of chauffeuring his mother to the bank or the accountant or the cash-and-carry. And a couple of times someone had seen him out on the sandhills with a pair of binoculars, supposedly bird-watching, but more likely spying on the courting couples.

"I don't see why you're doing a job like this, anyway," Mary Reilly continued. "I expect you were a college girl, weren't you? I'd of expected you to work in an office. Receptionist, something along those lines," Mary Reilly said, as they walked together along the Front towards the house where she and her feller had a room. Elsa, whose day off it was, had bumped into Mary Reilly in the shopping mall and been invited back for a cup of tea. Though she hadn't wanted to accept, Elsa had done so for fear of offending; Mary Reilly, offended, could be very unpleasant indeed.

As they walked, she pointed out the various hotels that she had worked in, described the goings-on. Here, she'd spent last summer in the stillroom until she'd had to leave because the assistant manager was always groping her; there, she'd been taken on as a chambermaid, only to find herself thrown on to a bed and practically raped by an importunate male guest during her first week.

"Bloody men," she said wonderingly. "If my feller had ever got to hear of it he'd have lamed them."

It was possible, Elsa supposed – she was probably not much more than thirty-five and, without the disfiguring bruises, might be considered attractive in a ripe, coarse sort of way – but she suspected fabrication, and wondered if the bruises could be due to the fact that "my feller" *had* been informed, in a deliberate attempt to make him jealous.

He was away for a couple of days, visiting his mam in Nottingham; she was poorly with this illness that made you swell up and your head loll to one side. Or so he said. "If I find out that he's back to his old tricks," said Mary Reilly, fumbling for her key, "I'll swing for him."

Elsa breathed in at the threshold of the room, and then tried not to breathe in again, too deeply, for the duration of her stay. The smell was an almost solid entity and derived from a variety of sources: insufficient ablution of both human body and habitation, the smoke from countless cigarettes, an unvaried diet of fried food, windows left unopened, and – perhaps most pervasive of all; certainly the most visually sickening – a long-unemptied tray of cat litter in the corner.

Once inside it was impossible to refuse the offer of a cup of tea and to drink at least a drop of it, though the teacloth with which the cup had been dried looked as though it doubled as a duster. Mary Reilly fondled the tabby cat that blinked nervously before settling to lick at the balding, mange-mite-infested patches on the inner surface of its thighs.

"He's as narky as hell, these days, Des. It's with being skint. It takes away your self-respect. Half the time he can't be bothered to shave himself, and if I say a wrong word he's up in a minute, shouting and blaggarding. Still," she said, "what can you expect, banged up in here, day in, day out? It's as bad as the nick. We've put our names down with the council. Some hope! It isn't as if he hasn't tried for work. You've no chance when they find out you've done time."

"*You* managed to get a job."

"Oh sure. Whoever else would she get, the old cow?"

After a moment Mary Reilly realised that she might have been tactless. She pushed back the swathe of stark-black dyed hair from her forehead in a gesture of embarrassment. "Look, I didn't mean . . . I expect if it wasn't for you being divorced . . . What did he do, *your* old man?"

"He made furniture, tables and chairs and so forth. Until the business went bust."

"Funny, isn't it? You wouldn't have thought, with a trade in his hands, he'd have gone down."

Ah, but his furniture was beautiful: handcrafted, slow in the making, expensive. However, it took off; there were customers queuing for it. He employed other craftsmen, bought new premises. The VAT man entered our lives. Secretaries were employed, distant orders dispatched. Money was made, even more was spent. We put Dad into a cripplingly-expensive nursing-home for a month and toured the Greek Islands. Then the trend really took off and the big concerns stepped in, churning out the cheap imitations upon their factory lathes, filling their high street store windows with enticing displays. At first only those who couldn't distinguish veneer from solid wood were attracted, but soon investment and development enabled them to produce the real thing – albeit of inferior quality – at competitive prices. The world and his wife flocked to the shrewdly-situated, brightly-coloured emporia and the self-assembly outlets. And instead of behaving cautiously, the firm attempted to spend its way out of trouble while the VAT man adopted a persecutory mien. Distraint warrants were issued; the bailiffs prepared the way for the official receiver. And my old man grew thin and shouted in his sleep and bit his nails down to the knuckle and, eventually, saw a chance of salvation and took it.

"You're better off without," Mary Reilly said.

How sweet the outdoors tasted, the salty air overlaid as it was with the odours of fast food manufacture. But then an area populated with glue factories or gas-works would have been an improvement upon the rancid vapours that circulated in Mary Reilly's bedsit. Having made her escape, Elsa walked quickly away from the cafés and the funfair and the amusement arcades, down by the side of the Floral Gardens and along the sea-wall to the marsh road where, they said, Rodney Speakman satisfied his voyeuristic appetites.

"An Easter this forward," they also said, shaking their heads ruefully; it boded ill for the rest of the season: too good, too soon. But the weather held: a sky cobalt-blue and cloudless stretched tight over the horizon and the wind was warm. Young men wore those sort of sleeveless tee-shirts that exposed the muscle at the top of their arms and flaunted their premature suntans. Children on holiday from school dug in the sand. Elsa leaned on the edge of the parapet, watching the stumbling grace of their movements, listening to their shouts that were carried away on the wind and out to sea. "I was married, one time," Mary Reilly had said. "I had a couple of kids. They're in care. In Liverpool. St Theresa, the Little Flower, the home's called. I was born a Catholic, you know, and I had both of them done. The boy though, Wayne, well he wasn't my husband's. I'd never have let on if he hadn't been the wrong colour. He's thirteen. I think he might turn out to be a boxer. That's what his dad was . . ." Her eye grew cloudy with reminiscence. "I visit them sometimes, of a weekend, take them presents."

"Don't you miss them?"

"You can't let it get you down," Mary Reilly had said, as though one might have some choice in the matter.

Elsa found a seat, took her sketch-pad from her bag and turned her back upon the children who gambolled and shrieked on the sands below. The roofs of the hotels along the Front made a pleasing pattern upon the skyline. Pen and ink would be the appropriate medium and she had only charcoal – much too imprecise for her purposes, but she persevered. Perhaps she would be able to return tomorrow afternoon, hoping to find the same seat vacant. Although, as the season got into its stride, she would find peaceful out-of-doors seclusion harder and harder to come by. In fact, she realised with sinking heart as the bicycling figure approaching along the causeway came into clearer focus, it was starting already.

"Oh I say," Muriel Selby said, steadying herself with one foot on the ground as she brought her sit-up-and-beg to a halt, "that *is* good. Hidden talent! My friend Hilda draws, you know. She has tuition from a Mr Bernard Jones. He has a studio above Freeman, Hardy and Willis. Lots of local artists go there and every so often they have exhibitions. Hilda nearly sold her Langdale Pikes. She would have done if it had been hung in a better position." She breathed in and out exaggeratedly as though sea-air was quite a novelty and not a constant factor of her environment: rusting up her bicycle wheels, corroding the aluminium window-frames at Priory Lodge.

Muriel was on her way home after a day's typing at the Lodge to the flat above the dry cleaners' in Station Road that she'd shared with her friend Hilda for the last fifteen years, ever since Mother died.

"Got a lovely bit of rump in the market," Muriel said, fumbling among the various soggy parcels in her handlebar basket. "Look!"

She drew back the greaseproof paper to display the slab of meat, juicily red with its frill of yellow fat. Hilda had a good appetite and needed plenty of protein; she was always on the go. When not engaged in teaching gymnastics to the daughters of gentlefolk at St Monica's, she was hefting her easel and watercolours around the more clichéd of the beauty spots, or else exhausting Chappie, their West Highland terrier, by dint of marathon walks along the beach. Sometimes you wished she'd slow down for a minute or two. But only sometimes. "Don't worry, Mrs Selby," Hilda had said at the terminal bedside in Ward B, "don't worry, I'll look after Muriel," and Mrs Selby had smiled, emitted the death-rattle and died.

"Well," said Muriel, lifting one brogued foot on to her pedal, "best push on. Else I won't half get what for. Oh I say, isn't that Dr Rees's wife?" She shaded her eyes with her hand and peered across the Kiddies' Paddling Pool and the Ornamental Gardens to the Promenade where a few early holidaymakers strolled. "Look, there, in the forecourt of the Metropole."

Elsa, unaware that Dr Rees had a wife, let alone familiar with her appearance, was unlikely to be able to offer corroboration but nevertheless followed Muriel's pointing finger. There seemed to be something of a scuffle taking place on the hotel's forecourt. A woman was attempting to get into a car and two men, one in porter's livery, the other dressed in the morning-coat and pin-stripes of manager's attire, were quite obviously attempting to prevent her from doing so.

For a moment or two they wrestled beside the parked car, a dark-blue open-topped sports model and then the woman seemed to slump against its bumper and the man in the pin-striped trousers put his hand on her arm and ushered her gently towards the hotel entrance. "Can't *see* properly," Muriel complained, going cross-eyed in the attempt to bring the scene into clearer focus.

Elsa, however, could see all right. The woman in question was tall and slender. She wore a pale silk suit that matched her pale-blonde hair and carried a handbag which she occasionally swung threateningly in the direction of one or other of the men.

"Looks like she's making a show of herself again," Muriel said, her face sagging with disappointment as the three of them disappeared inside the hotel.

"Oh?"

Elsa had wanted to be left alone to finish her sketch before the light changed, but gossip was always hard to resist no matter how little you knew of its subject, and cared less.

"She's notorious," Muriel said. "Can't keep off it, apparently. They say she goes off on these cures but they don't seem to do her any good. I can't imagine how he manages to hold his head up. Last winter I believe they had a real hammer and tongs at the golf club dinner-dance. Had to be dragged off each other, swearing like troopers. You wouldn't think a woman of her background would use that sort of language, would you? Finishing schools and I don't know what. Her father made his money from marmalade. Owned half the town at one time. Course, that'll be the trouble – spoiled to death. She'll have been trying to drive home," Muriel said, "that'll be it. In that condition! And they'll have been trying to persuade her to take a taxi. She's known everywhere. Course, *he* puts up with it for the money. Cripes!" she said, consulting her watch and then looking up accusingly as though Elsa had been responsible for detaining her. "Is that the time? I'll get shot. Ta ta for now. See you on a seesaw." And with that, Muriel swung a stout thigh across her saddle and pedalled off, hell for leather, to regale Hilda with the story, no doubt.

Elsa persevered with her drawing until a dishevelled man – obviously the local lunatic – sat down next to her and told her that he was Jesus Christ Risen and had she noticed the

Russian spies lurking behind the sand dunes? His imprecations followed her as she walked away from him: "Whore! I hope you get killed in a train crash."

A local character, as familiar in the town as the station clock, the copper dome of the observatory, pointed out to the visitors in the same way that landmarks were indicated. Mrs Rees, by the sound of it, was just another of them: a good laugh, a free cabaret turn, her doings gossiped about and then forgotten. Unless, of course, you happened to be married to her.

4

Sunday tea at the Priory differed from the weekday repast in that cream cakes were served instead of what Mrs Randall called assorted fancies: sawdusty sponge cakes coated with violently-coloured icing and somewhat on the stale side – Mrs Speakman having an arrangement with a local confectioner to relieve him of his leftover stock at a special discount price.

The cream cakes were on account of the guests rather than the residents, for, if visitors came, they usually came on Sunday. Elsa cleared away tea things, trying not to eavesdrop. Though as there weren't many guests, there were few conversations to be intruded upon.

There never were many visitors. Relatives usually collected the old dears and extended their hospitality over the Christmas period, a couple of days at Easter and a week later on in the year. Surely they thought, conscience pangs righteously pacified, that demonstrated sufficient family feeling to avoid being cut out of wills. Only Mrs Cuthbert-Carew's family and Mrs Booth-Powell's son and daughter-in-law visited on a regular basis. Miss Vyner's friend from Chester drove over about once a month and Mrs Pendennis entertained what appeared to be an ancient beau at roughly the same sort of intervals, but the rest took a tea as devoid of congenial companionship as it was during the rest of the week, and had to rely for comfort on the superior cream cakes.

"Finished, Colonel?"

She had to tap him on the shoulder because he had his Walkman switched on and was beating time on the arm of his chair. When he'd first moved in he'd brought his gramophone and his record collection. Military music, it was, and it needed to be played loudly to obtain the proper effect, even if you weren't slightly deaf, which the Colonel had been ever since El Alamein. But complaints, some of them alarmingly ferocious – Mrs Booth-Powell had threatened to smash the records about his ears – had silenced him. He'd moped about for weeks until that queer cove Golding had pointed out these handy little gadgets in Rumbelows as they were walking back together from the Railway Tavern. Now he was as happy as a pig in muck, *Blaze Away* blazing away directly and exclusively at his auditory nerve; well, as happy as he could be since Maud went.

Elsa cleared away Mrs Pegler's cup and saucer and glanced admiringly at her handiwork. Mrs Pegler knitted with the ease and seeming inattention of the skilled craftswoman. She knitted amazingly intricate Fair Isle sweaters, gossamer-fine christening robes, exquisite layettes. Periodically, huge parcels were packed and dispatched to Ontario or New South Wales or Johannesburg; her three sons had separately taken off for new lands where their low-class antecedents would not prove to be a disadvantage. "Dad and I," Mrs Pegler said, expertly turning the heel of a minute baby boot, "we always loved Torquay. The Palace Hotel. Every year. The head-waiter always kept the same table for us. He was always that pleased to see us . . ." Her needles clicked, the diamonds crammed on to her podgy fingers caught fire as the shaft of sunlight changed its position. "I'll bet he was always pleased to see you," Mrs Crookthorne muttered sarcastically; she had the keenest pair of ears in the place and the strongest aversion to Mrs Pegler's impressive display of wealth: you could bet your bottom dollar *she* didn't lie awake at night worrying about the interest rate.

Elsa was not able to clear the table occupied by Mrs Cuthbert-Carew and her two granddaughters because the granddaughters were still stuffing their faces. "By the way, Grannie," said the larger one, sucking cream loudly from each of her fingers in turn, "thanks awfully for the postal order."

Mrs Cuthbert-Carew, who had not been partaking of food but rather gazing abstractedly at the opposite wall, slowly turned her head until her granddaughter's face came into view. She looked momentarily bewildered and then recognition established itself and she said, "What did you buy with it, dear? Something for your pony?"

"No," said her granddaughter, "I bought an LP."

Mrs Cuthbert-Carew looked mystified. Mrs Crookthorne who had attached herself to the fringe of the group in the hope of catching crumbs from the aristocratic table provided the translation: "Long-player, Mrs Cuthbert-Carew. Records, you know."

"Oh, Cliff *Richard*," Mrs Cuthbert-Carew said in the satisfied tones of one who has received perfect enlightenment, at which her granddaughters rolled about their armchairs in an ecstasy of mortified mirth.

"Cliff Richard, Cliff *Richard*," they moaned when at last they were capable of comment. "Oh, *Grannie*."

"Cliff Richard's very old hat," said Mrs Crookthorne, fairly smugly. "It's all Duran Duran and Boy George now."

They gazed at her, round-eyed, not unimpressed.

"Oh, Simon," breathed the larger of the two.

"As if Simon would look twice at you with your fat bum," the smaller one said, unwrapping a Mars bar and sinking her braced teeth into it.

Mrs Cuthbert-Carew kept blinking her eyes and shaking her head but neither of these actions served to disperse the fog that seemed to have got inside it. Two big fat pubescent girls sat beside her, stuffing their faces with sweetmeats. Perhaps one of them was Bessie. She hadn't seen Bessie for years and years, ever since – when was it? The fog wrapped itself round the connections in the circuits of her memory. Bessie? Who was Bessie? She closed her eyes, squeezing the lids together, trying so hard to focus her concentration while, unbeknown to anybody, small haemorrhages seeped within her skull.

"That would be so nice," Mrs Pendennis commented to her elderly admirer Roland Machin. "Yes dear, thank you, we've finished," she said to Elsa and leaned sideways to allow the table to be cleared. This enabled her to move her profile through ninety degrees while touching her throat with a slender forefinger. But it was from habit. She wouldn't have wanted Roland Machin with his turkey neck and mottled nose to come hither. How dreadfully unprepossessing old men were.

He'd been so good-looking once, one of the many men with whom she'd almost had an affair.

"We could go up to the Lakeside," Roland Machin droned on, "have some lunch. Do you remember, Marion?"

He quivered with emotion. When he was thirty-five he'd arranged to meet her there for a stolen weekend, an idyll; Jack Pendennis was away fighting the Japs. He'd waited for an eternity, not accepting until the last that she wouldn't show up.

"That would be nice," she said, stroking a curl back into place, "if it wasn't for my wretched hay-fever." She'd forgotten all about that broken date, of course; the promises she'd made. Oh, how *old* he was: his bottle-nose and that ridiculous bow tie. He'd looked at her like a dog all those years ago. How pretty she'd been. Why, oh why, did it have to fade? It wasn't even as if the photographs did her justice.

"We'll have to be going now, Grannie," chorused the scions of the Cuthbert-Carew family. They stood over her, reiterating their farewells. They were such a drag, these Sunday visits. "For God's sake, Leo, she's practically senile," Mummy kept saying but Daddy insisted.

She waved a hand in their general direction, anxious that they should be gone. They overpowered her, they breathed the air that she needed so desperately in order to clear her head. The creeping fog spread its clammy tentacles across the screen of her consciousness. Somewhere, at the edge of it, a wraith beckoned, beseeching to be remembered.

"Now take care, Gertie," Miss Vyner said, struggling to her feet to escort her friend from Chester to the door. "No speeding, now."

"Chance would be a fine thing," Gertie remarked, pulling on her driving gloves. Damn thing was falling to pieces, you couldn't get more than sixty at full throttle, it'd never get through the MOT and there wasn't a hope of raising the cash for the repairs. I should have married, Gertie thought, while I had the chance. I could have spent my declining years like some of these old dolls: totting up my share certificates, sending for my accountant, scrutinising my dividends.

"Never mind," she said, "we'll live till we die. I'll see you next month, Dot, all being well." Suddenly she recoiled, gave one or two investigative sniffs, then located the source of the smell that spread its bad-egg miasma throughout the lounge.

"Oh dear," said Mrs Pendennis faintly and reached for her scrap of a handkerchief. Not that it could do much good. "Bloody woman," Colonel Pritchard thought, and turned up the volume of his music as if this could drown out the stink.

Mrs Bannerman's flatulence was fast attaining the status of legend. Colonel Pritchard, who'd spent time in India, had never come across anything quite like it. Indeed Mr Golding, pressing his friendship too far, would nudge him knowingly and talk about vindaloo curries and real rip-snorters. "Phew!" said the smaller of the Cuthbert-Carews.

Only her grandmother was unaffected. The hand that had beckoned at the periphery of her blurred vision had come into focus. It wore an opal ring – so familiar. That, and the grey stuff sleeve and the cameo brooch and the smiling face, rosy beneath its frizz of hair and frilled cap. "Bessie," said Mrs Cuthbert-Carew silently. "Oh, Bessie." Terrified in the night, and no mother to come, but Bessie was always there. Paid to care, she had loved away your fears. She reached out an arm. So. Not dead these sixty-odd years after all. Not dead of the Spanish flu. You'd yelled and screamed and tried to drag her back into life and after that nothing was quite the same. But no, not dead after all. "Oh, Bessie," she repeated, silently, and then all the small haemorrhages became one huge explosion of red and the fog rushed in everywhere.

Many of the old folks dozed off after tea. It was likely that Mrs Cuthbert-Carew had been dead for a good ten minutes before anybody noticed.

"Oh no," he said. "*I* can't write out a certificate. For one thing she wasn't my patient – as far as I know there's no history. You might have been putting ground glass in her tea for all I know."

Mrs Speakman tapped her spectacle case on the edge of her desk. She could cheerfully have murdered him. The sort that revelled in making life difficult for everyone. No wonder his wife drank herself senseless.

"Come on, Nora," he said. "You know as well as I do . . ."

She flushed crimson. They'd known each other years ago when she was a staff nurse and he was walking the wards at a teaching hospital in the Midlands. He knew more about her than most, but that didn't give him the right to presume intimacy.

"Who *is* her doctor? Drummond-Forsyth? Get on to him."

"Sunday evening?"

"It's not my problem."

And it was no good arguing with him; he was that way out. He'd had that same stubborn look all those years ago, that cut-his-nose-off-to-spite-his-face attitude. And a chip on his shoulder the size of a plank.

"In that case, don't let me detain you," she said, drumming her fingertips impatiently on the blotter. They regarded each other steadily, locked in a battle of wills.

As soon as she'd realised what had happened she'd cleared the lounge as rapidly as possible, trying to contain the panic that bubbled beneath the surface. Silly old sods. They acted as though death was some sort of aberration, as if time wasn't bound to take its toll now and again within a community of persons, average age seventy-five. Rodney and the new lad had carried Mrs Cuthbert-Carew over to a sofa. She'd had to threaten Rodney, he was so squeamish. Always had been. Thank heavens she'd started the lad, Norman's replacement, the day before, though she didn't much care for the look of him: that sort of streaked, tattered hair that they affected nowadays and an earring. But a pair of strong young shoulders was necessary nevertheless.

"Oh, I don't suppose there's any reason not to," he said at last, opening his case and unhooking his pen. That was the way he always operated: liked to have you on a piece of string. "Emlyn the Gremlin," his contemporaries at St Mary's had nicknamed him, all those hearty young men who thought it a huge joke to expropriate the odd penis from the dissecting room and produce it, grey and wizened, from a pocket at parties. Sour-faced swot, they'd called him too. But he couldn't afford their antics, their nonchalant attitude which embraced failure as easily as success.

"I'll get on to the undertakers, then," she said. "Oh, while you're here, Rodney needs a prescription for Ventolin. He had a couple of attacks last week."

Rodney had been a martyr to asthma since childhood. Its potentiating factors were many and various: animal hairs, pollen, grasses, tension, excitement. It had been for the sake of Rodney's health that she'd moved to the seaside, hoping that the climate would suit him better, but so far there had been no improvement.

"Righto, then," she said, taking receipt of the prescription and directing a dismissive nod in his direction. But he seemed inclined to linger, took a cigarette from his packet and looked round for an ashtray in which to deposit his spent match though he knew full well there wasn't one. You'd have thought he'd have more sense. Talk about physician heal thyself!

"*She* kept her head at least, your assistant," he said, flicking his ash into the compost surrounding a vibrant red begonia; Rodney's Mother's Day offering.

One gave thanks that it hadn't been Marguerita or Rosa who'd made the discovery, either of whom would have felt obliged to scream blue murder.

"Where did you find her?" he continued casually. "She seems a cut above the usual."

"She was the best of the applicants who answered the advertisement. Why?"

"Oh, nothing," he said, extinguishing the cigarette, half-smoked.

Nora scooped it up with fastidious fingers and threw it into the wastepaper-basket. At St Mary's fornication had been rife among the housemen and nurses, but he'd been too busy studying. Now, it seemed, he was trying to make up for lost time.

"Here," Elsa said. "I've put plenty of sugar in it." She handed the mug of tea to the young man who drank it down gratefully. Brandy would have been in order but there didn't seem to be any alcohol on the premises except, so Marguerita and Rosa informed her, stashed at the back of Mr Golding's wardrobe. Bottles and bottles of it. There were books too, with dirty pictures.

The colour gradually returned to the young man's face. "You don't usually expect to have to deal with a stiff on your second day at work," he said. "Blimey! She weighed a ton. I thought that other bloke was going to puke."

She'd brought him up to the first-floor pantry where there was an electric kettle and provisions for making early-morning tea. Mrs Speakman probably counted the tea-bags and the sugar-lumps, but this surely qualified as an emergency.

"I think he very probably did."

They'd laid Mrs Cuthbert-Carew upon a sofa and covered her with a rug. Her denture had slipped, making a clicking sound as her neck hit her chest. The young man had paled, though not quite so dramatically as Rodney Speakman who had turned the colour of processed cheese.

"Is it always like this? People popping their clogs all the time?"

"I don't know. I've only been here a couple of weeks. I hope not."

He hoisted himself on to the edge of the sink unit, took a tin of tobacco and a packet of papers from his pocket and began to roll a cigarette. He was about nineteen or twenty, she supposed, with thick dark hair that had once been highlighted but was now growing out unevenly. A small gilt cross hung from his left earlobe and his tee-shirt, baggy, faded and fraying at the edges, proclaimed "I'm for Ronnie Reagan". (Colonel Pritchard, catching sight of it earlier on, had thought: well at least *some* of them have got some sense.) He was slim enough and lithe, but still there was a cherubic air about him: as though baby fat had only just been shed, as though he had tried every means at his disposal – a pubescent moustache, the stubbled chin, the raggedly-cropped hair – to establish his maturity.

"I've never seen anyone dead before," he said baldly.

Dad had gone in exactly the same way as Mrs Cuthbert-Carew: alive one minute, dead the next. She'd come in from hanging out the washing and she'd said, "Would you like a cup of tea?" and said it more loudly because his hearing wasn't what it used to be. Then she'd noticed that his eyes were closed and she'd leaned over to make his pillow more comfortable and realised that something was not quite right.

She'd started to shake him, over and over again, calling his name louder and louder, as if sheer effort of will was enough to bring back the dead.

"I thought I'd been employed to peel spuds and so forth, not to cart corpses around."

His comment roused her from reverie. She smiled at him and he smiled back. A nice smile. An attractive lad, she thought, despite all the attempts to uglify himself in deference to fashion. He was an ex-university student, a drop-out, whom Mary Reilly had met when he moved into an adjacent bedsitting-room, and introduced to Nora Speakman as being a suitable replacement for the incarcerated Norman.

"Well, thanks for the tea," he said. "I'm sorry, I don't know your name."

"Elsa."

He pushed his cigarette-end down the plughole and swung himself to the floor. "Mine's Nick," he said.

Her heart gave a jolt and the pain came back as raw as when you ripped a plaster from a wound. It was the same every time; that same jolt followed by the sharp piercing pain. Perhaps it would always be so.

5

She had misheard. His name was not Nick, it was Mick – short for Michael. Michael Wynn. He donned Norman's canvas apron and scoured out the pans and peeled the vegetables and emptied the swill-bins. He cleaned the windows and humped in the groceries and mowed the back lawn because old Clegg who was responsible for the gardens had upped his rates and Nora Speakman hadn't been put on to this earth to be ripped off by tradesmen. He mended a fence and repaired a vacuum-cleaner and he clambered up into the loft and did something vital to the ballcock in the cistern. He worked at top speed, attacking the pans with wire wool almost before they were emptied, heaving the half-hundredweight sacks of potatoes about with ease. Mrs Randall, who had earlier pronounced disapprovingly upon the subject of lazy drop-outs, began to change her opinion. "Beat you into a cocked hat any day," she was heard to say to the two workmen as she handed them their tea. A fortnight, they'd been, replacing a bit of guttering. "Weary Willie and Tired Tim," she called them, claiming by way of justification that the lad was worth ten of them.

But she might have been less well-disposed towards him had she known why he had to have every second Wednesday morning off. It was so that he could sign on.

"Aren't you running a terrible risk?" Elsa had asked. "Drawing Social Security while you're working?"

He'd shrugged. "No more of a risk than she's running," he'd said, gesticulating in the direction of Mrs Speakman's office, "not paying my stamp and so forth. Everybody's doing it," he said. "They call it the black economy."

"I know what they call it. I also know what the penalties are if you get caught."

"You worry too much, Elsie, you're a worry-guts."

Elsie, he called her, said that Elsa sounded like someone's German au pair, or one of those mad Middle-European professors' daughters in a Thirties B-film. "I didn't know people were called those sort of names anymore."

"I'm sure they aren't. We are going back a bit."

"Of course. I forgot you're just about due for your pension book. You should be *living* here, not working here."

He treated her as a contemporary, probably because – apart from Rosa and Rodney Speakman (with whom the likelihood of compatibility must have been in some doubt) – she was the closest in age to him. And because she was the only one upon whom his jokes and odd cultural references were not wasted. Mrs Randall couldn't understand what was funny about the roast duck and the dessert being in close proximity to each other on their respective silver serving-dishes; Mary Reilly, talking about her feller's mistreatment at the hands of the law, said, "Eh?" when he enquired about the number of heads that had been nailed to coffee-tables during the course of Des's criminal career; and Marguerita backed away in alarm when he quoted *The Waste Land* at her as she carried in sprays of lilac from the garden. "Are you taking the piss?" Mary Reilly had said, while Mrs Randall just thought it was criminal that a good education had been thrown away: "Your mum and dad must have been heartbroken."

"My mum and dad," he said, chopping the blackened bits off a heap of cauliflowers (Mrs Speakman had come to an understanding with a local merchant concerning substandard produce), "couldn't give a shit."

"Language!" said Mrs Randall automatically, but you could tell she was thinking: poor lad, he looks like nobody owns him: his backside practically hanging out of his trousers, all his belongings crammed into a rucksack, the army greatcoat that had very probably been through the Battle of the Somme.

He regaled them with tales of the drunken roisterings indulged in by Mary Reilly and her feller: pitched battles, foul abuse; told of the night that she had fled into the street with her hair on fire; the early hours of the morning when he had been awakened by the sound of glass breaking to see Mary

Reilly's feller standing below heaving half-bricks at the front elevation. Elsa suspected exaggeration but laughed all the same.

He made them all laugh, in fact: clowning about in the kitchen, imitating the mock-cultivated accents of Mister Rodney, his mother's stately gait. The residents liked him too – even though he imitated *them* most wickedly. His good looks cancelled out what they considered to be the bizarreness of his appearance, and he reminded them of a son: in Australia, or long dead, or grown old and fat and unfilial. He was a huge success but Elsa sometimes detected strain beneath the bonhomie, was occasionally irritated when his joking spilled over into silliness, and suspected that, in childhood, he'd gone short of a good smack.

The good weather continued to hold. Mick exchanged the Ronald Reagan tee-shirt for thinner, skimpier models, was even seen sporting a pair of jeans cut off at the knee when he worked outdoors, until Mister Rodney saw them and had a word with his mother. Mister Rodney wore the same dark-blue blazer and grey flannels whatever the weather. The residents appreciated smartness. But perhaps it was not inconceivable, Elsa thought, noticing a spark of excitement in one or two pairs of pale old eyes, that they appreciated the sight of firm young flesh even more.

However, on Mrs Speakman's orders, he was obliged to cover his lower limbs as he climbed aboard the petrol mower and roared off down the garden (toying with the idea of striping the grass with an outlined obscenity), as he set out the tables and chairs upon the terrace, erected the garden swing and, in a blaze of petrol, exterminated the ant colonies that threatened to disturb the residents' outdoor pursuits.

They came out cautiously at first, the old ones, filmed eyes blinking tearily, hands cupped above their spectacles against the sun's glare, shawls and extra woollies at the ready. Mr Golding donned his alpaca suit, Miss Vyner exchanged her thick tweed costume for one of marginally lighter weight, and Mrs Pegler sported a silk hat adorned with roses, a hat of the sort that had once looked so becoming at the thé dansants of the Palace Hotel, Torquay. Wife of a scrap-metal merchant she might have been, but she'd had chic all right, unlike some of these toffs who were born to it: Mrs Booth-Powell in her everlasting Pringle jumpers and her Burberry macs; the late Mrs Cuthbert-Carew and her dinge-coloured skirts and cardigans, her tarnished silver kilt-pins and cairngorm brooches. (Though one mustn't speak ill of the dead; Mrs Pegler had taken to attending Evensong at St James's now the warm weather was here; Dad had always said that religion was so much codswallop, but best to be on the safe side.)

It was not so strange, Elsa supposed, that death at close quarters had stimulated many of them into renewing attentions to their faith. Colonel Pritchard, who was a sidesman at St James's, was quite surprised to see not only Mrs Pegler but also Mr Golding in the congregation at Evensong – having been under the impression that the fellow was a Jew. Miss Johns, who sang in the choir at St Simon's, looked up during the Nunc Dimittis and spotted Mrs Pendennis attracting a lot of attention from old Edward Green, the people's warden. Mrs Booth-Powell who was a lapsed Welsh Presbyterian unlapsed herself. Mr Gentile tottered off to Our Lady, Star of the Sea. And Mrs Crookthorne in the Elim Pentecostal Church sang, "Wait not till the shadows lengthen, till you older grow. Hurry now and sing for Jesus everywhere you go." She sang it with gusto, together with the rest of the congregation which contained a fair number of members of an ethnic minority, in much the same enthusiastic manner that her husband, Bertie, had once chanted, "The Yids, the Yids, we've got to get rid of the Yids," as he marched through the centre of the town in his black shirt.

Yet the one who was most in need of preparing her soul to meet its maker appeared to be blithely unconcerned, spent the Sabbath morn with a copy of the *Mail On Sunday* on her knee, and was heard to remark, "What a racket!" whenever they switched on *Songs of Praise* in the evening. Mrs Bannerman had the best set of teeth in the place: white, regular, all her own – her late husband had been a dentist – but her teeth were probably the only part of her that had not succumbed to age and decay. Her limbs were knotted with rheumatoid arthritis, her swollen ankles and the pouches beneath her eyes proclaimed dropsical tendencies, her chest played her up dreadfully in winter, her sinuses in the summer. A chronic haemorrhoidal condition necessitated a régime of suppositories and long, long sessions in the lavatory. None of these afflictions was directly life-threatening, but now it seemed that her flatulence – which everyone else had regarded as either a reprehensible lack of self-control or else a cause for hilarity – suggested to Dr Rees a symptom of something more sinister.

"I'm going to send you for some tests. To the infirmary," he told her, as he drew down her nightdress. "I'M GOING TO SEND YOU FOR SOME TESTS. To the INFIRMARY."

"All right. I'm not deaf."

As she swung her legs over the edge of the bed, her pendulous belly strained against the silk of her nightgown: pure silk, it was, trimmed with handmade lace. Bill had always liked her to have nice undies. Refined, romantic, not sexy. He'd worshipped at her shrine, his hands gentle, his kisses tender. Which was why it had come as such a shock when she'd found those magazines after his death. Not just sexy, she could perhaps have accepted that, but downright filth: women being penetrated with all manner of inappropriate objects, being flogged, branded, urinated upon. She'd stood in the meticulously clean loft, the collection spread about her, and shivered from head to toe though it was July, before bundling them together and rushing them down to the incinerator at the bottom of the garden.

"I've been having a bit of bother for a while," she told Dr Rees, "in the nether regions." Bill had always called them the nether regions. "I thought it was just old age."

"How's the constipation?" he asked.

"Terrible sometimes. It takes me ages. And with the others waiting. I haven't a toilet en suite, you see," she explained. "I have to apologise. Though I can't help noticing that they always seem to need it when I'm in there. Oh, Doctor," she said, "what it is to come to: old age and poverty!"

Poverty! He doubted that she could begin to grasp that the word meant something different from not being able to afford a toilet en suite. But his hand was gentle as he assisted her to her feet. What he suspected was wrong with her he wouldn't wish upon his worst enemy.

"Time she was on her way?" Nora Speakman asked him

when he came downstairs. She could do very well without another of them being carted out feet first in the space of the same month. And there were plenty of applicants waiting to take her place.

"Don't know yet. It may not be anything." Damned if he'd give her the satisfaction of knowing until the knowledge had to be made public.

"It's not very nice, you know, for the other residents . . ."

"If the odd fart is the worst they have to put up with, then they're very fortunate."

She looked as though she might have a retort ready but then thought better of it and smiled; a smile of such pure condescension, acknowledging that his circumstances prompted uncouth behaviour and allowances must be made, that it irritated him beyond measure.

It was three o'clock, and there was no earthly reason why he shouldn't go home. However much he took on: extra surgeries, stints in the path lab at the Infirmary, voluntary clinics for this, that and t'other, the time always crept to the moment when there was no reasonable excuse not to go home.

The woman: Edna? Enid? *Elsa*, was turning out of the drive as he got into his car. From the back you'd have thought her a girl, perhaps seventeen or so: narrow-hipped, slim-shanked, but the little lines on her face betrayed her years. Not that it wasn't a pretty face. Or would be if she smiled a bit more. Then he caught sight of his own reflection in the driving mirror and grimaced. Pots and kettles, old son, he thought.

James Owen, his partner when he'd had the practice in Oswestry, had said, "Have you never thought of divorce, Emlyn?" There'd been incidents in the local pub and talk was beginning to filter through concerning a woman entering in hotel registers a name to which she had no legal right. "We all appreciate your problem," James Owen had said, "but that isn't the way to solve it, surely?"

He'd moved soon after that; he could cope with gossip, but not interference masked as concern. "A clean break," his colleague had spoken of: a fresh start. Sometimes he'd allowed himself to fantasise: a "normal" marriage, children, compatibility, support, peace, but he suspected that it wouldn't turn out that way. All his affairs had ended disastrously and in all probability would have done even if he'd been free. The marriage he had was probably the one he deserved. Besides, he wasn't the sort to give up on anything. God knows he could have done that ten times over during his lifetime.

But he never spoke of it, the self-sacrifice. Even Diana hadn't known his background. It wasn't shame that prompted his reticence, but rather that a sort of fastidiousness in him recoiled from reciting the clichés: the mining town hovel where the most strenuous of hygienic efforts could not hold back the grime, the scholarships, the wrists poking from the sleeves of the outgrown, outdated sports jacket, the social gaucherie, the thin-skinnedness that detected condescension where none had been intended, the final academic success – and, to cap it all, marriage to a rich man's daughter. "I don't believe you were ever young," she'd once yelled at him, and he'd had to admit the truth of the accusation: the carefree irresponsibility of youth lay entirely outside his experience.

The woman, Elsa, waited at the bus stop. He drew to a halt and opened the passenger door.

"Can I give you a lift?"

"That depends on where you're going."

"Where are *you* going?"

"Into town."

"No problem, then. Jump in."

He sought for conversational openings. "You coped very well the other week with – old Mrs Whatnot, the cerebral haemorrhage."

"My father died in the same way last year. I found him."

For a moment he saw the memory of pain flicker across her features. His own father had died the previous year too. He'd sent his sister Olwen a cheque to cover the funeral expenses but he hadn't gone back. There would have been no point.

"Were you very close?"

"He'd had a stroke that partially paralysed him soon after my mother died. He'd lived with us ever since."

Us? He stole a look at her left hand which proved to be bare of identification. "On your way home?" he hazarded. It was hard going but he persevered; there was something infinitely appealing about the angle formed by the line of her jaw and the curve of her neck.

"No. I live in at the Priory."

Which meant, of course, a single status, or at least a husband out of the running.

"I wouldn't have thought," he said, changing down for the roundabout that heralded the main street, "that *that* was a good idea for one's private life."

"I don't have one," she said. "And it's cheaper than a room outside."

"I've no doubt. But surely . . ." He'd seen those staff attics at Priory Lodge: as spartan as they must have been when the place had been a private residence and the tweenies had been housed up there.

"I need to save money," she said, "and this seems to be the best way of doing it."

All too soon – despite his taking full advantage of every red light – the centre of the town was upon them. "Oh, here, please," she said, indicating a side-road. "This will be fine."

She lifted her bag from the floor. It was a wide hold-all with a shoulder strap, open at the top. He saw cartridge paper inside it and a box of crayons. "Bit of sketching?" he said. "Not much of a view, surely, round here?"

"No," she said. "But if you go on to the marsh road, near the headland . . . Well, thanks very much. Goodbye."

He watched as she slung the bag over her shoulder and disappeared into a throng of holidaymakers. Was the fact that she had informed him of her precise destination significant? Had she maintained eye-contact for a moment longer than was absolutely necessary? Was he succumbing to the myth of his reputation: an unsatisfactorily-married middle-aged man who couldn't resist anything halfway decent-looking in skirts and saw sexual invitation in the most neutral of behaviours?

He drove back to whatever awaited him in the house beside the golf links. She was certainly enigmatic, though. And he'd never been able to resist a mystery.

6

As Dr Rees supposed, the attics at Priory Lodge had been subdivided to house servants long before Nora Speakman took possession of the place. A few mementoes of those days remained: rows of rusted bells marked "drawing-room" and "study" and so on, marble washstands, the odd flower-patterned ewer and basin. But for the most part Mrs Speakman had furnished her staff quarters with job lots bought from auction rooms: plywood furniture riddled with worm holes, greasy moquette armchairs, and mirrors mottled and de-silvered to the extent that they tendered you a reflection of dermatological decay. Rosa and Marguerita decorated these comfortless cells with family photographs and garish souvenirs and innumerable icons: Sacred Hearts and Virgin Marys and plaster statuettes of St Jude covered every available surface. Beyond unpacking her suitcases, Elsa had done nothing except to move a rickety rattan table closer to the window so that the source of light fell directly upon the drawing-board that it supported.

There was another small window set high in the wall that separated her room from the one next to it on the right-hand side. (In the room to her left Marguerita snored loudly and with an irritating lack of rhythm.) Elsa, lying in bed on her first night, had puzzled over its function until she realised that, due to partitioning, the room next-door had probably been deprived of a window of its own and therefore depended upon the borrowed light that the small pane afforded. It was kept locked, that room, as were several of the others – storerooms, she supposed – though Mick eagerly supplied a more sinister explanation. After exploration and trying each of the handles in turn, he reckoned that the Unspeakables, as he called them, *mère et fils*, stored their ill-gotten gains in there: residents' furniture, their valuable personal effects, their teeth and hair probably, their skin for lampshades. "Imbecile daughters," Mick said, drooling grotesquely, "mad wives, the ghosts of defrauded guests."

But the idea of ghosts didn't bother her. The dead stayed dead, she had already discovered, despite the most strenuous efforts to call them back.

Part of the attic space had been converted into a bathroom of which Elsa enjoyed a virtual monopoly. Marguerita and Rosa, perhaps daunted by modern plumbing, preferred to wash in the privacy of their own rooms, utilising, presumably, the marble washstands and the antique ewers and basins. It became her habit to take a bath after returning from an afternoon's sketching, as that was the time at which most of the residents retired for their naps and were therefore unlikely to be draining off the hot water. She'd wander back and forth between bedroom and bathroom, half-clad, unconcerned; after all there was no one other than Marguerita or Rosa to observe her déshabillé.

Until the afternoon when, having bathed, she was back in her room, towelling herself dry and heard a crashing sound issuing from the room on the right-hand side.

She pulled on jeans and a blouse and went out to investigate, curious rather than alarmed. It was the middle of the afternoon and even Mick would have had difficulty in accepting that the paranormal would manifest itself in such a noisy fashion.

As pale as a ghost, they said, though Rodney Speakman, who was coming out of the room next-door at exactly the same moment as she stepped into the corridor, hardly fitted the description; his face being suffused with the crimson blush of extreme embarrassment.

"Oh," he said, his voice cracking. He cleared his throat and moistened his lips and tried again: "Somebody piled up the trunks any old how," he said. "They came crashing down soon as I touched them . . . Didn't frighten you, I hope?"

Elsa could see sweat on his forehead. "No," she said, regarding him steadily, "you didn't frighten me."

He stared at her imploringly for a moment longer, then

turned rapid tail and fled down the stairs. So precipitate was his departure that he left the key in the lock.

The thud of his feet receded. She opened the storeroom door as gingerly as if expecting the more outlandish of Mick's monsters to leap out at her, but was confronted with nothing more threatening than a collection of trunks and suitcases.

It was only when she was back in her own room that she remembered the small pane of glass that afforded unimpeded visual access from the room next-door, or at least it did if the observer were to climb on to something high enough to provide such a view – a pile of trunks, perhaps . . .

She kept waiting to feel afraid. But there was a bolt on the inside of her bedroom door and she also kept remembering the expression on Rodney Speakman's face: as though he had been frightened of *her*. She didn't think he'd try it again, but if he did, she would threaten to tell his mother and, she suspected, thinking of the mixture of fondness and hostility which seemed to characterise that relationship, the threat would be enough.

"You're joking?" Mick said. "Are you sure?"

"I'm not *sure*. It might have been perfectly innocent but he *looked* as guilty as hell and they say he goes in for that sort of peeping Tom thing."

"Dirty old Rodders," Mick said. "I must say he looks a bit of a wanker. What are you going to do?"

"I've done it."

She indicated the picture that now obliterated the window.

"You don't think he'll have another go?"

She shook her head.

"No," he said, "you're probably right. They're usually shit-scared, aren't they, that brigade: the peepers and the flashers and the knickerpinchers; they run a mile if anybody catches them at it."

They were both off-duty and sharing a pot of tea and two stolen Chorley cakes. "I could always warn him off," he said, with a deliberately casual unconcern. "If you want me to?"

"No, I don't think so. Best let well alone."

"Oh, by the way," he said, "message from HQ: Nellie Macpherson's sister is ill so she won't be coming in tomorrow, so Rosa'll have to do lunches, and *you*, according to Big Nurse Speakman, will have to get up for morning teas. *Comprendo*, as Rodders would say?"

Elsa groaned. Her free periods were subject to constant erosion and often the time off in lieu didn't materialise. Still, she was managing to salt away a good proportion of her wages, and it wouldn't do to rock the boat.

"Nellie's sister, Florrie," he said idly, scattering crumbs all over the scatter rug. "What dreadful sort of un-thought-out names they always gave them in those days."

"They had such large families. I expect, by the time they'd reached the seventh or eighth, inspiration had dried up."

"Is that what happened with you?"

"Shouldn't think so. There *was* only me."

"There was only me too," he said. "Hell, wasn't it?"

She hadn't thought so, had never found the full focus of attention overwhelming, had – despite the inevitable periods of loneliness – relished her status as an only child. Apart from anything else she'd done rather better in terms of new shoes and bicycles than her friends: siblings who had to make do with hand-me-downs.

Mick, however, hinted at an altogether less satisfactory state of affairs: a childhood characterised by trauma, compounded of equal measures of spoiling and neglect, mediating in marital discord where his allegiance was alternately sought with blackmail or bribery.

And not just his home life: school too had been a purgatory, and university had just about succeeded in fucking his head up altogether.

"So you dropped out?"

"God," he said, grinning, "that's a lovely old Sixties' expression."

"I'm a lovely old Sixties' person. Grew up with a picture of Paul McCartney pasted under my desk lid."

And was drawn to Robert because he looked a bit like Paul McCartney. She remembered the art school dance: fancy dress; he'd worn a stetson and a Zapata moustache. She'd thought it was false, pasted on for the occasion, until she'd ended up in bed with him and found it to be real.

He was the star of the final year. Off to London to do a

postgraduate course in furniture design. She'd been flattered, and ready to be in love. But neither so flattered nor so love-hungry that she hadn't been desolated when she'd found herself pregnant and married to him in fairly rapid succession, her art school days perforce at an end. Even now, more than ever now, she regretted the waste. And considered Mick's behaviour: the *wilful* wastage of opportunity, as being almost criminally perverse. "The best time of your *life*," she said vehemently, looking back on her own student days, seeing them in an idealised glow as some sort of lost Golden Age.

He said it wasn't like that. "You really do have this weird idea," he said, "all rag weeks and deeply intellectual discussions. It's not like that. Students are the biggest bunch of boring creeps going. They're all into *computing* and working towards *junior management* positions and planning to do courses in *business administration*. They're either so straight they're practically invisible, or else they've developed posing into an art form and they're terrified to act spontaneously in case they damage their street cred."

"As an alternative," she said, "I wouldn't have thought that this was much of an improvement."

"It's a job. Till I get my head together."

The year before, during the summer vacation, he'd worked on the dodgems at the funfair. He'd returned to the town, hoping they'd take him on again but all the vacancies had been filled so he'd been obliged to take the first job that offered itself. Nobody could expect you to exist on the fortnightly Giro.

"You should have gone home."

"I tried that. All I got was: did I realise how much it had cost to keep me in education, and how was she going to tell her friends, and had it sunk in that I'd ruined my life? It just went on and on. Rabbit, rabbit. When she wasn't turning on the waterworks."

"What about your father?"

"He blamed her for spoiling me."

Suddenly irritated by the conversation he got to his feet, peered into the piece of looking-glass that was propped on the mantelpiece, and ruffled the plume of hair that hung over his forehead. "Christ!" he said, peering more closely, "have I suddenly developed a rash of zits, or is it this mirror?"

"It's the mirror."

"Makes you look as though you've been dug up." He grimaced grotesquely. "Speaking of which, *The Evil Dead*'s on at the Coliseum. D'you fancy it? Or we could grab a takeaway. I could kill for a curry. I said to Randall the other day when she was doing that everlasting mince muck, 'Why don't you ever do a curry, a really hot vindaloo, get 'em all going?' She gave me this funny look. I think she thought it was a sexual perversion."

"I want to finish my sketch."

But she was tempted: to run round the town with him, as carefree as a kid, as the student she'd once been before living demanded its dues.

"It can wait," he said cajolingly.

"No, it can't. I need to get a portfolio together for my interviews. I told you."

"You've got very high hopes of this college business, haven't you?" he said sulkily. "There still aren't any jobs at the end of it all, you know. Particularly for people your age," he added cruelly.

"Perhaps not. I shan't know till I try though, shall I?"

She found three old dears seated on a bench on the marsh road near the headland; marvellous detail: lard-white, pillar-like lower limbs knotted with navy-blue varicose veins, wedding-rings jammed tight on to swollen fingers, a complicated tracery of wrinkles on parchment skin, hooded eyes and dowagers' humps – all of this set against the fretworked effect of the Promenade skyline. She was pleased with her effort, and had even been capable of accepting their comments with equanimity: "Ee, Hannah, do I really look like that? No offence, love. It's right good. It is that, Edie, she's caught you to a tee. I bet you wished you'd put your teeth in before we came out. Get away with you!"

"We're three widows," they'd informed her, as though she needed to know their status in order to do them full justice. Her portfolio was growing thick with drawings of widows: Mrs Crookthorne captured dozing in a recliner on the terrace,

Mrs Pegler, the knitting wool flying through her fingers, Mrs Booth-Powell, her face empurpled in the Gloucester Room as the television set portrayed a scene of simulated sexual intercourse. "Studies in Ageing" she would call them. Elsa was beginning to discover after her short time at Priory Lodge that ageing was a depressingly democratic process, not one whit kinder to Mrs Cuthbert-Carew or Mrs Booth-Powell than it was to the three ex-mill-workers from Bradford enjoying their once-a-year breath of ozone.

They hobbled back towards the boarding-house and she surveyed her work with mild satisfaction. She'd been terrified, when first she tried again, that the facility might have deserted her – she hadn't picked up a pencil with any serious intention since she'd married Rob, there hadn't been time – and, at first, her hand had stuttered upon the page, tentative, clumsy, afraid to risk disappointment. But soon there was a flow, a spontaneous movement, as memories reasserted themselves and forgotten familiarities were recalled. "High hopes," Mick had said. "You might be wasting your time. There *are* no jobs, you know." But he had missed the point. She had an interview in a month. For the first time in years she had made something happen.

Pen and ink had been her chosen medium, but perhaps the sketch might translate into a painting – a gouache, perhaps – whenever she had the means and the opportunity to work on it. (So many materials with which to reacquaint herself: the act of creation was one thing, technical mastery quite another.) A lot of pale-blue and gold was needed, and gamboge or ochre or something, to capture that bronzed tone of elderly skin. Or perhaps she should treat the sketch as an entity separate from the circumstances of its execution; perhaps it would work better in the sombre tones of a winter afternoon . . . She pored over it, irritated that it was not within her capacity to make the experiment immediately. And then a shadow fell across the paper and she half-suspected before ever she looked up the identity of its substance.

He raised his hands, Dr Rees, cupped them together and called through them: "Captain! Here!" and the large black labrador which was snuffling around on the beach pricked up its ears and started to trot towards them.

"Good boy. Down!"

It greeted him rapturously, shook itself and sprayed sand liberally in all directions while Elsa hastily moved her drawing out of harm's way. Having rid itself of irritants, it thrust a large wet nose into her lap and raised its eyes, red-rimmed, mournful, to hers.

"He likes you."

"How can you tell?"

"If he doesn't he bites your leg off."

"Ah."

"May I look?"

She'd rather he didn't but he was already looking, composing the remark that would convey a measure of admiration untainted by sycophancy. She forestalled it: "It's just a preliminary sketch. I'll probably turn it into a painting later on."

Obviously relieved that he had been spared from expressing enthusiasm, he sat down beside her.

"You don't mind if I join you for a minute or two? I've walked him from the fog bell. I thought it might tire him out. It hasn't, but it's certainly knackered me. Have you had some training – the drawing, I mean?"

"I went to art school years ago. I'm hoping to take it up again in October. If I get accepted."

"Here?"

"No. I want to do a degree course: art and design. I've applied to various places, but I'd like Manchester, preferably. There's someone there who used to teach me. Of course I'll be pleased with anywhere . . ."

"So here is just a stop-gap?"

She nodded.

"I thought you looked out of place at Priory Lodge."

"People have to compromise and do all sorts of jobs that don't suit them in the slightest these days."

"Oh yes, quite."

They sat silently for a while. Strains of the *Merry Widow* waltz floated across from the Floral Gardens. The family on the beach below began to pack away the paraphernalia of their day out: hamper, windbreak, primus stove, toddlers both sticky and irritable. A yacht, its sail bellying, glided into view at the far end of the boating lake. His labrador sighed deeply and settled itself to sleep.

He is paying me attention, she thought, with a little shock of recognition that was accompanied by a measure of either nervousness or excitement – she found it impossible to distinguish between the two. She hadn't been paid that sort of attention for years. Except for once when a furniture-making colleague of Rob's had pressed her up against a lathe in the workshop, thrust his leg between her knees and his tongue into her mouth. He'd evidently interpreted her total lack of response, which was due to astonishment, as being due to frigidity or lack of interest; at any rate the experiment had never been repeated. And if there had been other evidence of attraction, it had eluded her. But then she'd never been particularly adept at reading the signs: until Rob had actually kissed her during the art school dance she'd been convinced that he was pursuing her friend Pauline.

However, a gambit this obvious could hardly be misinterpreted. Intrigued and somewhat flattered, Elsa looked at him out of the corner of her eye. Grey hair, and a face that proclaimed its age (Rob had stayed as young-looking as that early portrait of Paul McCartney; thin, harassed, though still with that sinful choirboy look which women found so appealing), but nevertheless not unpleasing. The green eyes, flecked with gold, darting, dancing, and then slumbrous, proclaimed him to be a womaniser while the thin line of his mouth told a different, puritanical story. Wasn't that supposed to be a disastrous combination?

"This *is* pleasant," he said, leaning back and raising his face to receive the benison of the fading sunshine. "In a month the place will be seething with grockles and no peace for anybody."

"Grockles?" she said. One of his hands was spread across the thigh of his corduroy trousers, the other lay on the wooden slats of the seat between them. She was terribly conscious of it: its thinness, the dark hair that grew upon its knuckles, its impeccable cleanliness.

"It's what the locals call holidaymakers."

He met her sidelong glance. The dog moaned in its sleep and thumped its tail on the ground.

"Have you tried the park?" he said. "There's quite an interesting plant house – if you go in for that sort of thing."

Her portfolio was certainly lacking in plant drawings and perhaps few of the grockles penetrated as far as the park.

"I take Captain there sometimes when I've a free afternoon." His hand moved slightly, advanced, then, finding no reciprocal movement, retreated. He got up to go and they said goodbye. She walked slowly back to Priory Lodge. The play having been made, she hadn't the slightest idea whether she wanted to respond to it.

7

"Are you a Welsh speaker?"

He nodded, his lips pressed against the apple-blossom fragrance of her newly-washed hair.

"Say something in Welsh."

He moved his cheek against hers. The faint abrasion reminded him that philandering always required a keener attention to the sharpness of one's razor. "Cariad," he said.

"Oh!" she exclaimed, disappointed at his lack of originality, "even I know that." And know, although it sounds so lovely, that it couldn't possibly be true. "Is that bougainvillaea?" she said, gesturing with her free hand towards the purple sprays trailing above their heads.

"Could be. Who cares?"

He sought her mouth, drawing from it all the sustenance that, for the time being, he required. Kissing was enough. The discovery of texture and sweetness and corresponding eagerness seemed sufficient in itself. Though not for long, he knew; appetites less delicate in their manifestation would lead him to suggest a more private place of assignation, would oblige him to force the pace, rush him headlong to the conclusion.

But now was the kiss and the kiss was enough. Garlanded with trailing bougainvillaea (if that was what it was), obscured by giant curling fern fronds, concealed from spying eyes by the whitewashed windows of the greenhouse, they clung to each other. A half-finished drawing of an arum lily stood propped against the wall. Alert to the sound of the first intrusive footstep, they gave over their other senses wholly to the voyage of discovery, to the time of transition between strangeness and familiarity. The best time.

"You smell of lemon."

She had washed her hair for him and he had applied a new cologne for her. In a week or two they would come to prefer their natural odours, the mingled scents of their skins.

"I'm on duty at six."

"And I've a surgery at five thirty."

Though they would not be too distressed at parting. They could savour the delight of their meeting, rerun each of their embraces, from the tentative to the truly committed. He would inspect diseased tonsils and peer at inflamed eardrums and listen for arhythmic heart-beats, thinking all the while of the softness and slenderness of her within his arms. She would pour coffee: black for Colonel Pritchard, cream for Mr Gentile, sweeteners for most of the ladies; she would feel the glancing touch of Mr Golding's hand on her bottom as she bent to lift the tray (light enough to have been accidental should anyone complain) and remember *his* touch as, with gentle fingertips, he read her face like Braille.

"I thought you were terribly prim. When I offered you that lift . . ."

"And I thought you were terribly brusque. Poor Mrs Crookthorne and her dwindling assets."

They laughed with condescending amusement at these false selves that others – insignificant commonplace others – had signally failed to penetrate. And then their laughter was silenced abruptly as mouth found mouth and discovered a sweetness beyond compare.

A hundred yards away Miss Vyner, who had been kissed once after a barn dance at St Luke's church fellowship when she was seventeen and hadn't cared for it at all, hobbled beside the lake. A fine drizzle wetted her tweed coat and blurred the lenses of her spectacles but so many cubic centimetres of fresh air per volume of lung capacity per day was a goal she had set herself. Otherwise . . . She shuddered, the consequences of the alternative being too awful to contemplate.

She tried to fix her attention on the aesthetically-pleasing scene before her: the rain rippling the lake, the mallards bread-hunting at its rim, the willows weeping to the ground, but the view kept being displaced by the image of Mabel Bannerman, crippled, dropsical and, recently, lying in her room with mortality written large on her brow. Soon Dr Rees would order her into a public ward of the general infirmary (Mabel Bannerman had no private health insurance), where they would remove her teeth, put sides up on her bed and drug her to death. No one would be able, with any certainty, to state the degree of pain that she would be subjected to before she died, and she herself would be in no position to offer enlightenment.

"You could always come to me, Dot," Gertie had told her when she'd expressed her fears that the arthritis might lead to immobilisation, but the expression on Gertie's face made it plain that the offer, though polite, had not been sincere. Best to go like Maisie Cuthbert-Carew, before your independence was totally eroded. Locked in the top drawer of Miss Vyner's bureau, back at the Priory (a lock that had proved impervious to Mister Rodney's attempts upon it with a hairpin), was a letter to Exit. She had been plucking up her courage to post it for weeks; what deterred her was the account of some trial she had read, involving the use of polythene bags. Should she decide to frustrate the intentions of nature with regard to the date of her demise, there was no way (as they said these days) that she could end it all by means of the use of a polythene bag. Dignity, at least, must be preserved – otherwise why bother?

"Come on, Dorothy Vyner, pull yourself together," she said sternly, attempting to straighten her bowed shoulders, to strike out purposefully with her walking-stick. Morbidity was a rare indulgence; she had a meeting of the Women's Standing Committee that evening, and a Bach recital in the art gallery at lunchtime the following day. There was the *Times* crossword still to be solved and – Wednesday, was it? – kedgeree for dinner, hurrah! You could worry yourself into the grave if you weren't careful, without needing the assistance of any organisation promoting the cause of euthanasia.

And, anyway, her attention was distracted from any further brooding by a couple of incidents that she witnessed on the way home.

First she saw Dr Rees and the girl Elsa coming out of the tropical plant house, separately but in such rapid succession that it was impossible to misinterpret the situation. Well, well, she thought, mildly surprised. She hadn't had much truck with the doctor but he had struck her as a miserable piece of goods – the Welsh were a dour race at the best of times – and the young woman kept herself very much to herself.

Miss Vyner didn't approve: adulterers rarely managed to keep their adultery sufficiently discreet to avoid hurting others. And invariably they hurt themselves. (She remembered Gertie and the assistant bank manager all those years ago; oh the tears and the anguish, out of all proportion to the importance of the affair in the general scheme of things.) But neither did she violently disapprove, realising, though she had never been vulnerable to it, that certain people had a pathological need for that spurious state of being they called romance. She, Dorothy Vyner, had escaped the affliction; having been deprived of a marriage partner by the war (she'd had to admit a slight measure of relief on this score), she'd concentrated her energies upon getting on in the Service. Father's illness had prevented her from advancing at the rate of which she was capable, it was true. But never mind, she had her pension and the satisfaction of a lifetime's useful effort and, if God should show mercy, a dignified end.

Then, walking along the Esplanade, she caught sight of the boy, Mick, prone upon a sand-dune. It was hardly the weather for it; tough old birds like herself could walk in the rain with impunity, but the young were prone to coughs and colds. She thought of hailing him and advising him to seek shelter, but then decided against – he looked so very dispirited, and unlikely to welcome her interference. And as she watched, he heaved himself to his feet and ambled over the brow of the hill and disappeared. Perhaps some girl had stood him up. The sand-dunes seemed to be the local trysting place: during the good weather, or after dark, their undulations provided concealment for sexual intimacy. Once, during the course of an evening stroll, she had caught sight of Rodney Speakman in flight along the beach. He was being pursued by a young man who shouted and gesticulated angrily before abandoning the chase. The implication – that he had been caught at his spying – was fairly obvious. The exertion had brought on an attack of asthma: that night at dinner he'd started to wheeze and sweat had beaded his forehead. His mother had put it down to cat hairs, Mary Reilly having been discovered feeding a stray tom with kitchen scraps at the back door.

Miss Vyner felt sorry for the boy, Mick. He seemed a pleasant enough lad, but somehow pathetic. Not that she'd had much contact with him: a word here and there as he weeded a flower-bed or carried the kitchen refuse down to the compost heap. She'd asked him if he enjoyed his job and he'd looked at her in amazement – *enjoy* it? Jobs were not for enjoying; they were for earning the bread to keep body and soul together. There was no virtue in work for its own sake.

She'd kept silent, afraid that if she spoke it would be sharply, with indignation; the virtue of work for its own sake was the personal philosophy that had sustained her for a lifetime.

That evening, Miss Johns, who had kept up her botanical interests ever since childhood, sat in the Gloucester Room, pressing a batch of marsh gentians and covertly scrutinising Mrs Pendennis's latest admirer.

Everyone was scrutinising Mrs Pendennis's latest admirer and had badgered Miss Johns, who was the only one who knew him, for information. But the information she was able to provide was disappointingly sparse: his name was Edward Green, he was a widower and had been elected people's warden of St Simon's at the last meeting of the parish council. She had a feeling that, rather than being a committed Christian, the church fulfilled a purely social need for him. But then that was so often the case and – she had to admit it – was preferable to the aggressive sort of evangelism that was occasionally inflicted upon the congregation: those bands of guitar-playing, tambourine-shaking, born-again creatures. Her father, who had inclined (just ever so slightly) towards Rome (liturgical deviations, a biretta, a regret, she felt, that he had married; a relief that, quite soon, he was able to devote himself to celibate widowhood), would have had a fit.

Edward Green was besotted. This much was obvious to everyone. The men were astounded. The women sighed, but were mostly beyond envy. Mrs Pendennis had kept as many of her looks as anyone could reasonably expect to at the age of seventy, without recourse to the surgeon's knife, and a woman who had had looks worth keeping was bound to be granted a prolongation of masculine interest. Generally, the women considered her welcome to it. Men were bad enough when they had something to offer you in terms of their bank balances or their splendid physiques; past it and impecunious, they weren't worth the bother.

Colonel Pritchard got up to go for a snifter at the Railway Tavern and Mr Golding, having anticipated his intention, was waiting for him in the hall, already clad in his overcoat. "The Railway? Oh no, old chap," Colonel Pritchard said. "Not tonight. I've a ward meeting at the Conservative Club."

He'd never had any connection whatever with local politics, considering those who did to be a bunch of old women, but Golding didn't know that; his face fell and he took off his coat.

Mrs Pendennis wore her grey silk blouse with its pie-crust collar and leg o'mutton sleeves, and a jet brooch pinned at her throat. Mr Green thought that she looked like Queen Alexandra.

"How would it be," he asked, "if you and I were to go out for a spin some Sunday? There's a little spot in the Lakes that I'm particularly fond of. I'm sure you'd love it too. Do say yes."

Mrs Booth-Powell blew her nose in her usual foghorn fashion and Mr Gentile sucked noisily at a caramel. Mrs Pendennis winced. Perhaps it would be nice to have a day out. And this one was distinctly better-looking than Roland Machin.

"I have a friend," she said, "a Roland Machin, who was going to take me to the Lakeside . . ." She said it wistfully, as though Roland Machin, the cad, had let her down.

"Oh, I'm sure we can do a lot better than that. The *truite bleue* at the Old England . . . A little lemon sorbet . . ."

Mrs Pendennis's gastric juices flowed. She eyed him quite fondly. And the looking-glass on the opposite wall had just tendered her such a generous reflection: hair softly waved, three-quarter profile violin-shaped, not a day over fifty-five.

"I'd love to come," she said after the appropriate moment's hesitation, touching Edward Green lightly on the back of his freckled hand. She hoped that he wouldn't turn out to be a fumbler. Roland Machin sometimes essayed the odd fumble. She'd write to him and tell him not to visit for the meantime as she was going to stay with her sister-in-law on the Isle of Wight.

Suddenly Mrs Booth-Powell leaned forward and bellowed at Mrs Bannerman (unnecessarily, it was felt; Mrs Bannerman might be a little deaf, but Mrs Booth-Powell was sitting directly opposite her): "Are you all right, dear?"

She was far from all right. She'd had a session in the toilet that morning which had nearly crucified her and had only come downstairs in the vain hope that the novelty of Mrs Pendennis's new admirer would take her mind off the pain that gnawed at her lower intestine with the insatiability of a starved rat.

"Elsa!" bellowed Mrs Booth-Powell, again unnecessarily, as Elsa was standing barely two yards away. "I think you ought to ask Mrs Speakman to ring for Doctor. I don't like her colour at all."

"I've to go for the tests next Friday," Mrs Bannerman protested feebly. But Mrs Speakman wasn't risking another stiff on the premises. Her telephone message, received by the doctor's housekeeper and delivered to him at the dinner-table, was terse and to the point; Mrs Speakman had had too many years' experience not to recognise that crucial moment at which the rate of progress of a disease begins to accelerate.

"They're dropping like flies," Mrs Randall said, looking over the top of her glasses, the better to focus on the local paper. The potatoes were boiling, the cabbage was steaming and the casserole of chicken was simmering in the oven (all thighs and wings, of course; mention the word "breast" to Nora and she turned pale), so she could allow herself an indulgence. She read out the headlines to the kitchen at large as she came to them: "'Brownies Raise £120 For Lifeboat Appeal'; 'Visit of Syd Lawrence And His Orchestra'; 'Imposter Threatens Elderly Resident'. You're not safe in your beds," she said. "Fancy! Pretending he wanted to look round the house – 'with a view to purchase' – and then assaults her. They should bring back the birch. There was a case last year out at Saltlea. Makes you think, doesn't it?"

Mick combed his hair. "They've opened a new wine bar behind the Esplanade," he said. "We could try that."

Elsa cleared the tea trays. Discovering that they had the same night free, they'd decided to go out for a drink together – she saw that he'd brought a pair of respectable-looking trousers and a jacket to change into – but that arrangement had been made before Dr Rees had been summoned.

"Would you mind dreadfully if we postponed it? I'm feeling a bit off-colour."

She saw then that he had had a close shave too and, in place of the customary torn training shoes, he wore a pair of leather moccasins. Efforts had been made.

But perhaps she had overestimated the importance of her companionship. "No sweat," he said. "Another time. I quite fancy the disco actually, go and dazzle a few of the local chicks."

I was only doing you a favour. Dazzling the local chicks is far more to my taste than escorting un-chic ladies of mature years around the staider of the town's nightspots.

He didn't say so, but she suspected it was what he hoped to convey. "Go on to a club afterwards," he said. "Hey, Mary," he called across the kitchen, "might see you and Dinsdale in the Top Hat later on?"

"Not unless you're paying, lad. I'm skint. And I know he is."

Mary was not in a good mood. She'd tried a new hair dye and it had come out with a bilious green cast to it, the landlady was threatening to prosecute because Des had been fiddling the leccy meter, and the cat had worms. Again.

The gloom was general. Marguerita had received a letter that morning telling of her grandmother's death; Rosa had been obliged to slap Mr Golding's dithery old wandering hand and was now terrified that he might report her to Mrs Speakman; and to cap it all, Mrs Randall's daughter Doreen was experiencing marital problems a mere six months after the lavish wedding reception that had all but cleared out her mother's post office savings book.

And Mick combed and combed his hair, pretending that he didn't give a toss when people decided to let him down at the very last minute.

Elsa quivered with anticipation. She had been deprived of excitement for so long that she had forgotten the potency of its appeal.

"I'll collect the trays, Rosa," she said, having heard the sound of a car in the drive and judging the approximate period of time he would need to examine Mrs Bannerman. Rosa acquiesced gladly and returned to her Portuguese newspaper.

Her timing was impeccable. Mrs Speakman had gone down ahead of him to order an ambulance. He saw Elsa approaching from the end of the corridor and held open the lift door until she joined him. She laid the trays down inside and he manipulated the handle so that they came to a halt between floors then, with his free hand, pulled her close to him.

A saucer cracked beneath his foot. Kissing her, he released his pressure upon the handle and the lift shuddered and then moved slightly, a shudder and a movement that were echoed in his body. "Oh God," he groaned into her neck. "When? Where?" he implored, finding his desperate exploration foiled by the gusset of a pair of tights.

"Soon. I don't know."

It was all that he could expect, but his erection persisted.

"Tomorrow? In the park?"

She nodded, and with her assent he allowed the lift to judder to the ground floor.

He held his case in front of the incriminating area of his anatomy and barged past Mr Golding who was waiting to ascend. Lucky fellow, he thought, too old to be troubled by inappropriate physical reactions.

He stood in the deserted hall, waiting until he achieved calm. As a young man he'd been too busy, too terrified of rejection and too unsure about his own attractiveness to risk much sexual experimentation. Then there had been ample opportunity. Now, when temperance was demanded of him and age might have been expected to dull his appetite, his body betrayed him, reacting just as violently, albeit with a finer discrimination, as it had in adolescence. At that point the lad: kitchen-hand, general factotum, newest member of Nora's band of slave labour, came through the kitchen door, stopped in front of the hall mirror, gave his reflection a critical glance and then ran lightly down the steps. "Dr Rees?" he heard Nora Speakman call. Go to it, lad, he thought grimly. All too soon you'll be as old as I am, still feeling as young as you are now.

8

The morphine dosage administered to Mrs Bannerman was gradually increased. Under its influence she dreamed the sort of lucid dreams that linger all day in one's memory. Mrs Bannerman, however, was never awake long enough for this to occur: one dream was succeeded by the next without the interval necessary for conscious examination of it.

Had she remembered she would have been mortified by the scenes that were played out behind the deceptively demure appearance of her closed eyelids. "'Bill,' she keeps saying," one nurse reported to another, raising her ear from Mrs Bannerman's murmuring lips, "I suppose that was her husband."

The nurse had guessed correctly, though in her dream Mrs Bannerman's Bill was behaving as he had never behaved in life. In life he had treated his wife with respect and tenderness. Only in the loft with the magazines did he adopt an entirely different sexual persona: brutal and dominant. Fuelled by the pornographic pictures, his ejaculations were explosive, magnificent – oh so very different from those feeble dribbling emissions that dampened the sheets of the marriage bed.

"Yes, Bill, oh yes. Like that," urged Mrs Bannerman of her husband, in her dream. "Hurt me!" she demanded. Never, until the occasion of her dying dreams, had she admitted to herself that she found her husband's sexual attentions insufficiently dynamic. Only now could she own up to the excitement that had quite overpowered the disgust attendant upon her discovery, after his death, of the pornography in the attic.

The ratio between the effectiveness of the morphine and the viciousness of the pain changed over the period of her dying.

Miss Vyner had not been too inaccurate in supposing that the final oblivion would come not by the grace of God but from a syringe. Yet who, except the most blazing fanatic, could object if the only alternative was howling agony?

She died on the last day of May. Dr Rees – coincidentally, he was visiting another patient – was there at the time of her death. He remembered lectures in medical school, earnest debates, concerning the ethics of mortality. He remembered how fervently he had argued against the medical man adopting a god-like stance; "No one has the *right*," he'd argued. But he'd never seen an advanced case of cancer of the bowel then.

He left the social worker attempting to rustle up some distant relation; how easily it could happen that only the vicar and the undertaker were present to witness the casket sliding noiselessly towards the furnace doors.

For instance, should his sister Olwen not survive him, he would find himself in that position. Apart from Diana, of course. And as he drove along the coastal road past a busload of schoolchildren out for a day by the sea, he was subject to that pang which occasionally surprises even the most child-hating of the childless; the knowledge that their line has no prospect of continuation.

Apart from Diana. He was surprised to find her at home. She was off it at the moment, and when she was off it she usually attempted to occupy her time with outdoor pursuits: golf and tennis in the summer, photography and bird-watching in the winter – the detritus of discarded hobbies that littered the house!

She'd never cared for housewifely pursuits. During the early, happy time of their marriage (for there had been a happy time – difficult though it was to remember – when they had, briefly, transformed themselves into what each desired of the other), though she'd tried hard, he'd realised that she was bored to distraction by the routine. Child of privilege, it had come as a shock to her to discover that chores, once completed, soon need to be tackled again.

Unseen, he watched her through the kitchen window. He didn't think she'd have been aware of him had she spotted him, so deeply absorbed did she seem in her book. It was their housekeeper's day off and the breakfast things had been merely pushed to one end of the table. An avid reader of novels all her life, she read in the way that a child does: head supported on hands, fingers running through her hair, totally absorbed. At her elbow stood a pot of the marmalade that still bore her maiden name upon its label (although the firm had been taken over long since), toast crusts littered the tablecloth. It would never have occurred to her to clear the crockery and *then* read her book; she was as impatient of gratification as a child.

"You should give her some kids of her own," her father had told him just before he died, when it became obvious that procreation was not the foremost priority of their marriage. "What's up?" her father had said. "Can't you make kids?" He was a vulgar old man and nothing would have given his son-in-law greater pleasure than to answer him in the same vein, but he was dying and, besides, the truth of the matter had to be kept from him: that his lack of grandchildren was due not to Emlyn's second-rate spermatozoa but, rather, the result of his daughter's illegal termination.

She had been lovely. And wilful. Prey to the first rascal who promised her heaven in order to persuade her to part her legs. Terrified when she found herself pregnant at seventeen, she'd consented to an abortion. He'd aborted her, all right, that struck-off doctor, unqualified medical student – whatever he'd been, plying his trade on a kitchen table covered with oilcloth – but he'd left her with the salpingitis that eventually blocked her fallopian tubes and rendered her sterile.

She was no longer quite so lovely. Drink and dissatisfaction had distorted her loveliness, leaving only hints, echoes, of the girl in the white dress to whom he'd been introduced twenty-three years ago by a colleague who had had the honour that year of escorting her to a May Ball. She had seemed haughty and unattainable, quite beyond the reach of his most towering aspirations. Because of that he hadn't tried, and because he hadn't tried she'd been intrigued. He was real, she'd told him. So refreshing after all the poseurs and the playboys, the silver-spoon merchants. He was a dedicated man, a man of principle, devoting his life to the alleviation of suffering.

She had made him sound like Florence Nightingale. Whereas in those days he was much less interested in the patient than the disease. But the unexpected gift of her expensively-nurtured flesh had silenced his mouth, except for the unfamiliar purpose of murmuring endearments. His dedication, like her dream of becoming the power behind his throne, was a myth. Later, after she became a full-time drunkard, she would cry and castigate herself for having been the cause of blighting his career. That was another myth; he was competent and conscientious but, as a general practitioner in the provinces, had reached the level for which his talents most exactly fitted him.

She didn't look up until he was standing within a couple of yards of the table. Once he would have aroused her from absorption with a kiss. Now their touching took place only – and infrequently – in bed.

"Oh! I didn't expect you home. I've not done any lunch."

He had told her, quite distinctly, before he left. These lapses were becoming more frequent. She would give every impression of according him her undivided attention; half an hour later she would deny ever having been given the information, but whether because of genuine forgetfulness or contrariness, he couldn't decide.

"I'll get you something."

She tipped over the marmalade jar in her anxiety to atone. "It's all right," he said, moving towards the fridge.

He took out a carton of eggs. If I had been different, he thought, for the million and somethingth time, so would she.

"Omelettes?" she said brightly.

"I'll do them."

She couldn't boil an egg without leaving the kitchen looking as though World War Three had been fought in it.

"Good book?" he asked, as he took the crockery out of her hands and, quickly and neatly, cleared the table and reset it.

She shrugged. "He's going off. Getting old, I suppose." She stretched her arms above her head. Even when drunk her gestures were fluid, graceful; she should have been an actress, a dancer – if only she had been able to act, or dance. She should have been – *something*.

"Getting old," she repeated. "Like me."

He beat the eggs in a bowl, flicked out the glutinous speck of bloody germ, the speck which indicated that fertilisation had occurred. Nowadays, blocked fallopian tubes could be unblocked. Or the sperm and the egg could be conjoined without it being necessary for any journey to be made via that route.

"How've you been?" he asked. The techniques of in vitro fertilisation had been developed too late to be of any use to them. She was undergoing an early and troublesome menopause.

"Not so bad. I took the tablets. Oh, not for me," she said, seeing him about to divide the omelette into equal portions.

He looked at her suspiciously. Lack of appetite was usually one of the earliest signs of the return of her alcoholic craving. But she returned his gaze steadily. "No need to panic. I'm trying to diet. Bad enough to have my hormones dwindling away, I refuse to turn into a fat sow yet awhile."

But she had kept her figure. Made-up, elegantly-dressed, she could still turn heads. And yet, only once had she been unfaithful. She'd told him. She told him everything. He wished to Christ that she wouldn't.

"Is it warm outside?"

"Yes, very."

"I might do some sketching this afternoon," she said. "I haven't done any for ages."

"I thought you had an AA meeting this afternoon." He quaked, imagining she and Elsa finding themselves seated next to one another, producing their individual versions of the view and eagerly making each other's acquaintance.

She grimaced. "They're so boring. And so earnest. It's like Billy Graham."

"Oh *do* go, Diana. You know how important they are."

She wandered into the sitting-room and put a record on: the "Missa Luba", sacred music transposed into a tribal chant, her latest enthusiasm. She played it at full blast. "Kyrie Eleison," yelled the Bantu tribesmen. A good job we live in a detached house, he thought. A good job for many reasons. "You *will* go, Diana?" he persisted.

She moved her body sinuously to the rhythm of the chanting. "There's no *point*," she said. "It just brings it all back. And what's the *point* when it's over now?"

The omelette turned to ashes in his mouth. How many times had he heard *that* before?

The residents of Priory Lodge contributed towards a wreath for Mrs Bannerman. Mrs Booth-Powell made enquiries at various florists and proclaimed that the best bargain was to be had at The Flower Basket: "Eight pounds sixty-five," she said. "By my calculation, that means if we all contribute, it will be seventy pence each. I shall make up the extra twenty-five pence myself," she added magnanimously.

There were general murmurings of consent except from Mrs Crookthorne who, if they passed the hat round, had hoped to get away with donating ten pence.

"I've no change," she tried at first, but Mrs Booth-Powell, briskly ticking names off her list, said, "That's no problem. I've plenty."

Strapped for cash, Leonard Golding thought to himself, as he watched her fumbling in her purse. Or thinks she is, more likely, tight old bat. There had been animosity between them ever since he'd walked into the Gloucester Room on his first evening and found her asleep with her mouth open, snoring volubly, though he wasn't aware of either Bertie or Bertie's political persuasion, and she couldn't have known that only a generation ago, before the journey was made from Whitechapel to Golders Green and thence to rural Cheshire, Golding had been Goldstein.

He volunteered to attend the funeral, or "committal procedure" as Mrs Speakman called it, which sounded to him as though Mrs Bannerman was being sent to the loony bin or for trial. Having been both up for trial and in the loony bin himself, as a young man, this put him off a bit. But he attempted to straighten his shoulders in imitation of Colonel Pritchard's military bearing and told himself that a male presence was necessary and there was only himself to provide it, what with Gentile being a left-footer and the Colonel unwilling to attend send-offs because they reminded him of Maud and upset him terribly.

In the end, on the day of the funeral, attendance was sparse: Miss Vyner was an atheist, Mrs Pendennis was having her day out with Edward Green, and Mrs Grey was visiting her sister; so there was just Mr Golding, Mrs Booth-Powell and Miss Johns who, in her capacity as rector's daughter, always attended such functions.

Though, to Leonard Golding's way of thinking, you couldn't consider a cremation to be a proper funeral: a couple of quick prayers, a brief spouting from the vicar, a snatch of sacred music as the coffin, covered with its pathetically few wreaths, slid through the curtains. The only surviving relative – a distant cousin who was looking very pleased with himself at the unexpected windfall ("Who? Oh, old Auntie Mabel. Oh yes, I remember her vaguely; she came to visit when I was a kid") had arranged a cremation because it worked out cheaper.

In the Garden of Remembrance a council worker padlocked his bicycle against the end of the wall upon which were placed several funerary urns. "And may the love of God, the grace of our Lord Jesus Christ and the fellowship of the Holy Spirit be with you and remain with you for evermore, amen," gabbled the vicar, hitching his cassock on to his shoulder and leading the way out of the chapel. He probably had another cremation to preside over in ten minutes' time. Leonard Golding, who rarely considered himself to be anything other than a gentile, thought, "These Christians, they have no sense of ceremony, no understanding of the annealing power of ritual. They scurry through the most important occasions of their lives as though they are ashamed of being human."

"Well, that's that," Mrs Booth-Powell pronounced, sighing deeply. Her mauve-powdered jowls trembled for a moment or two. However casual your acquaintanceship with the deceased, however perfunctory the funeral service, you couldn't help but be upset. The distant relation shook hands with all present, heartily and rapidly, tipped the undertaker and departed without offering anyone a lift. "Lovely day," Miss Johns said vaguely and irrelevantly. She'd seen too many funerals at too close hand to be upset.

"Would you allow me to buy you a sherry?" Mr Golding said suddenly, greatly daring, as they stood outside the chapel, feeling like three spare parts. It was what the Colonel would have said. He knew how to treat women: with just the correct mixture of firmness and gallantry. Of course, the Colonel had been married and had, no doubt, had sexual intercourse – experiences of which Mr Golding was totally innocent.

He ordered a taxi and took them to the lounge bar of the Railway Tavern, hoping that it would be considered suitable for the entertainment of ladies. Mrs Booth-Powell just about managed to conceal the fact that she judged the place to be rather low-class. Miss Johns blushed with a mixture of nervousness and exhilaration. It gave him the confidence to order the drinks and carry them back without spilling a drop. "Now then," he said, smacking one plump thigh with the flat of his hand. "Your very good health." The Colonel always said that, so it must be all right.

Here he sat, in the company of two women. Not the most attractive members of their sex, but women nonetheless. Music played in the background, gentle, undifferentiated music. The barmaid had smiled at him. Mrs Booth-Powell pursed her lips and tilted the glass to her mouth. Miss Johns, who loathed the taste of alcohol, read the jokes on the beer mats and hummed along to the tune. How easy it was. He understood now, too late, at the age of seventy-three: you simply asked and they accepted. If only he'd known all those years ago he'd never have been obliged to attempt to satisfy his curiosity by exploring little girls, never needed to spend all that time in the Retreat, never felt that his experiences had barred him for all time from essaying what they called a "normal relationship". Why, he wondered, gazing into the tawny depths of his glass, were the lessons always learned when it was too late for any practical application?

The music meant that you didn't need to strain to make conversation. The odd pleasantry, and you could hum along to it while you gazed out of the window and watched the world go about its business.

Though sometimes the business of the world was close to home and prompted conversation. "Isn't that the doctor's wife?" said Mrs Booth-Powell, peering, raising her bottom from the banquette, the better to see.

"It is," said Miss Johns, who was sitting nearest the window and had suffered no impairment of vision. As Mrs Crookthorne acted as the ears of Priory Lodge, so Miss Johns provided the eyes.

She had come roaring down the street in her sports car, the doctor's wife (sometimes she drove barefoot, it was said), and shrieked to a halt upon a double yellow line and jumped out leaving the door open and the key in the ignition as she disappeared into the off-licence and came out again some moments later carrying a large brown paper bag in both arms.

"Back on the juice," Mr Golding commented and thought what a waste of a fine-looking woman. He patronised the same off-licence and drank his purchases in his room. Sometimes the room rotated and the bed floated when he lay down to sleep, but he didn't consider himself to be a toper. Trouble was, alone, you drank far more than you did in company. At the Colonel's elbow he was quite content with a couple of pints of bitter of an evening.

Miss Johns marvelled that anyone could enjoy the taste of the stuff sufficiently to actually buy quantities of it. She held her breath and took a sip of her sherry. It seemed so *childish* to order orange squash.

"I thought they'd been told not to serve her," Mr Golding said. He watched her wistfully, as she swung her long legs into the driving seat.

"What would be the point?" said Mrs Booth-Powell. "She'd simply go elsewhere for it. It's a sickness, you know," she told them as if there was no likelihood that they could already be aware of this. "Just as well she has a position in the community and her escapades can be hushed up. Otherwise she might well have found herself up before the Bench."

Mr Booth-Powell had been a magistrate. Drunk and disorderlies had provided the main bulk of his clientèle.

"It's the reward you reap when you bring your child up badly," she told them. But since Diana Rees's father had died before he could reap any reward, and given that the knowledge of Mr Golding and Miss Johns concerning children was very limited indeed, the profundity and aptness of this remark were debatable.

9

Elsa had supposed that since she'd turned down Mick's offer of escort, no further invitation would be forthcoming. After all, however well they seemed to get on, superficially, he was scarcely more than a lad and needed companionship nearer his own age. And she was too old, in her attitudes as well as in years, to enjoy what she supposed he would enjoy.

She knew he'd gone out to the clubs and got legless the night she'd cancelled her date with him; Mary Reilly had reported back (apparently she and her feller had raised the money for a night out from somewhere – the electric meter, probably): "Paralytic. Silly lad. Des had to carry him back."

The story Mick told, however, which involved discos and dancing partners of astonishing pulchritude mad for carnal knowledge of him, did not tally. "Please don't try so hard to impress," she wanted to tell him, as a mother would gently rebuke a small child for showing off. She found his personality such a curious mixture of the childish and the mature: it was he who had comforted Marguerita, drawing on his meagre knowledge of schoolroom Spanish, when she'd received the news of her grandmother's death; it was he who had lent Mary Reilly the tenner that prevented her and Des and the cat from being thrown out into the street. Yet news of Mrs Bannerman's death provoked a stream of lavatorial jokes, and exaggeration, she suspected, came more naturally to his lips than did the plain truth.

"I've got the chance of a motor," he told her, the morning of the day Mrs Bannerman died. "Nice job," he said. "If he'll come down a few quid."

"Oh yes," she'd said, supposing that this was one of his stories: the Harley Davidson that he'd ridden right into the chemistry lab at school, the Swedish film starlet ("Honest to God!") with whom he'd spent last summer's vacation, his job as a roadie with "The Worm In The Bud" before they struck lucky and decided to call themselves something else.

But on the afternoon of the cremation – his day off – he poked his head around the kichen door and called to her: "Elsie! Come on outside. I want to show you something."

It stood next to the Speakmans' Rover; an ancient Jaguar, battered, half-rusted away. The offside rear door was blue, the rest of the bodywork was maroon and the number plate had been tied on with a piece of string.

"All right, isn't it?"

Pride of ownership shone from his every feature.

"Does it go?"

"Of course it goes. Engine's been stripped down, hasn't it? The guy who sold it me's a mechanic. Does this sort of thing all the time. You don't want to go by appearances."

She'd always wondered what, if you oughtn't to go by appearances, you were expected to go by, since most situations demanded a decision long before all the relevant facts and hidden snags became known.

"Judge for yourself," he said. "It's your day off tomorrow, isn't it? We'll take it for a spin."

"It's not your day off, though. Is it?"

He tapped the side of his nose. "Going to be not well tomorrow, aren't I? I reckon I'm due a slight malinger. How about it?"

"Have you a licence?"

"Christ, I hope the man from Littlewoods never comes knocking on your door. You'll spend so long enquiring about his credentials that he'll change his mind and piss off somewhere else."

"What will you be ill with?"

He rolled his eyes and staggered. "I dunno – how about twenty-four-hour Lassa fever? I'll think of something. Are you on?"

Why not? There might be an age gap between them, but surely enjoyment of each other's company made that irrelevant?

Young people enjoying themselves, Mrs Pegler thought, as she trotted through the front gate on her way back from an appointment with her broker. She smiled and waved at them, but then felt wistful. They reminded her of children and grandchildren, distant, dim in her memory, despite the glossy colour photographs and the letters sent at religiously regular intervals. She could afford first-class travel, her display of diamonds elicited attentive and respectful service, but she was old, too old. She needed them to come to her, just as Mrs Cuthbert-Carew's family had surrounded her and sustained her in old age. But that was tradition and the only tradition that flourished in the Pegler family was a striving for betterment and that still in its infancy.

She went up to her room and unhooked her corsets (custom-made by Cammell Laird's, Dad used to joke; they were custom-made, of course, but by Ambrose Wilson) and kicked off her shoes (shaped to the specifications of her own personal last) and sank her well-fitting, non-NHS dentures into a marron glacée (hand-confected in Belgium). Life was full of sadnesses, she thought, but sadness could be assuaged – to a degree, as long as you had your health and strength – and money.

"How much will the petrol cost?" Elsa asked next morning, standing with her hand on the door, afraid that if she tried to open it it would drop off.

"We'll worry about that afterwards."

He wore a pair of very dark wrap-around sunglasses, the inevitable jeans and a jacket in that fashionable stuff they called distressed denim. She considered that his ordinary jeans – aged and tattered – fitted the description far more accurately.

"How much?"

Fashionable new clothes and cars – however decrepit – did not come cheap; it was difficult to believe that Nora Speakman's wages, even supplemented by the state, could run to them.

"Elsie, Elsie," he said, opening the passenger door from inside, "relax and get in. We'll monitor the petrol consumption to the last gramme, or whatever it is, and then we'll divide it precisely by two. All right?"

"All right."

But when he stopped at the petrol station she was horrified

by the amount that clicked up on the pump. She remembered then, from what Rob had told her, that these cars tended to go cheap in old age because of their enormous petrol consumption.

"Wouldn't you have been better off with a smaller car?" she asked, as he flung the credit card counterfoil in through the window where it fluttered to the floor, as carelessly as though credit card counterfoils had no connection with the day of reckoning. "A Mini or something?"

He grinned derisively. "A Mini? Give over. I wouldn't be seen dead."

"Why are you such a *misery*," Rob had said, when he was trying to convince himself and everybody else, by dint of frantic bouts of spending, that the business was not plunging downhill fast and she was counselling caution. "Why do you *never* look on the bright side?"

She'd been appalled by his insensitivity. "Life," she'd said, her face in her hands, "has not given me much occasion to look on the bright side."

"I know, I know. I know what's happened. But we've got to go on living," he'd said, hoping that where sympathy had failed, his callousness might jolt her into animation.

That conversation had taken place two years ago and ever since she'd tried to suppress the pessimistic, overcautious side of her nature. A new status, fresh surroundings, a job, an uncritical response to the promptings of sexual desire, they were all part of her attempt to transform herself, to close off the past. But one thing remained, would always remain. "Can I ask you something?" she enquired of Mick.

"What?" He was unwrapping a packet of Benson and Hedges with his teeth as he started up the car and reversed out of the garage.

"Not to drive too fast. I get frightened."

"I'm a very good driver."

"I've no doubt. It's just – a phobic thing, I suppose. Please?"

"OK. I'll drive the way the Unspeakable Rodney drives the Rover – like he's taking it to a funeral."

And it turned out that he had very little option to do otherwise. Road works were taking place on the motorway, the traffic was filtered into one lane and the volume of it made anything more than a hearse-like progress impossible.

"Where are we going, anyway?" she asked, somewhat belatedly as, stationary yet again, he flicked through the radio band until he found something sufficiently cacophonous to perforate their eardrums.

"Blackpool, of course. Isn't that the aim of all vulgar days out round here?"

Of course. Perfect. From the first whiff of ozone to the last greasy newspaper-clad portion of chips. Blackpool, where you shrieked and sang and made a spectacle of yourself and nobody noticed because everybody else was doing the same; Blackpool, which your parents would never have chosen as their holiday destination because the other holidaymakers were so common.

"What's the difference between vulgar and common?" she asked him idly as they edged forward another few yards.

"I dunno – maybe vulgar's having bad taste, whereas common's having no taste at all."

The wind blew the little cotton-wool clouds inland. White bordered waves frilled and broke on the beach. The sun climbed high and when they breathed there was salt in their nostrils. He parked the car and leaned over the Promenade rail, filling his lungs. His plumed fringe streamed away from his forehead. He took her hand. "Where first?"

"A tram ride?"

"The funfair?"

"A bag of cockles?"

"A stick of rock? A paddle in the sea?"

All of them. But first there were the finances to be arranged. She took two ten-pound notes from her purse and pressed them into his hand. "Keep a count and you can give me the change afterwards. Otherwise I'm going straight back."

"You'll have a job on, m'duck. Unless you want to hitch. They tore up the railway years ago. Mrs Randall was telling me. She calls it a damn shame. 'I call it a damn shame,' she said."

"M'duck?"

"It's what we say where I come from."

"Where *do* you come from?"

"The Black Country, den oi?" he replied in grossly exaggerated accents and then began to run. "Race you down to the sands. If your old legs'll stand it."

They screamed as the first of the waves lapped icily at their ankles. The sun was high and bright but the water was as cold as death. He hopped from foot to foot, howling, and retreated. Small children wearing water-wings ran past him and into the water without so much as a shudder.

"Nesh," she taunted him.

"Nesh, my arse," he retorted, taking off his jacket and distressing the denim even further by drying his feet on it. "Your balls could drop off. Look," he said, as they trod back to the Promenade through the soft sand, "you don't have to go halves. I'm all right for cash."

"I'd prefer to."

He bought two tubs of potted shrimps to sustain them until they found somewhere for lunch. "I got the impression you were saving up madly for this college thing," he said.

"I am. I'll probably get a grant but it won't be a full one." There was a little flutter of excitement when she thought about it: her interview, in a fortnight's time.

"Your timing's rotten, isn't it?" he said, digging into his shrimps. "You should have applied before Maggie's lot got in, or moved to where there was a Labour council. You wouldn't have had as much trouble then."

"Maybe they'll let me have the proportion of yours that's been wasted," she said, feeling suddenly nettled by his know-all tone.

"Fair enough. OK. Anyway, how come your ex doesn't contribute? What happened to alimony? The papers are always full of letters from second wives whingeing on about how unfair it is that he has to pay out for their predecessors. I thought you lot were all on a meal-ticket for life. Or is that only the ones with kids?"

"There's got to *be* money before there can be any question of leeching," she replied. "And he hasn't any. So that's that."

"I thought you said his girlfriend wasn't short of a bob or two."

"She isn't."

"So why doesn't that count?"

"It might. Except that they moved to Scotland and the two legal systems are separate. I've got no claim on him there."

"Oh," he said, crushing his empty tub and kicking it into the stratosphere. "Knackered then?"

"Totally knackered."

"Still," he said, "it means you retain your integrity, and that's what matters."

"Is it?"

"So everyone says. Personally I reckon it's more important to be able to eat. Integrity's usually what those who are in no danger of going hungry tend to preach about, all that 'how degrading' stuff and 'I'd starve in the gutter before I'd . . .' Nellie Macpherson says that: 'I'd starve in the gutter before I'd . . .'"

". . . strip twice nightly for my living."

". . . offer hand relief in a massage parlour."

". . . model for a centrefold."

Nudging each other delightedly, they made their way down the Prom, past the seafood stalls and the rock shops and the waxworks and the many only genuine daughters of Gipsy Petulengro and the hamburger bars and the souvenir shops and the places where you could have your ears pierced or your tee-shirt printed with a slogan, the booths where they stuck your head through a hole in a seaside postcard painting and took your photograph, past the Winter Gardens and the funfair and the Tower Ballroom and all the piers. Everything that wasn't vulgar was common, and everything appealed. After they'd eaten, they retraced their steps and sampled every one of the garish delights: they fed coins into the maws of amusement machines, they blasted space invaders and crossed off numbers on Bingo cards, they inspected the zoo: a lethargic puma, comatose polar bears. They sucked at pieces of rock fashioned in the shape of false teeth (which reminded them vividly of the contents of the tumblers that reposed at so many bedsides in Priory Lodge); they were photographed as evil seducer and female prey: "The Unspeakable Rodders," Mick said, "twirling his moustaches," and leered magnificently. They screamed on the waltzer and shrieked on the log flume and rode painted horses buoyantly to the music of Johann Strauss. He bought an earring in the shape of a small gilded skull to replace the cross that he normally wore even though she warned him that it would turn his ear green. He bought a very rude postcard which he sent, anonymously, to Mrs Booth-Powell. He bought candyfloss which evaporated and encrusted their faces so that they had to spit on each other's handkerchiefs and perform rudimentary ablutions.

In her old life she'd enjoyed a glass of dry white wine and a Mozart horn concerto, the autumn quiet of the walled garden, a soft spring rain; an ordered routine, the knowledge that resources were being husbanded wisely. In her old life. Now she spat on her handkerchief in the midst of the shrieking, jostling, malodorous throng and dabbed at the sugar crusts on his chin. She watched him spending her money with glorious abandon. She was hot and rumpled and dirty, and she was enjoying herself. "Poor lass," Dad had said, "there's not much enjoyment for you, is there?" "Why are you always such a misery?" Rob had said, before leaving her for one whose relentlessly ebullient nature smothered the first faint trace of gloom, and whose bank balance enabled him to pull himself out of the mire.

A tram ride took them from the petered-out desolation of Squire's Gate along the Golden Mile, past the parades of boarding-houses and private hotels, to the residential roads of prosperous Bispham. In one of the private gardens a woman dead-headed her early roses. It was a well-stocked garden, and reminded Elsa of her own in the old life. "Domesticity," Mick said, following her gaze. "Dolls' houses. I suppose you had one?"

He said it with the sort of intonation you'd employ to describe a prison cell.

"Yes." Mature, well-stocked gardens. Four bedrooms (we needed the extra for Dad), close to local schools and amenities. "It had to be sold, when the business got into difficulties. We moved into a rented flat." And when he left I discovered that the rent hadn't even been paid for the last three months.

"He sounds a real creep."

"No. He was just scared."

Like you, I suspect, she thought, stealing a look as he gazed out to sea, shading his eyes with his hands – the chic sunglasses, now forgotten, pushed back on top of his head. Scared and running; it's something you recognise, like a smell. "Can't you go back to university?" she asked impulsively.

"It's not irrevocable, is it? Couldn't you change your course?"

He closed his eyes as though to blot out an unwelcome prying presence. "It's not really a question of that . . . Anyway, shut up about it. I'm just sick and tired of trying to do what other people want me to do . . ."

The tram approached the stop and he got up from his seat. Her approach had been wrong, she realised; "for your own good" was the tactic that could always be relied upon to alienate whoever it was whose good concerned you.

The fortune-telling booths opened on to the pavements. They were partitioned off to provide little antechambers where the clients could wait their turn. They were furnished with gilt and chintz and sprays of artificial flowers. Testimonials from famous names of stage and screen papered the windows and crystal balls (presumably spares) reposed on lace tablecloths. Where trade was slack, the current Gipsy Rose Lee or the Only Authentic Petulengro sat at the entrance, raising her face to the sunshine and touting for custom.

They had scoffed at them, reading aloud the reckless pronouncements: "Your problems resolved"; "Your heart's desire can be granted"; "A reading may change your life", craning their necks to identify the faded likenesses of the forgotten celebrities who vouched for the clairvoyant powers of the proprietors.

"Only a pound," the gipsy women chanted whenever they spotted a potential punter. "A pound reveals your destiny," and then, if their offers were ignored, returned to their sunbathing.

"How can they *all* be the only authentic whoever it is? Load of con merchants," Mick proclaimed. But in a side-street, the beckoning of one particularly exotic crone seemed so personally directed that it was difficult to resist. "Come on," he said. "Let's have a laugh. Let's hear her two-penn'orth."

"One pound fifty's worth, actually. No thanks."

But the crone continued to beckon, fixed him with an implacable dark eye, and began her sales pitch, delivered without inflection: "Your future revealed only one pound fifty your problem solved . . ."

"Come on!" he urged, hesitating at the threshold.

She shook her head. "I don't want to know, whatever it is."

I don't want to know because accepting that it's all laid down beforehand makes a nonsense of trying to *make* it happen.

He had hesitated too long. The old woman drew them inside. "Come on in, lovey, nothing to be afraid of."

She had greasy sausage curls and chipped nail varnish and an accent cultivated in some Lancashire mill town. With one hand she took his money, with the other she took his hand and held it close to her myopic gaze. A cluster of gilt bangles slid down her arm to her elbow and the sleeve of her variegated gipsy-type robe fell back to reveal a Marks and Spencer's acrylic jumper. She spoke again in the same wearied tone: "You're the artistic type but you haven't yet found what you're looking for in life, you've been ill as a child and you had an operation when you were seven, isn't that right, lovey?"

"Yes, that's right."

"There was a girl last year, she went away to another country. A 'J', I think: Jenny, Janet? Aquamarine is your lucky stone and you was born this month, weren't you? Aren't I right?"

The atmosphere in the cabin was stifling. Incense mingled with the woman's smell. The chanting continued: "You've a friend, a good friend . . . A woman will bring you luck . . ." Mediums, Elsa had heard, spoke in the same inflectionless monotone – until they were taken over by their guides. She yawned until her eyes watered and the woman glanced at her sharply and then back at Mick's hand which, Elsa noticed, was criss-crossed with tiny lines. Men's weren't, usually; Rob had had only a very few: clear-cut, deeply-scored; she tried to think of Emlyn's but could remember only the touch of it and not the way that it looked.

The woman was speaking more quickly. Urgently. Her face, hitherto bland and bored, took on a pinched, keenly-focused expression. He tried to draw his hand back but she held on. "There's trouble. But not if you leave now. Go home. There's two tall men and a woman in black. There's black all round her. There's a blade and trouble. You go home. You'll be all right."

It was momentary, the change, over almost before they'd registered it. Her speech slowed, her face cleared, the chanting re-established itself: "Monday's your lucky day. You've just had a windfall, aren't I right, lovey?" And that was that.

"Dear Christ!"

They collapsed, giggling, against each other, repeating her cryptic comments. "Dear Christ!" he said. "The gipsy's warning!"

"Beware the woman in black!" she said in sepulchral tones.

His face was pale though, and they giggled not so much from amusement as from nervousness.

"Well, I suppose it's a variation on the woman in white," he said, pulling her into Yates's Wine Lodge. "Jesus! I think I definitely need a drink."

"But not too many?"

There was the return journey to be negotiated and he'd had plenty already.

They'd finished the road works and the traffic lanes were clear. She sat rigid beside him, watching the luminous green needle moving clockwise around the dial of the speedometer, pressing her foot against the floor as though she expected the brake pedal to have miraculously changed its position. The sun set spectacularly ahead of them, the wind whistled through the open quarter-lights, and the needle continued to climb.

She closed her eyes and prayed. He talked, and seemed unconcerned that his chatter provoked no response. Sometimes he took a hand off the wheel while he fumbled to strike a match on the box clutched between his thighs and she felt the steering waver and sweat beading her forehead. Trees and fields and houses and petrol stations flashed by and she clenched herself tightly, trying to prevent the scream escaping from her throat.

Suddenly there was a noise like a pistol shot and the wheel pulled at his hands as though it had developed a will of its own. She heard him say, "What the fuck!" as he fought for control and they careered towards the crown of the road. And then the screaming could no longer be contained and ripped through her throat and out of her mouth and she closed her eyes because she could not bear to witness the moment when they would crash into the central reservation barrier looming up ahead.

10

"I told you I was a good driver."

He held the cup to her lips because her hands were still shaking. Her teeth chattered on its rim but eventually she was able to swallow a little of its contents: tea, very hot and sweet, the same sort that she'd brewed for him after he'd had to carry the dead weight of Mrs Cuthbert-Carew across to a sofa; her last resting-place in Priory Lodge.

"Can I get you something to eat?"

Elsa shook her head; the tea scalded her throat which felt sore – from her screaming, she supposed.

"You *are* all right?"

He peered at her anxiously, afraid that she might be in need of medical attention, that authorities might have to be alerted. By a stroke of luck, the blow-out had occurred only a few yards from a service station and he had been able to push the car on to the forecourt. "Oh God!" she'd said, when he'd told her that it wasn't insured; but, badly shaken though she was, it occurred to her that this news was hardly surprising.

"I was going to insure it in the morning. I *was*. Christ, I didn't know the tyre was due to blow, did I?"

It was the front nearside tyre that had gone – of all four the one most likely to cause a serious accident. But, miraculously, that particular stretch of road had been free of traffic and he'd regained control just in time. He was, as he said, a good driver.

Her shuddering became spasmodic. Tentatively, she lifted her cup and found that she could hold it steady enough to drink from it. He watched her closely, enquired if her vision was normal, whether her pulse rate had slowed down and was she absolutely sure she didn't fancy a sandwich, a plate of egg and chips, a quarter-pound beefburger?

"No!"

It came out as a harsh croak. Her vocal cords felt as though they had been sandpapered, which was hardly surprising given that her scream had echoed inside the car long after he'd brought it to a halt.

"What will we do?" she enquired of him; his unblinking scrutiny made her feel uncomfortable.

"Change the wheel. No sweat. Look, I'm dead sorry," he said. "This can't be the best thing for someone who's scared in cars. She pulled like you wouldn't believe," he said, unable to eradicate the self-congratulatory note from his voice. "I could see eternity looming. I say, old whatsit the fortune-teller never foretold this, did she? I reckon I ought to ask for a refund. Unless this is what she meant by a woman in black. Perhaps I was due to snuff it and you would be climbing into the old subfusc in order to mourn at my graveside. Obviously she hadn't bargained for my quick-as-lightning reflexes – Oh Christ, what's up?"

Tears were falling. Like rain. From her eyes into her teacup and all over the tabletop. And the more she tried to contain them the faster they flowed. A woman clearing the neighbouring tables paused with a pile of saucers suspended in mid-air and gaped.

"Elsie!" he hissed. "For Christ's *sake.*"

"Elsa!" Rob had hissed when, once before, her tears had flowed in a torrent, when embarrassment had, briefly, overcome his grief.

"Is it shock?" Mick asked. As long as he was able to classify and categorise, it seemed, he felt capable of handling the situation.

Gradually she achieved calm. She mopped her face and blew her nose and attempted to breathe deeply and rhythmically. He kept darting little glances at the door as though he would dearly have loved to leave her, change his wheel, and roar away into the night. Granted it had been a bad experience, but hardly enough to warrant the sort of over-the-top performance she was staging. She owed him an explanation for her behaviour. No. That wasn't it; she *wanted* to tell him.

For the first time in four years she wanted to tell. Because of what had just happened. And because the recipient of the information, unlike most of the people who had had to be told, would not have at his disposal a fund of the stock sympathetic responses that made you want to scream and keep on screaming until their stupid faces registered the knowledge that there wasn't anything anyone could say which could be of any comfort; not even in the smallest degree.

"I'm sorry," she said, as the sobs became sighs and she caught the last tear as it dripped from her chin. "The reason that I'm scared of cars and speed is that I had a child who was killed in a road accident, and I know I have to get over it, the fear I mean – everybody told me that – and I think I have, mostly, but obviously something like this brings it back . . . Rob made me get into a car straight afterwards. I wasn't going to, I was going to walk to the funeral. But he made me. I was yelling and shouting and fighting him, but I can see now that he was right . . . What I didn't realise," she said, staring at her distorted reflection in the back of a teaspoon, "was that it was bound to be worse for him. He couldn't yell and scream and have hysterics. I just thought he was callous and told him so. It was unforgivable, so I shouldn't be surprised that he never forgave me. It's funny, isn't it, that when we say 'unforgivable' we never really think of it meaning that. But sometimes it actually does. It's bound to."

She stopped talking and there was silence. She felt, illogically, that his next comment was crucial, that he knew it too and was struggling for the right words, impossible though that was. For she'd heard them all: all the fake, fulsome (and genuine) expressions of sympathy.

"What was his name?" he said at last. And of course that *was* the correct comment to make, implied that her son had been not just a statistic, victim of a tragic accident, reason for hushed voices and doleful countenances, but an individual, a *person*, with a name and a history, however brief.

"Nicholas. We called him Nick."

"What was he like?"

Where to start? Podgy at first, as a baby, with bracelets of fat round his ankles and wrists, and then thin, big-eyed, a fledgling, growing out of his clothes so fast that we could hardly keep pace. He kept a pet frog in a teapot and had an imaginary friend called Lewis who was responsible for all the acts of naughtiness that took place. I used to read to him in bed at night and sometimes I'd yawn and say I felt tired and he'd say, all rosy-faced from his bath and solemn, "That's all right, you can bundle in with me." His hair was thick and dark and tufty and he hated having it washed. He also hated: buying new shoes, the swings in the park, big dogs that jumped up at him and having to wait. He watched *Blue Peter* and then attempted to make those intricate models that they put together out of balloons and papier-mâché and washing-up-liquid bottles and, sometimes, if he couldn't get them to work, he'd stamp on them in a rage. His temperament was volatile: tantrums one minute, smiles the next. He wrote a story when he was five years old, typing it out, his tongue between his teeth, on Rob's old portable. It was called *Robert and The Ring of Singing Owls*. I kept it for ages, but then it got lost, the way things do. He called us "Muv" and "Farv", until he grew up and became sophisticated, when he'd manage to manoeuvre conversations so that he didn't have to call us anything. When I took him to school on the first day, he stood in the doorway, calling, "Muv, don't leave me, Muv." But I had to. Those words ring in my ears still. One afternoon, when I was engrossed in trying to balance the firm's books, he dashed in from school and dashed out again because he'd heard the ice-cream van. He was seven years old – that age which is all dash. He dashed out into the road and in front of a car. The driver had no chance, they said, was not at fault in any way, but I would have killed him with my bare hands had they let me near him.

Some of this she told Mick, her tea cooling in front of her, tried to convey to him the way she had loved: unreservedly, totally, and with a purity that transcended any other form of love.

He ground out his cigarette to nothing. "Why didn't you have more children? You know, the way you said your husband made you get back into a car straight afterwards, well, wouldn't it have been the same: having another child? In a way, I mean?"

"My father was living with us. He was semi-paralysed. Even

if I'd wanted to, I couldn't have coped with him and another child. And I didn't want to." The idea of a replacement had been abhorrent. Besides, she'd stopped menstruating for ages after Nick's death. And by the time her periods had started again, Robert was no longer interested: either in her or another child.

Mick took some matches from his box and arranged them in a pattern on the tabletop. "There's supposed to be a method where you move just two matches and form a square. I've never been able to do it."

She pondered for a moment and then solved the puzzle.

"I've always been good at things that don't matter."

Solving puzzles, keeping the house clean and tidy, rendering an aesthetically-pleasing version of the view on a piece of paper – aesthetically-pleasing, but no more than that. She had no great original creative talent. Neither for art nor, it would seem, for human relationships: a good mother would have kept her son safe, a good daughter would have noticed in time and prevented her father from overdoing it, a good wife was one from whom no husband would desire to stray. Or so she supposed.

He made designs with the matches. "I've got ten O-levels and four A-levels," he said, "all at grades A and B. I've a photographic memory and obviously, judging by my IQ, a talent for analysis and synthesis. Everybody thought I couldn't go wrong."

"So what did go wrong?"

"Nothing particularly interested me. Plus I couldn't get the whole thing together. I mean, there was this bit of me that could do things dead easily and another bit that couldn't make head or tail of anything. And just because I could do all those things easily, everybody expected me to be thrilled to bits about it. It was just a knack, that's all. How could you get thrilled about a knack? It was just words and lists and stuff on paper. It never meant anything. I never got *absorbed*, you know, the way people say they sometimes do. You look at their faces and they're really *into* it, they're interested, they *care*, and you're sitting there, yawning your tonsils out, not giving a shit because none of it matters . . ."

"Does anything?"

"Well, only people, I suppose. And I always seem to make a balls of *that*."

"You're young yet," she said, as he swept the matches back into his box, all save one which he struck against his thumbnail – as if to demonstrate to her that there was no end to his useless talent – and held to the tip of his cigarette.

"Does that make a difference?"

Smoke hid his face from her scrutiny. Tomorrow, she knew, they might behave as though this strip-Jack-naked session had never occurred. "It means," she said, "that, generally speaking, there's the chance to make good your blunders. Pick another path, if you like."

"I once read this horrible story by O'Henry," he said, "where this guy got the chance to try all the paths – and they all turned out to be the same."

"Go on!" Mary Reilly said. "The nerve! What did you say?"

"I said that I wasn't aware that I was required to clock in and out, particularly on my day off," Elsa replied.

"That was a good one," Mary Reilly said. "That'd put her in her place." "Aware", she repeated in her head, and "required", attempting to store them for future reference – they would have more impact than any ordinary four-letter abuse – while Elsa described her late return the previous evening and how she'd been obliged to ring and knock until Nora opened up, all because keys were not issued to the resident staff.

"Cheek!" said Mary Reilly. "Still, you put her in her place."

Actually she'd done no such thing. A timid: "It *is* my day off and it's not all *that* late," was the best she'd been able to manage.

"And then she tore you off a strip?" Mary Reilly prompted, scraping out the last of a jar of salmon paste on to a slice of bread.

"Not really. She said that she thought I'd understood that late hours were not expected because of the nature of the job."

"Bit like the nick, this place," Mary Reilly said. "The way she starts shoving them off to their own rooms soon as *News At Ten*'s over. That Mrs Crookthorne, she doesn't have a telly of her own and she likes to sit up to watch the late film, but aul

Nora does that much clearing of the throat and bashing of the cushions that she soon gets the message and buggers off. You know, by rights, she should employ night staff – the prices she charges." She wiped the sweat from her forehead with her salmon-paste-spreading hand. "Jesus, Mary and Joseph, how many more?"

They were making sandwiches for the buffet supper provided for residents and artistes after the annual concert put on by the girls of St Monica's. Hilda Leggat, their games mistress and Muriel Selby's boon companion, was the organiser, liaising with Miss Vyner who had appointed herself unpaid, unsolicited, social secretary. That few of the residents were keen on being subjected to a ninety-minute demonstration of lack of talent was by the by.

The two of them, with Muriel Selby dancing attendance, walked about the Kent Room, instructing Mick to move this table here, those chairs over there – or, no, as you were! This table *there*, I think, don't you?

"Here?" Mick enquired. "Or there?" He dropped the trestle to the floor. He had splinters in his fingers and Hilda's bloody dog, who accompanied her everywhere, had worried his ankle until he'd taken advantage of its owner's absence to boot it across the room. He hummed *My Generation* loudly as he moved the furniture, vocalising when he came to the line: "Hope I die before I get old." But it was lost on them.

"Here," said Hilda Leggat.

"There," said Miss Vyner.

"Why don't you put it midway?" suggested Muriel Selby, but no one paid her any attention.

Apart from issuing dire warnings concerning the parquet and the furniture (a cigarette burn last year in an armchair! So much for gentility; they were as bad as the kids from the comprehensive), Nora Speakman kept well out of the way. Her first instinct had been to put her foot down – if they wanted entertainment they were perfectly well able to go out and pay for it – but second thoughts had prompted her to agree. What was the cost of a few sandwiches if it kept them happy?

Hilda Leggat blew a shrill blast on her whistle and called the roll. She might be getting a little bit long in the tooth for cavorting on the wallbars, but the stentorian powers of her voice more than made up for that. "Louisa Parker and Joy Fletcher, Piano: Mozart's *Turkish Rondo*, followed by *The Harmonious Blacksmith*. Emma Beverley, Recitation: *The Ancient Mariner* . . ."

"What!" whispered Miss Vyner, blenching.

"Oh . . . abridged," Hilda Leggat corrected herself. "Penelope Fielding and Ruth Meadows, Piano Duet. Marina Morgan, Dance . . . Marina Morgan! Where is Marina Morgan?"

A minute child, dressed in Neapolitan peasant costume was pushed to the front. "The *Tarantella*," boomed Hilda Leggat. "Have you brought your music?"

The child drew in her breath sharply and her eyes widened, then she shook her head and giggled.

"Well, we *are* a silly little girl, aren't we? However are we going to dance the *Tarantella* without musical accompaniment?"

Marina Morgan shook her head again. She carried a tambourine decorated with ribbons which she bashed against her leg forlornly as if to emphasise her plight.

"I don't suppose our accompanist can play a *Tarantella* without sheet music. Jeanette Roberts!"

Our accompanist, Jeanette Roberts, indicated, with some glee, that such a feat was indeed beyond her capability. "Oh well," said Hilda Leggat. "Nil desperandum. You shall demonstrate the steps and we shall clap in rhythm."

This proved to be the high point of the evening. Colonel Pritchard, returning from his snifter at the Railway (Golding's company was preferable to a lot of little girls torturing their tonsils), came in just in time to catch it. The rest of them, too cowardly, too idle or lacking in resourcefulness to absent themselves, had successfully drowsed their way through the *Turkish Rondo* and *The Ancient Mariner* (abridged), even through the choir's fortissimo rendering of *Sheep May Safely Graze*, but the sight of Miss Leggat lumbering on to the dais, her baton tucked under her armpit, instructing them to clap in time to the rhythm while Marina Morgan performed, jolted the most somnolent of them into wakefulness.

In the kitchen, the door of which, when ajar, gave access on to the revelries in the Kent Room, Rosa and Marguerita were united for once in their perplexity. The English and their incomprehensible rituals! Looking oh so embarrassed when the little child did her dance and yet applauding loudly when she made a big mistake and fell down on her bottom. "Poor little lass," said Mrs Randall sympathetically and remembered tearfully how her Doreen had once had a get-up like that for a concert. Her Doreen had had nothing but the best of everything and look how things were turning out with her and Les: marriage-guidance council and I-don't-know-what.

"I don't know about clapping," Mary Reilly said. "There hasn't been a decent tune you could sing to in the whole thing."

And Mick rolled around the floor in hysterics.

"Get up. It's not *that* funny. If Nora comes in she'll blow a gasket."

Elsa prodded him with her foot. His shirt had come unbuttoned and she saw that there was a growth of hair upon his chest. The signs of masculine maturity, be it chest hair or a couple of days' growth upon his chin, always came as a surprise; somehow she thought of him as a boy: smooth-skinned, pre-pubertal. Which of course was ridiculous. He was, patently, a young man. And a good-looking young man at that. Perhaps all the stories of fighting off avid young women at discos were not flights of fancy after all.

11

The day after the concert Rodney Speakman was prostrated with asthma. For the week he was subject to daily attacks Rosa and Marguerita were obliged to take trays up to his room, in between the bouts of extra cleaning that his mother had instructed them to carry out in case allergens had somehow secreted themselves within the walls. She couldn't be sure that they were thorough in their investigations, but they reported no animal life or drifts of pollen or colonies of dust mite upon the premises. The problem with asthma was that its triggers were so often psychological. After a week she sent for the local herbalist (as a nurse, she had a healthy disrespect for orthodox medicine) who recommended an infusion and, whether because of its efficaciousness or by coincidence, Rodney slowly began to recover.

During the times when Rosa and Marguerita were off-duty Elsa had been called upon to deliver his meals. It was their first direct contact since the storeroom encounter – he had done his best to avoid her during the intervening weeks and she had grown accustomed to receiving instruction from him via a third party: "Meester Rodney, he say . . ." Now, whenever she carried in his trays he pretended to be asleep and she would place them on the bedside table and beat a retreat without ever attempting to call his bluff.

As Rodney recovered, Mick succumbed to infection and on the Monday came into work with a streaming cold. The weather had changed. June, it might be, with sunbathers on the beach and windsurfers on the lake, but there was a nasty little chill north-easterly blowing. In the Gloucester Room they were pulling their chairs closer to the log-effect electric fire while Mick continued to wear the same skimpy, coming-apart-at-the-seams tee-shirts, despite Elsa's warnings. "I notice that stupid old bat of a gipsy never predicted that I was due to get double pneumonia," he complained when the temperature and the insufficiency of his clothing finally combined to lay him low.

"Perhaps she thought you had more sense than to invite it."

She boiled water and poured it over Friar's Balsam in a bowl. "Here," she said, beckoning him across to breathe in her concoction.

He blew his nose into a length of kitchen towel. "It smells vile."

"You don't have to drink it. Just inhale it."

She bent his head to the bowl and covered it with a towel. Beneath this tent-like arrangement she heard him coughing and complaining.

"Best remedy out," Mrs Randall said.

"Aye," said Nellie Macpherson, "that and a raw onion."

"My mam always put goose-grease on our chests," was Mary Reilly's contribution.

They fell to discussing home remedies. Between inhalations, Mick moaned loudly that he was suffocating, but Elsa held his head firmly, preventing him from moving. Then Marguerita came into the kitchen and gestured that she was wanted.

"Who is it?"

Marguerita shrugged, her eyes fixed upon a spot of air just above Elsa's head. Rosa externalised her foul temper with shoutings and hissings, but dumb insolence was Marguerita's forte.

In the hall Mrs Pendennis stood at the public telephone box, the receiver to her ear. "I think it's for you, dear," she said.

"Please don't telephone me," she'd asked Edward Green. "I hate the telephone." She'd said it with a little shudder, as though it was the crudity of this newfangled communication that offended her sensibilities rather than her inability to hear the messages it transmitted. So he wrote to her instead. Daily. Roland Machin wrote too. He said that he hoped his letters would be forwarded to her sister-in-law's on the Isle of Wight since she'd forgotten to give him the exact address.

Elsa took the receiver, her hand trembling slightly. As far as she knew there was no one who had the right, or the knowledge of her whereabouts – or indeed the inclination – to telephone her. And her instinct was to fear the worst. A romance, Mrs Pendennis thought, treading softly away. The young woman could have been pretty, if only she could be bothered to make the best of herself.

"It's like getting through to God," the voice said. A deep voice with a strong Welsh intonation.

She gasped. "Whatever would you have said if Mrs Speakman or Rodney had answered the phone?"

"I should have asked whether I'd left a jar of urine-testing strips on their premises."

"Have you?"

"I've left them somewhere," he said. "However, as Nora Speakman is, at this very moment, standing in a queue in Barclay's bank, and Rodney is waiting outside for her – illegally parked, I might add – the need for subterfuge becomes redundant."

"How do you know?"

"I'm standing in the phone box opposite Barclay's bank."

He's done it before, she thought, a good many times judging by his smooth grasp of the stratagems. But this knowledge was not off-putting. Rather the reverse: it made her role in the affair somehow less deserving of censure.

If there was to be an affair.

The pips went, and by the time he'd inserted another coin she caught only the tail-end of his sentence.

"What?"

"Your interview. You said you had an interview in Manchester next week. I was wondering . . . were you planning on staying overnight?"

"Well, hardly. Not when I can be there and back in a couple of hours or so."

"But you *could*?"

Well, of course she *could*. From a life where every movement had had to be accounted for and strictly apportioned between child, husband and father, she had made the transition to a form of existence where – apart from the obligations inherent in earning her living – she was accountable to no one.

A country hotel, he was speaking of, somewhere in Cheshire. A night together. A better chance might never present itself.

She thought of the secret of his body beneath the sober suiting; of the promise conveyed by those green cat's eyes, and the brief but electric touch of his hand as he'd attempted to caress her secret flesh. She thought of how the prospect of meeting him would colour and make even more fraught the ordeal of the interview, the outcome of which was so important to her. She thought of how quickly the strangeness of him would become familiar, and how difficult that familiarity might then be to renounce.

"Think about it," he said. "I'll be in tomorrow afternoon. Oh, here she comes," he said, "with your wages by the look of it – Nora, in full sail. Till tomorrow," he said. "Cariad."

Back in the kitchen Mick still sniffled under the towel. She crossed the room and uncovered him.

"Am I supposed to be better now?" he enquired grumpily.

"I don't think it's quite such a miracle cure as all that."

"Oh shit!" he said crossly, touching the top of his head. "It's melted all me bleedin' setting gel."

"Never mind," she said, "I'm sure it won't spoil your beauty." And with a sudden movement she leaned over and brushed her lips against the limp softness of his hair. His blush – as thorough-going and crimson as Rodney Speakman's had been – surprised her. But she didn't give it much thought. For reasons that she couldn't fathom – and the implications of the decision that she must make demanded very serious consideration – she felt like kissing everyone: Nellie Macpherson upon her faded rose-petal cheek, Marguerita's whiskery upper lip, even Mary Reilly who had a cold sore. She laughed as he blushed. Light-hearted and headed, it never occurred to her that the decision had already been made.

Mrs Grey screwed the top back on to her Frank Cooper's Oxford marmalade preparatory to carrying it back to her room. Priory Lodge marmalade was supplied in catering packs and bore only a passing resemblance to the oranges grown in Seville. And this was quite apart from the fact that you required the patience of Job and a knack in order to release the khaki-coloured substance from its vacuum-packed plastic container. Jams and spices and relishes were hoarded in the residents' rooms; Colonel Pritchard had his Lea and Perrins, Mrs Booth-Powell her acacia-blossom honey, Mrs Grey her Oxford marmalade. All were carried down for breakfast and then taken back afterwards.

Mr Gentile mashed his cereal into a pap before sucking it from his spoon. Mrs Booth-Powell wrestled with the *Daily Telegraph* and stared through Mrs Pegler who had remarked pleasantly that it was a pity that the quality newspapers were not produced in tablet form; she herself read the *Mail*. Her stars, she noticed, were very good for today. She was Aquarius, the water-carrier. Dad used to say it suited her down to the ground; they'd never been able to go on a coach trip because of her weak bladder.

Mr Golding (Virgo; "What else?" he sometimes thought, shrugging his shoulders so high that he reminded himself of the Smyrnese pedlars from whom he was descended), tried to cajole Rosa into providing him with an extra rasher of bacon. To his surprise she complied with alacrity; sweet-natured compliance being the tactic most likely to dissuade him from conniving at her dismissal. He would have been astonished, and then horrified, if he had known of her fears.

Mrs Crookthorne (born on the cusp between Aries and Taurus, sharing her birthday with the Queen of England and Adolf Hitler – Bertie would have found this highly significant, had he known of it) saw the furtive transaction and made up her mind to complain to the Speakmans. It wasn't as if he couldn't afford to pay for extras, coming from a wealthy family like that, with a chain of shops across the country.

Mrs Pendennis (like Mrs Pegler an Aquarian, but with Libra rising – explaining her good looks), was too elated to notice what was going on. She had peeked at her stars in Mrs Pegler's *Mail* before it was collected from the hallstand, as she did every morning, and had been agreeably surprised to read that great news hovered on her horizon: opportunity, cause for rejoicing. She marvelled at the perspicacity of the forecaster when she opened Edward Green's letter and discovered that it contained a proposal of marriage.

". . . I find it easier to write this than to speak of it," he had written. "And I feel that, whatever your answer is to be, you too will prefer to avoid any embarrassment . . ." (How considerate he was.) "I feel I know you so well, Marion, even though it is barely a couple of months since I introduced myself. How forward you must have thought me!" (Not at all; she'd found his boldness refreshing. So often, in the past, she'd been left wondering whether so and so cherished a secret passion for her because he was too shy to make himself known.) She read on with a rising sense of excitement: "One of the reasons for my choosing to write to you rather than speak to you is that I must make sure that we understand each other regarding what I will call the 'intimate' side of marriage. Marion, I respond to your attractiveness as any red-blooded man would do, and I know from my reading and all these television programmes that that side of life can continue, long after the younger folk suppose us to be 'past it', but unfortunately, despite an operation . . ."

Then came a reference to his prostate gland and what seemed to be a rather complicated exposition of medical matters which she skipped.

". . . I'm comfortably off, Marion, and I would undertake to make your happiness my goal for as long as I live. (Apart from the prostate, I'm fighting fit, or so my doctor assures me.) I thought, after Mrs Green was taken from me, I'd never meet another woman for whom I could feel as I felt for her. But life is full of surprises . . ."

And so on and so forth, with many more extremely pleasing references to her looks and her youthfulness.

She skimmed over the endearments, folded the letter, replaced it in its envelope and sat tapping the envelope against the edge of her teeth. Roland Machin was forever proposing. She had to tell him to stop being silly. And others before him. "Why on earth should you want to marry me?" she'd asked them, though the reason was always the same and as plain as the (often stupendously unattractive) noses on their faces. She'd had the misfortune, she realised, to be born into a sex-mad generation. Early in life she'd supposed that the menopause called a halt to the whole messy business, but apparently not. And she'd never been lucky enough, before, to meet a man with a malfunctioning prostate gland.

"I'll see you in the lounge, then," Esmé Grey repeated, as she passed by Mrs Pendennis's table on her way out. On Tuesday mornings they usually visited the library and then took coffee in The Spinning Wheel. She was a shallow, vain woman, Marion Pendennis, without a cultivated thought in her head. Once she, Esmé Grey, had discussed existentialism with young graduates, but these days one had to be grateful for any sort of mildly compatible company.

"Sugar?" she repeated later, when they were drinking their coffee. "Dear me," she said. "You *are* in a brown study."

Mrs Pendennis sipped her sugarless coffee. It might be an idea to start cutting down a little on the carbohydrates: she had noticed of late that her girdle, rather than simply firming the flesh, was confining what could only be described as flab. Just in case. Edward Green might be incapable of sexual intimacy but he would surely expect to share a bedroom, and he wasn't blind. She remembered, unwillingly, her first wedding-night: a fairy-tale, everyone had said, yards of tulle, stephanotis and silver horseshoes, a spangled Juliet cap upon her chestnut curls, white kid shoes enclosing her size-two feet, church bells and the voices of choirboys, a suite at the Negresco, silk lingerie and the dusk falling like navy-blue velvet. And then, suddenly and horribly, the dream becoming nightmare as she was subjected to an ordeal of clutching and grabbing and pain. Edward Green, she thought fondly, Edward Green who would worship at her shrine without desiring to penetrate it.

"Have you never thought of marrying again?" she asked Mrs Grey, looking at her closely for the first time in their acquaintanceship. Not in the same league, of course, but there was no denying that her companion must have been a pretty woman some thirty years ago.

Esmé Grey snapped a Marie biscuit between her teeth and winced. I *must* make an appointment with the dentist, she reminded herself. But the wince was only partly due to the pain of vegetable matter coming into contact with a partially-exposed nerve. Marriage, she knew, was a wonderful institution, but who – as Mr Golding joked – would want to live in an institution? Of course, as a lifelong bachelor, he was hardly qualified to joke about it and not for a minute would she have considered admitting that her marriage was one of the exceptions that proved the rule (thirty years of subjugation by a sadistic bully). Though her certainty about the rule had been subject to waver as widowed friends opened up in a way they could never have done as wives. "Frankly, Esmé," they told her, concerning the demise of a husband, "frankly, I can't say that I was sorry."

She shook her head and spoke quietly. "I've never been asked."

"One misses male companionship," Marion Pendennis said, instantly dismissing Colonel Pritchard, Leonard Golding and Mr Gentile as insignificant members of the male gender. Idly, she took an everlasting flower from the arrangement on the table and began to dismember it, petal by petal: "Yes I will, no I won't." The last of the petals yielded a yes. It was as good a way as any to decide, life being too short for soul-searching. And besides, she had got out of that habit a long time ago.

12

"I didn't bargain on you wanting *two* days off," Nora Speakman said frostily. "It's *most* inconvenient. Why on earth should you need two days off to get from here to Manchester?"

"Manchester? Not Manchester, *Chi*chester. You must have misheard. And I only want one and a half. I'll be back by Thursday evening. I've a day owing from Whit. Well, actually, I've four days owing if you count Easter – "

"Yes, all right," Mrs Speakman said rapidly. Bank holidays, they proliferated yearly, thought up no doubt by somebody who held a grudge against employers. "You haven't forgotten Mrs Pendennis's engagement party on Friday?" Seventy years old and an engagement party! It was pathetic.

"No, I haven't forgotten."

While Mrs Pendennis had sought guidance by demolishing an everlasting flower, Elsa performed no such active experiment, and merely allowed normal events to act as obstacles or otherwise to her will: Nora might have put her foot down. Nellie Macpherson had left for a week's holiday, Marguerita had a gum-boil and Mick was incapacitated by his cold to the extent that she'd been obliged to send him home with the instruction to stay there until he was recovered. It wasn't nice for the residents, to have someone coughing and sneezing all over them like that.

She might have put her foot down but she didn't. Coincidentally, three of the residents had decided to take their holidays at the same time: Mrs Booth-Powell was staying in a villa in Ibiza with her son and his family; Miss Vyner had joined Gertie for a few days, determinedly touring the Cotswolds; and Mr Gentile had been collected by an official from the society of expatriate Italians, or ice-cream sellers, or whatever it was, and transported to Herne Bay to spend a week in their holiday home.

This meant three fewer beds to change, meals to serve, wants to be attended to. Rosa could see to the dining-room and Marguerita, gum-boil or no gum-boil, would have to cope with the bins. She was a big hefty girl, after all.

"Don't breathe your germs over *me*, either," Elsa said when she went to visit Mick, bearing a bottle of cough linctus, a packet of tissues and a few of the more basic foodstuffs. His cold was still in full spate and, to stem its tide of mucus, he kept producing a handkerchief of such noisome aspect that the sight of it made her feel faint.

"I've brought you some of that vitamin stuff and Mary's going to look in when she gets back to see if you need anything."

"I'll look forward to that," he said with heavy irony.

"I'll call in again on Friday – if you're not back at work by then."

"If I'm not dead by then." He emitted the sort of sepulchral cough that can be either an indication of very serious chest trouble or else a trick one learns during one's schooldays to relieve the boredom of dull lessons.

"Let me call the doctor," she offered, "if you're feeling that bad."

"Haven't got a doctor."

"I'm sure – whatshisname – Dr Rees – would oblige if I rang."

"How come? Does he always drop everything when you get in touch?"

She felt herself blush though there was no possible reason for him to suspect anything.

He didn't. He was merely being unpleasant. "I don't want a doctor," he said. "I wouldn't want to put *anybody* to any trouble."

"You'll live," she said, refusing to fuel his self-pity. "Well, aren't you going to wish me luck?"

But Mick pretended ignorance. When she reminded him, he said negligently, "Oh, *that*. Yeah, right, have a nice time."

"A nice time?"

"Well, whatever. I hope you get your heart's desire. And I hope you find it *is* your heart's desire when you get it."

She pushed the last of her offerings – a carton of orange juice – towards him and left him: a sullen-visaged, huddled picture of misery, ignorantly, unintentionally, saying her sooth.

In the privacy of the Speakmans' attic her newly-assembled portfolio had looked rather impressive: pastels and gouaches and drawings executed in a variety of styles but, she thought, bearing sufficient of an individual stamp to proclaim them as the work of one unique talent. (She had noticed that the order of their arrangement had been altered between one day and the next: Rodney Speakman, she'd supposed, and resignedly rearranged them; it seemed that his voyeurism was symptomatic of a general and insatiable curiosity.) That had been two days ago. Now, pulled apart and propped around the life-drawing studio that was being used as an interview room, she was less sure. "Original", "innovative", "accomplished", were the adjectives that had suggested themselves in the Speakmans' attic; other words seemed more appropriate now: words such as "inept" and "over-ambitious", words such as "derivative" and "hackneyed".

There were three of them on the interviewing panel, three people who did not include her old tutor – he was away with flu, she discovered. The omens were not good. Not only did her work appear pathetically amateurish, but the expected questions for which she had carefully prepared intelligent-sounding answers were never asked. Other questions were sprung instead, questions which exposed her ignorance or seduced her into pretentiousness. At the beginning of the interview she had felt that only the woman – a middle-aged *jolie-laide* of the imposing sort – seemed hostile; but by the end of it she was certain that her male colleagues – one bearded and grizzled, the other pale, pretty and androgynous – felt the same way too.

She made a moronic comment about the influence of German expressionism, confused Ben Shahn with Ben Nicholson and, standing up to indicate a feature on her *Three Widows From Bradford* drawing, managed to drop a heap of preliminary sketches from her lap to the floor. "Tom Ewing taught you?"

the grizzled man said, as if to imply "the poor devil", and then all three of them, as if in response to some invisible signal, smiled at her radiantly and said they would let her know their decision in a fortnight or so. And before she knew it she was out in the street, struggling to fit the slippery portfolio under her arm, not knowing whether to be cast into the depths of blackest despair or to jump for joy.

She had arranged to meet him in the station buffet. She cast a preliminary wide-ranging glance around the room, then, as she queued for her coffee, conducted a more thorough investigation. But he wasn't there. She struggled with coffee, portfolio and overnight case to a table in the corner, already attempting to produce some convincing excuse for being able to travel to and from Chichester so rapidly. For, of course, back she would have to go if he didn't turn up; she had neither the means nor the inclination to keep a one-sided tryst in a country hotel.
"If I could draw, I would draw you. I'd call it, 'How to worry yourself into premature wrinkles.' I'm terribly sorry. I got held up and then I couldn't find a parking space."
She had chosen a seat with a good view of the main entrance, but he had come in by the side door.
He bent over and kissed her robustly and matter-of-factly on the cheek. "Did you think I wasn't coming?" he asked.
"I hadn't noticed you were late," she said.
"Well, how did it go? Tell me all about it. But not here," he said. "Unless you want to finish that coffee? No? Anyway, I'd better shift the car before *they* do."
"Can't you put up one of those 'doctor' signs?"
"I could," he said, ushering her forth, "except that I feel discretion ought to be one of the watchwords of this little outing."
She moved away abruptly from his touch. "How did it go, then?" he asked, unaware of his blunder.
"Quite well, thank you."
I can go back, she thought. I can lug these articles on to platform fourteen and board the homeward-bound train. I am not obliged to continue with this arrangement, this "little outing". Calling a halt would be the most sensible thing to do.

"What's the matter?"

Ignoring her protests he took the portfolio and case and halted her progress with his other hand. "What is it I've said? About being discreet, is it? I meant as much for your sake as mine." He took hold of her chin and turned her face so that she was obliged to look at him. She hadn't yet come to a conclusion on the debate as to whether he was infinitely pleasing of countenance or thoroughly unprepossessing. This afternoon she was rather inclined to the latter view.

Prevented from looking away from him, she made the most of his green-eyed attention. "You've done this before," she said.

"Yes."

"Often?"

"As often, I suppose, as anyone else who keeps on hoping."

They began to walk out of the station. "Hoping for what?" she asked. If he'd said, "No, never," or "I never wanted to until I met you," she'd have disbelieved him, despised him for the banality of his smooth tongue, but all the same, part of her – the uncritical, wanting part of her – would have welcomed it and rejoiced.

"That there's more than one chance at life," he said.

It was what her every action since Nick's accident and her father's death and Rob's desertion had been predicated upon: the belief that you had more than one go at it, but she couldn't believe that he was motivated by the same hope. He would take her, she thought, for the same reason that his wife, presumably, took drink; as a temporary respite from the dissatisfactions and boredoms that formed the fabric of daily life.

"Light a cigarette for me, would you?"

He had stacked her case in the boot, next to his own, squeezed her hand and swung the car into the maelstrom of the city centre traffic. Lighting a cigarette was part of the ritual of a long-forgotten habit. Her doctor at home, years ago, after she'd had a particularly bad attack of bronchitis, had read her the riot act, warned her that smoking was endangering not only her own health but that of those around her, including her child's. Children were great mimics. Did she want to encourage him to wreck his lungs, weaken his heart, risk cancer, shorten his life? No, of course not. So she'd stopped.

He took the cigarette and inhaled gratefully. "I thought you lot were all anti-smoking," she said, "had all given up. It's what you're always preaching to us." After all, *she* had done everything possible not to shorten her son's life; everything except the one thing that mattered.

"Most of us have," he said. "About fifty per cent of the real addicts fill themselves with valium instead."

"Or booze, I expect. I remember reading somewhere that there's a very high incidence of alcoholism among doctors," she said before realising her blunder. "Like psychiatrists having the highest rate for going potty," she added lamely.

"Pressures . . ."

If he wanted to talk about it, she had provided the perfect opening. But "Yes, quite," was all he said.

He drove through the outskirts of the city and on to a motorway. "And have you?" he asked, glancing sideways at her. "Or is that too indelicate a question?"

"Have I what?"

"Done this before."

"No."

"Or wanted to, I suppose, is the real question?"

Yes, that was the real question, lack of opportunity being an important factor in the equation. She thought about it. Of course, if she had ever wanted to, she wouldn't have needed to think about it. "No, not really," she said eventually. Apart from opportunity being scarce, there hadn't been the time, what with motherhood and wifedom and filial obligation. Occasionally she'd fantasised about some actor or newscaster or a man on a train, but never more than idly. It was as if all those sort of wild, youthful, dangerous longings had, very wisely, gone underground, perhaps awaiting their moment.

"Responsibility, then," he said, screwing up his eyes against a sinking sun to read a road sign.

"I don't see why. I'm quite free to make my own choices."

"Nobody's free. If I wasn't here, you wouldn't be here either."

"But I might be somewhere else doing something equally inadvisable."

"The alternative," he said, glancing at his watch, "before we get deeply existential, would be tea at Priory Lodge, dispensed by Nora. Think of it! Tea with Major Armstrong."

"Who?"

"A gentleman who used to invite his guests for tea and lace the cream buns with cyanide."

"Before my time."

"Before mine too. Believe it or not. I suppose," he said, forestalling any other who might say it, including herself, "I'm only just not old enough to be your father?"

"Are you anybody's?"

He shook his head. "You can put it down to that if you like: displaced paternal affection. I wonder," he said, "how on earth people justified their actions before Freud?"

"Their good actions by reference to reward in heaven, I imagine; their bad ones to temptation by the devil."

"Oh, biblical," he said, suddenly very Welsh. "Where I come from they used to stone adulterers."

"Isn't it ingrained: all that hellfire-everlasting stuff?"

"I expect so. My Anglicisation probably provides only a thin veneer. One day it will all come rushing back and I shall take to flagellation."

"One day?"

"One day."

Their verbal fencing was as much part of the ritual as those complicated patterns of action that animals must complete before they can mate. She found it almost exhilarating, and would have been happy to continue as they sped along the byroads, the breeze on her cheek, black-and-white cows grazing in picture-book green fields. But the hotel was upon them too soon.

It was as picturesque as the cows and the fields: an authentic, done-up coaching-inn with cobbled yards and carriage lamps and low creepered gables and white-painted tubs filled with scarlet geraniums – the sort of place that, if anyone mentioned assignation, sprang immediately to mind, though you knew full well that the majority of assignations took place in Crest Motels or Trust House Fortes, big and impersonal, to ensure convenience and anonymity.

"I've passed it so often," he said, switching off the engine.

"It's lovely, isn't it? Ideal. These things usually end up in the Station Hotel, Middlesbrough."

"Is there one?"

"Bound to be. Full of Mr and Mrs Smiths. Not that anybody gives a toss nowadays."

Neither of them made any move to get out of the car. "It isn't *too* over the top, is it?" he said rather anxiously.

"I'd have preferred the Station Hotel, Middlesbrough."

"You wouldn't?"

"Yes. So that I could watch haughty receptionists watching you forging your signature."

But she saw, to her surprise, that he signed his proper name and address in the hotel register: E. F. Rees, 6 Southdown Road. He had booked them a double room. No nonsense, then, about them maintaining separate identities. Obviously he didn't feel that there was any danger of anyone attempting to contact him. She wanted to interrogate him on this point, having a horrid vision of his wife ringing him and her answering the phone. "Where is your wife?" she wanted to ask. "Where does she think you are?" But she didn't, of course. They were not sufficiently well-acquainted for those sort of questions to be put.

"Shall we have some tea first?" he asked, and indicated to the porter that he should take their luggage up to the room. She sensed that, immediately the words were uttered, he'd regretted saying "first". What must be accomplished in the antique carved bed before they left in the morning suddenly loomed as ominous as an examination, as her interview had done before she walked into the life-drawing studio. She saw him light a cigarette with twitchy movements. Perhaps he felt the same way. Perhaps the ambience demanded a standard of performance that paralysed all amorous inclination. Perhaps the Station Hotel, Middlesbrough, or its local equivalent, would have been a safer bet after all.

Tea arrived, in a silver pot, and tea-cakes keeping warm above a spirit lamp. Crumbly scones and fruit-packed jam and yellow cream. She remembered seeing an advertisement for this hotel in a copy of *Country Life* at the Priory; "Dad and I used to stay there," Mrs Pegler had observed, *en passant*.

She didn't know whether to eat lots of scone and cream and

jam in order to get their money's worth, or to go easy in case each item was charged separately, the way they counted up the cakes before and after you in cafés. Not that she had any appetite whatsoever.

"Dad and Mrs Pegler used to stay here," she said, pushing tea-cake morsels around her plate, and unable to offer anything more scintillating in the way of conversation.

"Who are Dad and Mrs Pegler?" he enquired politely. "*Your* dad, you mean?"

"No, Mrs Pegler's late husband. Mrs Pegler from the Priory. The lady with the white hair like cotton-wool and the Black Diamond mink."

"Oh," he said, "the one with diverticulitis? No wonder, if she used to make a habit of staying in places like this."

"Is that how you think of people?" she asked. "In terms of their diseases and disabilities?"

"I try not to. It's just something that's difficult to get out of after working in hospitals: all that 'the mastectomy in bed nine' and 'the pneumonia in Ward D' business."

The wife in Southdown Road, Elsa thought, the mistress at Priory Lodge. Or was "mistress" too formal a word to describe her role in his world? She tried to recall the sexual excitement she had felt during their chance meeting in the Priory Lodge lift, but the memory remained fugitive. A collection of organs clothed in cold flesh, she would accede clumsily to his demands, repay her share of the cost of the accommodation. Crumbs of tea-cake lodged in her throat. These affairs, she thought, should be spontaneous or not at all. Too much scene-setting, too extended a preamble and sometimes the players froze, corpsed, and forgot their lines. Unless, of course, they could rely on experience to carry them through and, new to the game, she didn't have even that standby.

He demolished scones and cream and jam as doggedly as if the consumption of them represented duty rather than pleasure. "Surly" they called him, the old dears at Priory Lodge, and that was how he seemed to her now as he enquired whether she had finished her tea. "No *manner* with him," they said, comparing him unfavourably with old Dr So and So or Such and Such.

Going up to their room in the lift they stood apart from one another. He concentrated stonily on the floor indicator, preceded her when the lift came to a halt, walked ahead of her, unlocked the door of their room and then finally turned to face her. "We aren't forced to go through with some sort of charade, you know. I can take you back."

"If that's what you want."

"It's not what *I* want, but it's obviously what you want."

He said it so certainly, with such an air of knowing condescension, that retort sprang to her lips: "How can you possibly know that? You don't know me. Any more than I know you."

Her case lay, unpacked, on a trestle at the end of the bed. She reached for it, he reached for her hand and for a second they struggled. She remembered the men on the hotel forecourt struggling with his wife, then he let go of her, she let go of the case and he looked down at the carpet and said, "How else, in these circumstances, can we ever get to know each other? I can hardly court you for six months before venturing my first kiss."

His pose was unconsciously elegant; his face, turned from her, more pleasing in profile. Her little outburst had freed her from paralysis, dissipated the animosity that had been building up ever since his tactless comment in the station buffet. She touched his sleeve and felt a small vibration start up, gain in strength, transmit a message that carried information of a sort that couldn't be learned in ten years of courting. Why, she wondered, as they came together, angle to angle, plane to plane, as if magnetised, why was it that sexual attraction was so roundly condemned as "mere"? Surely, she thought, its occurrence was so uncommon that, when it did happen, it ought not to be decried, but rather heralded as miraculous.

13

On Wednesday, June 13th 1984, the moon was full and the season approaching its solstice; there was no time during that night when darkness could be said to have fallen. As the light faded it drained colour and substance from their surroundings, but that was all. Even with the bedside lamps switched off and the curtains closed, the patterns of their features were so clear and so constant that it seemed impossible that they might ever fade from the memory.

They snatched sleep intermittently, alternately – fifteen minutes here, half an hour there – while the other kept watch, anxious to discover whether the sleeping self would yield up any more of the individual than was displayed during that other vulnerable state, the act of love. Once he moaned and twice she sighed and, when it happened, the other pressed closer, enfolding limb with limb, attempting that total penetration and containment of which sexual intercourse was merely symbolic, envious of the separate dream life that prompted such moans and sighs.

Every nocturnal sound was registered by her heightened responsiveness: the breeze in the tree foliage, the shriek of some small animal as it fell prey to a larger one, the odd lorry grinding its overnight way along the main road. She heard what she thought was the sound of a river and imagined their room as an island, water-bound, all boats and bridges and inter-connections cut; made impassable. Only the telephone, smugly silent, threatened. Earlier it had emitted a sort of whirring sound and she had tensed and clutched at him while he had stroked her hair and hushed her as one would comfort a nervous child.

Father and daughter perhaps, she had thought at first.

There were men, particularly childless men, who sought out child-women – vulnerable and dependent – from whom they could be certain of uncritical childlike acceptance. But in bed the fifteen years that separated their ages dwindled to nothing. He had a young man's sexual vitality and a sort of playfulness that she would never have guessed at from the cast of his outward appearance.

It had been an unpromising start, but inauspicious beginnings do not always go from bad to worse. She'd touched his sleeve and it was as if all the stress had flowed out of them and earthed itself on the carpet beneath their feet. He'd pulled her close, lifting her slightly so that the discrepancy in their heights was minimised; their hip bones had grated against each other and the thud of his heart-beat had reverberated through her ribcage. Their bodies had begun to make those slight, instinctive moves of adjustment in preparation for coupling, and then he had released her because, as she had told him, they did not know each other well enough to risk premature intimacy.

"Would you like to go for a walk? There's a lake, a mere..."

She nodded her approval and he put an arm about her shoulders as they walked through reception. One or two among the group of elderly American ladies who were booking in had looked at them and smiled nostalgically. She felt proud: proud that he should seek to enclose her so protectively in public, proud of the picture they made that she saw reflected in the glass of a showcase – she, young (well, young enough) and pretty; he, tall, soberly-suited, the cares of a responsible position upon his brow, the greyness of his hair as distinguished as that of a magazine hero.

The reflection was not the reality. But there were occasions when the illusion was more to be desired than the substance. She had come away because she found it necessary to escape, however temporarily, from the world of Elsa the divorcee, bereaved mother, maid of all work, aspiring student, and embrace a film scenario where every action obeyed the dictates of the sort of script appropriate to the genre.

But in the real world of common sense, stout brogues are donned for strolls around the damp rim of rustic meres. She stumbled in high-heeled sandals, her stockings drenched, her arm tight around his waist as much for balance as physical closeness. There were clumps of yellow flowers at the edge of the water and the fields beyond shimmered, a haze of gold. Cereal crop, she had supposed, wheat perhaps, or barley, but he corrected her. "Rape" they called it, stuff planted to restore the earth to its former fertility. "Country boy," she said and he saw her dreaming up for him a boyhood on some Welsh mountain-side, wild and free, whereas he had grown up in a place where the foreigner owned the land, the coal beneath it and the whip-hand. His place, had he owned up to one, was where subservience was bred in the bone, a place that, were you to escape intact, you were subsequently obliged to deny.

And it was lonely, having no place. "Land of my fathers," his wife sometimes sang derisively when she was drunk. She thought that insulting his heritage caused him pain, and did not know him well enough to realise that neither the land nor his fathers had ever been allowed to mean that much to him.

But while he walked beside the lake in the company of a desirable woman this could be forgotten. "It's rape," he could say and, playfully, hold her so tightly that she was forced to concede how easily the frailest man can overpower the most powerful woman in terms of sheer brute strength. He clasped both arms round her waist and bent over her, pressing his face against the fragrance of her hair, moving so that he felt the swell of her breasts, and the nipples hardening beneath the fabric of her dress. Had this been a genuine dream scenario he would have laid her down then and there among the yellow flowers and entered her, and felt his seed spurting endlessly, freely, gloriously, into the deep softness of her. No need to make clumsy enquiries about contraception in a dream scenario. In the real world you had to close the door and draw the curtains and mumble, "Is it all right? Do I need to be careful?" In the real world you had to bathe and shave yourself close and apply cologne and buy dinner and evince curiosity about her life and nature and personal history before you could, in all conscience, speak to one another in the only language that really mattered.

From the window, the lake had seemed a magical place, a place where lovers might stroll and kiss while butterflies danced above their heads. In reality, midges swarmed and hidden cowpats presented a constant challenge and he realised that she'd ruined her flimsy shoes and wondered how, without mortally offending her, he might offer to replace them. For she seemed very touchy. As touchy as he was. "Don't be so thin-skinned," his wife had urged so often during the early years of their marriage when he'd objected to the fact that she refused to live on his meagre salary. "Don't imagine that because you can't keep me that it in any way undermines your masculinity." Though he hadn't imagined anything of the sort. "We ought to be able to manage on my salary," he'd told her, "thousands of other couples do." So, for his sake and the sake of his manhood, she had agreed to try.

But before the week was out she was writing cheques on her own account. How could they possibly eat, entertain, drink, behave like civilised human beings, unless she did? His arguments had fallen upon uncomprehending ears. Never having been deprived of it, money meant nothing to her. She simply could not understand why he should wish to stand so rigidly upon a point of principle. And he had recognised then, with the cold shudder of true fear, that he must face the consequences of wanting her for what she represented rather than for what she was.

The young woman cradled in the crook of his arm had none of that expensive glitter which is bestowed along with the silver spoon. This young woman wore a chain-store frock and had a hairdo that probably cost less than his wife tipped her faggot stylist weekly. It was probable that she practised all those little economies that had long ago ceased to be within his experience: walking to the next bus stop and therefore the next fare stage, accepting that an indulgence this week would have to be counterbalanced by a denial the next, watering the milk, turning collars and cuffs on shirts, and sheets' sides to middle – all the stratagems that his mother had been obliged to practise. Though his mother had always been poor and, apparently, Elsa had not. Infinitely harder, he thought, to adjust to it, after you had been used to a certain standard of living.

Every night in his bed, since she'd agreed to accompany him, he'd fantasised about their coupling, as he always did with any woman to whom he was attracted, stifling his orgasmic groan in case it woke Diana – though, so often, Diana slept the unrousable sleep of the inebriated. When the time came, having envisaged them solely in terms of their physical charms, it was always a shock to discover that they could move him in other, less manageable ways. Sometimes it was a smile, a joke, an indication of a keen intelligence. With this one it was her air of vulnerability that disturbed him. He let go of her hand as they approached the hotel courtyard, suddenly wanting to hold back. To act in a dream scenario you had to abandon your identity and take on the attributes of myth: handsome prince, beggar maid, whatever. As soon as real identities and desire for true information began to intrude the dream faded just as fast as they could strike a film set: the lake became a swamp, the butterflies were moths, the pretty yellow flowers were actually known as rape.

"So what drew you to Nora's establishment?" he asked.

"Want of anything better."

They had bathed (each conscientiously respecting the other's privacy) and were now seated in the bar, prior to going in for dinner. He drank half a pint of beer slowly. He would be naturally abstemious, naturally fastidious, she thought, neat, orderly, well-organised. And if ever he lost control, it would only be briefly: a moment's unchecked hilarity, a howl of rage or pain swiftly curtailed, a few seconds – eyes blank, pulse beating in his temples – during the swoon of climax. Either that or he would lose control completely.

"I can't believe that," he said, lighting only his third cigarette since they'd met. Even the nicotine, which he obviously craved, was religiously rationed out.

"It's true. You've to be glad of a job at all these days."

He thought of his father, touching his cap to the pit manager. He had vowed then, spreading his books over the plush-covered table in the otherwise little-used front parlour ("Ssh! Our Emlyn's working at his books") that, never in his life, unless it was necessary for advancement, would he concede anyone's superiority. His mother had encouraged him. It had been obvious from the beginning that he was marked out to be different: his brains, his instinctive nice ways, his height. Bred out of generations of short Welshmen, he towered above his contemporaries. (For a bookish child, this was a distinct advantage, saved him from a good deal of the bullying that would otherwise have been directed at him.)

"Does she know that you'll be leaving come October?"

"With a bit of luck," she said, hushing him to caution.

"Of course you'll get a place," he said, as though other possibilities were too unlikely for serious consideration.

"What makes you so sure?"

"Because people who really want things, realistically, usually get them."

"Maybe you're aiming just a *little* bit high, Emlyn," he'd said, the headmaster at the Grammar. "They can take their pick, you know, these top-class medical schools. Many of the entrants come from families of medical men . . ." They'd had a redbrick in mind for him, some sort of general science degree, and failing that, a teacher training college. At his interviews, he'd sat in rooms with all those confident young men who stared so and drawled and sprawled and looked so *clean* – as though the greater part of their formative years had been spent wielding a loofah in a bath full of soapsuds. "What?" they'd said. "Sorry? Didn't catch . . ." though he'd practised toning down his accent for years. But he'd always known, even in the face of incredulity and condescension, that he could get what he really wanted.

"I hope you're right," she said, fiddling with the orange stick that lay in her empty glass. She'd drunk her drink too quickly and was afraid that he might have her down as another inebriate.

He ordered her a fresh one. "I wouldn't let on to Nora," he said, "that you're not staying. If she finds somebody permanent in the meanwhile she won't hesitate to give you the push. Not renowned for the softness of her heart, our Nora."

"Do you know her? I mean, apart from going to Priory Lodge?"

"I met her years ago when I was working in Birmingham. She was a staff nurse then."

"Nora'll give you a good time," they said, the young housemen, "I don't think! Christ, I bet she's got teeth up there!" She disconcerted them, lay outside their frame of reference:

a woman with no obvious charms who, it was reputed, though she called herself Mrs, had failed to provide her child with legitimacy.

"What happened to *Mr* Speakman?" Elsa asked. The drink relaxed her. To hell with whether she should stick to tonic water in order to be tactful.

"There never was one."

"What!"

"Apart from father or brother or whatever. She never married."

"Good grief! And Rodney?"

"Rodney is the son of the man with whom she had a years' long affair. A married man, very rich. When he died he left her enough money to buy herself a business. She started with a nursing-home, but I presume the profits are better if you don't have to employ qualified staff."

"Is this general knowledge?" Elsa asked, marvelling. Nora Speakman looked the sort who would cheerfully stone adulterers.

"I doubt it. She's always maintained the fiction of respectable widowhood, as far as I know."

"She watches over Rodney like a hen with a day-old chick."

"Maybe she's afraid that he'll make a similar sort of mistake. They say there's none so sanctimonious as the reformed rake. Besides, he's all she's got."

"He's all I have!" She remembered when, mad with grief, she'd howled it out to the unresponsive eau-de-nil-washed walls of the casualty department. There had been a policewoman at her elbow who had firmly restrained her when it seemed that she might go completely out of control, and start to hurl herself at those walls, simply because – as lunatics discover – physical pain is easier to bear than the other kind.

Perhaps Nora Speakman had once been close to losing her child, in which case her overprotectiveness was easy to understand.

"Shall we go in?"

Dutifully they gave their attention to the gourmet delights described on the menu. Food-hunger was not uppermost in terms of their sensual priorities, but they observed the niceties. The tone had been set and it was too late now to do anything but carry it through: a civilised meal and then an elegant coupling of the sort that you used to see in soft focus in foreign films of the Sixties, while the sound of a hundred violins soared in the background.

After dinner customers were urged into the lounge to partake of their coffee so that their tables could be relet. They sank down on to a tightly-stuffed sofa opposite a small man wearing gold-rimmed granny glasses who proceeded to examine them first through, and then above, his spectacles.

They tried to pretend that it wasn't happening. She felt the warmth of his thigh pressed against hers as he passed her the sugar and allowed their hands to touch, lingeringly, before he took it away. Despite observation, their eyes met and, pupils dilated, held each other in a gaze that excluded everything else. "Excuse me," the little man said, leaning forward, "but it's Randolph, isn't it?"

"I'm sorry?"

"Randolph Sergeant? Of course it is. I knew as soon as you walked through that door." He leaned further forward and peered more closely. "And Rose, isn't it?"

He had a thin, meagre-featured face which lit up triumphantly at his successful identification.

They shook their heads emphatically. "Of course it is," he said. "I'd know you anywhere. All those times at the Club! When did you leave Droitwich? I bumped into Tony Church and he said something about Nottingham . . ."

"I'm sorry. I can assure you that my name is not Randolph Sergeant, nor is this Rose. I'm afraid you've made a mistake."

For a second she wondered whether he was a private detective, whether this ploy was a well-known gambit employed by private detectives to trick their quarry into revealing their true identities. But the deflation that he displayed when it became obvious that a mistake had been made convinced her otherwise.

"Are you sure?" he asked, ridiculously.

"Absolutely sure."

Somewhere, in Droitwich, or possibly Nottingham, Randolph Sergeant and Rose, doppelgangers, lived lives that would never impinge.

"Well, all I can say is that you're the spitting image . . ."

He conceded his mistake but by that time had them trapped in conversation. A sadistic spider, he watched their polite but futile attempts to break free of the web – "Well . . . Well, we must go. Er . . . well . . . good evening" – each attempt baulked by another banal comment: about the restaurant, the hotel, the countryside, the weather. He had that habit, irritating in the extreme, of repeating back to you the ends of your sentences.

"Are you regulars here?"

"No, this is our first visit."

". . . first visit. I come once a month usually when my business brings me up here. Are you local?"

"No, just visiting the area."

". . . visiting the area. I'm from Leamington Spa."

They imagined him, haunting pubs and clubs and the edges of dance floors, get-togethers of lonely-hearts and coach trips to historic monuments, picking out his victims, attaching himself, limpet-like, until desperation forced a dismissal so curt that it couldn't be misinterpreted.

They smiled and nodded and drained the coffee-pot, half-rose from the sofa and then sank back into it as he prevented their departure with yet another question, or mesmerised them with his beady stare. And all the time they were being detained their desire for each other was growing. And the feeling was different from that which might be considered suitable for an elegant filmic night of love; it was urgent and ungainly and not amenable to postponement so that when they finally escaped to the haven of their bedroom, all the scene-setting, tone-enhancing preliminaries were forgotten. They simply took off their clothes and got into bed and came together quite nakedly, not worrying that their breath might smell of smoke or garlic, that age had slackened stomach muscles or caused the bosom to droop, that he or she might, theoretically, prefer this way or that. Knowledge of such detail seemed to be instinctive. Truth will out, they say, and the truth, the only truth, was that they wanted each other. Once they'd accepted that, it was easy.

14

There is a wonderful light-headed, loose-limbed, floating sensation that sometimes follows upon lack of sleep. It was because of this that her feet seemed to be not quite subject to voluntary control and slid across the damp, glistening cobblestones. It was raining. He said that it always rained the next morning and, with a smile, she agreed that this was probably the case. That he seemed to be such an authority on next mornings mattered not a jot. For a time, the night before, they had been as close, in the true sense, as it is possible for two people to be and, when that happens, what has gone before or may follow afterwards becomes irrelevant. Temporarily, at least.

"Back to the grind," he said, stowing their luggage in the boot of the car.

"And what does that consist of?"

"A visit to the General when I get back, a trip out to Merryfields – you know, the retarded kids' home – this afternoon and an evening surgery. What about you?"

"We have to get the place ready for Mrs Pendennis's engagement party tomorrow night."

"Good God," he said, fitting the key into the ignition – the engine turned over a few times but refused to start. And for an irrational moment, unmindful of the fact that there were buses and taxis and trains available to them, she willed it to continue failing. "They're gluttons for punishment, aren't they?" he said.

Combustion took place and he let out the handbrake.

"Don't you approve of marriage?" she asked.

"I neither approve nor disapprove," he replied, taking his foot off the clutch rather sharply so that they departed in a flurry of gravel.

Towards dawn, physically exhausted, they had talked a little, whispering to each other as guests in hotel bedrooms who have heard evidence of guests next-door always do. He had stroked her body, his hand coming to rest upon the one small scar that it bore, souvenir of childbearing, and he'd raised an eyebrow and she'd said, "I had a child but he died," and he hadn't pursued it, just held her very closely in the warm angle between his neck and shoulder. Earlier, searching in her handbag for a handkerchief, she'd tipped the contents on to the floor. Naked and laughing, they'd crawled about the carpet, retrieving combs and lipsticks and Polo mints and out-of-date dry-cleaning tickets. He'd picked up her bottle of sleeping pills and looked at its label and said sternly, "You shouldn't need these. You'll not require them tonight at any rate."

She hadn't done. Sleep had needed no cajolement. He had wakened her with his mouth, his tongue, arousing her, urging her to arouse him. "I'm greedy for you," he'd murmured as, astonishingly yet again, she'd felt him stirring beneath her touch. The greed was mutual. Sex with Robert had become such a routine affair that she'd forgotten the early days: the way you couldn't keep your hands off each other, the excitement sparked by a casual caress, an accidental touching.

"Cariad," he'd said, lean and dark above her, pulsing inside her, his face solemn with the effort of postponed ejaculation, his fingers working gently but urgently at that exquisitely sensitive spot where his rigidity was buried, became merged with her moist softness, now stroking her, now imitating his penile thrust, until the combination was discovered that brought her rushing to climax, coaxing from her throat a cry so resonant that he was obliged to cover her mouth with his own until it was over and his groan had merged, silently, with hers.

And then, drowsing in the aftermath, they had talked. She spoke of how her husband had deserted her for a woman who had the financial means to rescue him from ruin; he talked of how his wife had a sickness called alcoholism. He was married to a cripple, one no more responsible for her illness than a cancer victim or an arthritic. "My husband is a weak man," she told him, and he said that his wife was a woman who found it difficult to resist temptation – at least when the temptation came out of a bottle. There were crueller explanations, but love had made them kind.

And so they had talked, freely, spontaneously. The relationship between the man and the woman who drove out of the hotel forecourt spraying gravel in their wake was qualitatively different from that which had existed when they arrived. Exchange of information, as he knew from bitter experience, could be fatal: if ignorance was bliss, then knowledge meant concern. There was no way now that he could regard her merely as an attractive instrument. She was Elsa, known, a factor to be taken into account in his day-to-day existence. It was dangerous, he knew, to allow the development of that sort of recognition; it meant not only that you were liable to feel pity and care and tenderness and all those other intrusive emotions, but also that those vulnerable parts still present, lurking in the skin you'd grown for protection were exposed to another's caprice. If she chose, she could hurt him.

He rubbed at the inside of the windscreen as their breathing misted it up. The movement of the wipers mesmerised her gaze. The fine drizzle wetted everything more thoroughly than a downpour would have done: sodden grass and cows and pools in the road and overhanging branches that released gouts of water whenever they were stirred by the breeze. He frowned, peering ahead of him. "Would you do it again?" he enquired of her. "Marriage?"

Rob at twenty-two had been fun. And desirable. And something of a catch among the crowd she moved in. He had pleased her in bed and amused her when out of it. They had felt the same way about serious issues, moral and political. But later, before he finally plucked up the courage to leave her, she'd found him heavy, dull, humourless, banal in his opinions, tedious in conversation, ultimately unworthy of trust or respect. By then, of course, he'd had ten years with her and a hell of a lot of flak flung at him.

"I don't know. What about you?"

"I think I'd have made the same sort of mess of it whoever I'd married."

Or else why should his affairs, without exception, have ended so badly? You fancied a woman and pursued her until she yielded to you, or vice versa, and it was glorious. And then the closeness, the knowledge, started to intervene and you found it not cosy but threatening and began the arms' length treatment until either she told you where to go, or else you found you'd pushed her so far away that she'd ceased to impinge even peripherally. At least Diana, senses befuddled and anaesthetised, remained blissfully remote.

"What now?" she asked him as, after a return journey that had seemed half the length of its outward counterpart (though when *he* drove fast, she wasn't afraid), he dropped her off as arranged at the bus terminus for the second leg of the journey back to Priory Lodge. She had felt the emotional distance between them increasing as the miles were demolished.

"I'll ring you, of course," he said, handing her her luggage and kissing her cheek with a wary eye out for observers. "Failing that, I'll see you next Wednesday."

She had a feeling that it would be next Wednesday before contact would be made, that he would need that amount of time to consider the ramifications of their redefined relationship. She felt sad for a moment, and humiliated, then she remembered about her interview and it suddenly came to her that he was right in his optimistic prediction and she *had* got her place and she smiled at him quite merrily because whatever decision he came to, it wouldn't, in the final analysis, matter as much as she'd feared it might.

"Oh, I don't think we need to be *too* reckless," Mrs Pendennis said, with a little tinkling laugh. She had come into the kitchen to consult with Mrs Randall direct about the amount and variety of foodstuffs that needed to be prepared. And Mrs Randall, remembering a departed resident, rich and, unusually, generous who had occasionally presided over soirées to which her expectant relatives were invited, suggested smoked salmon, pâté and strawberries soaked in kirsch – it was after all the season. "Oh, I think not," Mrs Pendennis trilled, making a little moue to indicate that such profligacy was inappropriate to the modesty of the occasion. "Some of those little meat pies, perhaps? And I think that the tinned fruit salad you serve on Sundays will be more than adequate." This last was a little dig at Mrs Speakman who stood impatiently by, waiting to find out what Rodney must pick up from the market; the tinned fruit salad was usually passed off as being fresh.

"I always find that a boudoir biscuit goes down very well," Mrs Randall said as earnestly as if she had been the Savoy *chef de cuisine* in consultation over the menu for a royal banquet. "And some of them petits fours that we had at Christmas."

"What would that work out at?"

They bent their heads over the piece of paper upon which Mrs Randall had done the sums. "That, and a nice sherry," she said. "Or was you thinking more of a sparkling wine?"

"A very light sparkling wine," Mrs Speakman intervened. Amazing how quickly they became inebriated, these old folk. She wasn't having them collapsing all over the Gloucester Room.

"I shall leave it all in your capable hands, then," Mrs Pendennis said. Details of organisation were so tedious; she had always relied on her beauty and her charm to persuade others to deal with them. Besides, she had to get a letter into the post, a most important letter informing Roland Machin that his communications, written or otherwise, must now cease. "I am to be married," she had written. Fifty years ago, upon the occasion of her first engagement party, she had written those words, over and over again, to disappointed young men who could no longer hope to win her hand. Sad to think that, today, only one letter was required.

At the kitchen door she turned. "Oh, you said the boy would take care of the gramophone records? Miss Johns is borrowing some suitable ones from the library."

"The boy" enacted a dumb show of jeering insolence as soon as her back was turned. He had a wicked plan.

Mrs Pendennis put on her musquash to take her letter to the post. The box was perhaps fifty yards away from the Priory's front gate and the weather was clement, but it didn't do to take chances. She hesitated for a moment before she made the irrevocable movement of dropping it into the slot. At first, insanely, she had thought of changing the communication into an invitation: "You are invited to a party on Friday, 15th June, to celebrate the engagement of Marion Pendennis to Edward Green." But she'd had to reject the idea. He was an old man and the shock might be too much for him. She had been responsible for many a broken heart but never, as far as she knew, had she caused one to cease its beating.

"You survived, then?" Elsa enquired of Mick. He had turned into work that morning but Mrs Pendennis had come tittuping in before she'd had the chance to ask after his welfare.

"That's right," he said. "How was Chichester?"

"Ssh," she said. "It wasn't Chichester. I told *her* that because otherwise she'd have wanted me back by the first available train."

He peeled potatoes rapidly and with stagey flourishes. More peel than potato after he'd finished, as Mrs Randall complained, but you couldn't fault him on speed. He cast her a sly sideways look. "What *have* you been up to, Elsie?"

"Sorry to disappoint you," she said, turning from him to fold the tea-towels, "but I stayed overnight with an old schoolfriend. That's all. What about you?" she said. "When I left you were at death's door, or so you reckoned."

"Sweated it out of me, didn't I?" he said, with an accompanying grimace so spectacularly lewd that all possible offensiveness was cancelled out. "I got pissed off lying there so I went out to that new disco on the Prom. Lots of talent. Met a German girl. Best cure there is," he said smugly. "You ought to try it sometime, Elsie."

"I'll bear it in mind."

But when Mary Reilly came in later she reported that, after she'd got in on Wednesday evening, she'd taken him a cup of tea and found him so fast asleep that it had seemed a pity to disturb him.

"He didn't go out, then?"

"Only in his dreams, lovey," Mary Reilly said. "Only in his dreams."

Joseph Locke, Miss Johns had borrowed from the library, John McCormack, Anne Ziegler and Webster Booth. She'd used not only her own ticket but Mrs Pendennis's too and, kindly donated, those of Mrs Grey and Miss Vyner, so that she could borrow eight records in all, including a selection of Strauss waltzes.

They were heavy, but she stacked them in her shopping trolley on wheels which only presented problems when you needed to lift it up and down steps. Once, the bus conductors had cheerfully obliged, but now there were no bus conductors and the youths who might have been expected to deputise for them simply barged past or shouted out the sort of swear words that even now, after years of overhearing them, could still make her flush and sweat.

That evening she stood in the Gloucester Room, holding her glass of sparkling wine close to her chest, occasionally raising it to her mouth and pretending to drink from it. How lucky Mrs Pendennis was to have Edward Green who would protect her from the swearing, barging, staring youths who sometimes even commented loudly about old biddies who travelled free on the buses and therefore had no right to be depriving paying customers of their seats. But of course, as Mr Green had a car, this occasion for gallantry would never arise. So much that the married woman took for granted, Miss Johns thought wistfully. Once she had shyly confided in Dot Vyner, fellow spinster, her sorrow at never having been married and Dot Vyner had retorted briskly, "Save your tears, my dear; look around you at some of the ones who have and consider what sort of an advertisement they provide. As long as you've your health and strength and your pension, all the rest is just wishful thinking."

Miss Vyner conveyed her congratulations to the betrothed pair and then retired to a chair by the wall. Let the rest of them mill about, cocktail-party fashion; she couldn't manage it. She collected a plate of food and drink before she sat down: a meat pie, a mushroom vol-au-vent surrounded by a few limp lettuce leaves and a glass of the drink that most nearly resembled cider but was called something far more impressive.

From her vantage point she scrutinised Edward Green. He was well set-up, as they used to say, but she couldn't bear to see any man degraded by the assumption of that dog-like expression, so quite quickly she averted her eyes and concentrated on her food.

Mrs Pegler did the same. It amused her, the way these people complained so about the food. She, Ivy Pegler, had eaten at every standard from a slice of bread and dripping when she'd sat, shoeless, on the doorstep at home, to the Palace Hotel, Torquay. She raised her glass in the direction of the happy couple. "Cheers," she said and added, "May all your troubles be little ones," but neither of their faces cracked. They didn't know how to enjoy themselves, these toffs, that was the trouble. She remembered her own engagement party, the way they'd brought the piano out into the street (the lampposts were already decorated with bunting for the Royal Jubilee) and Alf's sister Cissie had played for them to dance. She could vamp as good as any of them in the silent pictures, could Cissie. A right old knees-up, they'd had. The day after they'd all gone on a chara to Blackpool and Flo Redmond had lost her drawers under the North Pier.

Mrs Pendennis and her sweetheart were as refined as could be, but they'd never have that sort of fun.

Mrs Crookthorne, standing alone in a corner, surreptitiously wrapped three little meat pies and a couple of vol-au-vents in a paper serviette. Behind the screen at the other end of the room Nellie Macpherson (home early from her sister's in Knott End – they never *could* get on) was doing the same thing. That's me tea for tomorrow, Nellie Macpherson thought contentedly, together with a nice tomato. I'll eat those with my cocoa later on, Mrs Crookthorne thought. She secreted her parcel in her handbag. "Congratulations," she said to Mrs Pendennis and her dozy-looking swain. There ought to be more of these dos, she thought – not because she cared a damn whether people were crackers enough to want to get married, but simply because it meant the chance for some free food.

"And so I go to fight a savage foe," sang Joseph Locke, perhaps a trifle fortissimo, although with most of them being deaf they didn't realise it. "*So* nice to meet you," said Edward Green, shaking successive hands: gnarled, liver-spotted, palsied. "*So* nice to meet you." Leonard Golding, grimacing at his first mouthful of wine – it tasted like piss – thought him most impressive. Not perhaps in the same class as the Colonel, but certainly impressive. To be able to win and marry two women – well, that demanded a real way with them. Though why anyone in his right mind should want to marry Marion Pendennis was beyond Leonard Golding's comprehension. She was pretty enough, in an ancient sort of way, but so *vain*. Imagine, Leonard Golding thought, attempting to come between Mrs Pendennis and her mirror for the duration of your married life. If you wanted a divorce you'd have to cite her reflection as co-respondent.

Mrs Booth-Powell and Mrs Grey went into a huddle by the door. Elsa, carrying through plates of food and trays of glasses, caught snatches of their conversation which they fondly imagined was being kept sotto voce but which had to be conducted at a level that was mutually audible: ". . . more sense . . . you don't suppose . . . not at their age . . . not without, I gather . . . what *do* you think of Lily Crookthorne's present? . . . I'd be ashamed . . . fairground rubbish . . ."

The presents were arranged on a trestle-table. Cunning ploy, Leonard Golding had thought admiringly. An engagement party meant that if you had a wedding reception as well you could cop for two sets of gifts. Not that they'd get any more from him; that rose-bowl had cost him an arm and a leg, even though the assistant in Boots had assured him that it was a genuine sale bargain. You had to take your hat off though to old Crookthorne: a set of the sort of glasses that they gave away as consolation prizes at the fairground; cost: about forty pence wholesale.

Assorted fancies, Mrs Crookthorne thought, as fresh platefuls were carried in. Very nice. She took a couple: one for consumption and one for her handbag. The glasses didn't look so bad either, she thought, when the light caught them. Fifty pee, it had cost her, on the rifle range. She hadn't shot down a single target but the man behind the stall had taken pity on her age and infirmity. And her spirit. He'd wanted her to have a cuddly toy but she'd stuck out for the glasses.

"I think it's going very nicely, Marion," Edward Green said, returning from circulating about the room. The only problem, as far as he could tell, was that the food and drink seemed to be dwindling faster than had been anticipated. He himself hadn't consumed more than one tiny triangle of paste sandwich, but he saw that it would be as well if he stuck at that. For an hour now he'd carried the same inch of wine in his glass. Dear Marion, he'd have to teach her about wine!

"Goodbye, goodbye," sang Mary Reilly, "I wish you all a last goodbye . . ." She raised her glass and winked. "Bottoms up!" she shrieked and drank from it. "Come on, Elsa, join us in a drink, won't you? Come on, Elsa," said Mary Reilly, "don't be a spoilsport. Quick before aul Nora comes in."

She had whipped a couple of bottles of wine before they left the kitchen for the Gloucester Room, secreting them behind the tea-urn in the stillroom, tapping the side of her nose as she did so. And because of its hiding-place, the wine was not only unpleasant but warm into the bargain. Elsa sipped unwillingly at her glassful. "That's a grand tune," Mary Reilly said, dancing a few ungainly steps. "I like that tune."

"She's been at it ever since she came in," Mrs Randall muttered out of the side of her mouth. "Drunken tart! I hope she gets her marching orders."

But you knew that she would do her best to cover up for Mary, if necessary. Workmates were workmates, after all, and bosses were bosses.

It became obvious from the speed at which Mary's inebriation occurred that she had had plenty before starting on the wine. "Nasty-drunk," Mrs Randall had reported, basing her opinion on past experience, but Mary was, as yet, still at the loud and silly stage. "Come on!" she shouted, spreading her arms to enclose an imaginary partner as she waltzed round the kitchen to the overheard strains of "Roses From The South". "Come on! You're a bunch of miseries, the lot of yez. Them old dolls have more go about them than you lot. Da da da," she sang, horribly off-key, then collided with the shelf upon which a basket of cutlery was stacked and sent it cascading ear-splittingly to the ground.

At half past nine Mrs Speakman, with Rodney walking a few paces behind, emerged from her office. It was her duty as proprietor to propose the official toast to the health and prosperity of the happy couple. Fools! she thought. The excitement alone would probably finish them off. She was in a bad humour: Edward Green was taking his bride away from

Priory Lodge to live with him in his bungalow, and residents who weren't much trouble were hard to find.

At this point, while Nora Speakman stood contemplating her bad fortune, Mary Reilly gave a twirl, staggered and crashed heavily into the swing-doors separating the kitchen from the hall. She flailed about her for a handhold, finally clinging to the doorpost as desperately as if it were a floating spar in a flood-tide. "Oh Christ," she said, "I think I'm pissed." And with this acknowledgement, her mood suddenly changed. With eyes narrowed and focused upon Nellie Macpherson who was at that moment carrying in a stack of dirty dishes, she said, "What are *you* staring at?" And Mrs Randall, at the back door, nodded her head as if to say, "I told you so, I told you it would all end in tears." This was a mistake. Slowly Mary turned, gripping the edge of the sink to steady herself. "And what's ailing you, fish-face?" she demanded.

"You're drunk," Mrs Randall proclaimed, redundantly and unwisely.

Mary positively bristled. "Do you want to make something of it?" she asked, then noticed for the first time that Rosa and Marguerita were tittering. "What's so funny? What's so bloody funny?"

"Mary," said Elsa placatingly.

"Don't you Mary me," came the reply. "I want to know what's so bloody funny . . ."

In the Gloucester Room, Nora Speakman, having delivered an appropriate little homily which contained phrases such as: "never too late", and "in the sunset of one's years" (each of which made Marion Pendennis wince quite noticeably), raised her glass (which, having been involved in the purchase of the wine, she had no intention of drinking from) and declared, "Let us all drink the health of the happy couple: Marion Pendennis and Edward Green." "Marion and Edward!" she repeated, although she found that sort of familiarity distasteful in the extreme. And the assembled company raised their glasses, chorused "Marion and Edward", and there was a moment's silence inappropriately reminiscent of Remembrance Sunday and then the record-player was switched on and relayed not "This Is My Lovely Day" which Miss Johns had purposely set aside for this moment, but "Too drunk, too drunk, too drunk to fuck", rendered at full volume by what sounded like a pack of crazed hyenas.

He'd secreted the Dead Kennedys record among the rest of the *dreck* beside the hi-fi, the boy. Risking the sack was worth seeing the expressions on their faces. There wasn't one of them so deaf that the message failed to penetrate. They were stunned. Nora's mouth opened and closed like a captured cod's. But then everyone turned when, the very next minute, Mary Reilly staggered in through the door, demanding to know just when she was due a wage rise. She teetered to a halt in front of Edward Green whose modest smile adopted for the toasting of his health had not yet faded from his face, though his eyes were as startled as those of a rabbit caught in a beam. "You," she said. "Just what's amusing you?" And then she stopped swaying and there was a green cast to her complexion and she opened her mouth and a thin stream of vomit splashed over his shoes.

15

If Mary Reilly hadn't staggered in drunk Mick would have been sacked. Instead, despite entreaties from Mrs Randall, Mary Reilly was given her marching orders. "Not a bad worker, as a rule," Mrs Randall said, meaning "Better than nobody". "It's just when she's in drink . . . A silly girl more than vicious." Nora Speakman had looked up from checking the wording of Rodney's advertisement for a replacement and said that drunkenness confined to the kitchen was one thing, drunkenness over a guest's shoes in the Gloucester Room quite another.

"Bollocks," Mick said, when Mrs Randall came back with the news. He felt guilty. Though it was he who had calmed Mary down and taken her home (there had been another bout of aggression: "Who d'you think you're pushing about? Take your effing hands off me"), had it not been for him adding insult to injury she might still have her job.

She sat in the kitchen while they commiserated. "No budging her," Mrs Randall reported of Nora Speakman. "And, come on, Mary, you can't really expect much else, can you?"

"Was I that bad?" Mary asked with a sort of awed curiosity, as though enquiring about the doings of someone else.

Mick offered her a cigarette which she drew on hungrily. "Let's just say that it's debatable whether you'll get invited to any other engagement parties," he said. "Look, Mary, I *am* sorry . . ."

She held up her hand to silence him. "Ah, never mind, lad, it wasn't your fault. 'Twas a rotten job anyway. She can stick it up her jacksie. There'll be something else."

They were silent, each of them, including Mary who'd said it, reflecting upon the irrational optimism of the statement. All the "something elses" that, traditionally, had been relied upon to keep the wolf from the door had vanished from the market; positions of that nature being filled by exploited kids off some youth training scheme.

"Oh well," she said finally, finishing her cup of tea and buttoning up her coat, "better trot along to the SS, I suppose. *They'd* better not start their shenanigans, that's all." She pondered. "Or should I go on the sick?"

"Are you ill?" they asked concernedly. From being Mary Reilly, incompetent kitchen-hand, known thief and nasty drunk, she had become, since her dismissal, Mary Reilly, martyr.

"Ill?" she said, perplexed. "No, I'm not ill," as though being ill was not a prerequisite for signing on the sick. She had a tame psychiatrist, it seemed, who was willing to sign certificates stating that she was suffering from attacks of anxiety severe enough to prevent her from looking for work. He signed similar certificates for her feller. He was a bit mad himself, if you asked her opinion, but then you would be, wouldn't you, surrounded, day in, day out, with nutters? "That Mrs Rees," Mary said, "that one that drinks, she goes to him. Private, of course. She goes to his house. It's the big one near the park. I seen her there once when Des had to pick up a cestificate because he'd forgotten to leave it at the clinic. I see her in the off-licence too," Mary said. "She buys these bottles and bottles of lemonade – I expect that's when she's taking the cure. Other times I bet it's gin."

She laughed contemptuously. Getting pissed now and again was different from being a piss-artist which, let's face it, was what they meant, these toffee-noses, when they talked about having a drink problem.

Mary said she'd best be off and Mrs Randall said to pop in from time to time in case Her Ladyship relented or couldn't get a replacement and, after she'd gone, Nellie Macpherson said wasn't drink the very devil? And Mick, relieved by Mary's departure – it meant that he no longer had to act contrite – said, "Does this mean, Nellie, that you're not going to join in my birthday celebrations?"

She misunderstood him. "Eh lad," she said, "I'm too old for birthday celebrations. I don't count 'em anymore." She then went off into a long and rambling discourse about how, in her younger days, they'd never had the brass for commemorating birthdays; that you were lucky to get an orange and a peg-dolly in your stocking at Christmas-time. An oft-told tale which attracted an audience of one: herself.

"Which birthday?" Elsa asked afterwards.

"Twenty-first."

"When?"

"A week next Wednesday."

"So what's happening?" she asked.

"What do you mean, what's happening?"

"Well, aren't you having a party? At home . . . your parents . . . your friends?"

"Load of bullshit that," he said, "all that gold-watch stuff. You couldn't have a decent party anyway, not with family, not mine at any rate. Talk about spectres at the feast!"

"Your friends, though?"

"Too much hassle searching them out," he said, settling himself on top of the switched-off hot-plate with a copy of the *Sun*. "They're all over the place. No, I shall just probably get totally wasted. That's what it's all about, isn't it?"

"No, it isn't."

Short notice, Elsa thought, but she could ask Mrs Randall to bake a cake, have a whip-round among staff and residents. Something ought to be done to mark the occasion. Had Nick lived, she'd have provided him with the most spectacular party ever thrown. Never would he have stood alone, in a strange place, holes in his socks, the zip of his fly held together with a safety-pin, pretending not to give a damn because nobody cared enough to put themselves out.

Rosa spoke urgently in Portuguese. Marguerita didn't even bother to listen. "I no understand," she said, loudly and smugly. "I no understand that language."

It was good to get her own back. Rosa, being the pretty one, got away with murder.

But then that language changed into fractured English with only occasional lapses into incomprehensibility, due in the main to Rosa's agitation. The gist of it was that her purity was in peril. Marguerita stopped being perverse and started to listen. And so did Elsa. They were in the kitchen, scrubbing down the shelves.

"It is bad for me," Rosa said. "One – I give slap, so!" She demonstrated with the dishcloth against the edge of the sink. "Next one – I cannot because Mum will be angry."

"*I* slap," Marguerita said, sneering, "I slap all right." As if the situation was ever likely to arise.

First, it seemed, there had been Mr Golding, careless concerning the direction in which his hands strayed. Rosa had been obliged to deter him but had prevented him from shopping her to Mrs Speakman by means of granting his requests for extra food. Now Mister Rodney was starting to follow suit. Sexual harassment from all sides; they treated her as if she was an English girl.

Marguerita requested detail. Rosa demonstrated: "Mr Golding – there." She twisted so that her neat little rump was displayed. "Mister Rodney" – and now she hesitated and then slowly brought her hand towards herself until it came to rest about six inches away from her left breast – "here!"

Elsa imagined him creeping up behind her in his suede shoes, catching her unawares, then backing off as she whirled round towards him, backing off and rubbing at the cushiony part of his lower lip. "You slapped old Mr Golding," she said. "You must also slap Mister Rodney. Then he will stop doing it."

They both looked at her askance. As an immoral Englishwoman she had no business advising them on such matters. As for slapping Mister Rodney – Rosa shook her head violently; she would rather return to Portugal.

"The Unspeakable Rod, not content with trying to peep through my window, has been foisting his disreputable attentions upon Rosa," she told Mick when he came on duty that evening. She had expected that he would be avid for detail, that he would join with her in mockery. But, "Fancy", was the only comment passed as he walked into the pantry and started to drag out a sack of carrots.

She tried again: "He's persistent, I'll say that much for him. Do you think he tries it on with every female who comes to work here?"

"I haven't the faintest idea."

He took the chopping-knife and began to top and tail the vegetables.

"What's wrong?"

"Nothing's wrong."

"So why the 'we are not amused' expression?"

"I just think it's a bit unnecessary to keep taking the piss out of him all the time," he said, chopping away with an exaggerated degree of vigour. "Rosa isn't quite the Virgin Mary she pretends to be, you know – she can give the old come-on as well as the next – for all the shock-horror way she reacts if anybody takes her up on it."

"Oh, come on," she said, "Rodney's a creep and nobody should have to put up with that sort of harassment."

"Nobody should have to put up with that sort of cock-teasing," he said sanctimoniously, "but it happens."

"Oh, sorry I spoke," she said, and left him to his carrot-chopping and his contrariness.

She had arranged to meet Emlyn in the park on the Friday. Not in the plant house which, now the evenings were long and light and the trippers poured into town by the busload, was not the haven it had formerly been. Instead they had discovered a disused summer-house at the far end where the responsibility of the Parks and Gardens Committee ended and the rhododendron bushes gave way to the marram grass and copses of silver birch bordering the sand-dunes. Vandals had kicked out, or age had decayed the struts of the ornamental balustrade that encircled it and generations of graffiti artists had inscribed their messages upon its lime-washed walls. But now its existence seemed to have been forgotten and nature was encroaching rapidly: grass sprouting between the floorboards and ivy climbing to the roof.

She found the place spooky, nestling unseen, with its musty odours of rot and rank vegetable decay, and was glad when Captain's crashing and snuffling announced her lover's arrival.

The dog burst through the undergrowth and hurled himself upon her. She fended him off – muddy paws and drooling tongue – as best she could until his master's command brought him vaguely to heel.

"The rain's held off, at any rate."

"Yes."

"I'm a bit late. Surgery dragged on. I thought I'd never get rid of them."

They were shy with each other. On edge. He stared into the middle-distance as he spoke, as though his thoughts were elsewhere. At the beginning they had fallen into one another's arms, giving thanks for the opportunity of a meeting, however brief and unsatisfactory. Now it was as if such meetings were pointless. The delicious anticipation that had characterised them previously had been satisfied and, it seemed, all that such encounters could yield was frustration and the awkwardness which follows the first occasion of intimacy between a man and a woman who are obliged to behave towards each other in public as though sex has never occurred.

A single bell, somewhere in the distance, began to toll. Captain howled in unison.

"Are we being invaded?" he asked, calling upon the dog to cease its noise.

"Practice, probably."

"What for? A funeral?"

He sighed, gazing out to where a blurred blue line indicated the ebb tide. She chanced her arm. "Would you rather we called a halt to this?"

He turned slowly towards her as the implication of her words penetrated his obviously distracted attention. "What makes you ask that?" he said warily. She had hoped, she supposed, that he would say "No".

"You don't seem very happy."

"I'm not."

Captain, who had been sniffing about among a mass of tangled roots suddenly stiffened, shivered, and then went hareing away in the direction of the sand-dunes.

"A rabbit, probably," he said, by way of explanation, "or else a bitch on heat. I ought to get him done."

His mood lightened. "Perhaps I ought to get myself done at the same time," he said, smiling ruefully.

"Don't do that," she said, suddenly emboldened into stroking the back of his hand.

"At least I wouldn't get into states like this."

"Are you?"

"You know I am. And not a damn thing to be done about it."

"There's nobody else around, is there?"

"No, but . . . Oh!" he said.

The church bell tolled, the breeze rustled the pale leaves of the trees. She watched his face changing as she caressed him, the struggle taking place between control and response. The dangers inherent in what she was doing – at any moment someone could appear, without warning, over the brow of a sand-dune – added an edge to the keenness of his excitement. He thrust his handkerchief into her free hand, clutched at her breast and clenched his teeth to stifle his cry of delight. And she was exultant, revelling in the alteration of the balance of power between them.

"*You* weren't thinking of calling a halt, were you?" he asked anxiously afterwards, looking into her face as though, if he looked deeply enough, he would fathom the truth.

"Not if you don't want me to," she soothed, stroking the dry fall of hair out of his eyes.

"I *don't* want you to."

He kissed her thoroughly and was then taken with a bout of hiccoughs. "Hunger," he explained.

"Haven't you eaten?"

"Not yet. She has an evening class on Fridays. Photography."

"Is she good?"

He considered. "I think she might be. It's difficult to tell. She plunges into these things with such enthusiasm but, usually, loses interest quite rapidly. Photography's lasted longer than most. It keeps her occupied."

At that very moment Diana Rees was ruining a very expensive pair of Manolo Blahnik shoes as she trod across the damp ribbed sand that the ebbtide had uncovered in her attempt to get a good shot of the sun as it sank most dramatically beneath the horizon. Had she turned the incredibly expensive telephoto lens of her incredibly expensive Nikon camera through an angle of ninety degrees, she would have brought the sand-dunes into view, and if she had focused upon the place where a gap appeared in them and pressed the shutter, development of the film might possibly have revealed the shape of a summer-house and, within it, two tiny figures locked in their farewell embrace.

As it was, she narrowly missed an encounter with Captain. Had it not been for the rabbit he would have followed the scent that informed him of a familiar presence and hurled himself at her in an attempt to lead her back to his master. It reassured him to know that his family was safely together in the one place.

16

"His parents don't seem to want much to do with him," Elsa said. "It's awfully sad. After all, you're only twenty-one once, aren't you?"

Mrs Pegler nodded absently. Her sons had had marquees on the lawn, Joe Loss's band and gold watches galore. They had made speeches saying that if it hadn't been for Mum and Dad . . . Poor lad. She gave Elsa a fiver.

Mrs Booth-Powell said it was eighteen nowadays; twenty-one was old-fashioned, and offered fifty pence. Mrs Crookthorne apologised for having left her purse upstairs. She did that three times before Elsa gave up.

The sob story worked with Mesdames Pegler and Grey, Miss Johns and the Colonel. There was no point in trying it on the congenitally mean such as Mrs Crookthorne, or those who were openly so, such as Mrs Booth-Powell, or forthright Miss Vyner, whose reply to the tale of the supposed indifference of the Wynns, *mère* and *père*, was to say that perhaps it was in response to their son's lack of filial affection. Nora Speakman, approached, had said that she made it her policy not to contribute to such appeals, otherwise she would find herself continually with her hand in her pocket: birthdays, weddings, funerals – there was no end to them.

"You weren't thinking of having any sort of party here?" she said sharply.

"Oh no."

They planned to surprise him in his room, to carry there the cake that Mrs Randall had baked ("Not my best, mind you, it would need to keep longer, ideally"), a bottle or two of good wine and a present.

"What's going on?" he'd asked, once or twice, catching

them in mid-conspire, but they'd fobbed him off without too much difficulty.

His mood, so contrary on Friday afternoon, had changed by Friday evening. He'd been waiting for her when she got back from her meeting with Emlyn, had enquired pleasantly whether she'd enjoyed her free time, and asked whether she fancied a drink and a chat. It was a balmy evening, light still, and they had unfurled striped umbrellas outside The Prince Henry and, being Friday, there was a licence extension till eleven.

"Sorry about earlier," he said, as they sat outside the pub. "Things were winding me up."

Children who should have been in bed hours ago were running about, eating from bags of crisps, grizzling into their mothers' skirts. Smacks and subsequent howls ruptured the calm of the summer night. Easier all round to take the kids back to the boarding-house and put them to bed, but their parents were loath to sacrifice the last traces of a perfect day.

Before Dad's mobility had become severely restricted, Elsa and Rob had holidayed quite often on the Norfolk Broads. Dad had acted as babysitter, tucking Nick into his bunk and reading to him from *The Tales of Beatrix Potter* while they explored the quaint little pubs on the river-bank. Upon their return, they'd been obliged to creep about (in that exaggerated fashion so characteristic of the slightly-inebriated) in order that the noise in such a confined space should not wake him.

"A penny for them," Mick said, looking at her over the top of his beer glass. "Or my week's wages, whichever happens to be worth more."

"It's not *that* bad."

"Bad enough. If that's all there was to live on."

"Ssh," she said, looking about her so nervously that, had the garden of the inn been filled with off-duty Department of Employment spies, she'd have been bound to attract their attention. "I have visions of you ending up in court."

"You're too honest," he said, "that's your problem. And too fearful. You'd never make a criminal. Anyway, what *were* you thinking of?"

Moths performed their frenzied dance of death around the

lanterns hanging in the trees. The buildings on the Front were swallowed up by the dusk. She looked down into the dregs of her lager as though the liquid might yield images from the past. "I was remembering," she said, "that's all."

"Good or bad?"

"Good, of course."

"Yes, I suppose it *is* good," he said reflectively, "when it's remembered. Better than it was at the time."

Nick had not wanted to be left with Dad on the boat on the Broads when she and Rob had needed some time to themselves. He had kicked and yelled and they could tell that Dad didn't approve of them going off. "Your mother and I never left you, not once, when you were a child," he chided. But go they did, even though most of the pubs proved to be tastelessly commercialised and the bar prices astronomical. Upon their return, made affectionate by drink, Rob had wanted to make love, but the noise carried so and Dad slept so badly that she'd had to refuse him, in consequence of which most of the nights were blighted by his petulance. "When you go out," Dad said, "it gets ever so cold in here, in spite of that so-called central-heating. And the reception on the telly's terrible – all wavy lines." "Never again," she remembered saying to herself apropos holidays *en famille*. But they did, because hope always triumphed over experience.

More and more, these days, like jagged ice-floes appearing above a sea's deceptively tranquil surface, true recollections kept breaking through, calling into question the whole tenor of how she had chosen to remember her past, exposing memory for the fallible process that it was, as false, much of it, as the picture that she and Emlyn had made as they walked by the lake, among the yellow flowers.

"I'll walk you back," Mick said, as the landlord called last orders.

"Where's your car?" she asked, suddenly remembering its existence and the fact that she hadn't seen it for a while.

He dribbled a squashed Coca-Cola can along the pavement and finally booted it across the road where it came to rest in the gateway of the presbytery of Our Lady, Star of the Sea. "Something's wrong," he said. "I'll have to get it into a garage."

She suspected that he'd been sold a pup. He should have had someone experienced to advise him. His father, for instance. Rob had been a good father: teaching Nick to swim, to ride his bicycle, to kick a football. But Nick had not been an amenable pupil. Tempers had been lost. He wasn't athletic, he never did learn to ride a bicycle and, in the end, it was the instructor at the baths who had taught him how to swim.

Mick found a stone as substitute for the Coca-Cola tin, dribbled it along the Promenade, past the Marine Gardens and the Pier entrance and Smartyboots discothèque and the amusement arcade, and finally lost it by the boating lake. Young persons clustered at the entrance to the discothèque. Some of them were amorously entwined, some belligerently drunk, others vomited explosively. The deep bass beat of the music caused the surrounding ground to vibrate.

Mick moved on, slightly ahead of her, hands in his pockets, shoulders hunched. "Are you giving it a miss tonight?" she asked. He spoke so often of the conquests he'd made there.

"It's a dump," he said disdainfully. "Full of yobs and dodgy old boilers."

The moonlight silvered his profile. He'd had his hair cut fashionably short the previous week but his face was too chubby to carry off the effect and he reminded Elsa of a young and raw army recruit; his ears and the back of his neck pink and shocked at the sudden exposure.

"Whole flaming town's a dump, come to that," he said, pausing to hurl his cigarette-butt down into the depths of the lake. "I think I'll tell the Unspeakables to stuff their job after me next pay-packet. All those old sods get up my nose. That Crookthorne one, the other day, she was in a deckchair on the terrace while I was doing the lawn. You know how hot it was? I took my shirt off. She only went and told Nora, the old twat. 'I may be old-fashioned,' she said, 'but I think we see quite enough of that sort of thing on the television.' Tight old twat. Did you see those wedding-gift glasses of hers? Rosa was saying at Christmas she gave her a hanky out of the box that Mrs Pegler had just given *her*."

"I may be old-fashioned – but my purse is harder to get into than Fort Knox."

"*I* may be old-fashioned – but my pound notes are brand

new – I keep them safely guarded from the harsh light of day."

"What will you do?" she asked as they recovered themselves from the hysteria that impersonation of any one of the Priory's residents always provoked.

"Go down to London, I think. More jobs going down there."

"What sort of job?"

"Oh, I don't know. Pub work or something."

"And where will you live?"

"There's bound to be a floor somewhere."

The bleakness and pointlessness of it, the lack of foresight and subservience to chance appalled her instincts for order and comfort and purpose.

"Have you not thought again about reapplying for your university place?" she asked, again, bracing herself for his retort. But this time he was not hostile.

"No point," he said. "No jobs, even if I wanted to, which I don't. It's changed, Elsie, all that meritocracy stuff. It's the grey brigade who make it now, the ones who haven't an individual thought in their heads, who'll follow the party line, or the company line, or the Establishment line without question. They're the winners now. The rest is just a sop."

He vaulted the balustrade and crossed the lake precariously on stepping-stones, twirling every now and then to show off his agility. Young now and agile, mobile and hungry for change. But youth was short and there he was, wantonly wasting his talents, throwing away the keys. By the time he came to his senses and collected them up again, they'd probably have changed the locks.

Despairing of originality as the days passed, she capitulated and settled for buying him the regulation watch. Not the sort with which the Pegler progeny had been presented – if she'd collected in the Priory from now until for ever she couldn't have afforded one of those. This was a much more workaday affair, but sturdy and reliable and, for someone who didn't possess one, most acceptable, she thought.

The problem was to make sure that *he* had nothing arranged which could confound their careful planning. Elsa subtly sounded him out, attempted to sift what might be the truth from what was, in the main, wishful thinking. He had yet to decide, he told her, which lucky girl was to be selected to share in his celebrations. A meal, he said, an almighty pub crawl and then – well, did she want him to draw her a diagram?

In other words, she suspected, he had no hard and fast arrangement made.

She told Emlyn about it during their next meeting. Rain fell from the sky as heavily and regularly as though it might never stop. Only parts of the summer-house roof were waterproof and she had no suitable clothing against such foul weather. "Oh, but you're *drenched*," he said, rubbing her limbs briskly as though her very circulation was in danger. "Idiot!" he said. "Don't you have a proper raincoat?"

"I suppose I must have done once. But lots of things vanished after the house was sold."

"If I were to give you some money," he said, "would you buy yourself another?"

He felt her stiffening. "I beg your pardon?" she said, though she'd heard him perfectly well.

"Is it so odd, to want to give you a present?"

"Of course not. But there's a difference."

He cuddled her close while she explained. And it was then, while on the subject of giving, that she told him about Mick's birthday and their plans.

"Oh damn," he said, brushing dust off a few more inches of seat with his damp handkerchief and moving them both along because the rain had found another point of entry above their heads. "I was hoping to take you out on Wednesday. A meal, I thought, somewhere in the country."

Diana was going away. An old friend of hers, an actress, had just moved, with her play, into the West End and had invited Diana to the opening. It was unfortunate that his commitments prevented him from accompanying her.

"Couldn't you make it Thursday?" she implored. But Diana would be back by then.

At that point she understood, with a pang, the first law of clandestine relationships: that there can never be any leeway as far as arrangements are concerned, that missed trains or ill health or prior commitments cannot be incorporated into them without risk to the balance of their fragile structure.

"Surely," he answered testily, "the lad would be happier celebrating with friends of his own age?"

He reminded her a little of Mick: that same propensity to sulk if thwarted.

"He doesn't seem to have any. Not here, at any rate."

"Not even a girlfriend?"

His own twenty-first had gone uncelebrated, except for family cards and a note written in his mother's ill-formed script: "Get yourself something nice, lovey," in the fold of which had been placed four white fivers. There hadn't been a girl for him either.

"He's always going on about girls," she said, "but I don't know how much of it is fantasy."

Perhaps not so much as she thought. Since the Friday of his bad temper he'd taken to dashing through the tail-end of his work so that he could finish early. "See you in the morning," he'd shout as he bolted out of the back door. There were no further invitations to join him for a drink and, ridiculously, she felt a little pang of pique. She had enjoyed her role as confidante, guide, elder sister – or whatever he considered her to be. He had made her feel young and free instead of old before her time and detached from society. But she saw that his way of life could not be hers: the mammoth drinking sessions, the frenzied bouts on the dance floor, the pubs and the clubs and the staggering home at dawn to an unmade bed, and the inevitable hangover. She had reached the age when even the excitement of the clandestine can begin to pall, preferred now the luxury of a four-star hotel to a leaky summerhouse and her feet sopping wet and the knowledge that an arrangement for Wednesday night could not be rearranged for Thursday.

17

Breakfast at Priory Lodge was served between eight o'clock and nine, morning teas from seven thirty, breakfast in bed only upon request and at an extra charge. Rosa and Marguerita and Elsa heaved themselves out of deep sleep at about six forty-five or thereabouts and were blearily setting about preparing the trays by quarter past seven. Most of the residents would have been awake since dawn which, in the summer, could be as early as five o'clock. One or two of them (notably Colonel Pritchard and Miss Johns) came downstairs and wandered around until signs of staff life became apparent and then drank their morning tea in the Gloucester Room while waiting somewhat impatiently for the papers and the post.

On the Monday before Mick's birthday Elsa's usual early-morning languor was tinged with agitation. Today she could expect the letter, the one that might enable her to tell Mrs Speakman exactly what she could do with her breakfast preparation. (Not that she'd do it. She would, meekly, give a week's notice and, just as meekly, make her farewells.)

Miss Johns had appointed herself unofficial postal-sorter. It helped to while away the time until they opened the breakfast-room doors. Residents' mail was individually sorted and laid out on the hall table ("Nosy old bitch," Mr Golding thought. He considered it a presumption. What if one was to receive personal mail? He didn't; his books wrapped in plain brown paper were delivered to the poste restante at the GPO, but it was the principle of the thing!), Speakmans' mail was carried to the table outside Nora's office, and staff mail popped into the kitchen.

Elsa glanced at the clock. The postman usually delivered

around seven thirty. At seven forty, or thereabouts, Miss Johns's head (receding chin, beaky nose and rabbit teeth) would appear around the edge of the door. If I can fry all the eggs without puncturing a single yolk, Elsa thought, if the porridge thickens up evenly without me having to strain the lumps out of it . . . What nonsense, she told herself, to suppose that any action performed now could make the slightest difference to a decision taken at least four days ago.

"Miss Franklin?"

The head appearing round the door belonged not to Miss Johns but to Colonel Pritchard (well-barbered, precisely-shaved, complexion tanned and mottled by all the suns of the Orient). "You are Miss Franklin, aren't you, Elsa?" he said. "I thought you must be. You're wanted on the telephone."

He can't be ringing me from home, she thought, feeling her heart beat against her ribs. Diana hasn't gone away yet. Anyway, why on earth should he want to ring at this time of the morning? Unless, of course, some crisis has occurred?

Her ear attuned for Emlyn's voice, it took a moment or two for her to realise that she was speaking to Mick.

". . . can you get over here? They've got me down for mugging old women and I don't know what. And get me a brief and make it quick, for Christ's sake . . ."

He sounded hysterical. His words were gabbled almost too quickly for her to catch their sense. She begged him to repeat them, to explain.

"The police station," he said. "Can you get over here? And get me a brief?" There was that jagged edge to his voice which suggested a fighting for control over tears.

"A brief?" she said. "What do you mean?"

"One for you, dear," Miss Johns said, passing by on her way to the kitchen with the post.

"A solicitor," he said. "Before they put me away for good. Look, move it, will you? I'm only allowed one telephone call."

She'd once been delayed on her way to pick up Nick from school. When she finally got there he had been alone, save for the caretaker, sitting with his arms round his knees as rigidly as if the slightest movement might cause dislocation. There had been that same note of panic in his voice until relief at seeing her overcame it.

"All right, all right, keep calm. I'll come now. Oh," she said, "where is it?"

A reasonable question, she thought. There was no reason that she should be familiar with the whereabouts of the local police station. But he jumped on her as savagely as if she'd been pretending obtuseness: "It's in the precinct, for Christ's sake. Opposite the fire station."

"Right," she said. "Give me twenty minutes."

"You're what?"

She'd collected her coat before confronting Nora, the letter that Miss Johns had given her lying forgotten in her pocket.

"You're what?" Nora said.

"I'm sure Rosa and Marguerita can manage for once. It sounds as though he's in real trouble."

"I can't have my staff running off hither, thither and yon every time they take it into their heads – " She broke off and started to sniff. Elsa remembered, too late, a dozen slices of bread toasting beneath the grill when she'd been called to the phone. She fled from the scene of her crime. "I'll be back just as soon as I can. Someone's got to go."

It was a modern building, the police station, unforbidding. Had it not been identified, she might have mistaken it for the library or the town hall. Only the bars, set across the ground-floor windows, alerted her to its true function.

"Michael Wynn," she asked as she presented herself to the uniformed man behind the enquiry desk. Behind him, in a glassed-in compartment, a constable took off his hat and scratched his head and a policewoman drank tea. It was very quiet.

He consulted a book resembling a hotel register (and wasn't that dissimilar, she supposed, except that here you weren't issued with a key). "You'll want DS Fleming," he said and took up the telephone and exchanged a few words with, presumably, the aforesaid officer.

"Take a seat. He'll be down as soon as he can."

She sat. Identikit portraits of wanted men stared at her from the opposite wall. Surely, she thought, such faces did not exist outside freak shows?

The hands on the electric clock above the desk moved in

spastic jerks. At twenty past eight a posse of uniformed men, their shift presumably at an end, started to drift in, each eyeing her as he passed. At half past eight a lad in leathers came in to report the theft of his motor-bike. At twenty to nine an elderly man with a speech impediment and a limp limped in to say that that devil across the road was *still* continuing to obstruct the pavement with his invalid car and what did they intend to do about it considering that he, the complainant, paid his rates like everybody else? Men that she took to be solicitors, formal suits and briefcases, marched in and out, straight through the doors to the interior of the building without consulting the desk sergeant, though the desk sergeant, noticing their presence, was required to press a button which released the doors. At five past nine a slovenly-looking woman handed a Marks and Spencer's carrier bag filled with clothes across the desk. "Can I have his others, love?" she asked the sergeant.

He made his consultation over the telephone then said, "Do you want to hang on until he's changed?" and the woman nodded and came to sit down beside Elsa.

"Smoke?"

"No, thank you."

She opened the packet and withdrew a cigarette, lit it and flung the spent match to the floor though there was a bin not three feet away. "Like making you wait in these places," she said, needing only the slightest encouragement to relay the sort of information that in Elsa's view ought to have been kept to herself. The court was in session this morning and her lad was up before the magistrates. Hence the change of clothing. Some of them went in deliberately scruffy: two days' growth, tattered jeans, bondage trousers; "I don't give a sod for you" was the message conveyed by these anarchic garments, but that was silly, wasn't it, being as the magistrates were old fogies, far more inclined to believe misdemeanour unlikely in one who wore a blazer than his fellow who sported a tee-shirt with a provocative message? Her lad needed to make the best of impressions; he could go down for a long time if he wasn't careful.

"Miss Franklin? Detective Sergeant Fleming."

She looked up, feeling horrified that Mick should have

allowed himself to be associated in any way with this ambience: the criminal's mother with her evil breath and ringed eyes, the hardfaced policewoman who drank tea with relish, oblivious of her surroundings, the freakish countenances that lined the walls.

"Would you like to come this way?"

She followed him through the one-way doors to a little room that reminded her of a store cupboard. It contained a table, three chairs, a filing cabinet and a padlocked bicycle. She sat down, noticing as she did so a heap of papers on the table headed with the legend, "Charge Sheet", and realised with a jolt that this must be where suspects were brought for the purposes of interrogation.

Sergeant Fleming sat down noisily, leaned back in his seat and studied her. She realised to her astonishment that she felt very nervous – on her own account, as much as for Mick – as though he were about to subject her to deep questioning. But she forced herself to return his scrutiny nevertheless.

He was a big man, florid-faced, with thick pepper-and-salt hair that waved back from his forehead and eyes so light in colour that you felt you were looking into nothing.

"You're a workmate of his, I believe? We've tried to get in touch with his parents but apparently they're on holiday in Spain and not expected back until tomorrow."

Typical, she thought briefly. His twenty-first birthday imminent and his parents were unreachable.

"As he's only just twenty he should have some close relative or, failing that, a friend here to sort things out for him. I understand he wants you to arrange legal advice. We have a duty solicitor here who can advise him quite adequately. Or you can get your own. It's entirely up to you."

"Only just twenty?" she said. "He'll be twenty-one on . . ."

"What's that?"

"Nothing," she said. Why the lie, she wondered. Why? Was there anything these days that you couldn't do until you were twenty-one?

"Look," she said, meaning "Listen", "I haven't a clue as to what all this is about, why he should need a solicitor at all . . ."

His light-coloured eyes flickered over her face, then came

to rest in a constant regard. She felt herself twitching, was envious of the impression he gave of composure.

"He was picked up at two o'clock this morning," he said eventually, "attempting to gain entry to a house near the park. He's being held now pending further investigations."

"Was he drunk?" she asked. Relief calmed her trembling. They seemed to be making a lot of what seemed to be a drunken prank. Typical. Chasing silly children while murderers and rapists and robbers roamed free.

"He'd had plenty, certainly. The occupant of the house called the police and he was apprehended hiding in an old summer-house at the edge of the park."

Stupid sod, she thought, imagined his panic as the noise of the siren ruptured the alcoholic haze that fogged his senses.

"So – he'll be charged with – whatever it is," she said, "and that's why he needs a solicitor?"

"I'm afraid it's not quite that simple," he said.

It was the lack of inflection in his tone, the absence of expression in his eyes, that made her feel nervous. But they were trained to do that, she supposed.

"One of the arresting officers noticed a remarkable similarity to a man we're looking for in connection with other crimes. I'm waiting now for an officer of the Regional Crime Squad to get here."

"What crimes?" she said. The muscles of her mouth seemed to have gone into spasm and she had difficulty in forming the words.

"There have been cases in the area, over the space of the last year, of a man using the pretext of being a potential house-buyer, or threatening the occupant with a knife, in order to gain entry to houses for the purpose of burglary. Descriptions of this man fit your friend Michael Wynn very closely. I am now waiting for Sergeant Verity of the Regional Crime Squad to question him. In the meantime I suggest you telephone a solicitor."

He spoke slowly, as if to a half-wit. Under the table she clasped her hands together to stop them shaking.

"I can call the duty solicitor," he repeated. "Or, if you wish to engage your own, you can use the telephone at the desk."

"I'll get one myself," she said. The services so cursorily offered sounded as though they might be distinctly secondrate.

But she wouldn't use the phone at the desk. She needed privacy. There were two boxes outside the entrance. She waited for the first of them to be vacated, breathing in gratefully the petrol-laden air of freedom, noticing the procession of women with carrier bags, mothers and wives, presumably, bearing the sort of clothes for their errant sons and husbands that might favourably impress the magistrates.

"Surgery."

"Could you put me through to Dr Rees, please?"

"Dr Rees does not take calls during surgery. Can I help you?"

"No. It's Dr Rees I need to speak to."

"If you'd like to leave your number I'll ask him to call you back after surgery."

She had a not-to-be-argued-with sort of voice, and Elsa heard her own rising, becoming strident, whereas dignity and authoritativeness were what were required. She breathed deeply, steadied herself. "This is a matter of some urgency," she said crisply. "I would appreciate it if you'd put me through to Dr Rees now."

"Name?" came the response, nasal and snappish, and a couple of seconds later there was Emlyn's voice, low and cautious, trying, with the single word of his response, "Yes?" to communicate the need for caution.

She babbled: "Mick's in the police station and he needs a solicitor, do you know of a good one?"

He cut her short. "I've a patient with me now. If you give me your number I'll ring you back in a few minutes."

And no receptionist listening in. There was a direct line from his surgery.

The few minutes stretched interminably. A woman, impatient to use the phone, glared in at her. When it rang she jumped a foot.

"Well, what is it?" he said. She could tell that he was not best pleased. She tried to be succinct. "But why should it concern you?" he asked, with what sounded like genuine mystification. For a moment she was lost for words, then she said, "If I were in trouble, I should hope that you'd help *me* – "

"Hardly the same, is it?"

"There's nobody else. Don't you understand? Anyway, all I want is the name of a good solicitor."

"Geoffrey Lomax," he said promptly. "Penn, Butler and Beaumont. He's your man. Deals with all the criminal stuff."

"Do you happen to know his number?"

"I'll ring him. I'll probably get through more easily than you. You want him down there, I take it? Actually he might already *be* down there. The court is in session today, isn't it? Anyway, his secretary'll know. I'll tell him to seek you out. What's this kid's name? His surname?"

"Wynn. Michael Wynn."

"Geoff Lomax is a tall chap, heavily built, with specs," he said. "Anyhow, he'll find you. By the way," he said, as though all this business was just an irritating incidental, "I think I may be able to manage Thursday after all. I'll pop into the Priory tomorrow afternoon – I've got Mrs Whatnot's X-ray results – and let you know."

"OK," she said, though it occurred to her that there was no reason now that she would not be free on Wednesday evening.

She walked back to the police station and resumed her seat in what she identified as the reception area, though that phrase conjured up Turkey carpet and fresh flowers rather than the composition flooring and extruded plastic chairs that made up the reality of the place. One eye upon the clock and another upon the outer door, she awaited developments. Various tall, bespectacled men came and went but none looked as though they were searching for a woman of her description. Some of them chatted together as they waited for their automatic admittance to the inner sanctum. They talked easily of lunch and golf and holidays. Awaiting them in the cells, no doubt, were desperate souls whose chance of freedom depended upon their legal skills. But you'd never have guessed it.

"Are you Miss Franklin?"

The man who approached her was small and thin and not even noticeably myopic. "Mr Lomax?" she said uncertainly.

"My name's Parker. I'm Mr Lomax's clerk. He's in court at

the moment. I do the behind-the-scenes stuff, as it were. He's the front man."

The sergeant behind the desk smiled obligingly, as though he'd heard this explanation being delivered a thousand times before.

"Well, I've had a word with our young friend and he seems very confident about the whole matter – "

"*What* whole matter?" she interrupted. "I still don't understand properly – "

He continued as though she hadn't interjected. "Unfortunately, in my opinion and certainly against my advice, he's agreed to appear in an identity parade this afternoon. However, that's his privilege. He thinks it'll get him out quicker. Which may be the case, of course. He's had his rights explained to him and he's asked me to tell you that he's dying for a cigarette, so if you want to get him some, just hand them in to the sergeant here and he'll see that they're delivered. The parade is scheduled for three o'clock this afternoon. If you would like to come back then and, depending upon what transpires, get in touch with me, I'll be in a better position to enlighten you. Meanwhile I suggest you get some lunch."

She glanced at the clock and found, to her surprise, that it was past midday. Nora would be chewing the carpet. There was no way that she could now return to the Priory and expect to be allowed out again for three o'clock.

She went back to the kiosk outside and dialled the number that went through to the public box outside the Gloucester Room.

"Oh *hello*, dear," Mrs Pegler said warmly. Elsa cursed. Mrs Pegler was inclined to be vague. Vyner would have been a better bet. Or even Crookthorne; poisonous but quick on the uptake.

"Could you possibly give Mrs Speakman a message for me? Tell her that I've been unavoidably detained, but will be back by late afternoon."

"Yes, dear," said Mrs Pegler. "It's such a lovely day, isn't it? I don't blame you for having it off. I would, if I were you."

Elsa noticed, for the first time, the sun streaming in through the window: the police station had been windowless.

"No, I'm not having the day off. Mrs Pegler – " She

repeated her message, but the pips went before she could ask for anyone else and by the time she'd put in more money, Mrs Pegler had hung up.

She walked across to a newsagent's shop where she bought twenty Benson and Hedges which she delivered, as directed, to Mick via the desk sergeant. Then she found a café where she ordered an egg on toast and while she was waiting for the somewhat indolent serving-girl to bring it, she felt in her pocket for her handkerchief and found there the letter that Miss Johns had passed on to her and she opened it and discovered, to her mild delight, that the art college place she'd applied for was hers for the taking.

"What?" Nora Speakman said. She often responded to other people's utterances this way, not because she hadn't heard them properly, but as though she hoped that pretence of having misheard would prompt them into altering what they'd said so that the information conveyed the second time around would be more to her taste.

"Such a *lovely* day," Mrs Pegler twittered foolishly. "She deserves a day off. It'll put some roses in her cheeks. When we were young, we were always out in the fresh air."

She omitted to mention that it was usually because there were too many of them to fit into the squalid little hovel that all fourteen of them called home.

"Dad was a great believer in fresh air." Even after making all his money he'd missed going out in the cart. But you couldn't go out in the cart when you had a fleet of lorries to organise and a brand-new Rolls-Royce in your garage.

"Day off?" Nora Speakman said, between her teeth and under her breath. "I'll give her day off!"

A couple of miles away the subject of their conversation walked round the boating lake, not for the good of her health, but because she needed to while away the time until three o'clock and sitting still had proved an impossibility. Never had she been more conscious of the contrasts between outdoors and inside. "Inside," she said to herself. "Chokey, the nick, clink, the slammer." How could anyone joke about it? Though perhaps only by making a joke of it could you begin to cope with its horrid reality.

St Simon's church clock struck the three-quarter hour, followed, three minutes later, by that of St James. With mixed feelings she turned her steps in the direction of the police station. Presumably this identification business wouldn't take very long. She thought of the melodramatic versions she'd seen countless times in films and on the television screen. She thought of Emlyn saying, "Why should it concern you?" and wondered how it could fail to concern anyone who knew him; thought of the criminals' mothers, carrying in clothes, remembered once sitting on a bus in front of two women and eavesdropping upon their conversation. One had asked after the other one's son and the first one had said, "He's away, didn't you know? In Winson Green. They did him for nicking a camera and stuff out of Boots. It's a devil of a journey for me. Two buses after I get off the train." She had spoken fretfully as though merely put out by the problems encountered in travelling to see him. "He's a bad 'un," she said. "He always was."

But still she went to see him. And Emlyn, who had never had a child, wouldn't be able to understand why.

"It'll all be over in half an hour," she told herself. The witness would walk down the line, fail to pick him out and the assembly would disperse and afterwards he'd have them in hysterics with his impersonations of all concerned. Twenty-one or no, they'd have the party anyway, to celebrate.

She crossed the precinct towards the station, comforting herself with such thoughts. But she couldn't get one niggling worry out of her head: the memory of the man at the hotel who had been so certain that she and Emlyn were Randolph Sergeant and Rose. A cunning ploy, she had thought at the time, to engage them in conversation. Now she was not so sure.

18

Outside, tar bubbled on the road and ice-cream began to melt as soon as it was scooped out of its refrigerated containers. Dogs panted on pavements, their tongues dripping, their flanks twitching. Fair-skinned persons stripped, recklessly risking sunburn, and one small child, its vest burned to its flesh, had to be admitted to the infirmary.

Inside the police station Detective Sergeant Fleming had taken off his jacket. In his blue cotton-polyester shirt he looked cool and composed. His colleague, the man from Regional, wore a suede bomber-jacket but showed no sign of discomfort. Cold-blooded, perhaps, Elsa thought.

She sat once again in the store-cupboard-cum-interrogation-room into which they had ushered her. Fleming came in moments later. His colleague leaned nonchalantly against the wall. He wore jeans and trainers and a medallion round his neck. So that he could mingle among young persons unremarked, she supposed. She remembered Mick talking about such policemen. "Stick out a mile," he'd said. "Always about two years behind the times."

"There's been a bit of a snag," Sergeant Fleming said slowly, putting his shirt-sleeved elbows on the table, bringing his hands together prayer-like and leaning the point of his chin upon them. "One of our witnesses, a Mrs Russell, is too ill to attend this afternoon."

"So we've had to postpone," said his colleague.

"She hopes to be here tomorrow," said Sergeant Fleming, "so in view of this, it has been decided . . ."

"To keep your friend here until then."

They were a double-act, this pair: the one heavy, solid and reliable; the other thin, quick and darting. Verity, she remembered, Verity, that was his name.

"But surely," she said, "he doesn't have to stay here until tomorrow?"

They looked at one another above her head. They were different in build and type, but their eyes were exactly the same: you looked into them and all you saw was your own reflection.

"I'm afraid there's slightly more to it than you may think," said Sergeant Fleming. He leaned forward. "Last September," he said, "an elderly lady in Saltlea opened her door to a man who led her to believe that he wished to inspect her house, which was up for sale. Once in, he drew a knife and, before leaving, assaulted her. Five weeks and three weeks ago, respectively, two similar incidents took place in the town. The second time the man fled when a passer-by noticed him loitering at the door. But during the first incident the woman was threatened, assaulted and had money stolen from the house."

"An elderly woman," Verity said. "A lady in very poor health. He ripped her blouse and fondled her," he continued, demonstrating in the region of his Wrangler shirt and gold medallion.

"All three ladies got a look at him," said Sergeant Fleming.

"But Mrs Russell, the victim of the second assault, got a really good look," said Verity. "She was able to give us a first-class description."

"How old is she?" Elsa said, finding voice with difficulty.

There was a pause and then Sergeant Fleming said, "Seventy-two," and Verity said, "But she has good eyesight and got a damn good look at him. If she picks him out, we've got him, no danger."

"And you say she's ill?"

He hesitated, torn between wanting to emphasise the heinousness of the crime and needing to establish that her degree of illness was not severe enough to have interfered with the keenness of her vision. "Look," he said, "we're not trying what they call a fit-up or anything here. But the resemblance between your friend and the description we have is remarkably close. And his escapade last night fits in with the general pattern."

"What exactly *was* the escapade last night?" she asked. There seemed to be a conspiracy of silence where this was concerned.

"Banging and thumping and demanding entrance to a house in which only an elderly lady is resident," Sergeant Fleming said eventually. "Frightening her almost out of her wits, then running when he saw a police car arriving."

"But *he* must have had an explanation?"

"Oh, I daresay." The big policeman leaned forward again. "What sort of a lad *is* he? Have you known him long? Many girlfriends, has he? That you'd know of?"

The confidential tone, the switched-on agreeability nauseated her. "Not the sort of lad to do anything like that," she countered. "Anyway," she said, "you're talking about last year for one of these attacks. He wasn't here last year."

"Oh yes he was," Verity said quickly. "He was working on the fairground last year on the date in question."

She sat very still and straight and said, with as much dignity as she could muster, "I've worked very closely with him for weeks now. Don't you think I'd have noticed if he'd been doing this sort of thing?"

They exchanged pointed glances of frank amusement. Verity said, "I picked up a lad last month after he'd set fire to his grandmother's house that afternoon. Old lady was burned to a cinder. Kid, when I picked him up, two hours later, was eating fish and chips and watching *Top Of The Pops*, just like any ordinary day."

They had an answer for everything, these two. "I still don't understand," she said, "why you can't let him out until tomorrow."

Fleming shook his head ruefully. "Afraid our boss is opposed to bail. Serious matter, you see. *I'd* bail him, but . . ."

"Can I see him?"

"The boss? I don't think it'd make much difference."

"No. Mick. Michael."

"Oh, yes," they said, in tones that suggested surprise that she hadn't asked before.

They called for a uniformed officer who ushered her forth and led her along a corridor which ended at a locked door. He unlocked it, then locked it again behind them, and motioned her to follow him along a stone passage which was intersected with yet another door that had to be unlocked and locked again behind them. Their footsteps echoed in the quiet.

She'd never seen police cells before. Not first hand. They coincided exactly with the image conveyed by films and television. Except that they were much, much dirtier.

This one was, anyway, the one containing Mick. The policeman opened a door and he was framed in the space: sitting on the edge of a concrete slab that was covered with a kind of thin flock palliasse. Stained it was, and of a maggoty colour. One touch, she thought, and you might catch incurable diseases. The walls were stained too. With excrement. There was a seatless lavatory next to the bed and a grey blanket folded at the end of it.

"Thank God," he said. "I can have a fag now," as though, compared with being denied a smoke, the rest of his troubles were negligible.

The policeman stood outside the open door. Mick's hand shook so that the match would not ignite against the side of the box. She took it from him and lit it. "Why won't they let you have cigarettes all the time?" she asked.

"In case I might be a pyromaniac," he said, dragging on his cigarette so deeply that he choked.

It was a feeble joke, but more than she had expected. He coughed until he'd got his breath back. He spread his hands wide. "Can *you* tell me," he implored, "what the hell's going on?"

"Haven't they?"

"They haven't. They just keep asking where I was on such and such a date. I can't flaming remember. Last year, one of them was! And that solicitor chap just read me a sort of riot act, and now this bleedin' woman's not turned up. Or so I gather. Just what is the score, exactly?"

She explained briefly, playing down the seriousness of the offences, trying not to look at his hands that trembled so.

His voice trembled too. "So I'm stuck here until tomorrow?"

"I'm afraid so. Unless the solicitor can do something. I'll ring him now."

She looked away while he struggled to control his voice. He was scared. Badly scared. As she would have been in his place. Innocent people, they said, had nothing to fear. Except, of course, a miscarriage of justice – and that was not so uncommon, if the newspapers were anything to go by.

"What was it all about," she asked, "last night? Were you trying to get into somebody's house, as they allege?"

He brought a hand to his forehead and touched it tenderly as though everything inside there was unendurably sensitive. "Last night," he said. "Oh Christ. Last night's pretty much a blank."

"Too many sniffs of the barmaid's apron," was how the solicitor's clerk described it on the telephone. "He told me he was looking for a girl, mistook that house for hers. There's nothing much we can do until tomorrow, I'm afraid, Miss Franklin."

"But aren't they supposed to *charge* people?" she asked. "They can't just *keep* him there, can they?"

"They can keep him for forty-eight hours, then they must either charge him or let him go. Now, don't worry, he'll be all right. He's a big lad."

That wasn't the way it had seemed to her when she'd left him five minutes ago. Young, he'd looked, and scared. Just as Nick had looked that day she'd been delayed in picking him up from school, as though he felt that succour would never arrive.

"Is there anything you need, if – if the solicitor can't do anything before tomorrow?" she'd asked. Then she'd realised that she would be unable to bring it for him. Once Nora spotted her, she'd be stuck at the Lodge for the rest of the day.

"I wouldn't mind a few books – I'll go crazy otherwise. Oh, and a change of clothes and shaving gear, I suppose. If I'm allowed to shave," he said loudly, for the benefit of the attendant policeman.

"I'll get them to you," she said. "Even if *I* can't come, I'll send somebody with them."

Mary, she thought, Mary Reilly was the obvious choice. She'd know the ropes. It would mean everyone knowing, but everyone would probably find out anyway.

"Keep your chin up," she said. "We'll get you out. Until then, if they question you, just tell them the truth. They can't get beyond that."

"Right then, love," the waiting policeman said, consulting his watch. She withdrew. Her heart went out to him: the vulnerability, the appeal in his eyes. "They can't get beyond that," she repeated.

But all the way down the stone-flagged passage, while she waited for the doors to be unlocked and locked again, she was thinking of Timothy Evans, of James Hanratty, and all those other controversial cases where it was possible that the fallibility of the British judicial system had been displayed at its most blatant. And she was thinking too about the man in the hotel.

They were restless at the Priory. The good weather was back and the forecast was favourable. There was a holiday atmosphere in the air, but most of those who had the chance of holidays had already taken them. Only Mrs Pendennis's wedding provided a landmark in the dull plateau of days that stretched uneventful up to Christmas, and that was not scheduled until October.

Three months of nothing to look forward to except Mrs Speakman reviewing her prices, the interest rate falling and the cost of living rising (whatever these young whippersnapper politicians tried to make you believe) – the residents of Priory Lodge were avid for a bit of excitement.

No one knew who had first spilled the beans. Miss Vyner got it from Mrs Booth-Powell who reckoned to have got it from Marguerita, but that seemed unlikely because, generally speaking, Mrs Booth-Powell found Marguerita's English incomprehensible. A separate, apparently independent rumour circulated via Mrs Grey and Mrs Pendennis and had its source, so it was alleged, in a conversation that had taken place between Elsa and Mrs Speakman on the second-floor landing where, quite coincidentally, Mrs Pendennis had been obliged to pause, half-in, half-out of her bedroom, stricken with an attack of cramp. She couldn't help overhearing what passed between them, and couldn't resist sharing her news.

The two stories, which differed markedly in several crucial details, prompted lively debate. The casts of *Crossroads* and *Coronation Street* gibbered and gesticulated on the television screen in the Gloucester Room because, for once, the sound had been turned down while the forgotten art of conversation – albeit in the form of gossip – was revived.

"They're holding him overnight, that's what she said," Mrs Pendennis reported, "'they're holding him overnight.' I'm sure I heard the word 'rape' mentioned," she added. She hadn't, but the more she said it, the more convinced she became that she had.

"What nonsense!" boomed Mrs Booth-Powell. "The boy is suspected of burglary. Rape has nothing to do with it. Rape is just a fabrication."

They shivered, thinking of their possessions: their rings and brooches and bracelets and furniture and silver Hunters and gold cigarette-cases, so vulnerable while he, the marauder, had walked abroad.

"He didn't look like a rapist," Miss Johns said. Everyone – at least everyone who read books or watched television – knew that rapists always had staring eyes and a sort of tic in their cheek which started to beat when they felt the rise of that irresistible urge. But when Mrs Booth-Powell said mockingly, "What do rapists look like?" she answered feebly, "Well – sinister, I suppose."

Mrs Booth-Powell's late husband had been a magistrate, which added authority to her pronouncements, but Mrs Pendennis had her information, as it were, at first hand. The company was split into two camps, with many shifts of allegiance.

"I think we ought not to speculate," Miss Vyner said, "until we know the facts of the matter." The others looked at her scornfully: goody-goody, prig, spoilsport – forever setting herself up as the voice of their communal conscience. It was time she realised that gossip and speculation were the only spices available to them for garnishing the dull cuisine that composed their daily fare.

"He always looked a shifty customer to me," Mrs Crookthorne said. Her viciousness was idle, unspecific. Whoever had been under discussion, she'd have felt obliged to malign him.

Bloody women, Colonel Pritchard thought, waiting his opportunity to avoid Golding's all-seeing eye and slip out for a drink. Poor devil if he got a jury composed of *them*; they'd have him flayed alive and flung to the lions.

"You never know, do you?" Mrs Pendennis said. And no one sought to disagree with that.

Speculation in the kitchen was as rife but better informed.

This was due to the fact that Elsa, calling at Mary Reilly's rented room, had found it occupied only by Des, or Dinsdale, as she found herself calling him. She had expected a massive brute, handsome in a coarse sort of way, with a quick temper and a melting eye. She felt that her jaw might have been seen to drop when he opened the door to her; he reminded her of a jockey: large-headed, stunted, bandy, his face as wizened as though he'd spent a lifetime staring into the sunshine through the frame of a horse's ears. Mary, he'd informed her, when she'd stopped gaping and explained her business, was at Priory Lodge. That Rodney chap had come to fetch her in the big car on account of being short-staffed. Des had told her to tell him what he could do with his job. But Mary had said that bygones should be bygones; she'd do anyone a good turn, would Mary.

And so it came to pass that Mary was in the kitchen, peeling potatoes, when Elsa was obliged to ask her favour. And as everyone else was in the kitchen too, urging her towards confidentiality seemed a waste of time.

"You're pulling my leg," Mary said, potato in one hand, knife in the other, peel dropping with a splat into the sink, mouth agape to the extent that a dribble of saliva followed it.

"I'm not."

Frozen into a tableau: a sort of Pompeian frieze of work in progress prior to the cataclysm, they listened to the tale. Chickens awaited their basting in marge at Mrs Randall's hand, while Nellie Macpherson, a tray of cutlery resting on her hip, took the weight off her bunion. Marguerita and Rosa, respectively washing teacups and mixing mustard, went goggle-eyed, their command of English never so limited that they couldn't understand what one attempted to keep from them.

There was a little pause when she'd finished her story, then everyone spoke at once: "Well, I'm damned," Mrs Randall said, "Well, I'm damned," and attacked the chickens with the marge brush and the venom of a corpse-violator.

"They've got the wrong man," Nellie Macpherson said vehemently, endowing her very-bad-line-out-of-a-B-film-script with a moving sincerity.

Marguerita just said, "Police – very dangerous," and shook

her head as one who has cause to regret an involvement with the law.

Mary Reilly's flabber was gasted all right, but she recovered her composure more quickly than the others. "What's his name," she asked briskly, "the busy on the case?"

"Fleming."

"No," she said scornfully, "not him. They're just Toytown. The Regional man."

"Verity. Detective Sergeant Verity." She wondered if his name had led him towards such a career. Were there villains called Verity?

Mary's forehead creased as she searched her memory for associations. "My feller might know him," she said. "I'll ask him on me way back. Oh, don't worry, love," she said. "They're all mouth, them CID. Couldn't catch a cold, most of 'em. If you've got him a good solicitor he'll be all right. Now, if you give me the key, I'll get his clothes and that together and take them down there. I'll put a packet of fags in too. Some of them are OK – they'll let you have a smoke. Otherwise the nights are awful long."

She put on her raincoat and tied a multicoloured chiffon scarf over her rollers – she'd been in the middle of perming her hair when Mister Rodney had come to summon her back to work. "Shaving tackle, a change of clothes, ciggies," she recited. "And these books."

Assorted magazines and paperbacks, they were, that Elsa had purchased on her way back to work. Not knowing his tastes, she'd aimed for a catholic selection, but suddenly everything seemed inappropriate: a detective story, a *New Statesman* that contained an article on penal reform, a copy of *Crime and Punishment*. Car magazines and science fiction had seemed the least offensive options.

"Don't worry," Mary said. "I'll cheer him up."

"Put her great big foot in it, more like," Mrs Randall said, after she'd gone. "Poor lad – what he needs is sympathy, not her daft jokes. Eh, now I think on, what about his birthday? What'll we do with the cake?"

Put a file in it, Elsa was tempted to say. But she demurred. That he had lied to them concerning his age was one item of news that she considered was best left unbroadcast.

19

After breakfast next morning Elsa rang the solicitor's office.

"Mr Parker? Miss Franklin."

"Miss Franklin?"

"Concerning Michael Wynn. We met yesterday at the police station."

"Oh yes, that's right. Now . . . I've had a call from Sergeant Fleming. They're hoping to hold the identification parade this afternoon, if they can get their witnesses together. One of them, apparently, is in poor health and has been staying out of town with a relative. She's hoping to get back for this afternoon – "

"Hoping?"

"If she can't, then they'll have to postpone again until tomorrow."

"Oh, for goodness sake, this is ludicrous! They can't keep him there indefinitely at some woman's whim – "

"As I explained yesterday, Miss Franklin, they are perfectly within their rights to hold him without charge for forty-eight hours. Mr Wynn has agreed to help them and, at this stage, it wouldn't look too good if he changed his mind. Now, I suggest either you go down to the station after lunch, or else ring my secretary. You can see him, you know, whenever you like. Take him food or books. They're usually very obliging . . ."

Very obliging. And, if one was acquainted from time past, as Mary Reilly was with the one who had led her to the cells, informative too.

"John Verity, he's called, that detective. Really keen, Dodds said. Been after this one for a long time. There's cases in Preston and up near Lytham St Anne's they're trying to tie it in with. Normally they'd have bailed him, but there's too much resting on this one. Bert Dodds says he's the spit of the Photofit – but you know what them Photofits are, you'd not recognise your own mother from one. I told him to keep his pecker up and did he fancy some toffees or anything? He didn't; he'd just have a read of the books, he said. He was all right when I come away. 'Don't let the bastards grind you down,' I told him. I told him an' all not to put his name to anything without his solicitor being there. That's what they do, you know, keep you there so flamin' long that you'd sign owt just to get out. I think that's what happened to me," she confided in an undertone. Mary often spoke of personal incidents as though they concerned someone other than herself.

After lunch, Elsa visited the police station. She carried with her a punnet of fresh strawberries and a large luscious ripe peach, bought en route from a fruit stall in the precinct. These garden-party summer delicacies seemed out of place in the dirty cell. He ate them, one after the other, not so much gluttonously as abstractedly, as if he required employment for his restless hands. His eyes were shadowed from lack of sleep and he was badly shaved. There was no mirror, he told her; one managed as best one could.

"She hasn't turned up?"

But she knew the answer to that already.

"So it'll be tomorrow? It's got to be tomorrow. Or not at all."

Having disposed of the strawberries, he bit into the peach. Juice gushed down his chin. She handed him her handkerchief. "It seems like half a lifetime already," he said, mopping himself.

As long as he kept his hands occupied, she realised, their trembling could be controlled. He spat out the peach kernel and lit a cigarette.

"Are they still questioning you?"

"Every so often. Where was I on May 23rd and June 4th and September the somethingth last year? As if I could remember."

"It shouldn't be too difficult to think back, surely? If you were at work, then it'll be down on a time sheet, won't it?"

"A time sheet!" He gave her a scornful look. "As far as Nora's concerned, I'm not officially an employee, am I? If pressed, she'll make up some crap about part-time work – you know, too few hours to qualify for National Insurance contributions, etcetera – "

"But *we* know," she said.

"Can you honestly remember," he said, "even such a short time ago?"

He was right. Days merged with their fellows. Without benefit of a diary, it was difficult to recall the exact sequence of events. But there were bound to be landmarks, triggers: the day he started work, the day Mrs Cuthbert-Carew died, their trip to Blackpool . . .

"We can start off with last night. I mean the night before," she said. "You can't have forgotten *that* already. Those policemen said something about your mistaking this old lady's house for someone else's?"

He lit a fresh cigarette from the stub of the old one, seemed disinclined to pursue her line of enquiry.

"Some girl," she persisted. "They said you thought it was her house."

"It was just a girl," he said rapidly, looking past her. "She gave me that address. Or I thought she did."

"Well," she said, "if we could find her she could confirm it, couldn't she? What was her name?"

"I don't know," he said, smoking his cigarette in little quick drags. "Debbie."

"Debbie what?"

"No idea. Richardson. Or Robertson. Some name like that."

"And where did you meet her?"

"At that disco on the Front. Look, stop it, will you? You sound like them. Just leave it until tomorrow when they get these witnesses here and then it'll be over."

Bert Dodds, Mary had said, reckoned that he was the dead spit of the Photofit. Presumably the witnesses, including the invalid Mrs Russell, had been responsible for assembling the likeness. Therefore it was not his direct resemblance to the attacker that was to be tested, but his resemblance to the witnesses' idea of the likeness of his attacker. If he had been detained because he looked like the Photofit, and that Photofit had been put together at the direction of those who were coming tomorrow . . . She forced herself to stop this train of thought before it got out of hand, or its gist could be read from her face.

"Your parents?" she said tentatively.

"What? What about them?"

"I understand they're back from holiday today. Will they be coming here?"

He started to bite at his fingernails, though they had already been chewed to the quick. "They'd no sodding right," he said, "to involve them. What right did they have? I don't want *them* down here."

"You must have given the police their address."

"Pissed, wasn't I?" he said aggressively.

"And in view of your age . . ."

He looked at her sharply and she decided not to pursue that tack.

"Do you want anything else sending in?"

"Won't you be coming back?"

She tried to explain: that if she did not put in the hours today, then she would be unable to take the time off tomorrow. And tomorrow was obviously rather more important, wasn't it?

"I'll send Mary," she said.

"Mary Reilly, prison visitor," he said, turning from her, "what could be more appropriate?"

"Why should it concern you?" Emlyn had asked, and now she asked herself the same question.

"Well," she said, "if there's nothing else you need . . ."

"Oh, Elsie," he said, carefully keeping his back turned towards her, but she could tell by the break in his voice that he had exhausted the energy of whatever perverse motive it was that caused him to alienate goodwill, "I'm not sure I can stand it."

"Yes you can. Because you've the very best reason in the world for standing it: your innocence. Whatever they say, and however they try to twist things or frighten you, it's up to them to prove your guilt, rather than the other way round. And they can't *prove* an innocent person's guilt."

Mary Reilly, carrying back Bert Dodds's information, had also told some horror stories: blameless persons put away for years, bent policemen, promotion-hungry. The villains, Mary had said, weren't always them who found themselves behind bars.

Elsa waited at a bus stop for ten minutes or so then, edgy because she had already overrun her free time, started off walking. It seemed incredible that townspeople pursued their livelihoods, shopped, pushed out babies in perambulators, that tourists strolled or frolicked in the funfair or dozed in striped deckchairs, that the world had not changed one jot from the way it had appeared on Sunday. "They brought a woman in last night," Mick had said. "She was screaming. She screamed for about half an hour."

A group of young girls, giggling, barged past her. Two elderly ladies paused, their shopping trolleys at rest, to chat. The newspaper vendor bawled his wares. A young couple, arms wound round each other, posed narcissistically. Melodramatic perhaps – but she wanted to alert all of them, to wipe the smug innocence from their faces, to make them confront the underside of life that existed just around the corner, where women screamed and excrement befouled the walls and innocent people could be held upon the mere coincidence of a physical resemblance.

The bus passed her between stops. It was half past four when she got back. She ran up Rosedale Road, nearly stumbled and fell when the nearside door of a parked car suddenly opened and a voice addressed her: "Where *have* you been?" He sounded very put out, as though she'd stood him up publicly. "I was just about to leave. I'm on visits this afternoon."

People, she thought, running temperatures of a hundred and four, sucking in inadequate amounts of oxygen through clogged bronchii, gasping at pain that radiated down their left arms, all waiting for succour, while he in turn waited for her in order to organise an occasion of adultery.

"I've been in a cell."

He winced at her crudity. "I've been hanging on to tell you that it's all right for Thursday after all."

He'd persuaded Diana to stay over another night. There was a photographic exhibition that she was anxious to see, and she and Daphne had so much to catch up on, hadn't they?

"Seven?" he said. "In the park?"

"No," she said, "not the park." The idea of a rendezvous in the place where Mick had cowered, hoping to escape detection, was unthinkable. "Down by the headland."

"And if it's pouring?"

"Then we'll get wet."

They weren't able to look at each other properly, their eyes were too busy darting in all directions to ensure that they weren't being observed. This she found highly frustrating, not because she desired intimate contact with him but because she wanted to discuss Mick's predicament with someone trained to be objective, someone able to cut through the legal bluster. But a brief, "What's happening with the lad?" and "They've postponed this identification until tomorrow," and they were obliged to part: she to face Nora's wrath, he to resume the professional role that society expected him to enact at the same consistently high level whatever the vicissitudes to which his private life might be subject.

She woke on Wednesday morning and the butterflies in her stomach preceded her remembering the reason for them. Her sleep had been restless, invaded by snatches of nightmare featuring keys being turned in locks and knives and lurking figures who exhibited hideously jumbled features.

Colonel Pritchard there was, normally, and Miss Johns, prowling about early in the mornings. But this morning most of them were downstairs, huddled in front of the electric fire in the Gloucester Room, elbowing each other for the vantage position.

Elsa carried the breakfast things through to the Lancaster Room. She watched the residents watching her, their mouths moving relentlessly, and wondered which one of them would be the first to approach.

Not surprisingly, it was Mrs Booth-Powell. She approached very close. Only a dining-chair separated Elsa from the jut of that brocaded bosom, the protuberance of that long and determined chin.

"Have they brought him up yet?" she asked without preamble. "Before the Bench?"

Elsa laid a teaspoon beside Mrs Grey's Frank Cooper and

gave Colonel Pritchard's Worcester sauce a shake. "There is no question," she said coldly, "of the Bench. Michael, if that's who you mean, is merely helping the police with their enquiries, and is not being required to answer a charge."

Curious how quickly one slipped into effortless use of the jargon. But if she'd expected that Mrs Booth-Powell would retire, snubbed by the chill of her tone, then she'd underestimated the thickness of Mrs Booth-Powell's skin.

"It's the ID parade then, this morning?" she asked. Once, Basil, her husband, had been very thick with the Chief Constable, had got to know all sorts of spicy information, but that had been several Chief Constables ago.

"Mrs Pendennis," she continued, "has got this silly idea about rape into her head." She said it in a confidential, woman-to-woman, superior-intellect-to-its-equal sort of way, and laughed dismissively after she'd said it, as though inviting Elsa to join in her mockery of such an ill-bred desire for sensationalism. Elsa, tray thankfully empty at last, said, "Has she indeed?" and went back into the kitchen. She could hear the Booth-Powell dentures clicking exasperatedly behind her.

If I can remember who has tea and who has coffee without consulting the list . . . If I can carry this empty tray across the tiled floor of the kitchen without treading on the cracks . . . She had mocked herself for a superstitious fool on Monday morning when the letter from the art college was due, but then her behaviour had been a futile attempt at influencing a decision already made, whereas any decision concerning Mick was still wide open, and subject to the powers of recollection that were, in a couple of hours' time, to be put to the test.

"Clammed up," Mrs Booth-Powell reported back to her cronies around the fireplace. "They stick together, of course, these domestics."

"Probably in it up to her neck," Mrs Crookthorne said. She was altogether out of sorts this morning. Normally she came down before Miss Vyner and was able to sneak a little All-Bran from her packet while Colonel Pritchard and Peggy Johns were absorbed in their newspapers. Also she'd have a read of Mrs Pegler's *Mail*. But this morning both Miss Vyner and Mrs Pegler were up at cock-crow. So much for Dorothy Vyner's pretence of disinterest, and a very large pinch of salt to be added to Ivy Pegler's habitual passing herself off as everybody's idea of a benevolent old lady. They had smelled blood, in exactly the same way as she, Lily Crookthorne – at whom they looked down their noses – and were anxious to miss none of the gory details.

"No point in trying to keep it quiet," shouted Mrs Booth-Powell. "We'll get to hear about it. It'll be in the papers."

This morning the local paper was read from cover to cover, each one of the residents impatiently waiting her turn. "Her" turn, not "his". The men were not interested: Colonel Pritchard because he found more than enough to be digested in his *Times*, Mr Gentile because his command of English was not of a standard advanced enough to pick up the nuances of the local journalistic style, and Mr Golding because local papers always reminded him of the newspaper headline that he'd once been responsible for providing.

He'd thought those memories were as safely buried as he believed his booze and dirty books to be at the back of his wardrobe, was amazed that they could resurface so effortlessly, present themselves so vividly: the girl's parents, accusing; his own parents, disbelieving; the courtroom, the psychiatrist, his companions in the Retreat: Joseph, who hadn't spoken a word for twenty years; Fred, browbeaten by his internal voices; Archie, who'd got hold of a steel fork and stabbed himself through the throat. Blood on white walls, he remembered, the rattle of keys, the alienist, small and plump and smiling, who'd uncovered the shame that ought to have been kept hidden, his father, crying, his mother, hysterical, the child, unaware, trusting, allowing him to explore her . . .

Desperately he picked up the Colonel's paper and stared unseeingly at the Wimbledon report. "Are you all right, old chap?" the Colonel asked. The old biddies were all too busy at their gossiping to have noticed how waxen pale his complexion had become, how stertorously he was breathing.

"Fine. I'll be fine."

Pills, he had, that he placed beneath his tongue when his heart began to race. He took the box from his pocket. The Colonel looked concerned. They were pals. He thought miserably of all the other potential friendships that had had to be nipped in the bud because the resurgence of unpleasant memories had made it necessary for him to move on. Frinton, he had heard, was very select.

In the kitchen Elsa said, "Right then, I'll be off," and, having said it, lingered. She'd hurried through her chores so that she would be free for eleven o'clock and now that eleven o'clock had arrived she was loath to make the journey.

Nellie Macpherson rambled as she stacked dirty crockery beside the sink: "Drink is the very devil, trouble it causes. You tell him from me to keep out of the pub in future."

"Wine is a mocker, strong drink is raging," quoted Mrs Randall who often betrayed an upbringing that had evidently included constant repetition of the more quotable biblical strictures. "Hadn't you better get going, lovey, if you're to meet him out?"

Am I to meet him out, she wondered, as she waited at the bus stop, or is this sensation of someone treating my stomach as an elevator in any way significant?

And by the time she reached the enquiry desk in the station her legs were wobbling too. It came as absolutely no surprise, but was no less horrifying, when Detective Sergeant Fleming, having ushered her into an interview room, adjusted the cuffs of his shirt and looked at her *en face* yet obliquely (she'd have thought it impossible, had she not had the evidence in front of her eyes) and said, "Well, I'm afraid she's picked him out."

20

"A woman of seventy-two years old? An ill woman? And how long ago? I don't believe it. And what about the other witnesses?"

"Ah."

The other witnesses, it seemed, had dematerialised. A Mrs Boardman, from last year, moved now to Llandudno, unwilling to make the journey; a Mrs Lewis, practically blind and deaf; a Mr Mather, a passer-by, telephoned for assistance but reported as being unable to swear to an identification, his sighting of the suspect having been so brief.

"I don't believe it."

She repeated this at intervals while he quizzed her: had she any recollection of Michael's movements on any of the dates in question? Did Michael have any girlfriends? Had he always had a moustache and his hair at that length? Was she aware of any particularly noticeable alteration in his spending habits?

She shook her head now and then, or nodded, whichever seemed to be the appropriate response. "I don't believe it," she said at intervals, like a clockwork toy that has been overwound.

"What's going to happen then?"

He rose to his feet. "If you can hang on for a while? I'm waiting for a call from my chief."

He left the door open. She watched the comings and goings: solicitors being escorted to the cells, young constables horsing around, plain-clothes detectives running briskly up and down the stairs. She heard phones ringing and snatches of conversations: ". . . registration number GAR 42X . . . yesterday evening . . . Bob, have we had a bull-mastiff reported missing? . . . remanded until July 10th . . . Sarge? Was it *29* Rochester

Terrace?" And all the while she was thinking: he can't be guilty, he *can't*.

After twenty minutes or so Sergeant Fleming appeared. He was escorting an elderly lady down the stairs, taking the steps slowly, at her pace, and handed her over to the equally solicitous attentions of the desk sergeant. Then he ran back up the stairs, taking them three at a time, without casting a glance in Elsa's direction. On the next floor, she supposed, would be offices to which victims or complainants, such as the old lady – Mrs Russell, she presumed – would be taken. There would probably be potted plants, cheerful calendars, perhaps even a cup of tea. Whereas suspects, and their friends and relations, were thrust into bare distempered interview rooms and forgotten.

They would charge him, she supposed, and bring him up before the magistrates at the court which was now in session. The magistrates would remand him in custody pending trial and he would be hustled away in handcuffs, put into a van and transferred to Risley where the weak who showed their weakness were occasionally found hanged with their own bedsheets. His solicitor's clerk, met briefly beforehand (she was going in, he was leaving: "They'll let me know the outcome."), had said that, should a positive identification be made and charges preferred, then he would not ask for bail. "Not at this stage. If it's refused, and I think it would be, then a precedent would be set for any future application."

Mick wouldn't last a week in Risley. The trembling hand, the break in his voice, they would condemn him from the beginning.

The swing-doors opened and an elderly stooped solicitor in a heavy serge overcoat hobbled through. Before the doors closed behind him she glimpsed a man and a woman at the desk. The woman's face was paper-white, the man appeared to be exhorting her, none too gently, to pull herself together.

And then suddenly Sergeant Fleming was at the door and Mick was behind him, looking as startled as a hibernating animal pushed rudely into the light, and Sergeant Fleming said, "I'm bailing him until July 25th. In the meantime we shall be proceeding with our enquiries. Oh, excuse me – "

The desk sergeant was holding open the one-way doors, trying to attract his attention. Behind him stood the pale woman and the man who was grumbling at her. Mick turned and the delight that had just begun to be visible upon his face was wiped clear as abruptly as chalk would be wiped from a blackboard.

She was Mother and he was Daddy.

"Daddy's getting too old for driving these kind of distances," she said.

"Don't talk wet, woman," Daddy responded.

He had a tic that pulled the side of his upper lip in the direction of his ear lobe with a mesmeric regularity.

"What else did they question you about?" Mother asked, the colour gradually returning to her face. A pretty face, marred only by the peevishness to which its expression habitually returned. She was dressed – in her shantung costume and frilly blouse and matching bag and shoes – as if for a wedding rather than a visit to a police cell.

"Everything you could think of," Mick replied. His cigarette burned unnoticed.

"But what exactly?"

"Money," he said eventually. "They wanted to know how I'd managed to buy the car."

"But you told them, surely?" she said. "About Daddy and I paying into your banking account?"

He blushed. Not only the dole, Elsa thought, and Nora's wages, but also Mother and Daddy coming across. How easy to proclaim your scorn of conformity in those circumstances.

They sat in the lounge of the Highview Hotel drinking coffee. The Wynns had booked into the Highview, having picked it at random out of the AA book before they set off, not knowing how long they were likely to be detained. Coincidentally, they had been given the room that Elsa vacated when she accepted the job at Priory Lodge. Out of season it was advertised as a single room, which was what it was; in the summer it was let as a double.

A waitress arrived with a plate of sandwiches. By the time that Fleming had finished with the Wynns they'd missed lunch. So had Fleming, for that matter. "We have to be sure," he'd kept repeating. "You wouldn't want to think that we'd failed to investigate thoroughly in such suspicious circumstances." Elsa, waiting outside the room with Mick, could hear Mrs Wynn becoming gradually but relentlessly hysterical. At one point there was a burst of sobbing and Mick had blushed and pushed his hands deep into his pockets and stared wretchedly at the opposite wall. When Fleming came out he looked tired and strained, and as though the words, "I'm only doing my job," might just have passed his lips. For a second, despite herself, she felt almost sorry for him.

Now, over an hour later, Mother urged ham sandwiches upon her son and, although he refused them, continued to nag: "Do eat something, Michael. Just a little. Just for me," until he snarled at her and her husband said, "For God's sake, can't you leave him alone?"

Her lip trembled and so did a tiny tear upon her lower eyelid, before rolling down the track that had been made by the many others that had preceded it.

Daddy ate heartily. And noisily. Though the tic probably made that inevitable. Alone of them, he seemed to have maintained a fairly sanguine approach to the business. Either he was possessed of an enviable calm or else he was remarkably insensitive. A heavy man, with the grey complexion of the indoor worker with no outdoor pursuits, he looked like a clerk: in the post office, perhaps, or the gas board, and close to retirement – both of Michael's parents were older than she'd expected.

"What do you make of it, then?" he asked Elsa directly, having emptied the plate of sandwiches, cress and ornamental slices of tomato.

Mother sniffed and looked away. Apart from a stilted greeting when introduced, she had behaved as though Elsa was not present. "I think it should be quite easy to disprove the allegations," Elsa replied evenly.

The bail form lay on the table, beside the empty sandwich plate. Mick had been released on a deferred charge. The positive identification that the old lady was supposed to have made had been nothing of the sort. Mick had relayed what had happened in whispers as they waited outside the room where Fleming was being discomfited by Mother's tears.

"They brought her up the line twice," he had said. "She stared pretty hard at me, but she told them she couldn't be sure. They kept on at her though and, eventually, she stepped forward and touched me and said, 'This one's the nearest.' But that's all she did say. Which isn't exactly what you'd call a positive identification, is it?"

"Hardly," she'd said. "How did the rest of them look? Like you?"

"They were about the same age and height and so on. Apart from that, no, not particularly."

He kept shivering and his eyes were red-rimmed. They'd tried to con him, he'd told her. He'd been taken back to his cell and, ages afterwards, Fleming had come in and said that the old woman, in his office, had changed her tentative identification to one about which no doubt remained.

"In fact," Elsa said, "it was probably the other way round. They were trying to get her to say she was certain and she was giving you the benefit of the doubt. Thank God."

In the lounge of the Highview Mother searched in her handbag and finally brought out a packet of menthol cigarettes and a mother-of-pearl lighter. Rob had had an auntie, an irritating creature who wore flouncy frocks long past the age suitable for such attire and drank gin and orange and batted her eyelids and bummed cigarettes and said, "It's naughty, I know, but I don't inhale." Once, slightly the worse for drink, Rob had forgotten himself and replied, "Well then, why the hell do you bother?" And her face had crumpled like tissue and she'd sulked for about six months. Watching Mrs Wynn, Elsa was reminded of that aunt – in all her aspects, not merely in her mode of cigarette smoking.

"Four o'clock, is it?" Mother said, patting her smoke in Elsa's direction. "The appointment with the solicitor?"

They'd met Mr Parker, who seemed to spend his mornings toing and froing between his office and the law courts, as they left. He'd received the news of the bail without showing any surprise. "They might want him to go on another parade," Mother had said tremulously. But Mr Parker had shaken his head. "I doubt it. Unless they've something else up their sleeves, it sounds to me as though their case rested wholly on this witness and now that she's been unable to swear to it, it's out of the window. However," he had said, "we don't know what other evidence may exist, so it wouldn't do to be too cocksure . . ." He'd arranged an appointment with them. Elsa saw that her role as legal go-between was now at an end. It hadn't occurred to either Mother or Daddy to utter a word of thanks.

"Where is the . . . ?" Mother said, looking about her fearfully, as though deadly obstacles might bar her way to it.

"At the end of the hall, on the right."

"Could you?" she said, with an imploring glance.

There were women who needed to be guided here, there and everywhere, Elsa knew that. She'd been one herself, going straight from her parents' home to her husband's, confined to barracks first by pregnancy and motherhood, and then in her role as nurse/domestic. Only when Rob's business troubles had become too troublesome to be concealed, had she learned to enter into and cope with that unknown world of accountants and solicitors and employers; learned, of necessity, a measure of self-reliance.

In the pink-lighted Ladies' Room Mother emptied her bladder very quietly, washed her hands in the thorough way that most people do when someone else is watching and began to repair the ravages that upset had wrought upon her make-up. In her total concentration, she reminded Elsa of Mrs Pendennis; it was a narcissism beyond vanity. An uphill struggle nowadays, though. Mrs Pendennis had been a beauty, Mrs Wynn merely pretty and prettiness never lasts in the same way.

As she painted and powdered she sighed deeply. "I've felt," she said, "ever since he left university that there was trouble ahead, though Daddy and I knew that he'd never stick it. We hoped, of course. But he's never been a sticker: you know, must have everything he wants and then, when he gets it, doesn't want it anymore. He went missing, you know, after he left college. Daddy and I were nearly out of our minds with worry. Then he gets in touch. Only because he needs money, needless to say. He thinks it grows on trees. We try telling him that we have to save now Daddy's near retirement – *I* can't work – but it doesn't seem to sink in. He caused a terrible quarrel between my husband and I" (a queenly expression as she primped her hair) "when I surrendered my policy to send him the money for that car. He said if he had a car he'd be able to move around looking for jobs." She paused, pursed her lips for the application of her lipstick. "Daddy says it's all my fault because I've spoiled him, but you do, don't you, an only child? I wasn't able to have any more," she said, with a brief explanatory glance in the general direction of her reproductive organs. "Anyway, it *was* coming up to his birthday and I was so upset at not hearing from him for so long. He takes advantage," she said, suddenly quite cold and matter-of-fact. "He always has done. Causes trouble between his daddy and me and makes us feel guilty so that we'll let him have what he wants. Always been the same."

Children tried that, of course, and succeeded if you didn't stand firm. Nick had tried it, playing her off against Dad. Dad had spoiled him, but she and Rob had presented a united front. Then. Before the rot set in. Would it have remained that way? An image presented itself: she and Rob, ten years hence, together but estranged from one another, and Nick, grown but emotionally stunted, deriving a sadistic satisfaction from a policy of divide and rule.

"Michael's had his birthday, has he?" she asked casually as Mother began to pack away her array of cosmetic aids. "I thought it was today. I must have made a mistake."

"Michael's birthday was three weeks ago. June 5th." She snapped the clasp of her handbag, wriggled her skirt around her hips so that its seam hung central, and patted her curls. "That's a date I shan't forget in a hurry," she said. And Elsa cringed, knowing from past experience that that was the remark that always preceded a blow-by-blow account of a long-drawn-out-and-painful parturition. Why was it that everyone – apart from oneself – had always been subject to two-day periods of labour characterised by unendurable agony? Mother was still talking of scissors and forceps and undammable haemorrhages when they rejoined the men in the lounge.

There was a silence between them that denoted a recent exchange of sharp words. Daddy's tic beat remorselessly. Mother, apparently insensitive to atmospheres, sat down and said, "Now, Michael, we've given you chance to calm down and pull yourself together, we want the whole story. From start to finish."

"*What* story?" he said. "What are you on about?"

"Well, the police don't just pick up people at random, do

they?" she said. "There's got to be some reason, hasn't there?"

"Oh, it does happen. That's what all the fuss is about concerning the sus laws . . ." Elsa started to say because Mick had remained silent, but the words died on her lips. She realised, and saw that Mick knew it too, that as far as his parents were concerned, no certainty existed as to his innocence.

"I gave him the watch and the card," she told Mrs Randall and Nellie Macpherson and Mary Reilly and Rosa. Marguerita was involved in one of her marathon sulking sessions and was flinging cutlery into the sink.

"The cake," she said, "I think we'd better save for a more appropriate time."

Mrs Randall nodded. It would, as she'd told them, be all the better for keeping.

"Perhaps when all this business is over."

They nodded together. Celebrations were hardly in order with such worrying possibilities hanging over the poor lad's head.

"He thanked you all very much."

He'd done nothing of the sort, of course. She hadn't given him the chance. Mother and Daddy had got up to leave for their appointment with Mr Parker and she'd called him back and taken the watch from her handbag and slipped it into his pocket and said, "This is a present that we collected for at the Priory. Perhaps you could write a note thanking them all. I'm sure they won't expect you to do it in person." He'd gone as red as fire and started to stutter out some explanation, but she'd silenced him because there wasn't one and his parents were looking on curiously.

"Not much of a birthday, is it?" Mary Reilly said.

"Still," said Nellie Mac, who believed with an irrational fervency in the succour provided by families, considering that her relations with her sisters were so strained, "he'll be all right now his mam and dad's here."

"Aye," said Mary Reilly, nodding her head vigorously in agreement. They didn't agree on much, but were in total accord when it came to expecting a closing of ranks by one's immediate family in the face of external threat. If your own mam and dad couldn't stick up for you then nobody else could be expected to.

An aura of faint melancholy pervaded the kitchen as each remembered parents, either departed or too far away for regular contact. Even Marguerita curtailed her percussion concerto. The image of Dad, self-pitying, criticising, but loving, surely, at bottom, came into Elsa's mind. "Dad" she had used as an excuse for so long, as a means of refusing to face up to the unsatisfactory state of her marriage, her fear of stepping out alone into what had seemed a hostile environment. And he'd colluded in her self-deception. "Try," she'd said, offering him an arm for support – the physiotherapist had said that there was no reason in the world for him to be bedfast – but his legs had collapsed under him. Besides, with Nick gone, there had been nothing to get up for.

"Mary," she said abruptly, "when you finish tonight, would you come with me round these clubs and discos? I want to try to find out the whereabouts of this girl Mick was out with on Sunday." The past was unalterable, except by the distortions of memory. The present demanded action that could change the future.

Mary's face became animated, a sparkle returned to her eye. Most of her adult life she'd been marked down as a no-good and, mostly, conformed to this definition. Now, all of a sudden, she was being recognised as an authority upon the due processes of the law – it was she, wasn't it, who'd had to explain to them the implications of police bail? Prison-visitor, reporter, and now private detective. She hadn't felt quite so chuffed since Sister Imelda, in charge of the school choir, had told her mam that she, Mary, ought to have her voice trained (but her mam hadn't, of course, been able to afford the money for that kind of nonsense).

"As long as you explain to my feller," she said. "Or else he'll think I'm off on the batter. If you tell him," she said, "he'll know it couldn't possibly be owt like that."

Elsa pondered that statement all evening, unsure whether she ought to be deeply insulted or inordinately gratified. The prospect of the night ahead was distinctly unalluring. "Where the kids go?" Mary had said. "You'll need your earplugs." But it was worth a try.

21

Mary, head filled with pictures of the fearless girl-reporters of investigative journalism, *News of The Screws* style, had gone home first to dress for the part.

They'd begun their tour at the north end of the Promenade; stepping into rooms at the back of pubs, or purpose-built concrete leisure complexes, or down area steps into the vaults of short-leased properties, outside which flapping posters advertised out-of-date attractions and overflowing dustbins were subject to marauding by feral cats.

To every orange juice ordered by Elsa, Mary added a vodka. By the time they'd reached the War Memorial, midpoint along their route, Elsa's purse was considerably depleted and Mary was starting to wobble on her five-inch heels.

But intent on inebriation or not, Mary's company was invaluable. Completely lacking in self-consciousness, she could talk to anybody. She could approach, shaking her flesh on the dance floor, partnerless, entering into shriek-level conversations with those around her who paused in their grave-faced gyrations to stare. Alone, Elsa would have conceded defeat at the first hurdle. With Mary, it always seemed that a chance remained.

A very slim chance. Girls there were, by the score, brutal-looking in the current fashion: their hair brushed into parakeet combs and dyed in the colours of exotic plumage, or strangled into beaded dreadlocks, or shaved into hedgehog tufts; their puppy-fat emphasised by the skin-tight stretch denim meant only for the slenderest among them; their lips and eyes and nails flashing pearlised in the gloom. They drank their nauseous cocktails and smoked their cigarettes and chewed gum (simultaneously sometimes) and stared expressionlessly when questioned. "Debbie Robertson? Richardson? Never 'eard of 'er." Sometimes the stare lasted so long that they despaired of a reply, wondered if they had chanced upon a group of foreigners, or the victims of brain damage out on a spree.

"After you, Cecil. No, after you, Claud," Mary said, recalling some dimly-remembered Workers' Playtime patter, as she ushered Elsa into Smartyboots Discothèque (" mar boot Di c èq ", actually, the neon that proclaimed its existence and function being defective).

Two pounds, it cost, to enter an enormous room where refectory tables and benches flanked a dance floor and one stood almost ankle-deep in spilled beer in order to buy a drink at a bar too long to be served efficiently by two tee-shirt-clad, harassed-looking girls, and around which seethed a mass of impatient customers.

They attached themselves to the rear of this shouting, gesticulating throng. Pound notes were waved, orders recited; the barmaids moved in the dogged rhythm typical of weariness, resolutely refusing to meet any eye other than that belonging to the current customer.

"Get you two ladies a drink?"

The dance-floor hoverer, the chancer of his arm with any obviously-unattached female. It was years since Elsa had entered any place vaguely resembling this one, but he was unmistakable still: the short stocky lone male, sprucely unfashionable, immunised by rejection into no longer fearing it; middle-aged, and unmarried for all sorts of reasons. The chance of getting off with anyone as promising-looking as Mary was too rare to be missed.

Mary immediately began to preen, a reaction obviously as reflexive as a knee-jerk. "I'll have a vodka and orange," issued automatically from her lips. "Better him paying for it," she muttered out of the side of her mouth, "than us."

"Les", his name was. In Elsa's limited experience, they had always been called Les. Or Des. Or Trev or Kev. Always alone, predatory and monumentally boring. This one was no exception. Ignoring her, he subjected Mary to an account of the life and times of a pipe-layer in Saudi Arabia. "Fancy," said Mary at intervals. She wasn't listening to a word, but politeness dictated a pretence: if he was buying you drinks all night he was entitled to a show of interest, as well as a bit of a grope at the end of it.

Time was running out and with it any hope of locating Mick's girlfriend, or passing encounter, or whatever she'd been. The amount of alcohol being consumed by Mary and the appearance of Les on the scene made effective cooperation less likely by the minute. "That disco on the Front," Mick had said. She'd have asked him to be more specific except that he'd have flown off the handle if he'd suspected that she was checking up on him.

A ridiculous idea, it had been. And probably totally unnecessary. She yawned widely while Les looked on malevolently – no doubt he had had long experience of having his sexual plans thwarted by "my friend". "I'll go, I think, Mary," she said, but as she spoke the glittery-suited disc-jockey announced the next record over the public address and a troupe of girls came, barging and giggling, towards their table and sat down and she thought, What the hell, it's worth one more try. "Excuse me," she said, "but would any of you know of a Debbie Robertson or Richardson who had a date last weekend with Michael Wynn?" and there was the usual response of amazed silence as though she'd made an improper suggestion and then one of them looked at another and said, "Hey Debs, what you been up to?"

Debs was a small girl with the sort of prettiness – curls and dimples – that looked curiously antiquated among the quiffs and crew cuts and Sumo wrestlers' attire preferred by her companions. She was no less aggressive in her manner, however. "What's it to you?" she asked. She had a light, little-girl voice in which refinement fought a losing battle with the local accent. A girl, Elsa thought, that you'd find behind a supermarket till, picking the varnish from her nails in one of the more down-market chain-stores, serving orders in a hamburger restaurant. Seventeen or so. A girl with whom Mick would have nothing in common. Intellectually at least.

"Do you think I could have a word with you? Privately?"

The level of noise guaranteed that most words would be,

perforce, private; getting them across was the problem. Elsa looked round and decided that the Ladies' Room was probably the only quiet part of the building, and indicated this as her destination. The girl looked suspicious, consulted with her friends and then, reluctantly, followed. Mary was swallowing back vodka and nodding at Les's monologue, eyes too glazed with alcohol and boredom to register Elsa's activities.

In terms of hygiene, the ladies' lavatory might be considered as occupying the same category as the police cells. Perhaps they occasionally accommodated the same clientèle. From one of the half-dozen water-closets came the sound of prodigious vomiting. A girl, presumably companion to the vomiter, stood waiting, expression dazed, swaying a little, using the tiled wall for support. Debbie Robertson, or Richardson, inspected herself most critically in the mirror above the washbasin and then turned abruptly to Elsa and said, "What is it you want?"

Small, curvaceous, dimpled, pretty: it wouldn't have been the possibilities of intellectual rapport that had attracted Mick so much as the chance of carnal knowledge. "It's about Michael Wynn," Elsa said. "I understand you've been out with him? He was picked up by the police outside a house near the park – in Canterbury Road – on Sunday night, well, Monday morning, actually. He said you'd given him that address and he was trying to locate you. They think he was trying to break in."

"Picked up by the police?" the girl said. "I'm not surprised."

"Why's that?"

"Bloody nutter, in' 'e?" the girl said.

"Well, that's a matter of opinion. I just wanted to know whether you'd given him that address, whether he was under the impression that you lived there – 17 Canterbury Road?"

"He wouldn't stop pestering me," the girl said. "If I'd given him my proper address, I'd never have had him off the doorstep. I'm going out with another lad now. I told him, that Mick, but he wouldn't take the hint. Hey," she said, "what's all this about? I don't want the police coming round. You've no business asking me questions. Who are you, anyway?"

"Just a friend. What *is* your address, your real one?"

"Never you mind."

There was a wary look in her eye. Obviously of the age and class that regarded a policeman as a threat rather than a reassuring custodian of law and order, she wouldn't divulge either her real name or her address. But the police could find it out, if necessary, and could frighten her sufficiently so that she'd admit to having misdirected Mick, provide back-up for his story.

The vomiter gave one final gut-tugging retch, pulled at the defective lavatory handle and staggered out. "Oh God!" she moaned. Her friend swayed forward from the wall and together they tottered out. Debbie Whichever-her-name-was adjusted the strap of her handbag more securely over her shoulder and made to pass Elsa. "Incidentally," Elsa said, "why do you call him a nutter?"

She was striding towards the door, but the temptation to explain was too strong to be resisted. "All that talk," she said, sneering, "about what he's done. Load of rubbish. And writing them letters. 'Let's run away together.' Bloody barmy. As if I'd run away with him. And what he'd do to himself if I didn't. Soft sod! All that talk: shacking up with a Swedish film star and all them groupies when he was roadie with the Worms. Bloody superman. I wouldn't care," she said, "but he couldn't even do it. I've had a bigger thrill off a Tampax!"

"Eh, kid, why didn't you stop me?"

Mary groaned and shook aspirin tablets from the bottle into the palm of her hand and threw them to the back of her throat and washed them down with a gulp of stewed tea, wincing as the hot liquid passed over her cracked lip. The cracked lip was her penalty for arriving home after three with her make-up smudged and ladders in her tights and her buttons undone. They'd gone on to a club, she and Les, and then she'd had to fight him off in the back seat of his car. "What d'you take me for?" she'd asked, and then had the satisfaction of raking her fingernails down the side of his face when he'd told her.

"Still," she said now, shuddering as the pills left their rank aftertaste, "it was worth it, wasn't it? We found what we was looking for," as though she had been directly responsible for the ferreting-out of important evidence, and not drunk beyond understanding what Elsa had attempted to tell her after the interview in the Ladies' Room.

Good news indeed. And fair was fair. Without Mary's guidance, the information might never have been acquired. Good news which more than cancelled out the bad. "Take him back?" Nora had said, incredulous. She'd never been one to tempt fate. He'd worked well, no denying it, but she had her reputation to consider. She hadn't forgotten the stunt he'd pulled at Mrs Pendennis's engagement party. He could come in to collect what was owed him, but that was that.

Elsa told Mick that afternoon. He was wending his reluctant way to the Highview where he was to put up resistance to his parents' insistence that he should return home with them forthwith. Daddy had used up all his leave and although his firm was very understanding there was a limit to the time he could take off.

"They can wait," Mick said. "Come in."

Chill and cheerless on that rainy afternoon, his room seemed, but a haven nevertheless when compared to where he'd spent the previous two days.

She perched on the edge of the unmade bed. "What does your father do?" she asked idly.

"Works in accounts at a local furniture shop. We have ever such a nice home," he said, parodying his mother's refined tones. "The best collection of veneered chipboard and synthetic carpeting in the Midlands. We have to take off our shoes at the back door and woe betide my dad if he drops a crumb on the floor. Having seen my dad, you'll appreciate that he finds it rather difficult to avoid doing that."

Getting in the derogatory comment first: there's no way you can put them down more effectively than I've done a thousand times before, was the gist of his challenging stare.

"So Nora's given me the push?" he said. He looked dirty and tousled and there was a rash round his mouth. She imagined his mother, nagging him to make use of the bathroom facilities at the Highview and him refusing for no better reason than to spite her.

"I'm afraid so. But it's good news, isn't it, about the girl? At least that bears out your explanation for Sunday night. Why on earth did you run, though?"

He shrugged, without bothering to answer. Kids of his generation always ran from the pigs – it was a reflex response.

"You're not going back with them, then?"

Jobless, there seemed little reason for him to stay.

He shook his head. "Christ, no. I couldn't handle it."

"Well, then," she said, "I think we ought to do a little bit of investigating in the matter of these crimes you're supposed to have committed. I know it's up to them to prove your guilt but all the same . . . I thought I'd have a look in the newspaper office for the original accounts. Unless you and your parents . . ."

But she already suspected that the Wynns' energies would be deployed in crying woe and alack rather than doing something practical to clear their son of suspicion.

"Can't you leave it alone?" he said irritably. "I'd rather not think about it. It just brings it all back."

"All the more reason," she started to say and then thought better of it. She didn't need his assistance, and if it upset him so to contemplate the nasty business then she'd be better off without him.

"Better get going."

At the door he paused and blushed and took the watch, still in its presentation case, out of his pocket. "I don't know what I should do with this."

"Well, I shouldn't think I could get the money back on it, and even if I could, I'd hardly feel inclined to return all the various donations. So if I were you I'd keep it," she said crisply. Then she said, "Why on earth did you pretend it was your birthday?"

He made a great business of locking the door behind them so that he could avoid her eye. "I dunno," he said. "I didn't ask for all the fuss, presents and so forth, did I? I just wanted you to stop treating me like a kid."

She used to say that to her mother (when she was years younger than Mick; her mother was dead by the time she was his age), and her mother used to reply, "I will as soon as you stop behaving like one." But that didn't seem to be a tactful comment to make in the circumstances.

The back issues of the local papers were, it seemed, seldom subject to public scrutiny. She tried the obvious source first: the newspaper office, but an adenoidal counter-clerk told her to try the library.

Here she met with rather more success. From some back-room glory-hole the reading-room assistant heaved out the huge string-tied bundles that covered the relevant dates. They were tattered and ruffled and torn and extremely unwieldy. Most of their page space was taken up with advertising. Mindful of the priorities of provincial journalism, she skimmed the bold print: "Bank Manager Retires After Thirty-Two Years", "Record Turn-Out For Local Elections", "Water Main Burst Halts Traffic", in favour of the less prominent headlines. Eventually she found what she was looking for and, beneath the curious scrutiny of the local lunatics and vagrants who composed the main part of the reading-room's clientèle, carried over the relevant pages to the Xerox machine where, for the price of thirty pence, she obtained some dreadfully blurred but sufficiently legible photocopies.

"Ridiculous!" she told Emlyn, later that day. "Absolutely ludicrous! It could have been anyone. It could have been you."

"Thanks very much," he said.

"Well, you know what I mean. The descriptions differ so widely that almost anyone between the ages of twenty and thirty, with a full head of dark hair would fit the bill. Oh, and a moustache," she said, chewing idly at a breadstick while waiting for the first course of her meal.

"That rules me out then, thank goodness," he said.

"Your face would surely be a little too well-known," she said, "for you to get away with that sort of thing." She spoke jokingly, but noticed that his response was to look round nervously. Quite unnecessarily, she thought, as the restaurant was in a village at least twenty miles from where his face was so well-known.

"Seriously, though," she said, "I remember reading somewhere that people generally make appallingly inaccurate witnesses, and these descriptions certainly go to prove it." She relayed to him the details of the accounts she'd read, in order of detail given. Description one, provided by a seventy-eight-year-old woman who had opened her door on the afternoon of September 11th last to a man who'd led her to believe he wanted to look round the house with a view to purchase and who'd subsequently threatened and robbed her: a man of approximately thirty years of age, average height, stocky build, wearing a blue pullover and grey slacks. Dark hair and a little moustache. Description two, given by a sixty-three-year-old widow who'd been threatened with a knife when she was letting the cat out of her front door on the morning of June 4th, and corroborated by a passing pedestrian: a man in his early twenties, wearing slacks and an open-necked shirt. Height between five foot ten and six feet, hair dark, small moustache. Description three, the most detailed, obtained from a lady of seventy-two who, on May 23rd, had been threatened, assaulted and robbed of a hundred and fifty pounds: a man between twenty and thirty, medium height, slim-built, wearing a casual shirt and trousers and light-coloured shoes, round-faced, dark-haired, brown-eyed, small moustache, spoke with an accent that wasn't local. The second woman hadn't mentioned anything about an accent, being too concerned with the knife in his hand. A kitchen knife of some sort, she thought.

"And the picture, the Identikit!" she told Emlyn. It had been as incredible as those that had stared down at her from the police-station wall. "Anyway, look for yourself."

She passed him her sheaf of copies to which – unsurprisingly, as she'd already narrated the information they contained – he gave scant attention, preferring to try and attract the eye of the dilatory wine-waiter.

She persisted. "What do you think? Nothing like him, is it?"

He looked at the blurred features of the Photofit, holding it first close to his gaze, then at a distance. "There's a vague sort of resemblance, I suppose," he said.

"Where?" she said, snatching the paper back, piqued that he'd seen fit to argue with her.

"Around the mouth and the eyes. But don't forget I've scarcely seen the lad. You're right, it could be anybody, anybody with dark hair and a moustache. Adolf Hitler, Errol Flynn, Charlie Chaplin." The muscles at the side of his mouth tightened as he disguised a yawn. He'd worked non-stop all day so that he could take the evening off with a clear conscience and the last thing he wanted was to spend it discussing the wretched boy. However, unaware that he had found her account of amateur sleuthing so tedious, she prattled on, uninfectiously enthusiastic.

"Am I boring you?" she said at length. He took her hand. He was familiar by now with her less attractive qualities and loved her all the same. Just as he loved Diana and would have, no doubt, come to love his other mistresses had he not had the foresight to engineer the end of the affairs before it could happen.

"Not a bit of it," he said.

"Well, then, what do you think?" she asked, anxious to have her efforts applauded, her judgement corroborated.

"I think," he said carefully, "that the police are grasping at straws and you could safely leave it in the capable hands of his solicitor. Geoffrey Lomax knows what he's doing, you know."

"But he's not *doing* anything," she said heatedly.

"It may not seem that way, but I'm sure it's all in hand. And if his parents are here now . . ."

She fiddled with her food in the same way that Diana did because, in Diana's case, food merely provided an alibi for drink. It irritated him. "Eat up," he said encouragingly. Whatever else he'd imbibed with his mother's milk and since rejected, a horror of waste remained.

She put a forkful into her mouth and chewed rapidly. "They're dreadful," she said. "Her especially. Treats him as though he were a combination of small child and lover: petting him and urging him to eat up his meal one minute," she said (and grinned briefly, realising the parallel that she'd unwittingly drawn), "appealing for his assistance and guidance the next. No wonder he seems so confused. The worst of it is," she said, bolting mouthfuls in an attempt to match his rate of consumption and continue her narrative, "that, as far as his character and motivations are concerned, he might as well be a total stranger. She looks at him and you can tell that at the back of her mind there's a faint suspicion that he might just possibly be guilty of these ghastly crimes."

She laid down her knife and fork. "You haven't been listening to a word I've said."

He had, he assured her, he had, but seized the opportunity to attempt a change of subject. "By the way," he said, "shouldn't you have heard by now from that art school?"

"I have. On Monday. Didn't I tell you?"

Last week it had been maximum priority, now it seemed less so. "No," he said. "And?"

"I've got a place. Which reminds me," she said, "I haven't written my letter of acceptance yet."

He raised his glass to her and toasted her success and she said, "Oh, I *do* hope so," and talked a little about how she was looking forward to specialising in certain areas of design, how techniques had become a great deal more technical since last she'd studied them, and so forth. But within minutes she was back on her hobby-horse, her crêpes cooling in front of her, the record stuck in the same groove. "What do you think it means," she said, "when the police talk about pursuing their enquiries?"

They might as well have eaten in the local McDonalds for all the attention, never mind appreciation, that she accorded her food or the surroundings. There was a moment when irritation might have prompted him to remind her that this was a clandestine – and risky – meeting, but then it occurred to him that a measure of his irritation stemmed not from her refusal to be diverted from her theme but rather from her failure to be impressed by his meticulous organisation; no small feat, as she would realise, if she'd had any previous experience. He wondered if she, or any other of them, had appreciated just how difficult it was for one whose face was widely known to be anonymous. He'd heard of medical men who used their surgeries, the couches in their consulting-rooms, out of hours, for the purposes of seduction. But he'd always found the idea repellent, would have been reminded too vividly of female flesh as it was displayed for his professional scrutiny to be capable of responding to it erotically.

Then his irritation was allayed by the little frown that scored the skin between her eyebrows whenever she posed a question. It made her look childlike, vulnerable. "I think it means," he said patiently, "that depending upon how important these cases are considered to be – and I would think, not very, in the general scheme of things – a few questions will be asked of the various police forces in the towns where the other offences occurred. I don't think they'll have Fabian of the Yard up here working on it. I think," he said, as she made a little moue of silent remonstrance, "that I want more than anything in the world to make love to you. And I wish you felt the same way."

His planning, he reflected, had not been as meticulous as all that. He could have booked a hotel room, could still, he thought, consulting his watch, except that the lateness of the hour and their lack of luggage might arouse unwelcome curiosity. Nothing for it but to do what most young men had done in their youth and he never had until middle-age: seek out some secluded spot and park the car and press the lever that caused the seats to recline and hope to goodness that they wouldn't cripple themselves.

In the event it was she who made love to him. Female active rather than passive suited the limited accommodation best. Astride him, she looked out at the dark blur of the sand-dunes, while he saw phosphorescence glowing at the sea's edge and heard the dull roar of the incoming tide as it raced through the estuary.

The tide sighed and flowed and so did he. Drenched with her juices, his own spent into her, he remained erect inside her, his hands cupping her naked breasts which gleamed in the moonlight as bright as the phosphorescence on the water, reluctant to be parted from her for as long as it was physically possible to remain conjoined. A naturally reticent man, words tumbled from him nevertheless. Before the event you were expected to murmur the odd endearment, if only to encourage her ardour. But these were wild words, unconsidered phrases, drawn from him without conscious effort just as the ebb and flow of her movements upon him had drawn his seed into a headlong (if futile) rush towards the neck of her womb. "I love you," he said. "I want to be with you. I want to fill you full of babies. I want us to be together."

His seed was ultimately doomed, thanks to the good offices of the manufacturers of the intra-uterine device, to meet with frustration. Whether a similar fate awaited his involuntary verbal orgasm remained to be seen.

22

"Happiness is coming" it said on the front of the tee-shirt worn by the young man who walked past the bandstand. The double-entendre didn't strike Dorothy Vyner immediately; she supposed that the slogan meant something along the lines of "Jesus is coming", or whatever it was that these born-again Christians preached. The young man reminded her of Michael and she suddenly wondered how he was coping with the strain of being under suspicion.

Marion Pendennis, married for thirty-five years – for her sins – to a man with a robust sexual appetite (highly oversexed, she'd considered him), knew exactly what the phrase referred to and was revolted, not so much that sentiments of that nature should be bruited abroad, but by the ugliness of the boy's general appearance: the badly-made tee-shirt, the drooping, jodhpur-type jeans, the scuffed plimsolls. A thoroughly unmanly generation, she thought, parading its virility as though that was all that mattered, as though charm and urbanity and mystique all came a very poor second. She glanced at the television page of Peggy Johns's newspaper and saw that *Random Harvest* was being repeated on BBC-2 later that afternoon: Greer Garson and Ronald Colman. Now there was a man! He hadn't needed to flaunt his anatomy in order to have women swooning at his feet. She wondered if Ivy Pegler would let her borrow her portable; the set in the Gloucester Room was monopolised by Colonel Pritchard during Wimbledon fortnight.

What a pleasant message to carry on your tee-shirt, Peggy Johns thought, so much nicer than the aggressive, or obscene, or vulgar slogans that were usually displayed. She folded her newspaper so that Mrs Pendennis's view of the programme guide was obstructed. Not perhaps a very Christian thing to do, but really it was most annoying to have someone reading over your shoulder, and it wasn't as though she couldn't afford to buy a paper of her own.

"Time they got a move on," Gwyneth Booth-Powell said, and referred them to the town-hall clock. She'd dozed off for a minute or two and hadn't noticed the young man or his tee-shirt.

The clock struck two and the bandsmen began to tune up. About time, thought the ladies of Priory Lodge, eager for their money's worth. Normally the seats on the Parade were free but for the duration of the weekly brass-band concerts in the summer they cost twenty pence. Twenty *new* pence, as they often reminded each other, which was an altogether different proposition from twenty old pence. Worth it though; this season they'd already had the Brighouse and Raistrick and the Black Dyke Mills. Next month it was the Besses O' Th' Barn.

Today it was the Metropolitan Police Band and though they were unlikely to lay down their instruments in order to make arrests, Mrs Crookthorne felt edgy, wondered if, after all, she should have paid, rather than hoping to con the collector with a quick flash of an expired ticket. But if he approached, she would pretend that age and infirmity had made it necessary for her to sit down for a moment. Until that time arrived, she would lean back and enjoy the sun on her face and the opening bars of the "Poet and Peasant Overture", a square of Cadbury's chocolate – broken from the bar that she'd misappropriated from the edge of the confectionery counter in Woolworths earlier that day – melting in her mouth.

"Oh-oh," said Mrs Booth-Powell, nudging Peggy Johns. "Don't look now."

She meant Lily Crookthorne whom she'd just caught sight of at the opposite side of the arena, but Peggy Johns thought she was referring to Leonard Golding whom she'd just espied standing at the top of the library steps, looking about him in a wild way reminiscent of someone waking up out of a nightmare.

"Have we been spotted?" Mrs Booth-Powell said, out of the

side of her mouth, as though there existed the possibility that Lily Crookthorne might hear her above the trumpets of the "Grand March" from *Aida*.

"What?" said Miss Vyner, reminding herself that she'd meant to replace the batteries in her hearing-aid.

"Oh, I don't think he'll be joining us, will he?" said Peggy Johns. "He doesn't usually." Mrs Booth-Powell gaped at her and then peered rudely in his direction.

Common consensus was that he was a bit . . . well, you know . . . peculiar. A lifelong bachelor (unlike a lifelong spinster who could claim that she'd had no choice in the matter) was suspect these days, ever since homosexuality had received such a big press. And then there was the way that he tried to attach himself to Colonel Pritchard, always at his side like a little dog, as if a manly man like the Colonel would have any desire for his company.

As they watched him, he trotted to a vacant seat, sat down, got up and moved to another. This process was twice repeated, after which he stopped dead in his tracks, looked up at the town-hall clock and moved off briskly as though he'd just remembered a pressing appointment, and disappeared around the side of the library.

Miss Johns heaved a sigh of relief. She felt sorry for him but dreaded having to endure his company. She found the company of most people a strain, but his was especially to be avoided in case he should make the sort of coarse remark that, unlike most of the ladies at the Lodge, she found herself unable either to ignore or to parry.

"Alzheimer's disease," Mrs Booth-Powell said, in the manner of an experienced clinician having reached a considered verdict. She'd been reading about Alzheimer's disease, a form of premature senile dementia from which Rita Hayworth was suffering. Ignorant or unkind people confused it with alcoholism, there being the same sort of characteristics displayed: the clouding of the mental function, the lack of physical coordination, the personality changes.

He's having some sort of breakdown, was Miss Vyner's conclusion. She had noticed signs of derangement in his behaviour over the last week or so: encountering him at the back gate where she had found him engaged in loud and abusive conversation with himself, watching the peculiar ritual he now observed before he ate his meals. Apparently she was the only person, apart from Rosa, to have noticed him tipping out the contents of the sugar-bowl and salt-cellar and inspecting them suspiciously, as though for ground glass. She wondered whether she ought to have a word with that dour Welsh doctor on his behalf, but the habit of minding her own business was so deeply ingrained that she demurred. He'll get over it, she told herself, it's probably just a phase; as though he were an adolescent, not a seventy-three-year-old man with no further phases to grow into.

The band moved on from von Suppé via Verdi to the more stirring of the Wagnerian overtures. By the time that Mr Golding was moving out of earshot they were on to *Lohengrin*. He trotted faster until he could no longer hear it and then slowed down to an amble. Military music made him nervous. A vague memory edged its way into his mind: the day they had him up in court, a midsummer day, the smell of hay and horse-dung steaming, and the strains of the military band that was playing in the square. For years that tune had tormented him, running in his head, a perpetual counterpoint to the voices of the barristers and the final instruction by His Honour, Justice Someone or Other, that sentence was to be deferred pending medical reports.

He'd never been able to put a name to that tune but had always done his best to avoid brass bands in case any similar martial music should trigger associations that might cause even more unwelcome memories to resurface. And they came flooding back these days: always the unpleasant ones. He couldn't remember what he'd eaten for breakfast that morning, whether, in fact, he *had* eaten, but found that he could recall the face of His Honour, Justice Someone or Other in its every mottled, prawn-eyebrowed detail; the exact hue of the green wall of the cell in which he had been detained; the side-whiskers affected by his QC and the smell of the lavender cachous that he chewed for his breath. He remembered also the bronze sculpture of *Prometheus Unbound* that had rested on his alienist's desk, his face, sleek as a well-bred cat, ever-smiling, waiting, biding his time, knowing that it had to happen: the breaking down of defences, and the final loss of dignity that, amazingly, was construed as being indicative of the possibility of recovery.

Mr Golding had walked past the Priory as he mused and now had to retrace his steps. He'd woken up the other morning and thought he was back in the Retreat. All these years of coping in the outside world and his time of incarceration coming back clearer than yesterday! A remarkable piece of equipment, the brain. The Colonel had said that, said that he could remember names and events from his childhood easier than those of a more recent vintage.

Of course! The Colonel. *He* would help him to get it straight. He always felt calmer in the Colonel's company. A talk, man to man, while the old biddies were out listening to the band and chewing the fat, would be just the ticket. He turned into the Gloucester Room where the blinds were drawn against the sun's glare and Rosa with the trim little bottom would bring you a pot of tea and allow you a little feel without making too much of a fuss and the Colonel would help you to get it all straight.

But Colonel Pritchard's attention was riveted by the activity of the white-clad figures on the television screen. A brief acknowledgement of his presence and his eyes swivelled back to the idiot box. "Fifteen-thirty," said the commentator, "Gerulaitis serving," and a curly-headed fellow threw a ball into the air and himself and his racket after it, and there was a thudding noise and the commentator said, "That's his fourth ace," and the Colonel hit his thigh with the flat of his hand and said, "Played, sir!"

A fortnight there was; tennis from midday to mid-evening, and a replay later on. What hope was there of catching the Colonel alone and responsive? Always the same. He mounted the stairs. Tears ran down the channels provided for them by the deep folds in the skin between his nose and his mouth. Always the same. Ever since the time he'd woken from a nightmare and there had been screaming coming from his mother's room and in the morning there'd been a new baby and his mother hadn't had any time for him. Not then, and even less after the baby died and she suffered a breakdown from which she never really recovered.

In his room he made straight for the back of the wardrobe.

Alcohol had a bad effect upon the memories: muddled them and made them as vivid as nightmares, but eventually it blotted them out. Problem was, as the days passed, the blotting-out process required more and more alcohol. He unscrewed the top from the bottle and tilted its neck to his lips – no point in using a glass; more evidence for old Speakman to pounce on – and whisky mingled with the tears that ran into his mouth, and hit the back of his throat and damn near choked him, while downstairs the Colonel exclaimed, "Oh I say, what a dream of a shot!"

Mesdames Booth-Powell, Pendennis, Vyner and Johns debated about taking a taxi back home after the open-air concert. Votes in favour came from Pendennis and Johns. Mrs Booth-Powell was against: why waste a perfectly good free bus-pass? If they hurried, they could just catch the last free ride. Miss Vyner was torn: on the one hand incapable of hurrying, on the other, being unsure that once she sank into a taxi seat whether she would be able to get out of it again. The arrival of Lily Crookthorne, offering to share, decided the issue. They all knew Lily Crookthorne: "You pay while I fumble," and had no intention of providing her with a free taxi ride.
"Let's walk," said Mrs Booth-Powell and tossed her head rakishly as if she was aware of having made a rather scandalous suggestion. Miss Johns was all for it – she'd once been a great walker, and Mrs Pendennis thought of all the shop windows between there and the Priory which would throw back her reflection. Dot Vyner gritted her teeth and gripped her sticks and Lily Crookthorne, sound in wind and limb, thought: how mean can you get, but fell into step beside them.
"No need to stride away," Mrs Booth-Powell called irritably to Peggy Johns who hadn't realised that she was striding, but who subsequently did her best to adapt to the snail's pace at which the rest of them moved. How jolly it was, she thought; an outing, with enough of you so that no one noticed your lack of contribution to the conversation (it was the one-to-one encounters that she tried to avoid: after an enquiry as to health and well-being and a comment about the weather, what could you say?). How did you respond, for instance, to

Mrs Pendennis's apparently deranged comment: "Camel-racing on the sands"?

You said, "I'm sorry, I thought you said 'Camel-racing on the sands'," and hoped she wouldn't think that it was you who was deranged.

Mrs Pendennis nodded, indicating the poster which had prompted her comment.

"Oh, how cruel!" Miss Johns said automatically. She always said, "Oh, how cruel!" whenever she saw a donkey on the beach or a drayhorse that the brewery trotted out from time to time, complete with liveried driver, for publicity purposes.

Mrs Pendennis shuddered. Nasty dirty creatures. Jack had been in North Africa. Said they were running with fleas.

Bertie Crookthorne had been in North Africa too. Lily remembered some tale he'd told about camels doing it back to back. He'd told other tales, far worse, involving unnatural sexual practices. There'd been a side to him that she hadn't much cared for. There'd been quite a few sides, come to think of it, that she hadn't much cared for.

Mrs Booth-Powell sniffed: the lengths that the Publicity and Attractions would go to to draw the tourists! You might as well be in Blackpool. Bingo on the Promenade and fish and chips served out on paper trays to be eaten publicly: the atmosphere reeking, the pavements covered in litter, and private hotels once noted for quiet gentility now ablaze with neon.

They came up to the Highview, one of the worst offenders. Once a boarding-house, catering for a very genteel clientèle, now it had been extended and tarted-up (as Mr Golding would say) with little gilt lamps and plush-covered banquettes and a cocktail bar so vulgar in its conception that it would cause anyone who possessed the merest trace of refinement to feel quite faint.

In the car park, at the front of the hotel, a man and a woman were packing their luggage into a car. The woman was handing the cases to the man who, obviously in a foul temper, hurled them into the boot. His face worked furiously, whether on account of temper or because of affliction, they were too far away to make out. The woman seemed, quite literally, to be wringing her hands. A young man stood close-by looking embarrassed. The ladies were not so far away that they couldn't identify the young man as Mick.

"Well," said Mrs Booth-Powell, and bucked up tremendously. She hadn't expected the walk to yield such an unexpected pleasure. This was most definitely the horse's mouth. Compared with the horse's mouth, Marguerita's garbled version of the story was probably a mere travesty. She was about to turn in through the gateposts intent on direct questioning when Dot Vyner held out one of her sticks quite unmistakably attempting to bar the way.

"Do have a *little* concern for the proprieties," she said in that sort of icy tone that they could imagine her having employed to subordinates in the Ministry. Mrs Booth-Powell was, momentarily (to use a local term), gobstruck. When she regained her powers of speech she attempted to emulate Miss Vyner's tone of voice: "Are you addressing me?" she said, but it sounded merely pompous; she had, after all, never possessed authority in her own right.

"Yes, I am," said Miss Vyner. "Curiosity is understandable, but behaving like a pack of fishwives is not. Don't you think the boy has had enough to put up with already?"

"I would ask, what business is it of yours?" came Mrs Booth-Powell's rejoinder, less effective because of the delay entailed in thinking it up.

"And I would turn the question back upon the questioner," replied Miss Vyner with a promptness born of a sharper wit. And the newspaper seller, an amused audience of their altercation, said, "Now, now, ladies, don't get your knickers in a knot."

Miss Johns spoke hesitatingly, "I think, perhaps, that Dorothy has a point . . ."

Mrs Crookthorne broke off one of the last two squares of Cadbury's chocolate that remained in her pocket and smuggled it into her mouth. When it had melted sufficiently so that her words were intelligible, she said, "I think there's things we ought to know that we haven't been told."

Mrs Pendennis gazed out across the putting-green and the miniature railway and the golf links and out to sea. Later that evening she and Edward Green would drive slowly along the

Promenade and park the car and watch the sun set. He would take her hand and bring it to his lips. Only the lack of swelling violins would mar the scene; that, and the irritating tendency of old men to leave patches of stubble on their chins.

Sides had been taken, daggers were drawn. This consisted of each couple: Mrs Booth-Powell and Mrs Crookthorne, Miss Vyner and Miss Johns, attempting to leave the other behind, but as each partnership contained one sprightly and one halt member, neither succeeded in this aim, but rather drew abreast and fell behind alternately. Mrs Pendennis walked by herself, a neutral territory, smugly displaying no favouritism.

Oh dear, thought Peggy Johns, now there will be atmospheres. For weeks. Messages relayed via third parties; small acts of vindictiveness; the uninvolved unwillingly obliged to choose one camp or the other.

But she had reckoned without the police car parked outside the Priory. All differences were forgotten in the common flurry of excitement that this spectacle generated.

John Fox had left a bequest to Nora Speakman in his will. It had been his intention that she, his mistress, should set herself up with a business that would provide her with a good living and enable her to bring up their (unacknowledged) son in the manner to which he would have been accustomed had he been born on the right side of the blanket. He had no doubt that she would make a go of it. Apart from that one lapse (and her stubborn refusal to have him pay for the extermination of the life created by that lapse), she'd always shown herself to be an extremely practical woman, as well as a passionate one.

So Nora had invested her money in the one area of the growth industry unlikely to suffer from the recession, and, thanks to a natural flair, and a willingness to learn from her mistakes, she had prospered. Rodney had been privately educated, not at the best schools, perhaps, but certainly not among the hurly-burly of the state system. That he had no particular academic gifts or technical aptitude, and a difficult temperament, was a pity but could hardly be blamed on lack of opportunity. She'd hoped for scholarships or for him to make the sort of friendships that could lead to a position both well-paid and prestigious. But it hadn't happened. A series of small private schools had yielded reports that spoke of inattention and lack of enthusiasm and indolence, and he'd always been a loner, a trait which, she had to admit, hadn't been actively discouraged. Children (and their parents, for that matter) could be so inquisitive: "Where's your dad, Speakman?" "Does Daddy work away, Rodney? Mummy must get lonely. Though she's probably too busy to notice."

And she *was* busy. First with the nursing-home, then running Priory Lodge. Accumulating a nest-egg. As well as being academically inept and no great shakes at interpersonal relations, Rodney hadn't much of a business head either, so that it was necessary to make financial provision for his future. This aim kept always within her sights, she'd gone from strength to strength: after the first few months, never a vacancy; word of mouth supplying free advertising; up till the death of Mrs Cuthbert-Carew, never an unsavoury episode.

However, police cars parked outside the premises hinted at an unsavouriness far more disturbing than a death on site; policemen in droves conducting criminal investigations could have you in the bankruptcy court. She was white with fury, stormed outside to tell the uniformed driver of the (one) car to move it round the back, returned to assure the (one) plain-clothes detective waiting inside that she had no knowledge whatsoever of the movements of that wretched young man; she'd only employed him now and then – when the grass needed cutting or the windows required attention, and so there would be absolutely no point in consulting time sheets as he didn't feature on them. He could only earn a few pounds, surely the officer knew that? People in receipt of social security were only allowed to earn a few pounds, otherwise their benefit was withdrawn.

She saw him make a note of that, Victory, or whatever his stupid name was. He looked more like a criminal than a policeman. They'd probably do Wynn for making a false claim. Well, that was his hard luck.

The detective leaned back indolently in the antique chair that had been left to her by a grateful resident.

"Would there be any point in talking to the old folks?" he asked. "Or are they all a bit too ga-ga to be of any use?"

"Certainly not," she was about to say, but then realised

that vouching for their mental agility was not the tactic to pursue if she wanted to get rid of him. "They get confused," she said, "can't remember what day it is, let alone what happened last month. I'm afraid you'd be wasting your time."

And as if by prearrangement, Mrs Pegler, having knocked and received no reply, but being unsure of this because of her defective hearing, poked her head round the door and said, "Oh, I'm sorry, you've got company. It'll do later on – whatever it was, do you know, I've forgotten." She then favoured the detective with one of those smiles of incredible sweetness which sometimes mask the symptoms of advanced senile decay.

"Run this place on your own, do you?" he asked when she'd gone, Viceroy, or whatever he was called. He had the air about him of a man who expects a cup of tea but is gradually coming to realise the futility of his expectation.

"No," she said stiffly. "My son assists me."

"Is he here?"

"No. He collects catering packs from the wholesaler on a Tuesday afternoon."

And I want to get rid of you before he gets back, she might have added. Rodney hated strangers invading their private lives.

"Well, if you – or he – should happen to recall anything about Wynn's movements on those dates I gave you . . ."

"I shall be in touch," she said briskly, getting up and ushering him to the door.

"Oh, one other thing," he said, coming to an abrupt standstill so that she almost went careering into him. "Noticed any knives missing recently? This character, according to his victims, always arms himself with a bread-knife, or similar. That is," he said, suddenly weary, as though the hours of listening to inaccurate statements from rambling witnesses were taking their toll, "if any of them could agree on the description of a bread-knife. To some, it's the big one with the serrated edge. Now I call that a carving-knife. The bread-knife's the straight one with the teeth – "

"No, there are no knives missing," she said. She checked the kitchen stock monthly, otherwise they'd be taking it home with them or else indulging in an orgy of breakage, but even if she hadn't been sure she'd have said no, just to get him out of the place.

"Good-day to you," she said, and practically pushed him before her through the hall, smiling encouragingly at one or two of the residents who were looking on curiously. "Just a detail I needed clearing up," she'd tell them if they asked. "Something to do with the Watch Committee. Licensing, you know." Most of them would swallow it, except perhaps Booth-Powell who could be a damn nuisance with her "I know the law" attitude.

She closed the door behind him and saw them going into a huddle, Booth-Powell prominent. Women! she thought. Generally speaking, men were a lot less trouble. A pity that they tended to die off before they required the services of this sort of place. Shorter life-expectancy. For them, anything over three score years and ten was a bonus. Mr Golding, she reflected, was over that age already. He'd been acting a bit peculiarly of late, but she hadn't realised how ghastly he was looking until this afternoon as she ushered the policeman out of the door. He was standing alone, at the bottom of the stairs, stock-still, eyes glassy, face colourless, as though he'd seen a ghost.

23

"Ralph and Laura have invited us to dinner next Thursday," Diana said. "I said yes, though I also said, as I hardly set eyes on you these days, that I couldn't be certain." Diana, his lady wife, off the juice and therefore sociable. It struck him as rather odd that she, a known alcoholic, famous for her embarrassing antisocial behaviour, had retained at least some of her friends, whereas he, sober, reliable and properly-behaved, found it difficult to name one person (apart from his current mistress) whom he would consider as occupying a role any closer than that of acquaintance.

"Thursday?" he said, consulting his diary, "yes, that seems to be all right." Ralph, their accountant, bored at a professional level, while Laura never missed an opportunity to quiz him concerning her multifarious minor ailments, and any social gathering had him on tenterhooks from the moment that drink made its appearance. But Diana – when sober – needed some sort of life outside, and he needed to keep her sweet.

Not too difficult at present. Her visit to the photographic gallery when she was in London had led to a meeting with a couple of the exhibitors; big names, highly regarded. Her actress friend, who made a point of knowing everybody, had introduced them. She had mentioned – hesitantly, as one would – her own interest in the subject, and because she was a beautiful, stylish woman had received the sort of attention that might not have been accorded otherwise. Now the kitchen table, instead of being littered with her current reading matter, was covered with countless photographs.

"I can't decide between these two, for my portfolio," she said, indicating to him two identical studies (he supposed she'd call them that) of the beach at sunset.

"They're both the same, aren't they?" he said, pretending a keener interest than was actually the case. Each of them, as far as he could see, showed the same ribbed sand, a glittering sea and the mast of a yacht sticking up in the left-hand corner.

"They're not remotely the same," she said, piqued that he should have failed to notice whatever subtle difference it was that distinguished one from the other. Women and their portfolios! He thought of Elsa, at work on the marsh road, producing those distorted-looking, warts-and-all portraits of the elderly. You tried to maintain a discreet silence in case your inability to appreciate the effect they were striving after offended them, but they couldn't leave it at that; they forced you into voicing an opinion and then of course were offended because it was, invariably, the wrong one.

"I think, actually, that this one is far better," she said, spurred by her annoyance at his lack of discrimination into making a choice, and placed it carefully in front of her with the rest of the chosen few. Passing the other side of the table on his way to the sink with his breakfast dishes, he caught the edge of the reject pile and sent the contents spinning to the floor. Thankful for small mercies, he bent to retrieve them. Most of the photographs, he saw, were landscapes but there were a few portraits: three old ladies, seated in a shelter on the Front, legs eased into elastic support-stockings, gnarled hands folded round their identical capacious plastic handbags, facial expressions stoical. It might be pouring with rain and blowing a gale but they had come for a holiday, and enjoy themselves they would. Were they, he wondered, Elsa's old ladies? Feeling a sudden queasiness, he thought of those shared pre-Raphaelite mistresses who must, on occasion, have been privy to the same scene or theme or whatever being handled quite differently by different of their artist paramours and quickly turned to the other studies.

The first showed the local lunatic, in mid-proclaim, mouth open, eyes wide, gesticulating wildly; the second, two mongol children, holding hands, water-melon grins bisecting their moon faces. The last time that he and she had been to London together she'd dragged him to see an exhibition by some American female who, it seemed, made a speciality out of photographing freaks: the deformed, the damaged and the insane had glowered or grinned out from their private worlds. During the course of his career he'd seen most of the sickening tricks that nature or man's interference with nature can play upon humankind, but those pictures had appalled him, had spoken of nothing more than a morbid curiosity of the pathological sort. He hoped that Diana was not aiming at the same effect, and was reassured when the next print showed two Alice-in-Wonderland children, beautiful, grave-faced, flowers in their hair; the sort of children that, had it been possible, he'd have wanted for his own.

Perhaps it was as well, with such an attitude, that it hadn't been possible. You couldn't choose, after all; you had to love what you were given. He looked at his wife more fondly as he always did when he remembered how traumatised she must have been by the knowledge of her sterility. Though, apart from her disappointment at not being able to make him a father, she'd professed herself to be relatively unaffected by the news. "I'd have made a rotten mother," she'd said. "Can't stand brats. And I'm far too selfish to be able to make those sort of sacrifices you're supposed to make. Probably the best thing," she'd said. And he'd agreed, claiming it wasn't that much of an issue; most men fathered children because their women required it of them. But he knew at the time these remarks were exchanged that neither of them was speaking the truth. Not exactly, anyway.

The last of the photographs that he picked up from the floor showed an image of alarm: a man, suddenly startled, or in flight. She looked over his shoulder. "Looks as though the devil was at his heels, doesn't he?" she said. "I took that a few weeks ago. I was walking back to the car – I'd been finishing off a roll of film in the Ornamental Gardens – and he came flying round the corner of Beach Road. I was a fugitive from a chain-gang," she said. "Except he doesn't look like Paul Muni. He looks more like – I don't know – one of those spoiled-boy, Latin-looking ones who were in vogue just before the war in those bi-op musical extravaganzas."

"It's Rodney Speakman," he said.

"Who's Rodney Speakman?"

"Nora Speakman's son. You know, Priory Lodge."

"Oh," she said. But she'd lost interest, returned her attention to the photographs that still remained to be sorted.

He continued to gaze at the print. Nora had a studio portrait of Rodney in her office. Doting mothers always did. His own mother had had his graduation photograph, silver-framed, displayed prominently among her tawdry ornaments on the mantelpiece. "My son," she'd tell strangers, "in his cap and gown," in case they'd failed to notice. Rodney, as far as he knew, had achieved nothing that could give his mother cause to be proud, but perhaps he was one of the fortunate ones and she doted on him regardless.

The residents of Priory Lodge took tea and passed round Mrs Pendennis's catalogues and brochures and samples of carpet and furnishing fabric. Edward Green's bungalow into which she was to move after the wedding was to be redecorated throughout. As it stood, she'd confided to Esmé Grey, she felt as though she were stepping into a very authentic stage-set for *Arsenic and Old Lace*: dadoes and plush tablecloths and jardinières and lino – lino! – in the kitchen. She shuddered, could not bring herself to mention that upon the lino stood a porcelain sink large enough for the immersion of a baby whale, and a sort of gas-boiler contraption that roared and showered soot every time you turned the hot water on. She'd hurriedly equipped herself with furniture catalogues and paint cards and the Yellow Pages to collect the names of reliable tradesmen. From now until October she intended to devote herself to the transformation of her future home. Interior design had always been her forte. "A beautiful setting for a beautiful woman," her admirers had said, unaware that the setting, like the woman, was meant to be admired, not handled; and that her first husband, Jack, had been refused the comforts of either.

"You won't know the place when I've finished with it," she'd told Edward Green who'd acknowledged her intentions with a rather pallid smile. All his bits and pieces, he thought, consigned to the dustbin, or the loft, if he was lucky. Not to mention the upheaval. All right for her; she could leave it, return to the Priory. He watched her, in rapt consultation with a painter and sighed deeply. He was too old for all this, and hoped earnestly that she was too.

But the challenge had given her a new lease of life. She handed round her brochures in the Gloucester Room, anxious for opinions, as self-opinionated people usually are, if only for the pleasure of subsequently rejecting them.

"I thought, for the bedroom, pink and cream," she said, remembering how she and Mama had shopped for sheets for the matrimonial bed in that bijou house to which she was to return after her first honeymoon. The sheets and the counterpane had matched her trousseau lingerie: a delightful shade they called Old Rose. The stain of her virginal blood upon them had matched too, she remembered ruefully.

"Grey, perhaps?" said Esmé Grey, unconscious of the pun, her mind boggling at the thought of Edward Green, very much a tweed and tobacco man, taking off his tartan carpet-slippers amid a vista of rose-pink satin. "That sort of pinky-grey? Like pigeons' feathers. Oyster, I think they call it. It can look very attractive."

Colonel Pritchard rustled his *Times*. Might as well have taken up residence in a girls' dormitory. Maud, bless her, had never been one for faffing around with the furniture. Not that she'd had much chance: they were forever on the move and had usually been assigned furnished accommodation.

Having rustled his newspaper, he then opened it full out to conceal himself behind it. Mrs Pendennis who had been going to ask him, playfully, for his opinion on décor, took the hint and desisted. She tried Mr Gentile instead, but he was asleep, his paunch rising up and down with a metronomic regularity, one of his fly buttons undone. "What do *you* think, Mr Golding?" she trilled merrily. As if he, a lifelong bachelor who'd lived in institutions ever since the death of his parents, would have a clue.

He'd been staring out of the window at the climbing-roses on the terrace. Thin cloud moving across the sun created a fitful light which dappled the leaves and plunged the trellis-work into shade. Easy to imagine shapes, lurking and sinister, out there; the same shapes that lurked in the folds of his dressing-gown and the recesses of his wardrobe, until the drink finally obliterated them. He jumped at the sound of his name and spun round in his chair. "I'm sorry," she said. "Did I startle you?"

"Startle" seemed an understatement for the terror in his eyes. Like an animal, cornered, a rabbit. Jack used to shoot rabbits. A lifetime of causing bloodstains.

Mr Golding didn't acknowledge her question, but merely continued to twitch: pulling at the edge of his jacket, drumming on the arm of his chair, scratching the stubble on his chin. (Why was it, Mrs Pendennis thought irritably, that old men could never shave themselves properly? Was it poor eyesight? Or trembling hands? Or a disinclination to invest in new razor-blades? She would send Edward to the barber.)

"Oh well," said Mrs Booth-Powell, preparing herself for the effort needed to get up from her chair, "time for forty winks."

Most of the residents took a nap between tea and dinner. A great creaking of joints took place as they rose in a body, and then limped, hobbled, scuttled or trotted into the hall and waited for Colonel Pritchard, striding tall, to fulfil his customary function as liftman. Having been in the Royal Engineers, he understood the mechanics of the thing. Mr Gentile was shaken awake and surfaced, blinking amiably. Mr Golding, roused from his reverie by the grip of Mrs Booth-Powell's hand on his shoulder, jumped and whimpered and looked at her blankly, but then trotted off quite obediently at her heels. There was a dazed look on his face. If it wasn't senile decay, Mrs Booth-Powell thought, then it was drugs. Basil had had to deal with drug offenders. "Human wreckage," he'd called them.

The first contingent, which included Mr Golding, assembled for ascent. Colonel Pritchard made his usual announcement: "First floor: Beds and Bedding, Household Linen, Carpets and Curtains; Second floor: Lighting, Furniture and Fitments, Bathroom Suites." Mr Golding usually added: "Third floor: Ladies' Underwear," but not today.

In the kitchen Mrs Randall had kept back two steaks of the cod that was steaming on the Aga. These two she floured and egged and breadcrumbed and deep-fried until they were golden-brown. A pile of chips and a good helping of garden peas filled the plate to overflowing. She handed it to Mick.

"Here," she said, "get that down you and you won't go far wrong. Take it into the storeroom in case Nosy Nora comes through."

She could hear his stomach gurgling. It was she who had told Elsa to tell him to sneak in of an evening. Lads of that age, left to their own devices, never ate properly. At least she could see to it that he had one square meal in the day. She'd made him an individual treacle sponge for afters. The rest of them were having raspberry condé (yesterday's rice pudding adorned with a spoonful of fruits from a consignment of damaged tins, sold off cheap at Tesco), though none of them cared for raspberries; the seeds lodged under their plates and required much disguised prodding and poking to dislodge them. But that consideration was immaterial when Nora had a bead on a bargain.

The guests came downstairs in the same way that they had ascended some ninety minutes previously. They had washed themselves after their rests and exuded a collective smell of perfumed face-powder and attar of roses and mothballed frocks. Everyone moved towards their tables with the alacrity that was only displayed at mealtimes, set down their individual gastronomic particularities: Worcester sauce, artificial sweeteners, indigestion tablets; waited impatiently for Nellie Macpherson to carry in the first course, and made small bets with each other as to what the menu would offer.

Nora came into the Lancaster Room as she always did at mealtimes, to check that all were present and correct and that Marguerita and Rosa weren't lolling around or Nellie Macpherson spilling the soup.

The first course was hors d'oeuvres, easily transportable without spillage, and both Marguerita and Rosa were off-duty. But all were not present and correct. "Where's Mr Golding?" she asked, clicking her teeth with exasperation. She liked to run a tight ship. "Elsa," she said, "go upstairs and get him down, would you?"

Elsa's first knock received no response. She knocked louder. To no avail. Curse it, she thought, I shall have to go downstairs for the pass key. Ever since the unseemly demise of Mrs Cuthbert-Carew, Nora had been mustard about checking residents' whereabouts. But the door yielded to the pressure of her hand and swung open and she saw that the room was empty. Of Mr Golding, at any rate.

Probably on his way down in the lift, she thought, at the same time as she had come up by the stairs. She walked along the corridor and saw that she had been half-correct in her assumption: he was in the lift, but it appeared to be jammed midway between floors and, from what she could see of him through the ironwork of the cage, he wouldn't be coming down for dinner.

24

Nora moved imperiously among the tables. "Everything all right?" she enquired brusquely of the diners. Most of them nodded, fixing their hopes on the pudding; on Fridays sometimes there was ice-cream, a bit waxy perhaps, it being the economy catering-pack sort, but sweet and agreeably soft nevertheless.

Elsa came to the door. Her face was colourless. She caught Nora's eye and gesticulated. And by the time she'd passed on her message, Nora's face had drained of colour too.

"Nobody around?" she asked as they ran up the stairs. For a heavy woman she could certainly motor. Elsa shook her head and Nora breathed a sigh that could be distinguished as signifying relief amid the sighing that signified shortness of breath.

Elsa hung back while Nora kneeled, craning her neck. Obviously the heap of clothes that was Mr Golding had fallen against the lift handle and caused the cage to jam. He was slumped in the corner, his head bowed, chin on his chest. From beneath his chin blood flowed, and dropped soundlessly on to the carpet.

For a second or two she stared transfixed. Then she moved into action. To Rodney. To the telephone. To the kitchen. Strong arms would be required to haul up the lift until it was level with the second floor, and time was of the essence. Mick, surprised with his mouth full of fish, chips and peas, attempted to conceal his incriminating plateful from her but she wasn't interested in illicit catering arrangements at that moment. Swiftly she ushered him up the back stairs, up to the loft where the winching gear was situated, and showed him how the cage with its horrific cargo could be hauled up to floor level.

Up it came, slowly. Movement shook a flurry of crimson drops on to the carpet. A red carpet, thank goodness, she had time to think, as they slid the door across and moved gingerly towards the heap in the corner. Dead or alive, they couldn't yet be sure, she and Elsa. Rodney had been posted at the top of the stairs to prevent anyone else from coming up.

"All right," she called quietly up the lift shaft to tell Mick that he should cease winding. The contraption came to a halt with a jolt and the bulk of Mr Golding, extinct or extant, fell forward, almost into her automatically-outstretched arms. Elsa bleated in alarm, but the edge of the door saved them from an unholy embrace.

"Jesus!" Mick said, having secured the lift and run down the back steps. "Mind out of the way," said Dr Rees who, having been intercepted by Mary Reilly in the hall, had run up the front staircase without further ado.

"Ring an ambulance," he said abruptly. "Why the hell didn't you ring one in the first place?"

Because ambulances did not arrive incognito. There were sirens and lights and heavy-footed stretcher-bearers who could not stop to think that a person's reputation might be ruined by an incident like this. But his tone brooked no argument so she went across to the second floor extension to do so.

There was a knife by the side of Mr Golding's body. A kitchen knife. "He's cut his throat?" Elsa said. Her hands were splayed across her face. She peeked through her fingers like a child watching a frightening television programme. The blood was everywhere: on the floor, on the side of the lift, all over Emlyn's sleeve.

He shook his head. "It's only a nick." He turned to Mick who stood, mouth agape, for assistance. "Can we get him out of here and into a bedroom? Here, take his arm over your shoulder – that's it. It's all right. There seems to be a lot of blood but it's scarcely more than a scratch. Cutting your throat demands more knowledge of anatomy than most people possess. Particularly when drunk."

He took Mr Golding's other arm across his own shoulder and together they hauled him across to his room, Elsa going ahead of them, and dropped him on to his bed. Nora came back from the phone. There were times, she knew, when you had to accept that fate was against you: Mrs Cuthbert-Carew, the Wynn affair, and now Golding. It had to end sometime. But who could tell what harm would have been done by then? "Right, Nora," Emlyn said, and she felt as though she were back at St Mary's, anticipating his commands as she'd done so efficiently when they'd worked together in Casualty.

Pressure was applied at the relevant points, the faint beat of his pulse sought for, his eyelids rolled back and the pupils inspected. Commands were issued which they ran to obey: a damp towel! undo his buttons! check the contents of those bottles!

Empire port, Elsa read from the labels, Rémy Martin, Johnnie Walker, Ativan. "Were they full?" Emlyn called, squinting across at the pill bottle. She shrugged. Perhaps Rosa would have been able to enlighten them but she was out learning the fundamentals of English syntax at night-school.

He held his hand out for the pill bottle and read the date on the label. "I prescribed these two months ago," he said. "Though, if he saved them up . . . Duw," he said, "where is that ambulance?" Mr Golding's blood had ceased to flow, Elsa saw, daring a quick glance, and was congealing stickily in the folds beneath his jowl and soaking into the fabric of his suit. "Looks worse than it is," Emlyn had said. She shuddered to think of the amount that must flow if you succeeded in what Mr Golding had, pathetically, failed to do with the knife that Mick had picked up out of the lift and now held, looking for all the world as the police had alleged he must have looked on the afternoon of May 23rd and the morning of June 4th and various other dates too, striking terror into the hearts of defenceless old ladies.

When the ambulancemen came it was as noisily and as publicly as Nora had feared. "An accident," she told them all as they crowded at the door of the Lancaster Room, their raspberry condés forgotten. "Mr Golding has had a slight accident. Could you please use the back lift for the time being until we clean up the other one?" Vomit, she hoped they'd assume, or incontinence. She might be able to flannel them short-term, but explanations would eventually have to be given. Inquests, the coroner's court, publicity. And her blood ran cold as she awaited the telephone call that would decide her financial future.

In the kitchen, democracy prevailed. Strong tea was brewed and heavily sugared. "Here you are, Doc," Mary Reilly said, handing him a mug. Elsa and Mick sat close together, side by side. They shivered while their chattering teeth made castanet-like noises against the sides of their cups. Lord love them, Mary thought, for a couple of kids, as green as the grass. She'd seen some sights herself, in the nick. It hardened you, that place. Eventually the Doc gave them a tranquilliser each from the miniature pharmacy that he carried in his case. Gave Rodney one too. Though he hadn't actually been at the scene of the crime. His mother always tried to protect him from unpleasantness.

Nora, unusually, was lingering in the kitchen too. She sat with her hands together as though in prayer. She probably *was* praying: "Dear God, don't let him croak, because if he does, I'm in the shit." Not exactly a selling-point, was it? "High-class establishment for retired gentlefolk – elderly resident just topped himself – mind the bloodstains in the lift."

"When will they know?" Mrs Randall asked. Nobody had explained anything properly. Mary had said his throat was cut from ear to ear, and dozens of empty bottles found scattered across the bedroom floor. Trust Mary! Not a bit like that. She listened as Elsa told the story. The Doc had gone to the phone. Lots of blood, apparently, but it issued from a cut not much more dramatic than that which might be sustained during the course of shaving. (A razor would have been the obvious choice for cutting one's throat, but Mr Golding shaved electric and had been obliged to steal a kitchen knife for the purpose. A blunt one, at that, silly bugger.) The question was: how much booze and how many pills, and of what variety, had he swallowed before staggering with his weapon to the lift? All sorts of ancient bottles had been found on his dressing-table. However, the promptness with which he'd been discovered made it unlikely that the dose would be fatal. They'd pump the poison out of his stomach, if necessary wash his bloodstream clean, and then transfer him to the psychiatric wing of the hospital. And Nora would manufacture some tale for the other old dears and be able to breathe freely again.

And that, more or less, was the gist of the message that the doctor brought back with him from the telephone.

Elsa watched him closely as he imparted this news. Never before had she seen him totally absorbed, oblivious of everything but the matter in hand. Never before had he seemed so sure, unvacillating, authoritative – she thought of Emlyn the lover, gasping with sexual excitement beneath her touch, out of control – and it was attractive, no doubt about it, the combination of private vulnerability and public assurance. I am having an affair, she'd told herself at the beginning, and there was such a glamorous aura attaching to the phrase that the person she was having it with assumed a subordinate role. Good sex, good company – and no skin off anyone's nose when it had to end. She'd had no experience with which to compare this new feeling, this sensation of looking at his by-now familiar face and seeing an attractive stranger. It should be the other way round, surely; first attraction, then familiarity? The weird thing was that, newly-strange, he seemed more real to her than he'd done when familiar.

They transferred Mr Golding to the psychiatric wing and then to a private mental hospital much more pleasant than the Retreat had ever been. Modern drugs and psychotherapy and enlightened attitudes had made this possible. Here there were no warders masquerading as nurses, but young therapists wearing dungarees and tee-shirts and no brassières because they didn't wish to be taken for sexual objects.

Miss Vyner got her friend Gertie to drive her to visit him and reported back that the place was bright and cheerful (and so it should be at those prices) and that he seemed happy enough – though not quite *with* the world, poor fellow. Apparently there was some history of instability. She took with her a card signed by all the residents of Priory Lodge, a pair of socks knitted by Mrs Pegler, a box of Rose's chocolates and a gruff message from Colonel Pritchard to the effect that he hoped he'd soon be up and about and out of the sick-bay. But Mr Golding didn't seem to remember who these people were.

Rosa scrubbed the lift carpet and the carpet in Mr Golding's room with One Thousand and One and gave periodic thanks to her patron saint Teresa for delivering her from the evil of his lustful ways. Marguerita crossed herself at the threshold and refused point-blank to use the front lift.

And so did most of the female residents, though Miss Vyner tried to set them a brave example and Mrs Booth-Powell strode into it, declaring that the rest of them were neurotic and Mrs Crookthorne used it as she always had done, without thinking; she was haunted by material problems and didn't give a toss for the supernatural. But the others stood firm and ten days after the incident Mrs Speakman bowed to the inevitable and called in a man to measure up for a new one.

But shudders were still exhibited, reports of feet walking over graves, sudden chills. The atmosphere was thick with intimations of the proximity of death and the possibility of afterlife. Mrs Pegler, who'd been toying with the idea of spiritualism for ever such a long time, finally took the plunge. Instead of St James's on Sunday evening (where the congregation consisted in the main of such snooty types), she went into town, down an alley that ran by the side of the Cooperative Hall and entered the corrugated-iron-roofed shed which served as home for the Spiritualist community in the area.

And a nicer bunch you couldn't wish to meet! Real friendly. No curled lips or raised eyebrows here when you missed off an aitch or mispronounced a word or made some comment that they (the snooty brigade) considered to be indicative of your low-class origins.

She told her new friends the sad tale of Mr Golding and prayers were said for his benefit. Perhaps, she was told, there might be a message for him, a message of comfort. There hadn't been one yet. There hadn't been one for her either. (Try as she might, she couldn't imagine Dad out of his corporeal body; there'd been so very much of it, after all.) Still it was early days yet. She had mentioned her involvement to Miss Vyner who had been very scathing, saying they're only after your money, but that was ridiculous. She'd been told right at the beginning that no compulsory payment was involved, though contributions, of course, were always welcome. Without these donations they could not continue to function.

So naturally she had contributed. And their gratitude had been so sincere. What Miss Vyner didn't understand was the comfort you derived from having a faith and friends who shared your belief and supported you and didn't make you feel like a social outcast just because you hadn't always sat on a cushion, sewing a fine seam.

On the subject of which, it was she who had taken Elsa's cardigan and mended the tear in the sleeve where Elsa had snagged it at some stage during the Golding drama. There was a tiny bloodstain on it too, so she darned, exquisitely, over it – blood being the very devil to shift from cloth.

As Elsa knew. She'd washed Mick's stained white tee-shirt, but the stains had simply run, producing a faded tie-dye effect and he'd taken one look and thrown it in the dustbin. Emlyn's suit – a lightweight, camel-coloured gaberdine – had been sent to Johnsons where the girl made a note concerning the nature of the stains and when it came back they were almost undetectable.

The bedsheets that had been bled over had to be burned. But the bedside rug came up a treat after an application of carpet shampoo. The new resident, booked to arrive in October, would never suspect a thing. As long as the rest of them observed discretion. Nora racked her brains to think of some sort of bribe that firstly, wouldn't cost too much and secondly, would be understood as the price of silence without it being spelled out as such.

Mick lay on the beach or, if it was raining, swam in the indoor swimming-pool and came round every evening to the Priory for his meal and said, no, shut up, will you, whenever he was asked by Elsa if he'd remembered anything that could corroborate his plea of innocence.

Generally speaking, the days settled themselves into the old pattern, except that everyone of them that was crossed off the calendar brought July 25th, the bail date, that much closer.

On the afternoon of July 23rd, Elsa went into town during her free time to equip herself with some fresh cartridge-paper and charcoal. Emlyn was away, at a conference on community health care in Harrogate and not due back until the following day. The week before there had been a couple of soirées organised by pharmaceutical companies that he'd had to attend, an evening on call and a social engagement. They'd managed one brief meeting, after dark, in his car parked on a lane that led off the marsh road. Moonlight and the flicker of his cigarette-lighter flame had shown her how tired he looked. "Where are you supposed to be?" she'd asked. "Looking for cigarettes," he'd replied. "Finding an all-night garage." He'd been edgy, abstracted. Did he, she wondered, still see the game as being worth the candle?

The price of drawing-materials made her wince. When she started at college she would be given an allowance by the education authority and be able to buy them at discount prices. She would have proper facilities for working. No more propping Mrs Randall's baking-board on a bentwood chair beneath Nora's twenty-five-watt light bulbs. Tables, there would be, and easels and models and light. Other people, to consult for advice, to learn from. She had received a list of accommodation addresses that morning. The award of a discretionary grant, to cover her fees and accommodation, had at last been confirmed, and her savings, supplemented by some part-time work, ought to cover her living expenses. An Elysian prospect. Or so it seemed. She hoped that she was not expecting too much. For most of her life she had expected too little, and there was a danger, she knew, of a reaction both equal and opposite.

She turned out of the art shop and into the Arcade, bought a cup of coffee in the Bakery and took it outside to where tables and chairs had been set beneath striped umbrellas and surrounded by massed banks of potted plants.

Very continental it looked: a fountain trickling, taped music playing softly in the background, tourists strolling and window-shopping. The sight of a large black labrador blundering through the grotto, stopping to cock its leg against a yucca plant, was incongruous. Several of the coffee-drinkers muttered that you'd have thought she'd keep it on the lead, at least.

He flung himself at her. All of a sudden. She had hoped that if she ignored him, he wouldn't approach her. She had tried to make herself inconspicuous: tightening her muscles, drawing her feet beneath the table, averting her eyes. But she might as well have called his name. She felt his paws in her lap, his great tongue dripping foamy saliva upon her forearm. "Captain!" called a voice: high, clear, cut-glass, "Captain! Get *down*, you idiot."

Reluctantly, he obeyed, but not before nuzzling at her and giving her a thorough licking. A nice dog, affectionate, but thoroughly undisciplined. They said that dogs resembled their owners. "I'm terribly sorry," Diana Rees said. "He hasn't marked your skirt, has he? He's not usually quite so pushy with strangers. He must have mistaken you for someone he knew."

Elsa looked up. She had to. Blushing furiously, she looked close up, for the first time, at her lover's wife: the woman who carried his blood-stained suit to the cleaners'; who accompanied him to social functions and fought with him publicly; who shared his name and his bed.

Striking, of course. She'd known that that would be the case. Tall and slim and classy. A bit haggard but blessed with that sort of bone structure that makes the process of ageing so much less destructive. Intelligent eyes. Expensive clothes. Style. Emlyn's prize: a beauty out of the top drawer, a constant morale-boost. How could he have anticipated the pickled liver, the barren womb? He had picked her first and foremost, no doubt, because of what she represented rather than for her own sake, just as she, Elsa, had taken up with Rob because he was the star of the school and all the other girls were envious. But her ego was perhaps less fragile and Rob had swiftly become just Rob, a man not an aspiration, whereas she felt certain that, despite his disillusionments, Diana had remained for Emlyn in some way the girl he still couldn't, realistically, have hoped to win.

"It's quite all right," she said. "There's no damage done." And folded her shaking hands so that they concealed the marks on her skirt.

"Well, at least let me buy you another coffee."

In the throes of fending off the dog's friendly assault, Elsa had knocked her cup over. Captain was now slurping the spilled liquid from the ground.

"No. No, really," she said, but the woman had already disappeared inside the café.

She closed her eyes and tried to control the rhythm of her

breathing and the tremor in her hands. Why had it never occurred to her that a nightmare situation of this sort was, if not inevitable, then highly likely, this being a small town and there existing a network of acquaintanceship to link them? September, she thought, Manchester, and repeated the words in her head like a talisman. Too much was happening, too quickly: Mick's arrest, Mr Golding's suicide attempt, and now confrontation with the wife of her lover. I came here, she remembered incredulously, for rest and peace and quiet. If only I'd known.

"Sugar?" said her lover's wife, lowering her sunglasses from the top of her head to their proper position and thereby disconcerting Elsa even more; at least the eyes, naked, could be consulted for clues as to whether any suspicion was being harboured. Now the scrutiny could only be a one-way affair.

"I took him to one of those training schools," said Diana Rees, "but they asked us to leave." She reached down and patted Captain's head vigorously as though, despite her disapproving tone, she was rather proud of his intractability. Elsa clenched her hands beneath the table, awaiting the dreadful moment when she would say "my husband".

"My husband says that I have only myself to blame because I've spoiled him. I'm sorry, did I not bring you the right coffee?"

She hadn't yet dared to reach out her hand to her cup because of the trembling. Now, beneath that inscrutable dark stare, she was obliged to do so. Perhaps she'll think I've got a hangover, she thought, as the cup shook and the coffee spilled. Unfairly, she, Diana, the alcoholic, lifted her cup with never a quiver.

But her attention was distracted by the antics of the dog. She'd snapped his lead on to his collar and trapped the loop of it beneath her chair leg and he had settled to licking his genitals. But now he was chewing at the foliage of some exotic-looking plant with evident relish.

"Oh God!" she said, tugging him away. "It looks as though I shall have to buy that too. You don't have a pressing need for a ghastly-looking greenhouse plant, do you?" And she grinned widely, a schoolgirl grin, and Elsa thought with surprise that perhaps, in different circumstances, we'd have liked each other, been friends, and then wondered why she'd been surprised: the women who attracted the same man were likely to share some of the same characteristics.

She made the most of her opportunity to gulp down her coffee, but almost choked herself in the process and was taken with a fit of coughing. She felt Diana's hand on her back, patting her, as she struggled for breath, swallowed down gratefully the glass of water that she brought.

"All right?"

She nodded, cleared her throat, wiped her eyes.

"Horrid, isn't it, when that happens?"

A pleasant woman, helpful; difficult to reconcile her with the figure who had struggled with the hotel staff on the forecourt of the Metropole. For a moment Elsa felt only pity: for this pleasant woman, in the grip of addiction, and for Emlyn, having to observe her personality changes, to watch out for the little signs that heralded their approach, scarcely ever able to relax his vigilance, and finally for herself, unlikely to escape, as she had once thought she would be able to escape, unscathed, from her predicament.

25

Mrs Pegler was chuffed. On Tuesday evening in the Meeting Hall, via the channel provided by Mrs Ethel Moore, medium, Dad had sent a message. First of all when Mrs Moore had said "Alfred", no bells had rung. She'd called Dad Dad for such a very long time. But then Mrs Moore had said "Tommy" and Tommy was of course the old horse that Dad, "Alfred", had had when he first started up in business for himself. Tommy, it seemed, having gone over, was now also residing in peace and tranquillity on the other side.

"Yes, yes," she said excitedly. "It's me. It's Dad." And they had smiled indulgently. First-timers always got het-up.

Dad's message was, in essence, to keep cheerful, and to make sure that her broker kept an eye out for them commodities. She'd smiled. Just like Dad, he'd always had a business brain. To come, as he had come, from rags to riches, demanded more than luck, whatever anybody said to the contrary.

The second part of Dad's message was more disquieting. She was not to hesitate any longer, but to gather her belongings and move from that "bad place". Dumbstruck, she looked at her companions. Or fellow-conspirators. (She'd forgotten that she'd told them about the Golding business.) She was to move to more congenial surroundings. Only idleness had prevented her from doing it before now. Wasn't that so?

It was. And so she went back to the Priory and gave Mrs Speakman a month's notice, pleading health grounds and the need to establish herself in a warmer climate before the approach of winter. She then went down the road to make enquiries at a rival establishment, Grey Towers.

She met the lad, Mick, as she walked back, and stopped to

chat. "How did you get on?" she asked, "with that police to-do?"

She'd only just remembered it herself. The upset with Mr Golding had put the other business out of everybody's heads. Miss Vyner, who'd been to see him, said that Mr Golding had gone doolally, but nobody seemed to know what had triggered it off.

"I surrender my bail tomorrow," the lad said.

He looked scared to death. Had she remembered, she'd have asked Mrs Moore if there was any message concerning the matter – intercessions in the spirit world were, apparently, not uncommon – and perhaps been able to offer him some authoritative reassurance. As it was, all she could do was to wish him well on her own behalf. "You'll be all right, you'll see," she said. "Everything'll be gradely."

But he didn't know what that meant. And neither did Elsa when he mentioned it the next day. "Sounds like something from your era," he said. "One of those quaint phrases that you elderly ladies use."

"No idea," she said. "Of course, when you reach my age your memory goes."

Wan jokes. Born of tension bordering on hysteria. Every few moments he would ask her what the time was. He'd put his clock into a drawer, saying that he couldn't bear to be reminded.

But reminder would come soon enough. At five thirty his parents would arrive from the Highview to collect him (Daddy had had to beg time off again. Michael probably didn't realise just what trouble he caused others by his irresponsible behaviour) and together they would make for the police station where, at six o'clock, he was due to report. Mother and Daddy had been told, in no uncertain terms, to keep away until then. "You really shouldn't have banished them like that," Elsa said. "They must be every bit as worried as you."

They were pretending to play cards. Pontoon. Of which she had only a vague knowledge. To which neither of them could bring the necessary attention. "Twist," he said. And then, "I mean stick. Nobody," he said, "could be as worried as I am."

She had recited, once again, the platitude that had been

used from the beginning to reassure him: that innocent, he had nothing to fear. And he'd said sarcastically, "Do you really think so?" But this time, at four thirty on the afternoon of Wednesday, July 25th, the question was not accompanied by a sneer but asked quite sincerely.

"Yes," she replied. "I really do."

"What's the time?" he asked.

"Five minutes later than when last you enquired."

"Oh Christ. Oh Christ. Oh Christ." He lit a cigarette from the stub of another, paced the room, kicked at the scarred furniture. Outside the sun blazed. You could see right across the bay to the Cambrian Hills. Perhaps exercise would take his mind off things – a good long walk along the beach. Or would that make the prospect of potential confinement even more horrendous?

"Surely," he said, for the umpteenth time, "if they had anything else on me, they'd have picked me up before now? After all, I could have fled the country, couldn't I?" And for the umpteenth time she agreed with him.

"You're sure?" he said, picking abstractedly at a skin blemish until he'd transformed what had started out as a minor eruption into a major disaster area.

"I'm sure," she said, and took his hand and held it fast. "I tell you what," she said. "A week this Friday the Unspeakables have to go to Torquay for the funeral of some relative. She told me this morning. They'll have to stay overnight. She'd give anything not to, I could tell, but she's probably due for an inheritance or something. Anyway, she's leaving me in charge – she's written me out about a million instructions: what to do if there's a fire, or a burglary, or somebody has a heart attack. Screeds of it. Anyway, I thought, we could hold that party, you know, your un-twenty-first birthday party. We could get Mrs Randall to wheel out the cake she made – I mean, it no longer matters that you *aren't* twenty-one. It's so long after the event that they'll have forgotten. A celebration party. What do you think?"

"I think," he said, removing his hand from her grasp, "that you're tempting fate even by *mentioning* celebration parties, and I wish to Christ you'd shut up."

At ten past five they heard the front door open. "I told them half past," Mick said. "I told them half past," and kicked so savagely at the rickety old sideboard that two of the drawer handles fell off.

But the feet that climbed the stairs were not Mother's feet, nor yet Daddy's. Size twelves, by the sound of them, shod in stout leather, steel-tipped, and followed by a slow, doom-laden knock.

They stared at one another. She saw that he was incapable of movement and went, on his behalf, to answer the summons.

A uniformed police constable, shirt-sleeved, unthreatening-looking, stood outside. "Michael Wynn?" he said, as unsinisterly as if he'd come to enquire about a dog licence.

"Come in," she said. But he wouldn't.

"No," he said, "I'm just going off-duty. Can you fetch him?"

So Michael Wynn had to propel himself, on feet that felt weighted down, as if in a dream, towards the landing, where his business was obviously to be discussed for the benefit of any other of the residents who cared to eavesdrop.

"Message from Sergeant Verity," the constable said. "He can't make it at the station for six. So you don't need to bother going in. As far as he's concerned, you've answered bail."

Elsa, hearing this information through the gap between the door and jamb, wondered for a second if wishful thinking had transformed message announced into message received. But Mick was saying, "So that's it, is it, then? I'm cleared?"

"You've answered your bail. That's all I know," repeated the constable, obviously anxious to be off and make the most of a beautiful evening's leisure. "He'll be in touch, I expect, Sergeant Verity. OK?"

OK? OK. O very much K. Mick turned back into the room. "It's all right," she said. "It's all right." And hugged him tightly and waltzed with him until they both collapsed with dizziness and, breathlessly, he kept repeating, "It is all right, isn't it? It's not a mistake or anything, is it?"

"No. No, no, no! It's all over. It's finished. I'm sure."

But Mother could always be relied upon for the pouring of cold water upon hope recently kindled.

They arrived early, after all. Just a few minutes after the policeman had left. The glad news was gabbled at them. Daddy's tic went into overdrive and Mother's colour changed violently. Then she cried. Which was understandable. Then she held Mick close in a hug. And that was understandable too. And then she wiped her eyes and asked him to repeat what the policeman had said, *exactly,* and he did, and then she said they'd better get in touch with the solicitor before he left his office. Mick said he'd ring, but she said no, they'd do it – they were paying for his services after all – and they went downstairs to the call box and when they came back it was to counsel caution: Mr Parker had been speaking to Sergeant Fleming and enquiries were still under way. "You can't afford to relax totally just yet, Michael," she said, as if by not relaxing he could in any way alter the outcome of those enquiries.

But the moment was too good to be spoiled. For him, at any rate. Even when she said, "You see, Michael, we don't know *which* charge is being deferred. After all, you *did* do wrong. If only you'd be more open about things a lot of trouble could be avoided. You can't imagine what this last month's done to us – your father and me. I've had to have pills from the doctor."

She tried to make him look at her but he wouldn't. Elsa looked instead. Her expression was not that which you'd expect to see on the face of a woman whose son has escaped wrongful arrest. That trace of uncertainty which Elsa had seen in the beginning still remained. She was not convinced. She never would be.

"Are you going to come back home now?" she urged. She looked at him hungrily. She'd never feel sure about him, or safe with him, but he was hers and without him her life was undefined. "I've had your room redecorated," she said. "And that friend of Daddy's boss – you know, I told you about him – Mr Howard of Howard and Pearson, thinks he might be able to find a vacancy for you in his office. Accountancy's the thing these days, Michael. Look at Steven Smith you were at school with . . ."

"I have to go," Elsa said, but if anybody heard, nobody paid her any attention. As she left, she understood that no, he wasn't going back with them, and thrice no, he wasn't going to become an accountant. And why was it that, just for once, they couldn't stop nagging him for long enough to be glad about the news? Mother was saying, "*You* try to knock some sense into him, can't you? Instead of standing there like a yard of tripe." But Daddy was gazing through the window wearing the expression of a man for whom only death can provide merciful deliverance.

She imagined the strained dinner that he would be obliged to suffer through while Mother enquired of him when he was due to come to his senses, and he told her to keep her nose out of his affairs and she asked why Daddy could never back her up and Daddy said, "Don't speak to your mother like that," and, "For God's sake, woman, leave it alone, can't you?" before he eventually walked out on them.

Mick would leave too, mingled irritation and guilt churning his stomach like acid. Why, oh why, he would ask, as he betook himself to some pub to drown the acid with the alcoholic variety, why does it never change? Why don't *we* ever change? Why can't we prevent ourselves from slipping into the roles of antagonist and martyr, bad son and dutiful parents? Are all families like this: breeding reluctant affection out of guilt, clinging dependence instead of instinctive fondness, forcing each member, in turn, to act either sadist or masochist, or both? No, he'd say to himself as he swilled beer down his gullet, they can't be. If they were then there wouldn't *be* any. We would all live solitary lives, coming together only to reproduce, treating each other with such superficial politeness that neither love nor hate could ever be sustained. There must exist, he'd think, motioning the barmaid to fill his glass, the possibility of love untainted by the corruptions inherent in the nature of love. He'd always believed that beyond the gloomy confines of his home – where the very walls absorbed tensions and guilts and sulks and frustrations and exuded them as vapours which chilled and dampened despite the most efficient of central-heating – there must exist the possibility of happiness.

"Last orders," the landlord would call and he'd push his glass across for a refill and purchase a clutch of cans to take out, remembering how he'd always believed in that possibility; how, once he grew up and free of his parents' dominion, he would be able to make a life for himself quite different in quality from anything he'd known. What he hadn't realised was how difficult it would be. No example, that was the problem. He could never give of himself, totally, in the way that would attract reciprocity, because he was terrified of his vulnerability being exploited. They thought of him as cold and manipulative, his friends, or else smothering, demanding; they rejected him, or drifted away from him, finding his selfishness, or his pathetic desire to impress, or his suspiciousness, or his infidelity just too hard to take.

"Time!" the landlord would shout and Mick would drain his glass, grab his cans and stumble out into the night, a warm night, scented with stocks and pinks and other aromatic flowers that favour a seaside habitat, trying to clear his head, to shake free the memories of all the friendships and the love-affairs that he'd sabotaged: all the girls he'd have died for, who'd either ignored him or laughed him to scorn or told him, kindly, to pull himself together: Julie and Jackie and Tracy and Sarah and Victoria and Penny and Jennifer and Emma and Lucy and Anne; declarations made and threats issued: "If you don't love me, then I'll . . ."; "Leave me alone," they'd said, "Push off," they'd said, "Don't be so *silly*." Even Jo, the one he'd really cared about, the one who'd represented for him the possibility of a mature relationship at last had rejected him. "You won't let me *breathe*," she'd said. "I'm being suffocated." She was doing American Studies. The second year was exchange year. From Berkeley she'd written the Dear John letter. And after that he'd dropped out of college. It was a place imbued with the essence of his love for her, poisoned now; he couldn't step across the campus without suffering contamination.

He'd pause on his way back to his room, smelling the flowers, breathing the warm night air. Too warm and too light to go home. And anyway he was restless. He'd steady himself against one of the mock Corinthian columns on the Front, holding himself rigid until a wave of nausea had passed. And then he'd turn his steps in the direction of Rosedale Road.

Elsa worked on a line drawing: a sketch of the pier at sunset, the tracery of its wrought-iron structure etched against the pale wash of an evening sky. She drew and erased, over and over again, unhappy with the perspective. In October she'd begin to learn the rules and techniques. At last. She would learn etching, lithography, printing, graphic design, sculpture, drawing and painting, and how to prevent ungovernable emotions from distracting her attention, dramas from demanding her participation. She would take up the reins of her life gently but firmly so that it realised, at last, who was in control.

The cartridge-paper was being worn away by constant erasure. She put the drawing into her portfolio and yawned widely. She would make herself a cup of cocoa, read a chapter of *The Meaning of Art* and go to bed. But as she got to her feet she heard the rattle of stones against her window and crossed over to it and pulled back Nora's flimsy bit of chintz (good enough for the staff) and saw, by the light of the lamp that illuminated the back entrance, the figure of Mick, stooping to scoop up another handful of gravel.

She raised the sash and looked out. "Ssh," she whispered. "I'll come down."

Down the back staircase, treading softly in that sleeping household. In half an hour Nora would make her final rounds and lock the doors: front, back and side, stout burglar-proof mortice locks, heavy bolts, security chains.

He *was* drunk. He lurched and giggled. "Go away," she said, "before you cause any more trouble."

"I've brought you a drink," he whispered, "to say thanks for everything."

"Tomorrow."

"Oh, come on, Elsie. Be a sport. Tomorrow's not the same."

Suddenly he seemed sober. Reasonable. She knew how it felt to have good news and no one to share it with at the time when it mattered. She could let him out later. The spare key was hanging on a hook in the kitchen.

The boards creaked. His cans of beer clanked together. He had the hiccoughs. And then his exaggerated attempts at soundless ascent made her giggle too. From the second floor came concerted snoring and one single brief but harrowing cry. Miss Johns, he thought, whispering, being visited by her nightly incubus. Mrs Crookthorne, he said, forgetting to whisper, dreaming that her purse was open and all the moths had flown out.

Still giggling, she got him into her room and shut the door behind them.

"Glasses?" he said.

"Haven't you had enough?"

"Probably, but what the hell! No glasses? Beer from a mug? Ugh! Better from the can."

Particularly when the mug said "HM Prison Dartmoor". "Catch," he said and then tilted his own can to his mouth and drank from it. But she poured hers into the prison mug which at least she knew to be clean. Squeamishness had been too long ingrained for her to change now. A desire to keep everything spotless masked, she suspected, a terror of loss of control. Only by taming the external world could one hope to suppress the unruly world of the interior. Always a tendency that way – overregulated as a child, perhaps – and worse since Nick's death: the ultimate mess, blood and brains smeared upon the highway, and herself, staring mad but a little sane/insane part of her thinking: if I could only clean him up, he'd be all right.

"Afraid you'll catch lergy?" Mick said. "I always used to think you could catch syph off cracked glasses. I read this Maigret book when I was about fourteen where Maigret goes into a bar and gets a cracked glass and wonders about contracting pox, and I thought: well, Simenon must know what he's talking about, and for ages after I used to inspect every glass in every pub I went into."

"What made you stop?"

"Too many threats, aren't there?" he said. "Herpes and AIDS and Legionnaire's disease and asbestosis and radiation sickness. You'd go bananas if you tried to guard against them all."

A wartime philosophy: if the bomb, bullet or shell had your name on it then no amount of running or hiding or protecting yourself could alter it. A rational philosophy, from one point of view: you couldn't exist, and keep your sanity, in a world which presented so many pitfalls. You had to ignore some of them. But from the other point of view, it was a philosophy that entirely exonerated one from attempting action upon the environment.

She drank from her mug. "Don't you think," she said, "that it's somehow significant, this – reprieve?"

He took a long swallow from his can, burped and frowned. "A reprieve?" he said. "A reprieve is what they give you when you're guilty but they've decided to let you off."

"I'm sorry, wrong word. Exoneration is probably what I mean. Anyway, whatever the word, I think it's significant."

"In what way?"

"By making you appreciate everything you took for granted, making you reassess your position to see in what direction, if any, you're headed . . ."

"You mean getting a proper job?" he said, but without the belligerence that usually characterised the remark. Perhaps because he was drunk. She hoped her words would penetrate through the drunkenness and lodge, to be recalled when he was sober.

"If I promise to have a think about it," he said, "will you promise to shut your gob? Here, have another can, and let's drink to my deliverance from the long arm of the law."

They drank. And then they drank to his *continuing* deliverance from the long arm of the law. And then to her artistic career. And then to whatever direction in which his future lay. She began to feel slightly woozy. He, who'd had a good head-start, swayed every time he raised his can and rose to his feet. The toasts got sillier: "To the health of Mrs Crookthorne's bank balance: an ever-rising rate of interest."

"To Mr Gentile, the Emperor of Ice-Cream."

"To the Unspeakables' expectations: a happy will-reading in Torquay."

"To Mary Reilly's Des: and twenty-three other offences to be taken into consideration."

Suddenly he shivered and sweat glistened on his forehead. "Oh God," he said. She thought he was about to be sick and dived across the room for a sort of rose-bowl ornament that stood on the window-sill. But when she got back she saw that it was not sweat but tears on his face and that his mouth was working as furiously as his father's did when he suffered emotional stress, except that Mick's was twitching and grimacing in the attempt to prevent his tears from flowing.

He failed and they flowed. Reaction. And a good thing too. He sought for a non-existent handkerchief. She handed him a box of tissues. "Cry," she said, "and, as my Dad used rather vulgarly to say, you'll pee less." She put her arm around him, stroked his hair smoothly and rhythmically while his sobs subsided. She felt enormously protective towards him.

"I'm sorry. I feel such a wally."

"Ssh," she said, soothing, rocking, crooning.

He trembled. It was well past midnight and there was no heating in the attics. "I never said it, Elsa," he said, "but – thanks. It was only you that kept me going."

The words were slurred, punctuated with yawns and hiccoughs. Exhaustion and the rhythmic movement of her hand in his hair were propelling him towards sleep. "Oh Christ," he mumbled, "I'll never get back."

It was no good pretending innocence. She must have known – when she agreed that he'd never make it and helped him to take off his shoes and tucked him into her bed and curled herself into the armchair with a blanket over her – that though she regarded him as a child to be comforted and protected, he had come to see her in terms quite different from the maternal. Her blindness to this fact was inexcusable, and unconvincing. Hadn't she been flattered? Just a little? Hadn't she found him attractive? Else why close her eyes to what had become patently obvious?

At dawn the effect of the drink had worn off. He woke and groaned and she woke too and called, as a mother would call to a child, "What's wrong?" and he croaked back at her that he had a throat like sandpaper and a raging thirst and she fetched him a glass of water just as she'd fetched Nick so many glasses of water in the night. But when he'd drunk it he reached out for her arm and pulled her towards him and started to kiss her and gather her to him with the obvious intention that she should reoccupy her bed, but not for the purposes of slumber.

If she'd thought about it she'd have been more diplomatic. She'd have thought back and perhaps realised that her behaviour could have been interpreted in a way that made his overture inevitable.

But her reaction was immediate and instinctive. She had gasped and hissed and pulled away from him and generally presented such a figure of outrage that, semi-comatose though he was and dreadfully hungover, he had little option but to put on his shoes and stumble out of the room and down the stairs, fumble for the key on the hook in the kitchen, unlock the back door and, presumably, go home.

26

Nora couldn't make head or tail of it: the key in the back door, the back door unlocked. She questioned everyone. When she got to Elsa, Elsa said, very brusquely for her, "I went out for some fresh air early this morning. I must have forgotten to lock it behind me. I'm sorry," and moved off before she could be properly chastised.

More to it than that. Nora was distinctly ill at ease. She wished not only her departed cousin in hell (he was probably there anyway, having led a most dissolute life), but also the funeral arrangements which forced her to travel to Torquay, leaving this evidently unreliable woman in charge of her bread and butter. Consequently her list of instructions and contingency plans grew daily. At intervals during the week before she was due to leave she called Elsa into her office and they went through it, item by item. Several times she had to speak to the young woman quite sharply to regain her attention. Like most staff, after all: so enthusiastic when first appointed, but give it a few weeks and their interest began to flag. She'd had every known variety working for her, every time-wasting, corner-cutting, skiving variety of the species and she'd thought she could recognise them a mile off and that Elsa wasn't one of them. Something on her mind, obviously.

"You will lock the door at midnight," Nora said, "and make sure that it *is* locked. At no time, when in charge, will you leave the premises. Do you understand?"

"Perfectly," Elsa said. "Can I go now? I was supposed to be off-duty at three."

She didn't wait for dismissal. Work, Nora thought, they didn't know the meaning of the word, remembered her probationer days: slogging, day in, day out, for a pittance, at everybody's beck and call and having to study for exams whenever there was a spare minute. Glad of the opportunity. Cleaning bedpans considered a privilege. Gone, those days. Sixteen-year-old kids now, ditching work experience: "They expected me to sweep the floor!" If only, thought Nora wistfully, and not for the first time, there was some lucrative business that could be run as a one-man band. One-woman band. She'd kick them all out tomorrow.

Elsa wrote a note and handed it to Mary to pass on to Mick. She'd written: "Can you call round to the Priory on Tuesday afternoon? Matters to discuss. Elsa." Terse. Neutral. Just in case Mary took it into her head to read the message before delivering it. She then ran like the wind down Rosedale Road and just managed to catch the number nineteen bus. She had a rendezvous and she was late. Which made a change.

They had reverted to the summer-house on the edge of the park for their meetings. It seemed to be the only spot where their privacy was assured, and now that Mick had been cleared of suspicion, its unpleasant associations had begun to fade. Curious how quickly they *did* fade, those associations. So many things she had thought that she would be unable to do, hold, look at, after Nick's death. Funny thing was, you always did, held, looked at, quite inadvertently. *Then* you remembered. But, after a shorter time than you'd ever have believed possible, you did and held and looked at and forgot to remember.

"So sad," Emlyn said. "Why so sad?" He'd been reading a newspaper and smoking a cigarette, oblivious to everything, and only started when she appeared in the gap between the trees. They'd rustled when she walked through the path between them but they rustled anyway.

He began to kiss her, framing her face between his hands, kissing her eyes closed, the tip of her nose, the curve of her earlobe and the place behind her ear that made her shiver and caused her lips to open and allow his tongue entrance to the warm moist depths of her mouth. Never a good idea to start what couldn't be finished, but they couldn't help themselves. And to think, she thought, as he pushed himself into her as though wanting alone could cause the barrier of clothes to dissolve, that once a kiss was enough.

Eventually the pitch of their frustration drove them apart. He lit another cigarette. His hands trembled. She supposed that she was responsible for the increase in his smoking. But he was a doctor and ought to know better. He was forty-six years old and ought to be able to arrange something more satisfactory than frustration at the edge of the park.

"Nora and Rodney will be away on Friday night," she said. "Can you come round?"

And lie beside me, lie, for the last time, in a bed beside me, so that we can explore every inch of each other: the smooth places and the soft, the rough and the angular, so that we can distinguish with our eyes closed the different textures that merge one into the other, so that we can play, light-heartedly, and cry out dramatically, with no one to hear except Marguerita who sleeps like the dead and who might not, anyway, recognise an orgasmic cry if she heard one.

"I'll try," he said. "I can't promise, but oh I will try."

They talked a little then, about the heavy workload that had awaited him on his return from Harrogate, about the necessity for her to inspect digs in Manchester and whether perhaps he might be able to find the time to chauffeur her on this trip. Then he asked again why she looked so sad and she debated, as she'd debated constantly with herself, whether she should tell him: about seeing Diana, about the fiasco with Mick, about her concern to know whether the sentiments he'd expressed on the beach, in passion, were to be taken seriously.

She debated again, and again decided against confiding in him. The Mick affair was none of his business and he wouldn't be able to understand her anxiety anyway: "So he made a pass at you. What's the big deal?" – uncomprehending of how that pass and her tactless rejection of it might have wrecked a relationship which, in its way, had become as important to her as the one she shared with him. More so, in its way. They had been – *copains*, as the French said – *chums*. Good chums.

As for telling him about Diana: that would scare him to death, the idea of his wife and his mistress in close proximity. Men scared easily; she knew that much, most particularly at the prospect of being found out, of having to admit to being in the wrong. Male pride seemed to depend, to a great extent, on never being exposed to *that*.

And before she had quite decided to broach the third subject of her concern, the birch leaves rustled. Startled, they both looked up. The only disadvantage of their hideaway was that the merest breeze set the frail branches swaying, creating the sort of sound that convinced you, if only momentarily, that you were under surveillance. Though perhaps, she thought, in view of certain of their activities, it was as well that approach should be so heralded.

It had never happened. And, please God, it never would. But the strain was intolerable. For him, anyway. She felt him go rigid in every muscle and then relax, tension exhaled in a great sigh. "This is shortening my life," he said. "We'll have to have some different sort of arrangement," as though this unsatisfactory state of affairs was entirely her fault. But she was beginning to realise that his peevishness, seemingly externally directed, was actually aimed inwards; that nobody could be as hard on him as he was on himself.

"Not much time left for that, is there?" she said, unsure when saying it whether she expected him to agree or disagree. So much remained implicit and therefore subject to misinterpretation; openness was no more a natural instinct for him than it was for her.

"Oh," he breathed, a long-drawn-out sigh into her cheek as his mouth edged towards hers and hers, in perfect tropism, moved to meet it. Verbally, they might hedge and fence and attempt to protect themselves from hurt, but their bodies would have no truck with such cowardly tactics and spoke true.

"OAPs' Fun Afternoon" it was called. Organised by Dorothy Dainty, who wasn't, but rather presented a somewhat formidable figure. Every Tuesday, during the season, in the gardens of the Marine Pavilion ("Indoors, if wet"), Dorothy organised her crowd of senior citizens in games and talent contests and singalongs with Eddy Horton at the Hammond organ. Multifariously talented – she sang, full-throatedly, a few ballads, a little light opera, cracked a joke or two, tap-danced or kicked her height if required – she bullied them into participating.

Sometimes, the ladies, during the course of their afternoon constitutionals, would pause and lean over the railings and look down upon the activities in the gardens: old men taking out their false teeth, old women being induced to move their friable bones and stiffened joints in a parody of dance, off-key choruses of "Show Me The Way To Go Home". Mrs Booth-Powell summed up what was a fairly general consensus of opinion: "Vulgar beyond words," she said; only Mrs Pegler's foot tapped in rhythm as she looked wistfully at those common folk off the chara, in their synthetic clothes, taking out their badly-fitting NHS dentures, clapping their red hands together, shrieking the choruses of music-hall songs in their mill-town, sea-port, slum-dweller accents. Enjoying themselves. Perhaps, when she became a resident of Grey Towers and found companionship of a more congenial nature, she would go down and join them.

Mick passed by on his way to the Priory. "Now, come on everybody!" Dorothy was bellowing. "I can't *hear* you. You'll have to do better than that. Last week we had a crowd in from Rochdale and they phoned up from Lytham St Anne's to ask what all the row was about. You don't want to be beaten by Rochdale, do you? Come on, give it all you've got!"

Obediently they threw back their heads and made loud quavery noises: "You put your left leg in, you put your left leg out. You put your left leg in . . ." A couple of game old birds, up on the stage, shook it all about. One of them had gone a very worrying shade of purple in the face and was due, that night, after disembarking from the charabanc, to suffer a mild stroke.

". . . you do the Hokey-Cokey and you turn around, and that's what it's all about, oy!"

Mick lingered, leaning over the rail. Old Dorothy, he thought, watching her curls bobbing as she led them in "She'll Be Coming Round The Mountain", Old Dorothy, doyenne of the providers of good clean family fun. Last year he and some of the lads off the fairground had stood barracking her turn. She'd been singing "Once I Had A Secret Love", in shrill soprano. When she'd finished and handed over to Eddy for his medley on the organ she'd come up the steps and confronted them. "Piss off, you!" she'd hissed. Close up you could see the crow's feet that even make-up plastered on like Polyfilla couldn't conceal. The fairground lads had backed off, jeering "Old cow!", while he'd marvelled at how artifice and subtle lighting and the requisite amount of distance could lend such enchantment.

Corruption everywhere. Appearances that misled. How were you to know? He turned his steps, reluctantly, in the direction of Rosedale Road, had a gander in the Job Centre on the way, but there wasn't anything this late in the season. Couple more days – and he'd pack his bag and hitch down to London. He had no close friends, but a great many acquaintances, some of whom lived in London and had floors where he could doss down while he looked for work. He'd have gone weeks ago, had it not been for the police business. The solicitor had reported no definite resolution to the affair: the charge deferred might yet be brought. Well they'd have to find him first because he was pissing off. No reason to stay. No reason at all.

His pace slowed as he approached the Priory. Better to have kept away rather than having to listen to her raking up the events of the other night, going on and on, as was her wont, worrying everything to death. "I was pissed," he'd say, to avoid the worst embarrassment, to prevent her from realising that he'd meant to do what he did, "I was pissed." Which was the truth. But not all of it.

She was in the kitchen, dipping the cutlery in a solution of tarnish-remover, rinsing it and buffing it on a soft cloth. The everyday cutlery was stainless steel of an inferior sort; the silver had been dug out and was being cleaned because Nora, after her return from Torquay, was planning a gourmet evening. It was to be her little treat, or bribe, for the guests, to wipe from their minds the dreadful memory of the Golding episode. It would coincide with the installation of the new lift. Everyone was looking forward to the dinner – except Mrs Randall, of course – who was expected to produce it.

The silver solution was magic. You dipped the tarnished forks into it and, in a matter of moments, the stains vanished. Both of them watched, fascinated, then he said, "So what's with the cryptic message?" and, finding his sunglasses in his pocket, rather belatedly put them on.

Nothing more disconcerting, she thought, in a fraught

situation, than having to enter into dialogue with a concealed expression; she had realised after her meeting with Diana just how much information is communicated by the eyes, the mouth itself being a more crudely obvious but still infinitely inferior instrument.

So, deprived of feedback, she talked without looking at him, busying herself with the kettle and the teapot. "Have you eaten?" she asked ferociously, quite prepared to be told that food had not passed his lips since his parents went home. But he nodded. His parents, realising that the solicitor's bill might not be so hefty after all, had sent him a cheque. "You can stick your money," he'd told them so often, but they continued to send it and he continued to spend it. Pieces of silver; a forlorn attempt at compensation for the botch-up they'd made of parenthood and, as such, he felt entitled to accept whatever bribes came his way.

"About the other night," she hazarded, trying to control the blush that made a nonsense of her matter-of-fact, let's-be-adult-about-this tone. "I wouldn't want you to go away with the wrong impression."

"No sweat," he said, head bent over his lighter flame. He exhaled a plume of smoke. Shades obscured his eyes, smoke now shrouded the rest of his face. "I was pissed," he said.

No. Not when the overture was made. Concealment notwithstanding, she could tell that that was what he wanted her to believe, but she refused to fall in with the deception. There had been enough self-deception involved in his short career – fantasies, tall stories, belief that anything worth having could be won without effort – and to collude with him for the sake of salvaging his pride would be doing him no favours. "Well, that's as maybe," she said. "But what I wanted to explain was me, not you. I wouldn't want you," she repeated, "to get the wrong impression . . ."

"But you're old enough to be my mother. Or you just don't fancy me. Why should you? Never apologise, never explain, as somebody said. Who was it said that?"

She didn't know, and thought it one of the dumbest quotations she'd ever heard; a recipe for a lifetime of bewilderment.

"Yes," she said, "the age difference makes that sort of relationship – well, unlikely . . . But that's only one facet of it.

What you may not have understood is me, my personal hang-ups . . ."

Scarred, she said, by her son's death, her husband's desertion; women who bore those sort of scars often found that their interest in – that subject had faded. And so, the fact that she had rejected him was no reflection on him personally. "I'm too old for you," she said, "and too – frozen up for contemplating anything like that for ages yet, if ever again. I need to recover. That's why I came here, to recuperate. I'm just not ready for the sort of commitment that comes with a sexual relationship. Oh, it might not mean commitment for you, or anyone else your age, but for me it would – and I couldn't cope with it. I need to be able to sort my life out without creating any more complications. Do you understand?"

Convincing? His look, what there was of it to see, was one of irritation at being obliged to endure this tedium. Hers was the analytical generation: endless self-examination in college rooms over glasses of wine or cups of cocoa, amateur psychologists all; whereas he and his contemporaries, aware of the futility of such absorption, just went ahead and did, without either soul-searching beforehand or post-mortem afterwards.

Was it right, she wondered, what she was doing? Did it matter that much to him that she needed to lie to protect his pride from hurt? One minute he cried like a child in her arms, the next he shrugged his shoulders and looked at her with amused condescension.

"No sweat," he said. "Why should we fall out over it? Anyway," he said, "I'll be going down to London, I think, next week. Look for a job."

"I'll miss you."

And she would. Terribly.

"Oh," she said, suddenly remembering offers made and subsequently forgotten, "about Friday – " Oh God, she'd talked of a party, hadn't she, and, oh God, she'd asked Emlyn to come round, hadn't she? Would it be possible, with precise – or lucky – timing, to honour both those promises?

"Hell," he said, "I'd forgotten all about it. I've arranged to take the car over to Wigan on Friday evening. There's a chap who answered my advert who's interested in buying it. He hasn't any transport so I'll have to take it to him, and if he decides to have it, I'll have to train or hitch back. Look, I am sorry, if you'd arranged anything. I just didn't think you would have done after . . ."

Diplomacy or embarrassment caused the sentence to peter out. "You don't rate it very highly, our friendship," she said, "do you, if you think I'd be so dog-in-the-manger?"

He raised the sunglasses so that they rested on the top of his head, just as Diana's had done before she had entered into conversation. Perhaps both of them needed anonymity in order to operate effectively. But sometimes a gamble could be taken, the personal and unconcealed statement made: "I told you," he said, "I really appreciate the way you've stood by me these last weeks. You've never given me any shit. I *do* rate it highly, Elsa, honest."

Everybody gave everybody shit, she told herself in mitigation. Most people understood that and could cope with it. And she was not responsible for the fact that he was an exception.

27

How slowly Mr Gentile ate! But never so slowly, she was certain, as on Friday evening when each mouthful seemed to be subject to endless mastication before being assisted down his gullet with a sip of water. Between mouthfuls he smacked his lips and fiddled among his gold fillings with a toothpick. She wanted to pick up his fork and push food into his mouth, pinch his nostrils together and force him to swallow, regularly and rhythmically, until every morsel was gone, and then hustle him out of the Lancaster Room, pour coffee down his throat and order him up to bed.

In the kitchen Nellie Macpherson consulted her bunion which, it seemed, when prone to twingeing, heralded electrical storms. Marguerita and Rosa, made irritable by this atmospheric tension, squabbled with each other about whose turn it was to serve supper. Elsa settled the dispute by telling them to share the duty. If only one of them did it, then the other might go out and there was no telling precisely when she might return and who she might bump into.

Marguerita launched into a tirade conducted in Catalan Spanish while Rosa giggled maliciously (actually it had been her turn) and responded with a flood of Portuguese. Mrs Randall said, "Do shut up, the pair of you," and Elsa, for the first time ever, imposed the authority that had been invested in her and told them to control themselves and get on with the washing-up. And, after gaping at her in astonishment, nice quiet Elsa suddenly acting boss, they did.

"After ten," she'd told Emlyn. "They're usually in bed by then." But at this rate, she thought, they wouldn't be in bed, neither the residents nor she and Emlyn, before dawn.

"Nervy," Mrs Randall observed, as she handed Elsa her

supper and noticed her restlessness. "You want an iron tonic."

"She wants something else," murmured Mary Reilly who had waited expectantly all these months for a man to materialise in Elsa's life and had been disappointed. Not natural, to live celibate for so long. No wonder she was twitchy. They were a pain in the arse, men, gave you no end of grief and aggravation, but who could manage to get through the night without a little cuddle?

"See ya in the morning, love," she called from the back door, then suddenly remembered an anecdote concerning Des and a consignment of cloth that had fallen off the back of a lorry: "Did I tell you? Good quality, he reckoned. Mohair. Pal of his give it him. Another mate, Joe, knows this tailor, Morry, that'll make it up for him into a suit, cheap. Well, he can do with a suit, Des. His other – you can see your face in it. Well, this Morry, he makes it up and he brings it back and puts it on and it's bright bleedin' purple! You never saw such a sight in all your life! Seems this cloth it was for pop stars' suits or summat and they're all colour-blind, Joe and Des and even Morry. Laugh, I could have cried!"

But Mary laughed. Interminably. Then she coughed until she choked and had to clear her tubes with a cigarette. Elsa clenched her fists until her fingernails left indentations in the flesh of her palms. In the distance she heard a faint rumble of thunder.

"Now, mind you lock all the doors," Mary cautioned, in parody of Nora. Then she said, "I'd 'ave orgy if I were you, love, while I 'ad the chance."

Peggy Johns bit the sheet and held her breath and counted in her head between the lightning flash and the clap of thunder; the shorter the interval, she had been told, the closer the eye of the storm, and the intervals were getting progressively shorter. At the point when the crashing seemed to come from directly overhead she had to smother her cries of terror in the eiderdown. "Mother," she sobbed, "Mother," but Mother had died when Peggy was ten and could offer no solace.

Most of them, however, sedated with Mogadon, slept through

it. Mrs Booth-Powell dreamed that she was in the Anderson shelter with Basil and there was a raid on. "Basil," she said, "please don't breathe so noisily." Exertion had always resulted in heavy breathing – some sort of adenoidal problem not corrected in youth. In the dream he made more noise than the falling bombs. Mrs Crookthorne awoke, turned over and slept again to dream that she was dancing naked in a field full of daisies and God looked down and smiled at her. Colonel Pritchard, awake and reconciled to it, switched on his light and picked up his book to read eye-witness accounts of the Battle of the Somme, the thunderstorm to end all thunderstorms.

Every time the lightning flashed, Elsa, like Miss Johns, held her breath and only released it after the subsequent thunderclap. But, unlike Miss Johns, when she bit the sheet it wasn't from terror, but to curtail her cries of sexual ecstasy.

Afterwards, as it was dying down, they got out of bed and opened the curtains and watched the sheet-lightning flashing on and off like neon over the sea, and the occasional jagged fork hurtling downwards into the sea itself. They watched as though it was a show put on specifically for their delectation, the light coming and going, illuminating their nakedness to each other and then plunging it back into darkness.

"Magnificent," he said, unable to understand her fear. There were some natures like that, she knew; they thrived on excitement. Quiet lives destroyed them, drained their vitality. Perhaps it was no accident that he had chosen as wife a woman whose actions were unpredictable. Yet another challenge, perhaps; an extension of the series of challenges into which his life had been arranged. He talked when, physically sated, they lay loosely in each other's embrace; talked of his past, describing to her the lonely misfit boy that he had been, with nothing but a pushing mother and a belief in his own abilities to sustain him, described the drab philistine joylessness of his background, the realisation, early on, that he must move up and on or wither like a plant condemned to a dustbowl. "You can't imagine," he said, "how it feels to be alienated for as far back as you can remember, never, ever, to feel as though you belong. I think I clung on to that adolescent fantasy about being a changeling until I was in my twenties and my mother died." His accent had grown progressively more Welsh as he talked. She stroked him: his smooth shoulder, the hair, dark still, that curled on his chest, the hair, drained of its pigment, that fell across his forehead, hoping to soothe his painful memories as he had soothed her fears.

"And then what happened?" she murmured, prompting him. "After your mother died?"

He sighed. He sighed a great deal, she had noticed, for one reason or another. "I think I learned a little about the nature of love," he said. "I began to realise that all the sacrifices she'd made for me, all the pressure she'd put upon me – which I'd so resented at the time – was not necessarily for selfish reasons but because she knew as well as I did that I'd never be happy unless I found a better place for myself. And she was terrified in case I blew it."

"We can't do right for doing wrong," she said, "mothers."

He pressed his lips against her forehead as if to kiss away the hurt of the memory. "You never had the chance, did you?" he said. "You can have no reason for self-reproach."

Not understanding, how could he, that the reasons for self-reproach started as soon as conception had been established: I smoked, or I drank, or I didn't want it, or I was so sick that it's a miracle I didn't dislodge it?

"Anyway," he said. "I'm boring you."

"No, you're not. I'm interested." She traced his face as he traced hers, as blind persons familiarised themselves with the features they could never see.

And she *was* interested. It had happened, despite her certainty that distance could be maintained. Once you became interested, you forfeited the distance that kept you safe. From him. Even from yourself.

"She must have been so proud of you, your mother," she said. He had after all done everything that could make a mother proud: worked hard, gained status, made money, married well.

"I suppose she was."

The graduation photograph, the exam results, cut from the newspaper and preserved at the bottom of the box where she kept their birth certificates, the notice of his fellowship, a photograph that he had sent her of himself and Diana at a

BMA do. All she had lacked was wedding souvenirs – they had married, on impulse almost, in a registry office, without entourage or celebration, merely calling upon two propinquitous acquaintances to act as witnesses. It was a great shame, his mother had felt, but she'd understood. The idea of his side of the family mingling with hers at some fashionable church, some fancy reception, was unthinkable.

"I'm sure she was," he said, "but I never gave her much chance." Infrequent visits made alone. (Diana, who had come to loathe her father for reasons that seemed different but which were actually the same, never expressed the desire to accompany him. Families were a blight, in her opinion, once escaped from, best forgotten.) "Why don't you ever bring her, your wife?" his mother had asked, but not often. She knew why, and she knew that it was she who had made him a snob and that was why he would never forgive her. She, it was, who had been responsible, initially, for sowing the seed for that schizophrenic splitting between the way he felt and the way he behaved. He thought of her when, in the depths of winter, he advised some impecunious old age pensioner to live in one room until the coming of the better weather, thereby saving on fuel costs and guarding against the constant threat of hypothermia; he thought of her when he next visited Priory Lodge, for which he collected extra fees, to inspect rich women's minor complaints, saw the minks and the musquashes and the sealskins hanging outside their wardrobe doors; thought of her when he drove his expensive car and ate his expensive meals cooked by his expensive housekeeper and rooted out his wife's bottles of drink, the price of which would have paid several old age pensioners' fuel bills. He thought of her constantly, in fact, and could not shift the guilt attendant upon the knowledge that never once had he tried to use his talents in the cause of redress of the inequality that horrified him.

She had neutered him, his mother, led him to betray his class, to defect from the weak to the strong, and he'd thought, for that, he couldn't forgive her. But after her death he'd begun to understand her motivation and, as they said, you couldn't understand without forgiving too.

Which was what all those who questioned his determination to stay married to Diana were unable to grasp.

Diana, he thought, as he turned towards his mistress, stroking her limbs as though sculpting them. Diana, be happy. If not for your own sake, then for mine. She'd been dry now for longer than ever before; there was talk of an exhibition of her photographs in a West End gallery. If he could keep her on an even keel, then, if it was a success, that would encourage her to stay on the wagon and she would be able to concentrate upon her hobby, her art, whichever it was, with, possibly – and for the first time – concrete results. Keeping her on an even keel depended in part upon constructing convincing alibis. He hoped they were good enough.

His mistress's limbs were cool and smooth and soft. He had made them so with his caresses. "What about you?" he said. "Tell me about you."

She started to talk: about the prim, rather elderly child she'd been, apple of Daddy's eye (taking her little-girl drawings to show off to his colleagues at work, parading her before them in her Sunday best), never a foot wrong until flattery drew her towards Rob's bed . . . But all the time she was talking he was planting butterfly kisses, on her breasts, her belly, in the crease of her thigh and down and down until they were no longer butterfly kisses but rather delicate tracings with lips and tongue of the convolutions of her inner self. And then his tongue became more urgent, opening her and opening her to fit him, releasing her honeyed juices, and she could no longer speak but felt for him, drawing him upwards, to fill the space he had created, and it almost felt that there was too much of him, that he would hurt her. But he didn't. His penetration was as smooth and fluent as ever it had been; the more he grew, so did she to accommodate him, and when they were joined and could go no closer, he motioned her to look down at where he was buried deep in her, the point at which their separateness ceased to be and she did and was overwhelmed anew with wonder that two people could become one. It was as miraculous in its way as the psychological union that had occurred when they finally acknowledged each other's irreplaceability.

She said, "Emlyn," as they began to move together in the rhythm that had come so effortlessly from the very beginning, and he said, "Elsa," but then there were footsteps in the corridor and a tap at the door and her heart-beat stuttered and he experienced such rapid detumescence that they were no longer joined and she thought, whoever can it be, it's the middle of the night?

But it was scarcely eleven o'clock. Living in an old people's home, where the residents retired early, gave one a false impression of the timescale operating in the outside world. For some, she realised, the night had barely begun.

Again there came the knock and this time her name was called, low and urgently. It never occurred to her to lie still and offer, when later called to account, the explanation of deep sleep. Instead she slid from beneath the weight of her lover's body, reached for her dressing-gown and called to him that she was coming.

She clambered out of bed and crossed the room. She was aware of Emlyn's face: a white blur of alarm. She fumbled for the key, found it, unlocked the door, stepped out into the corridor and closed it behind her.

She stepped right into him. Mick. He had switched on the corridor light. She was about to ask him how he'd got in when she remembered that, having left the back door unlocked for Emlyn, she'd forgotten to lock it behind him; incredible though that seemed, after Nora's interminable warnings.

Hoist, higher than ever before, with her own petard, she confronted him. He was drenched, his hair slicked to his head, his moustache drooping like a little drowned animal.

"You weren't asleep, were you?" he asked, rhetorically. "Only you said to come round if I could make it. I tried the back door and it wasn't locked so I presumed you'd left it open for me."

"You sold the car then?" she said. Her throat was so dry that the words emerged in a croak. She tried to edge him away from her door.

"Oh yeah. I thought: me luck's changed at last, and then I get back and find this in the letter-box!" He dug into his pocket and produced an official-looking envelope.

"What is it?"

"It's a summons, that's what it is. For being drunk and disorderly on the morning of June 25th. Bastards! I've to appear in court on the 31st. Petty bastards! Look," he said, shaking the rain from his face, "I could murder a cup of coffee. It's OK, I don't expect you to produce the birthday feast. Just a coffee would be terrific."

She saw a chance, of sorts. He'd moved towards her door, but she led him away from it, cautioning him to silence as they tiptoed down the stairs, as he whispered, "What's up? Why are we going downstairs?"

For it had been her custom to keep a jar of coffee in her room and to boil a kettle in the pantry along the corridor. Many cups of coffee they'd shared during the summer, while he prowled about admiring himself in the piece of tarnished mirror propped on the mantelshelf, poking in her portfolio, extracting drawings from it, making mock of her artistic efforts.

"I've run out of coffee," she said when they were safely down in the kitchen. She filled the kettle and took two mugs from their hooks while he rubbed at his streaming hair with a tea-towel. "Christ," he said, "you're trembling like mad! What's wrong?"

"You woke me from a nightmare." The lies, once embarked upon, came easily.

She fixed her gaze on the kettle and then, remembering how watched pots never boil, looked away from it. All her concentration was focused, all her will brought to bear upon getting the coffee down him and then getting him the hell out.

"Bastards!" he said again. "I was leaving on Monday too."

"Well, so you can," she said, "as long as you're back for the 31st."

"With this hanging over my head? What's the point? And if I get a job, what do I say: please can I have some time off as I have to appear in court? Jesus, you wouldn't think they'd be so petty!"

She gave him his coffee and held out her hand for the letter. The document was couched in the usual incomprehensible legalese, saying very little in a great many words.

"Tomorrow you'll have to get in touch with your solicitor. I mean Monday." Tomorrow was Saturday. She wondered fleetingly what happened to those who had the misfortune to be arrested on Friday night. Did they have to wait until Monday for legal advice, or were solicitors like doctors, obliged to make themselves available during antisocial hours? And the hour must now be getting very antisocial. Diana, waiting at home. Emlyn, trapped on the third floor. She tried to force Mick, telepathically, to down his coffee.

But instead he started to roll a cigarette and requested another cup.

She began to yawn, artificially at first, and then, as her yawning reflexes were activated, quite genuinely. The thunder had died away and the wind was getting up. She heard it moaning in the chimney; the workmen (finished at last, to Nora's general dissatisfaction) had replaced a cowl but replaced it wrongly so that now the wind whistled and the chimney smoked. "Do you think," she said, "that we could postpone all this till tomorrow? I'm absolutely jiggered."

"The burden of authority," he said sneeringly. "You'll never make a boss, Elsie. Nora does this every day and you never see her yawning. Perish the thought! I'll bugger off then, let you get back to bed."

But he didn't. Not until he'd drained his cup and finished his cigarette. The wind, fiercer now, was whirling in the chimney, whistling along the path at the side of the house. She hated the noise it made almost more than she hated the sound of the thunder.

She got to her feet and crossed the kitchen and grasped the door handle. "Come round tomorrow," she said. "We'll discuss it then."

He lifted his jacket from the back of the chair. It was as wet as when he'd taken it off. Slowly, ensuring that this fact was not lost on her, he donned it and zipped it and then slouched towards her, casting glances from beneath long-lashed eyelids that might even have melted the heart of Nora, had she been the one holding the door open.

Not holding it securely enough. A sudden gust of wind tore it from her grasp and slammed it shut so that the sound reverberated round the kitchen, and probably through the whole house. "Wow!" he said admiringly, opening it again and sticking his head out into the gale. "What a night! When shall we three meet again . . ."

"Two," she said, "two," as he turned to say goodbye, and then she saw that he was no longer looking at her but over her shoulder, that his eyebrows had shot up to meet his drenched cow-lick above widening eyes and, if it hadn't been that such things only existed in the novelist's imagination, that his jaw had dropped. She felt the hair rise at the back of her neck and her heart beating in her throat, and she knew, in that instant, that it had been foolishly over-optimistic to hope that she would be lucky enough to get away with it.

He had mistaken the wind's slamming of the door for her closing it after Mick. He had dressed after she'd left him and crept downstairs, his shoes in his hand, like a character out of a French farce, and lurked in the hall, straining to ascertain whether it was safe to make his escape. He had puffed at his cigarette and glanced every few minutes at the luminous dial of his watch. And in a frenzy of impatience – for Diana's credulity would now be severely strained by even the cleverest of excuses to explain his lateness – he had mistimed his entry by a mere few seconds.

They remained frozen in tableau for a moment that extended itself into an infinity: Mick with his mouth open, Emlyn with his shoes in his hand, Elsa, feeling, ridiculously, that someone might enter from the shadows, calling, "Cut!" Real life. Farcical. Not funny. Mick's gaze gradually shifted until he was looking at her. "You bloody hypocrite," he said. He said it so softly that had she not been close enough to read his lips she might not have heard. No mistaking, though, the justified outrage that prompted him to say it.

28

"No, love," Mary said. "Not seen him since – oh, would it be Friday morning? I know he was going to take his car to somebody in Wigan later on. Did you want him for summat? Perhaps he's gone to visit his mam and dad before he goes down to London."

"He can't go down to London yet, he's to appear in court on the 31st."

"No!" said Mary, displaying the sort of incredulity that, if her accounts of wrongful arrests and malicious prosecutions and miscarriages of justice were true, was quite misplaced. "They're not doing him for that old lady's whatsit, are they?"

"No. Drunk and disorderly."

"Oh, that," she said, and waved her hand dismissively. Drunk and disorderly was neither nowt nor summat; an occupational hazard for anyone who stepped inside a pub. She, herself, had been done for that more than once.

"It may seem trivial but it means that he'll have a criminal record," Elsa said. "It means that he'll have even more trouble getting a job."

"Oh aye," Mary said. "Drunk and disorderly. Nobody'll take him on with a record like that. They'll be wondering when he's due to pull off the next big bullion job. Don't talk so wet!"

There were times when Mary was touchy concerning references to criminal activity. "*You* put your foot in it," Mrs Randall said later. "That Des – she was telling me – they've been questioning him about some robbery that took place in Nottingham when he was there. That lodging-house!" she said. "Police never away from it. She's a nice respectable woman too, owns it. We were on munitions together, her and I. Mind you," she said, "give a dog a bad name . . ."

Her opinion of British justice, like Elsa's opinion of it and Nellie Macpherson's and that of several others had changed during the last few weeks. Previously they hadn't realised how difficult it might be to establish one's innocence beyond doubt, how unlikely it was that one's movements should be recalled in precise enough detail to furnish an alibi.

Still, Mary's Des was undoubtedly a villain, whereas that Mick was merely a silly young lad who certainly didn't deserve to be stigmatised for all his days because of an act of youthful folly.

"I'm worried that he might have done a bunk," Elsa said. "I'm worried that he might not turn up for the case."

"Nay," said Mrs Randall. "He's got more sense than that. He'll be back."

But she didn't have much time to spare for reassurance. She was too involved in preparation for the gourmet night scheduled for Wednesday. Twice the menu had been altered when Nora discovered the price of certain delicacies, twice Muriel Selby had had to retype and reduplicate the fancy cards that were to grace the occasion – and they were now awaiting a message from a fishmonger acquaintance of Nora's concerning the market price of whitebait. Muriel, having crossed out *moules marinière* and *caneton à l'orange*, was poised to substitute *boeuf bourguignon* for *tournedos Rossini* (depending upon a consignment of fillet steaks that might or might not be due to fall off the back of a lorry and into the van belonging to a butcher acquaintance of Nora's), and hoped that it wouldn't be necessary as she wasn't too sure of the spelling.

Elsa was sent on a tour of the wine shops and supermarkets, with instructions to compare prices before purchase. She had been tempted to falsify them out of sheer contrariness but this plan was foiled owing to Nora's insistence that Rodney should accompany her: he always did the weekly Tuesday shop, after all.

Neither of them was keen on the idea. Embarrassment gripped their tongues. As he'd stood holding the car door open for her a seagull, swooping low, had deposited its bodily waste all over the gleaming nearside wing. Completely at a loss to produce any other sort of small-talk, she commented upon this as he drove slowly towards the centre of the town.

"Funny, isn't it, how bird crap on dark surfaces is always white, yet when it's on light surfaces it shows up dark?"

She shouldn't have said crap; the use of the word offended him. She could tell by the colour rising duskily to his cheek and a little quiver at the side of his mouth. But at least words had been spoken, the possibilities for conversation established. He moistened his lips and, never taking his eyes off the road ahead of him for the merest instant, said, "What's happening with Michael, then? I believe they've let him off?"

"Yes. I think he's going down to London to look for a job."

She gazed through the side window as they drove down Station Road, up the Parade, and turned towards the precinct car park, straining her eyes to catch sight of a dark head with a brutal haircut, a golden earring, a brief moustache, a jacket of distressed denim, a pair of Ray-Ban shades. All these there were, in abundance, but never the right combination, however much her imagination attempted to make it so.

An ache like toothache pervaded every nerve. The image of his face: hurt, outraged, betrayed, constantly invaded her mind's eye. She would have given anything to undo the doings of Friday night. If only . . .

"If only," she had cried after Nick's death, "I had instilled into him better road sense; I had been paying attention; I'd been a proper mother. If only . . ."

". . . we didn't live in the twentieth century, the combustion engine had never been invented," the psychiatrist to whom they'd sent her had replied. He had hoped to convince her that circumstances alone were to blame for what had happened. Fashionable, these days, to abdicate personal responsibility by blaming any and every external factor: the times, one's upbringing, drink, drugs, unemployment. But buck-passing was, ultimately, a futile activity; in a random universe one had to have some certainty, if it was only the knowledge of one's own accountability.

"Seemed a bit of a rum 'un," Rodney Speakman said, presumably apropos Mick. "We get all sorts, you know, coming for jobs. You never can tell who you're taking on."

"Is that a fact?"

It had been an attempt, she realised with amazement, to allow her into his confidence, to imply that she was no longer considered to be within the category of dubious employees, but had perhaps achieved the status of faithful retainer. He drove up the ramp of the car park and brought the car to a halt. She froze out what was evidently intended to be some sort of attempt at alliance, at persuading her to forget what had gone before. His lip quivered. He reached down to pull on the handbrake and, at the same time, she reached down to pick up her shopping bag and their hands touched and his recoiled as though having made contact with a live wire.

"We don't have to troop round the shops together," she said, moving away from him to avoid any other such accidental contact. "It'll take for ever. If you do Tesco and Sainsbury's, I'll do Safeways and Peter Dominic."

"But . . ." he said.

"We don't have to *say*, do we?"

The idea had been that he would keep an eye on her. And vice versa. That way no opportunity for fiddling could occur. Without prompting, the notion of rebellion would not have entered his head, but once planted, it was obvious from his flush of excitement that the idea appealed. He walked off with his plastic carrier bag in the direction of the supermarket and Elsa watching him go, was sure that she could detect a certain jauntiness in his step.

"What!" Nora said, when they got back with the wine. She always acted outraged as though a world conspiracy existed to contrive at her financial ruin. She was thoroughly out of sorts, what with that damned new lift costing a fortune and now this meal proving to be more expensive than she'd originally envisaged. A bad idea, she realised now. She'd have done better sending them off on a coach to see the Blackpool Illuminations (though that was tricky, what with some of them needing the toilet every five minutes). Rich food, on the other hand, would upset their digestions. They'd be belching and farting and requesting milk of magnesia for the rest of the week. And anything not nailed down Crookthorne would have wrapped in a paper serviette before you could say knife and up to her room to be eaten at a later date. Marguerita and

Rosa had already reported crumbs all over the floor. Crumbs attracted mice. As if the woodworm weren't bad enough; she'd had a quote from Rentokil that had almost turned her white. Mrs Cuthbert-Carew had started food-hoarding just before she died; it was usually an early symptom of senile decay. But Mrs Cuthbert-Carew had had licence that Mrs Crookthorne would not be allowed. She knew, by virtue of Rodney's – attention to detail, she preferred to call it, rather than snooping – the state of Mrs Crookthorne's financial health to the last digit and it wasn't robust enough for her to be granted any sort of latitude.

Muriel Selby sat with her hands poised above the typewriter keyboard, awaiting final instructions. She had a French/English dictionary at her elbow that Hilda had borrowed from school, but a brief inspection had revealed a dearth of culinary words and phrases. Perhaps the old ladies and gentlemen would be none the wiser, but Mrs Pegler and Mrs Pendennis had stayed in some very grand hotels and Colonel Pritchard had an army background and Mrs Booth-Powell's husband had been a JP and Mrs Grey was very cultured . . . She hoped fervently that the fillet steaks would come through: Rossini was no problem. Just like the composer. Hilda said, "It *is* the composer, you silly billy, it was named after him. Honestly!" There were times when Hilda could be a bit too bumptious and know-all.

> Mrs Nora Speakman, of Priory Lodge, invites her guests to partake of dinner on Wednesday, August 8th, 1984, at seven thirty p.m. The menu will consist of: Melon Glacé, Turtle Soup, Fried Whitebait, Tournedos Rossini with duchesse potatoes, broccoli, baby carrots and asparagus tips, Bombe Surprise à la Priory Lodge, Selection from the Cheese Board, Coffee and Mints. Black tie will be worn.

Muriel typed it and added an artistic curlicue or two around the edges of it. Hilda Know-all Leggat wasn't the only one who had talent in that direction. Then she carried a copy through to the kitchen where Mrs Randall said, "Bombe Surprise? Some surprise. She's told me to use that tinned fruit salad instead of raspberries."

Mr Gentile, who had never participated in any form of English social life, read the invitation and obediently fished in a drawer and unearthed a black tie and wore it with his grey suit and white nylon drip-dry shirt through which you could see the outline of his interlock vest.

She hadn't put "Medals will be worn", Colonel Pritchard thought wistfully. His dinner-jacket was going green but he kept his medals polished. He wondered if he should wear them. It wasn't the done thing to be proud these days. The young bought campaign medals out of junk shops and wore them as jewellery; louts purchased ex-army uniform and flaunted it on the streets: German trenchcoats, RAF flying-jackets, battle fatigues, puttees . . . He opened the box and breathed on his jewels: the Military Cross, the Burma Star, the '39–45 lot, and polished them with a soft cloth and then he put them back into the drawer. What would they mean to a lot of old women, a couple of foreigners and a milksop mother's boy who'd never even done National Service?

Black tie meant long frock. Didn't it? Or, at least, formal frock. Peggy Johns opened her wardrobe door and agonised. Cotton prints with peter pan collars and piqué cuffs she had galore, wool jersey dresses for the winter, a couple of tweed suits, but nothing approaching formal evening-wear. She could either pin a brooch on to one of the wool jerseys or else buy a new dress. But the idea of enduring the patronising attentions of a saleslady made her shrivel inside. It would have to be the jersey dress and a brooch.

Mrs Pegler, however (same measurements as Miss Johns, same dress size), was spoilt for choice. Her wardrobe was crammed with evening-frocks, stoles, fur capes, Dorothy bags, gold kid sandals. She spent a most enjoyable afternoon trying them all on. It wasn't often she got the chance to dress up, but now she was bound for Grey Towers it might happen more often. She settled for her dark-blue silk shantung. French designer it was. Exclusive. And to go with it the diamond and sapphire pendant that Dad had bought her for their thirtieth anniversary. He'd come through again last week, Dad. "Good girl," he'd said. "You done right." He was referring to her decision to move. She had somehow expected that his grammar would have improved, over on the other side, but it hadn't.

Mrs Crookthorne dug out the eau-de-nil crêpe-de-chine that she used to wear when she accompanied Bertie to the Masonic Ladies' Nights. She salivated when she saw the menu. Mints, it said. Not everyone liked mints, they gave you heartburn. And crackers with the cheese! They couldn't restrict you in the way of crackers. There would be good pickings to be had tonight.

Miss Vyner screwed up her eyes and clenched her jaw and concentrated all her will upon raising herself from her chair. It had been a mistake to sit down upon it. It and any other deep chair or sofa. She must content herself with perching from now on. Bed wasn't so bad; she could roll out of bed and on to the floor, the mattress being low and the carpet soft, but chairs and sofas must definitely become things of the past. Gourmet dinners! she thought, opening her wardrobe door and pulling out from the back of it her evening-frock which had seen service with the Soroptimists and the Business and Professional Women over more years than she cared to remember. Gourmet dinners! They'd end up paying for it one way or the other.

Next-door Mrs Booth-Powell shed one of her very infrequent tears as she contemplated black velvet and rust taffeta and gold brocade. When Basil had been a JP there had been such a social life: Golf Club dinners and Rotary dinners and the Inner Wheel and the Conservative Association and the Old Boys and the Sailing Club and the Law Society. How it had dwindled. She was lucky if she had an invitation to dine out more than three or four times a year these days – and that was only with her son and his wife who squabbled all the time regardless of where they were, thus ruining any prospect of enjoyment. She wondered who had arranged it so that old men died before old ladies, since it was plainly quite the wrong sequence of events: a man, however old and doddery, kept his social life while a woman, partnerless, was quietly forgotten.

Mrs Pendennis, however, had no intention of attending the dinner partnerless. A quiet word with Mrs Speakman concerning extra payment and she had arranged for her fiancé to escort her. "Show me your dinner-suit," she had commanded him, and he had produced the elderly greenish sort of garment that she'd expected. "Put it away," she'd said in the same sort of tone that Miss Vyner had employed when berating the flasher in the park, and then she'd taken him to Moss Bros where they'd hired a modern one. A well-fitting, stylish dinner-jacket could make the most unprepossessing of men look presentable. Edward Green admired himself mournfully. He wasn't sure whether he was going to be able to cope. His bedroom was being turned into a tart's boudoir and his lavatory paper matched his bathroom suite and she'd thrown away his carpet-slippers and bought him leather mules which made him trip up, and all his bits and pieces seemed to be disappearing, bit by bit, piece by piece. The first Mrs Green had not been a beauty but at least he'd had comfortable slippers and good serviceable Bronco in the bathroom.

It was with these rather rueful thoughts that Edward Green joined Colonel Pritchard and Mr Gentile in the hall. "Where's Golding?" Colonel Pritchard wondered out loud and then remembered and blushed. Funnily enough, considering that he'd thought of Golding as being nothing but a pest, he missed him. Of course that was often the way. Maud's memory had been cherished a good deal more fondly than ever had Maud in the flesh.

A half-decent sherry was being circulated by Marguerita in black with a white muslin apron. They sipped at it appreciatively. Through the glass doors of the Lancaster Room they could see starched napery and ice-buckets and table decorations fashioned from orange blossom. Music at subdued volume issued from the record-player (supervised by Rodney; Nora was taking no chances this time). Verdi's *Operatic Highlights* was being played; at the moment it was the "Chorus of Hebrew Slaves" from *Nabucco*. Mrs Pendennis and Mrs Grey inspected the album cover depicting an enormous Italian tenor in the costume of a character from a different opera altogether and Mrs Pendennis wondered if *Nabucco* wasn't that rather nice aniseedy drink that she'd had on holiday in Italy, the sort they put a coffee-bean into and then a handsome waiter lit it with a flourish. Mrs Grey remembered reading that at Verdi's funeral the vast crowd of mourners had burst into a spontaneous rendering of the "Chorus", and thought how little and pointless one's life and achievement seemed when compared with that; thought of her husband Ronald's funeral and how the crowd of mourners (schoolboys, in the main, his pupils, obliged to attend) had probably burst spontaneously, if sotto voce, into cries of delight.

Rosa carried round a selection of canapés. The eyes of Rodney Speakman followed the progress of her bottom about the room. Even when obliged to change the record, his gaze never wavered. She was aware of his scrutiny but no longer disturbed by it. A new job, in a home for incurables, awaited her at the beginning of September. The home was run by nuns and the incurables beyond fondling her flesh, or so she hoped.

Qualitatswein, though not of the most superior sort, cooled in the ice-buckets. Melon, marinated in port, intricately cut and adorned with slices of orange and lemon, was lifted from its bed of crushed ice. Bread rolls crisped aromatically in a low oven. And for once the butter came not in individual plastic containers, but potted into wholesome yellow chunks. Rodney, in a dinner-jacket far grander than any other on show, and with a white carnation in his buttonhole, presided silently, ready to usher the guests to their tables, keeping one eye on his watch and another on the progress in the kitchen, where things were less tranquil.

Mrs Randall, who calmly churned out fish pies and steak and kidney puddings and Swiss rolls, week in, week out, had suddenly turned temperamental and developed the jitters concerning the fluffiness of her duchesse potatoes; the succulence of her baby carrots; the tenderness of her steaks and crispness of her croûtons. Her Bombe Surprise had her in a frenzy of indecision: at precisely what point should she put it into the oven to brown the meringue so that total destruction of its frozen interior would not result?

Only Nellie Macpherson, blasé about the whole business, retained her composure, and launched into her monologue concerning the gracious days of the grand hotels. She described banquets for hundreds, waiters in white gloves, fifteen courses with fruit sorbets at intervals to clear the palate, crowned heads of Europe and rose-petals floating on top of fingerbowls, cobwebbed clarets and smilex by the furlong and training schools where they taught you to carry soup-plates full of water.

Having heard it all a dozen times before: how I served King Zog of Albania with melba toast, how Gracie Fields gave me half a crown and Robert Donat autographed a menu for me. And Margaret Lockwood. And Nervo and Knox. And George Formby. And the Princess Royal (though she hadn't signed an autograph, they weren't allowed to – but *so* stately!), no one paid her any attention. She sighed and hobbled off with a basket of rolls, wishing that she'd been born in China where the old were revered, their fund of experience accorded due respect and deference.

In the Gloucester Room, Nora, acting as master of ceremonies, encouraged her rather less aristocratic guests to mingle. At first they felt rather foolish, treating those they saw, day in, day out, as new acquaintances, making conversation, being polite. Colonel Pritchard found himself standing opposite Mrs Crookthorne, a feast for the eye in a green frock that had seen better days. The side seam had split, the zip had stuck three inches from its destination – she couldn't be bothered to seek assistance – and there were ancient sweat stains to be glimpsed when she reached up to adjust a kind of matching bow contrivance that she'd perched atop her thinning hair. As Rosa passed with her tray, she seized a canapé in either hand, thus sacrificing her glass of sherry. It was food she craved, not drink. He stood agog for a while, watching her jaw move up and down as she munched, and then he checked himself, remembered Ladies' Nights in the Mess, Brigadiers' wives to be entertained, and a little of that forgotten urbanity came to his rescue. "May I say," he said, "how striking you look this evening?" It wasn't really a lie; she did look striking, particularly when her headband/hair-ribbon/whatever it was fell over her right eye.

"Good feed, for a change," she said. "Let's hope. You've a job to get one these days. Do you ever go in The Chestnut Tree?"

The Chestnut Tree was a café of the nastier sort. He never did, preferring the rather more salubrious environs of Reece's, but a comparison of their merits and demerits provided a topic of conversation that lasted them well enough until they were summoned to take their places in the dining-room.

Edward Green chatted to Mrs Grey and the longer he

chatted to Mrs Grey the more he felt drawn to her. An elderly lady of quiet, pleasing appearance, charming manners, possessed of a lively mind and cultural awareness. He sensed that they came from the same sort of background: book-lined studies, a fondness for gardening, mothers who'd been the backbone of the WI, brothers who'd either been killed on active service or else ordained. He sensed that she would find rose-pink satin and matching lavatory paper vulgar in the extreme. She must have been a good-looking young woman and she was still pretty, in a quiet way. They had been discussing the stories of de Maupassant of which they were both particularly fond and now he asked her if she'd ever attended the French Circle. Her French was obviously good if she read authors in the original. "Oh, it's rusty," she said, going pink. "I'd thought of attending once or twice . . ."

"We have a really jolly time," he said. "Do think again. I'm sure you'd enjoy it."

Marion, delicious in lilac, was meanwhile engrossed in her usual ritual of head-turning so that no one should be deprived of the delightful prospect of every angle of her beauty.

"Perhaps I should," Mrs Grey – Esmé – was saying, "if there was someone there that I knew."

Miss Vyner shifted her weight from foot to foot, eventually crossed the room and leaned against the sideboard. That morning she had carried a letter to the post-box. The letter was addressed to Exit, but the post-box had been sealed, as were all the others – there was an industrial dispute – so she'd had to carry it back again. This evening, after her walk, she had no energy to spare for chit-chat; all of it was devoted to keeping herself upright and to containing the pain so that she didn't groan or shriek out loud.

Miss Johns had delayed her entrance until the last minute. She came down slowly. If they knew what hell social gatherings meant for her, they would never arrange them. Wherever you went, someone always arranging some get-together. Why couldn't they be content? There was only one worse hell that she knew of, and that was living alone. That would be even worse than scurrying for protection to the side of Mrs Booth-Powell, swallowing down sherry like medicine, not knowing how or what to reply to Mrs Pegler's seemingly-apropos-of-nothing remarks, feeling the blush spread from her neck to her forehead when Mr Green's glance wandered and innocently came to rest upon her person. The blushing, a curse since childhood, had become even more frequent during the change of life and carried on getting worse.

On this special night Mrs Booth-Powell made an exception and talked to Mrs Pegler, though the poor old thing's conversation consisted of uttering meaningless banalities, making communication very difficult to sustain. Poor old thing! She must be worth a mint, Mrs Booth-Powell thought, looking narrow-eyed at the pendant, the diamond-crusted fingers, the gold bracelet – so discreet, so costly. Scrap metal indeed!

Peggy Johns had a gold bracelet, though hers was a childish affair with charms dangling from it. They reminded one of those Monopoly counters that one used for identification: a boot, a ship, a flat iron. She played with them constantly. "Don't fidget, Peggy!" Mrs Booth-Powell said. They'd been put together for dinner and she wasn't going to have her enjoyment of the meal ruined by the woman's endless twitching.

For the gourmet evening Mrs Speakman had de-Rattiganised her tables. Guests were disposed in twos and threes. And much consideration had been given to the dispositions: Mrs Booth-Powell might deign to speak to Mrs Pegler over a sherry, but could hardly be expected to maintain the civility for the course of an entire meal, and so on. All in all, it was a task that demanded a diplomatic sense worthy of a seat at the League of Nations, but, after much juggling of the symbols that represented her guests – a walking-stick for Miss Vyner, a gun for Colonel Pritchard, a knife and fork for Mrs Crookthorne – she managed it.

And, loath though she was to tempt fate, she had to admit that it was all going swimmingly. Perhaps there had been just the hint of two minutes' silence for Mr Golding before they began, as they remembered another meal and its ghoulish interruption, but after that they fell to it with a will. Conversation flowed, lips were smacked, and glasses drained. Neither Nellie Macpherson nor Rosa nor Marguerita spilled anything, the melon was cold, the soup was hot, the whitebait was fresh (thank God! She'd had her doubts), the steaks were tender, and the Bombe Surprise was baked to exactly the right consistency and aroused such a cry of admiration that nobody noticed how it had been filled with the usual old fruit salad.

No one got drunk, or vomited, or fell victim to food poisoning. Crookthorne, of course, stole some After Eights and water-biscuits, but you had to allow for *some* natural wastage.

At the end of the evening Colonel Pritchard got to his feet and proposed a vote of thanks and they prevailed upon Mrs Randall to come through from the kitchen and join them in a glass of wine. (This invitation did not extend to her right-hand woman Mary Reilly who had been threatened with the sack if the lowest of profiles was not maintained – Mr Green had not seemed entirely at ease all evening.)

A success. Fate, for once, on her side. It could even have been argued that it had remained that way when Wynn smashed up the Gloucester Room. At least he did it after all the residents were safely in bed.

29

Nora and Rodney and Elsa inspected the wreckage: one small broken pane of glass in the French window that had given him access to the latch. A shattered television screen. A smashed mirror. Two coffee-tables overturned. Debris made the damage seem worse than it was. In the middle of the floor lay the watch which had either been dropped, or flung. There was a piece of paper wrapped round the face. Written on the paper were two words: "You bitch."

It was Rodney who unwrapped it and read out the message. Elsa's face flamed, though there was no reason for them to link the words to her. More likely, indeed, that they should assume the epithet was directed at Nora; it was she who had given him the sack.

They knew who was responsible. Nora, alert as ever, had been the first on the scene and had caught sight of a figure running down the path at the side of the house. She'd seen dark hair, a moustache, an earring. The watch clinched it. "Isn't that the one you bought him for his birthday?" she asked.

"It could be. I couldn't be certain. There are lots of watches like that around."

But she was batting on a sticky wicket and she knew it. "Come off it," Nora said. "I know he was a friend of yours, but protecting him won't do any good. I thought he'd caused trouble enough round here. What do you think brought this on?"

She was itching to tidy it up and with the edge of her shoe pushed shards of glass together. "Mind your feet," she said sharply to Rodney who was wearing his slippers. He was trembling, Elsa noticed, as though even the evidence of violence, without its physical manifestations, terrified him.

He was also starting to wheeze. "Get to bed," his mother

said. "And use your inhaler." In an emergency he was neither use nor ornament. She it was who would ring the police, clear up the mess, keep things running smoothly.

"I'll be up later," she said, as you'd say to a child. He looked a little like a child who'd been woken from a deep sleep: his eyelids drooping, his pupils dilated, his cheek flushed. Only the moustache suggested maturity. Without it, you could have knocked ten years off his age.

"Don't suppose we'd better move anything until the police have been," Nora said. She pressed her hand against her forehead, feeling a migraine coming on, the sort of migraine that would prostrate a lesser mortal, entail rest in a darkened room for hours; but she would have to press on, just as she'd always had to. "I'll go and ring them," she said. "I've got the number in my office."

"No," Elsa said. "Don't."

She said it with a steely authority that stopped Nora in her tracks.

"I'll make good any breakages."

One of which, she realised as she said it, was a television set, approximate price: three hundred pounds. Perhaps Nora would be willing to take so much a week towards the cost.

"What!" Nora said, in the same way that she said it when you asked for the day off.

"Don't ring the police. He's already been charged with drunk and disorderly. He's to appear in court at the end of the month and if they find out about this he'll really be in trouble. Criminal damage, I suppose they'll call it. And then there's that other business that hasn't really been satisfactorily resolved . . ."

"If you think I'm going to let him get away with this," Nora said, "you must be out of your mind." The headache was becoming more intense and her vision was blurred. The light glancing off the jagged edges of the smashed mirror caused a specific pain in her temple. "Do you think he should get away with it: drinking himself senseless, wrecking other people's belongings, terrorising old ladies – ?"

"He gets drunk," Elsa said, "and he's responsible for this – but there's a reason for this, and it's not directed at you personally. Indirectly, this is my fault. I'd rather not explain why, and as I've said, I'll pay for the damage. It won't happen again – but he never terrorised old ladies. Whoever did that is still at large."

The suspicion must have been building, subliminally, for ages. All of a sudden, it crystallised: "a man between twenty and thirty", the descriptions had said, "dark hair, medium height, a small moustache"; someone who might have trouble relating normally to the opposite sex, Sergeant Fleming had also implied; "It could be anybody," Emlyn had said, studying the Photofit, "Adolf Hitler, Errol Flynn, Charlie Chaplin"; surprising him outside the storeroom; Rosa complaining of Rodney's lustful attentions; the reputation he had as a peeping Tom among the sand-dunes; the massive asthmatic attack (said to be brought on by fear or excitement) that had followed upon the date of at least one of the crimes in question...

Nora had half-turned towards the door. Slowly she turned back. They stared at one another. Never had so much information been transmitted without verbal exchange. It came to me, eventually, Elsa thought, the acknowledgement of the suspicion; how very much earlier it must have occurred to her, his mother.

Word was not spoken, nor ever would be spoken. But neither would the police be summoned. They continued to look at one another. Old Nora: mean, grasping, slave-driving, totally lacking in compassion. Except in one area. Old Nora, the mother of a son who might or might not be responsible for attacks upon old ladies which seemed to indicate elements of a disturbed sexuality; a son financially dependent upon his mother, who might or might not have stolen money – perhaps not in order to spend it (he was not materially deprived), but simply to have it as his own; a mother's son of thirty years old who appeared to have no independent life, who appeared to be totally under her thumb, who dared only to satisfy his timid sexual curiosity with voyeurism or fondling foreign servant-girls too frightened of being given the sack to complain. Mrs Wynn might never be convinced of her son's innocence but that was because he was a stranger to her; whereas Nora knew Rodney, knew him all too well and was afraid for him.

She pressed her hand hard against her forehead and the migraine receded. "I can claim off the insurance for the damage," she said.

Tacitly, the bargain had been struck. Elsa read the messages from Nora's face: "Please," they said, "it's unlikely," they said, "but there's always been the possibility of something of the sort. We'll draw a veil over all this," they said. "In return for your silence, I too will be silent. Not that I seriously believe, but . . . He's all I have. You can't know how it feels: a mother, a son . . ."

She could. But that was none of Nora's concern. "I'll get a dustpan and a brush," she said.

Of the residents, only Miss Johns and Colonel Pritchard had heard the rumpus in the Gloucester Room, and Miss Johns had been too scared to leave her room.

"A break-in," Nora had told the Colonel when he came down to investigate. "But it's under control. The police have been called. Please go back to bed." The police hadn't been called, though then, before Elsa's intervention, she'd had every intention of summoning the law. She didn't want the residents being made aware of the fact that the attack might have been in the nature of a personal vendetta.

"It won't happen again," Elsa had said. Next morning, after breakfast, she asked for time off. She didn't need to say that it was to find Wynn and sort him out; the knowledge was implicit between them.

With her chin leading, she ran down the terrace steps and out of the back door. No more convoluted explanations. No more shit. She would tell him straight: that she had lied to him in order that his pride should not be hurt, that if he carried on like this, he'd find himself in real trouble, and alone. She cared for him. There had been rapport between them from the very first, but if he believed that he was mature enough for her to care for him in that way, then he had even more growing up to do than was already apparent.

She walked briskly down Rosedale Road. Past The Haven and St Ignatius's Preparatory School. Past Grosvenor Mansions and Grey Towers. So absorbed was she in her inner dialogue that she was only peripherally aware of the car kerb-crawling on the opposite side of the road, keeping pace with her own, and did not suppose that this was any more than coincidence. So deeply absorbed was she that the voice that called to her had called to her several times before she became aware of it.

"Excuse me," said Diana Rees. "May I have a word with you?"

She was leaning out of the car window, her sunglasses pushed on to the top of her head. Her expression was composed, her tone unthreatening but firm. "Me?" Elsa said foolishly, as though the pavements were thronged with passers-by and she had intercepted a message intended for somebody else.

"Yes."

Nothing for it but to approach the car, legs wobbling, heart beating almost as erratically as it had done the night that Mick had tapped on her door and interrupted a lovers' tryst. Her lover, this woman's husband. Mrs Rees. Entitled to his name, to sole and exclusive enjoyment of his sexual favours. Entitled to scratch out the eyes of any other woman who trespassed upon her private property. She had been foolish to delude herself into thinking that they might escape detection. It was bound to happen. Sooner or later. Sooner had no doubt been precipitated by Friday night's débâcle. The wreckage that she had interpreted as an act of vengeance had obviously not satisfied his bloodlust: after all, smashing up the Priory would not hurt her and might well rebound upon him. In the final analysis shopping them to Diana was undoubtedly the best revenge available to him.

She held open the passenger door. Upon the third finger of her left hand was the ring that proclaimed her entitlements, that allowed her to say, "My husband", the ring that caused Elsa a pang of jealousy so keen that, for an instant, it quite overwhelmed her fear.

"I wondered if we could talk?"

"Well . . . yes."

"Not here. I thought we could have a cup of coffee?"

It might have been a social invitation quite devoid of sinister undertones, such was the neutral way in which it was spoken.

"I think we ought to talk."

She accepted the invitation. Perhaps Diana Rees was planning on abducting her, perhaps she would drive the car to where there were cliffs and carry on driving over the edge of them – but it seemed to her that she had no option but to step inside and close the door behind her.

"Do you like the Metropole?"

She had to work her mouth, as though it belonged to a ventriloquist's dummy before her reply would emerge: "I've never been in it."

"Their coffee's drinkable."

The lights were changing against them. She put her foot down. Elsa closed her eyes, heard the voice: husky, calm, saying, "He closes his eyes too when I drive. He has no confidence in me. Did you know who I was," the voice said, "when my dog jumped up at you and upset your coffee that time in the Arcade?"

"Yes."

"Is that why you were so nervous? It struck me at the time, how you were trembling so. It's wives who are supposed to tremble. Other women are supposed to be very blasé."

But only, surely, if they feel that they have the upper hand, if the initiative has not been taken away from them. She was trembling now, would no more be able to cope with a cup of coffee than before. Mick had spoken of his ordeal in the police station, had said that he'd been able to make it bearable, intermittently, by going out of himself: pretending that it was happening to someone else, that he was a mere observer. She tried to imitate this technique, but found that she was anchored firmly within herself, in the situation, and in the forecourt of the Metropole, where she would at last be obliged to account for her actions.

I can run away, she thought; I can say, "I have nothing to say to you," and walk quickly in the other direction. I haven't committed a criminal offence. What can she do? Cite me in a divorce action? Well there's not much stigma attached to that these days. And by then I'll be safely elsewhere. The problems between them are not my concern.

But she walked obediently behind Mrs Rees into the lounge of the Metropole. She saw a porter raise his eyebrows to a receptionist, saw two waiters nudge each other before one rushed over and enquired effusively if he could get anything for them. She was not in the least self-conscious. If I had made an exhibition of myself like that, Elsa thought, I couldn't be dragged within miles of the place. Perhaps she'd been too drunk to remember.

"A pot of coffee, please," she said. "A good big one."

It arrived with remarkable promptitude. They might raise their eyebrows and nudge each other when she appeared on the scene, but they certainly rushed to satisfy her wants. She poured it with a steady hand, then rummaged in her handbag and produced a packet of cigarettes, offering one to Elsa.

"I don't, thank you."

She had a fancy gold lighter but it failed to ignite. Eventually she called over the waiter who provided her with a book of matches after lighting her cigarette with a flourish. She drew smoke deep into her lungs, exhaled it elegantly. Speak, Elsa thought, staring at the surface of her cooling coffee. Speak before I scream.

"I've tried to persuade Emlyn not to," she said, "but it's hard for a smoker to give up when he lives with another addict."

"Yes. I know."

She raised her eyebrows almost as high as the porter had done. "Are you married?" she said.

"I was. I'm divorced."

Which, no doubt, in your view, means that, having made a hash of my own marriage, I'm now available and anxious to break up everybody else's.

"Do you love him? Emlyn?"

It came as brutally and as unexpectedly as a foul blow. Soften them up, Elsa saw, and then pounce. Obviously she'd had previous experience.

But perversely, the question, in its directness, reminded her of those questionnaires which are meant to be answered without pause for thought: What is your favourite colour? Do you prefer Bach to Beethoven? It seemed that a snap response was required, positive or negative. But she couldn't provide it because neither of them represented the truth.

"Sometimes I feel that I do. Other times – I just feel annoyed about the whole business, that it's complicating my life, interfering with my plans."

She had answered as honestly as possible. There was a part of her that strangely welcomed the opportunity to grumble about being in thrall to the entanglement that they had woven between them while another part of her protested against this cosy, all-girls-together, hair-down, soul-baring. It seemed a betrayal of him, a diminishment of his importance: token male, husband, adulterer, what *shall* we do about him?"

"Do *you* love him?" Elsa asked, emboldened by her anger at having been seduced into contemplation of betrayal.

Perhaps that rocked Diana back on her heels a little. But only a little. She started sentences and abandoned them. Finally she said, "We've been married a long time. Since 1961. That's – what – twenty-three years."

"That wasn't what I asked."

They were fencing now. It was inevitable. But scoring points wouldn't get either of them anywhere. It wasn't as if the prize to be won waited passively for his claimant; it wasn't necessarily as if both – or either – of them, regarded him as a prize worth winning.

"The usual answer would be, I suppose, that it depends what you mean by love."

She smiled. She had a nice smile, which wasn't entirely due to good diet in childhood and private dentistry.

"We're entangled with each other," she said. "We've been through so many years and such a lot together that it's difficult to think in terms of him as a separate entity. 'Love,'" she said, and frowned. "It's hard to remember. I'm an alcoholic," she said abruptly. "I suppose you know that? Most people do. It affects your memory. He's very lovable," she said, "in that little-boy way that some men are – the way they act so grown-up and try to conceal it, I mean. But perhaps that's just some sort of frustrated maternal instinct. I can't have children – I suppose you know that as well? He usually contrives to make sure people know that in case they should assume it's his fault. No," she said, "that's unfair. He's never been unfair in that way. Do I love him?" she said. "Oh, I did when I married him. I was crazy for him. He was so serious and unknowingly sexy. He was also one of the few men I'd met who didn't appear to want me. It was a fatal combination. I couldn't rest till I'd got him. Most people," she said, "think our marriage is a farce. It is, in a way. But – on the other hand – it exists, and it's lasted all this time, despite everything. We know each other. He thinks he's kept himself secret from me, but he hasn't. He thinks he can't bear to come home but he does and sometimes we even laugh together.

Sexually, I suppose the thrill is gone, as it was bound to do, but we still suit each other, we still share the same bed –"

Well of course. A highly-sexed man is a highly-sexed man, doesn't just become one when in proximity to his mistress, whatever he might say; he has a wife, and a matrimonial bed. But the thought of that was somehow less painful than the idea of them laughing together.

"He's had the worst of the bargain, no doubt about it. Living with an alcoholic is no fun. We lie, we deceive, we change from placid creatures to raving lunatics, we pick fights – or match anger with anger; he has a terrible temper, you know, one of those flaring Welsh tempers. Don't provoke him whatever you do because when he loses control, he really loses control. I've had a few black eyes. But that was years ago. He's calmed down a good deal. Everything's calmed down. Of course, a new woman will invigorate him. Until the novelty wears off."

This was deliberate cruelty. But a cruelty, Elsa felt, directed more at him than at her.

"I can't blame him too much. He's had a lot to put up with, years of it: being humiliated, finding me collapsed in a stupor, vomit all over the place, bottles hidden everywhere he looked. It's over now. But I'm still an alcoholic. I always will be. And he *could* have left me, a dozen times."

But he never did. Ask yourself why, were the unspoken implications.

"He hates to let go of anything, anything he feels he's achieved. Once there was a woman who got pregnant, got herself pregnant deliberately, I imagine. I thought then – though I don't believe most men are excessively paternal until made so by fathering children, the *idea* of being deprived of the chance to reproduce yourself must hurt – I thought he might go. But she had an abortion. He arranged it. That's the great advantage of having an affair with a doctor: he can usually arrange for you to avoid the physical consequences of your actions."

So don't imagine that by neglecting to take contraceptive measures you will trap him into forsaking me. We've been through all that before.

"Have you spoken to – other women like this?" Elsa asked.

She dared at last to attempt her coffee. It was cold, skinned over. Diana raised a hand and the waiter came running across with a fresh cup.

"One or two."

Just in case you should get the idea that you're unique. He's done it before and he'll do it again. Because I don't supply what he needs. Because his ego requires constant reinforcement. Because part of what drives him is the desire to prove to himself that he can have any woman who attracts him. Because he's an incorrigible romantic to whom the excitement of the clandestine, the sadness of knowing that it can never be, are as necessary as food and drink.

"Why? Is it to warn me off? To threaten me? Why the confrontation?"

She lit another cigarette and smoked for a while before she replied. "I was curious," she said eventually. "Was there another woman involved in the break-up of your marriage?"

Elsa nodded.

"Weren't you curious?"

Curious? Of course. But curiosity had come so far down the list of reactions as to be irrelevant. Astonishment, there had been first, then pain and anger. Oh, most definitely anger. There had been times when, frustrated by her impotence to make Rob understand the heinousness of his betrayal, she'd have killed. Him first and then her. With no compunction. Like Emlyn, enraged to the point where control snapped and the red mist descended. And that, she realised, was what Diana's demeanour lacked: any trace of anger. Hostility would be absent in only two sets of circumstances: either when one was emotionally disengaged, or if one was totally confident that no serious threat was being posed. "He hates to let go," she'd said. Presumably he felt everything to have been too hard-won to be lightly discarded.

"I'm leaving next month," Elsa said. "So you don't need to worry."

Diana's reply was so elliptical that it seemed she hadn't heard. "He believes," she said, "that he stays with me for my sake. But that's not true."

"Isn't it?"

"No. I can manage alone. Now. I imagine you can too. He

can't. And he knows he can always come back after his little diversions. I doubt he'd embark upon them otherwise."

"You don't seem to have a very high opinion of him."

She smiled. "How old are you?" she said.

"Thirty-one."

"Perhaps when you reach forty-six you'll realise that lack of a high opinion isn't necessarily a bar to affection. Sometimes it's what generates the affection. It's only when you stop worshipping that you can start to care."

"I told you. I'm leaving in a few weeks' time. There's nothing for you to worry about."

Until the next one comes along.

"Does he know that you know?"

There was a song, wasn't there, that went something like that? Ridiculously, in view of the circumstances, she found herself trying to remember the melody, the exact sequence of the lyrics.

Diana shook her head. "Not until you tell him."

"Perhaps I won't."

"Oh, you will," she said. "You won't be able to resist it. No matter how conscious you are that it would be more sensible to keep quiet."

"Tell me," she said, "how you found out."

"Finding out's not difficult. People who imagine themselves to be in love also imagine – I can't think why – that they're invisible. Being in love must be a bit like being drunk, in that respect. Reason ceases to operate."

"But how exactly did you find out?"

"There were all the signs that I've come to associate with him having an affair: lateness, feeble excuses, silences. And then I saw you together. I followed you back to Priory Lodge. Finding out is not difficult."

"No one told you?"

"No. Nobody snitches on lovers. It's considered not cricket. Not directly. It's usually the lovers who do the snitching. Perhaps they want to be found out."

"You're sure that no one told you?"

"Of course I'm sure."

But – as the saying went – she would say that, wouldn't she?

30

Elsa walked through the drizzle from the Metropole to the house where, presumably, he would continue to reside until his court case was heard. Anger pumped adrenalin. The rain fell upon her without her noticing it. She didn't even seek the shelter of the verandahs.

The rain fell upon her and seeped down her collar and drenched her jeans. Occasionally she shook it from her face. She thought of Diana's explanation: I saw you together and I followed you back to Priory Lodge – it seemed to lack the true edge of authenticity: saw us where? So what? Why should that make you assume that we were lovers? And the timing of her approach was just too precise to be coincidental. Difficult – impossible – to believe that she hadn't been informed.

"Hello there," said Mary's Des, coming out of the front gate as she went in. Like Diana Rees, he had to repeat himself because she was too absorbed in her own thoughts to notice him.

"Oh, hello," she said. "How are you?" And he was just drawing breath to tell her all about his latest run-in with the law, but she had a face on her that would stop a clock. Some poor bugger was for it.

She had to bang on his door for quite a time before it was answered. All the time she was banging she was imagining him slowly emerging from his stupor: the pain in his head, the nausea, the vile taste in his mouth, the agony entailed in coming to consciousness, sitting up, heaving himself out of bed and pulling on his clothes. And she relished each agonising moment, every spurt of nausea, every jolting, jarring sensation involved in his resurrection.

"Christ!" he said. "You'll have the door off its hinges! What time is it?"

Tousled hair. A stubbled chin. Bloodshot eyes. A complexion of the sort that Mary Reilly described as resembling boiled shite. A ragged shirt that reeked of alcohol, with faint undertones of vomit and sweat, flung on over a pair of jeans distressed to the point of collapse. She recoiled in absolute distaste.

"What time is it?" he asked again, clearing phlegm from his throat, rubbing a hand across his eyes as if to remove sticky excrescences of sleep still blurring his vision.

She put her hand into her jacket pocket and took out the watch, still wrapped in the paper that bore the evidence of his rage, and handed it to him. "Here," she said, "consult that – if it's still working."

He had the grace to hang his head at least, and looked at her warily from beneath lowered eyelids. "I was out of my skull," he said. "I don't remember much about it."

Behind him, on the table, she could see empty bottles. Pernod, there was, vodka and Newcastle Brown. The money from the car sale would have bought a lot of bottles.

"The same way that you don't remember your other antics? You were right about your head being fucked-up. It's fucked-up to the extent that you aren't responsible for your actions. Either that or else you suffer from convenient bouts of amnesia."

"I was wasted," he said. "Out of my brain. It all boiled up: all that crap you'd given me about not being in the running any more for relationships, needing to recover before you could even *think* about them. I wouldn't care, but I believed it." He groaned. Even the effort of speaking caused him pain. "And then," he continued, "suddenly there *he* is, lover-boy, with his shoes in his hand. Has been all along, I expect. You could have told me. You didn't have to treat me like a half-wit, a bloody infant."

"You *are* a bloody infant: raging and throwing things and causing mayhem whenever you can't have exactly what you want. And why you should ever have supposed that I felt anything like *that* for you, I cannot imagine. Even if you didn't have a mental age of twelve, I'm more than ten years older than you."

"And what about lover-boy?" he said, curling his lip. "He's

got to be pushing fifty. You're more than ten years older than me? He's damn near twenty years older than you. But that's OK, isn't it, because he's all those things that you worship: settled and respectable and respected. I expect he did *everything* by the book, didn't he? Went to college and got his degree and did as he was told and fitted in and made sure he knew the right people and never put a foot wrong and now everybody thinks he's fucking marvellous. I wonder if they'd think that if they knew he was screwing you in his spare time?"

She raised her hand and slapped him hard on the right side of his face. The force of the blow made her palm sting and almost knocked him off-balance. The gesture had been so histrionic that they were both surprised by it. One of the residents of the upper floor came clattering down the lino'd stair and looked at them curiously.

He massaged his face and said, without looking at her, "I expected the pigs round here before now. I suppose old Nora's frothing, isn't she?"

The assault upon him had not dissipated her anger. Her legs were shaking, her mouth filled with venom. "I persuaded her not to call the police," she said. "I wish I hadn't. I wish I'd known what you'd done before I persuaded her not to."

"What do you mean: what I'd done? I smashed up that lounge, didn't I? I put my foot through the telly and chucked an ornament at that ghastly gilt mirror, I remember that. I thought you'd seen it?"

"Not that. It doesn't matter to me whether you drive a bulldozer into Priory Lodge. They'll put you away. Which is probably where you ought to be. I mean your rotten dirty vindictive trick. You didn't have to do that."

"Do what?" he said, his jaw dropping. It made him look imbecilic, enraged her even more. "Can't you come inside?" he pleaded. Other residents would no doubt be eavesdropping, relishing every minute.

"No. There's no point. I just came to say thank you, thank you very much for telling his wife."

"What?" he said again, and the only way to stop herself slapping his gormless face again was to turn on her heel and start to descend the stairs. "You heard me," she said.

289

"I didn't tell his wife. I don't know his wife. I've never met her. Isn't she the one who gets drunk?"

"Yes. You should have a lot in common."

"I didn't tell her. I wouldn't know her if I fell over her. I swear."

"Perhaps you forgot that, too," she said. His mime of innocence: eyes wide, shoulders hunched, palms upturned, perplexity in every feature, was almost good enough to be convincing. "Perhaps it's that convenient amnesia again. I must say, if I'd known how frequent it was, your amnesia, I might not have been quite so certain of your innocence in other matters."

"What other matters?"

A devil controlled her mouth. "You know what other matters," she said. "After all, there's no smoke without fire, is there? And as your mother said, the police don't pick people up for no reason, do they?"

The patch on his cheek flamed crimson against his pallor. He gave a grunt as though she'd assaulted him physically. Then he looked at her and he said, "Piss off. Just piss off, will you?" and his voice was rising on every syllable and held the same note of incredulity as Nora's did when she said "What!" Except that hers was usually assumed and it sounded very much as though his was genuine.

There was a phone box on the opposite corner. She went in, dialled a number and the same nasal voice answered her. "Surgery," it said. "Can I help you?"

She was in no mood for obstructiveness. "Put me through, please," she said, "to Dr Rees. My name is Franklin and this is an emergency."

"I'm afraid," said the voice, failing to conceal its glee, "that surgery is over. Dr Rees is on home visits now. Perhaps if you explain to me the nature of the emergency I can help?"

She slammed down the phone. Home visits. A small town, but huge when it came to tracking down one car: a maroon BMW. That was his work car. He had another one, an MGB, that he used for leisure or, in his case, to give it its proper name: screwing purposes. A sensible precaution, she thought.

She walked along the Front towards the area of the town in

which the health centre was situated. Presumably his visits would be conducted within a certain radius of it. She saw the bus which would take her there moving away from the stop. The stop was one of those that was not provided with a shelter, and the rain was heavier now, persistent. The overhanging boughs of a diseased elm tree gave little cover. "When is the next number thirteen?" she asked the youth who waited with her. He shrugged his hunched shoulders non-committally as though resigned to a long wait. Perhaps she ought to leave it, go back to the Priory, draw a line under the whole business. In less than a month she would pack her cases for Manchester. She was not obliged to be involved any further. With either of them.

But although she had always told herself that it must end, she had told herself that it must end in September, and had not bargained on being deprived of the three remaining weeks of August. Those weeks were necessary; for adaptation, adjustment to the prospect of willing his image to fade from memory without leaving too much of an ache in its absence.

After an era, or a season, or perhaps it was only ten minutes or so, the bus arrived and carried her to the far side of town. She had paid for a ticket to Pavilion Road where the health centre stood, but she forfeited at least a third of it because, as the bus turned the corner into Whiteside Avenue, she spotted his car.

It was parked outside one of a row of terraced town houses. She lurked in a driveway a few yards along the opposite side of the road, feeling as conspicuous as if she'd been the one under surveillance. Eventually the front door opened and he stepped out. A young woman and a child were framed in the doorway. He turned, exchanged a word with the woman and then, in one of those roughly affectionate gestures that characterise the manner of those who are not entirely at ease with children, he ruffled the child's hair, before moving briskly down the path.

Something melted in her. Tears pricked behind her eyes. Always upon seeing him when he was either ignorant or oblivious of her observation: when he was asleep, when, bespattered with blood, he had snapped into action during the Golding crisis, when, eyes closed, he bit his lip at the moment of climax, she was similarly moved. Ambivalence might characterise her relations with him when he was close and conscious of her presence, but always, when, unobserved, she had the chance to observe him, these gut reactions told of something positive and certain, and reminded her, in their intensity, of the brief time that remained to them before the opportunity to observe him, unobserved, would be lost for ever.

He was sitting in the car, sorting case notes, when she reached it. She tapped on the glass and he started and glanced up and looked alarmed. He thinks, she thought, that I've taken to following him, and is terrified at the idea of it. Like most of his sex he is afraid of confrontation.

He wound down the window then, reluctantly, opened the door for her. "This," he said, "is not a good idea. Most of the people who live in this road are patients of mine."

"Why?" she said. "I'm not your patient. You won't be reported to the Medical Council."

"That," he said, "is hardly the point . . ."

". . . and," she continued, "it wouldn't be worth anyone's while reporting you to your wife because she already knows."

The hand that had been irritably brushing the hair from his brow came to rest, thumb and forefinger pressed to his temples. She had a vivid mental image of the way that that hand had rested between them on the seat on the marsh road at the beginning of the affair: so casual, so deliberate. How she had longed to touch it, to feel the current of its desire flowing between them.

His eyes, beneath the shelter of his hand, were closed. And when he spoke his words were barely audible as though the mere speaking of them would confirm what might be considered, up till then, as a misapprehension. "How do you know?"

"I have just come from an interview with her in the Metropole Hotel – well, with a short interlude in between. She more or less kidnapped me outside the Priory, persuaded me to go quietly. She's got guts, hasn't she, your wife? In the same circumstances – even though I was out of my mind with rage and jealousy – I didn't have the nerve to seek out my rival in that sort of cool fashion. But then perhaps your wife doesn't see me as a rival."

An elderly woman, passing by, glanced into the car and then glanced again curiously, smiling at him. He raised a hand in acknowledgement of her greeting. "Christ," he said. "It had to be her. Equivalent to the front page of the local rag. I've got five more visits," he said, "and I'm already running late. It's my afternoon at Merryfields and there's a meeting of the Community Health Council at half seven. I *can't* stay and talk."

"You don't have the time for extra-marital activity, do you?" she said, reaching for the door handle. "Or has it suddenly dwindled, the time at your disposal? Ever since the going started to get sticky?"

"Rough," he said automatically, annoyingly. "The going gets rough. It's situations that get sticky."

"Is that a fact? Well, semantics apart, it appears that the time you can make available for me has dwindled quite dramatically ever since it began to seem likely that you'd be found out. Still, we had a good innings, didn't we? Pity they couldn't have lasted a few weeks longer. Pity that rain stopped play."

It was pouring now, steadily. As if in imitation – ridiculously, and to her total chagrin – she started to cry. Not in the whole-hearted, unrestrained fashion that usually follows upon shock, the way she'd cried with Mick after the blow-out on the motorway, but sparse, choked tears of pure misery.

"Elsa," he said, "oh, Elsa, don't." Eventually he took her hand. It was the only gesture of comfort that he could risk, even though the car windows had started to steam up so thoroughly that their doings would not be visible to passers-by.

He stroked her fingers, clasped her hand tight within his own, reached into his pocket for his handkerchief – fiercely white, the same handkerchief, perhaps, that had contained his ejaculations – and encouraged her to use it to blot her tears. It smelt of laundry. The semen stains had been boiled out of it just as the tear stains would be too. There would be nothing, no souvenir, not a trace to commemorate the connection between them. She had bargained upon it ending certainly, though she had not gone as far as to prepare herself for the knowledge that its ending would also cancel out its existence.

"I have to go. I've a schizophrenic girl, and an old man with emphysema and two suspected cases of mumps and a pregnant woman who's afraid that she may have been in contact with rubella. I *have* to go. Elsa? Can I meet you somewhere tonight?"

She scrubbed at her face with his handkerchief. "I'm not coming to that summer-house place. I'm sick of creeping round like a criminal. What's the point?"

"I won't humiliate her," he said sharply. "I won't do that. What's that pub?" he said. "The one near the roundabout at the bottom of Rosedale Road?"

"The Hawk and Bottle."

"Will you meet me in there at half past nine? I'll leave the meeting early if necessary. I'll run you to the bus stop now." He pulled the seat-belt across her shoulder and secured it. Decisive suddenly. He glanced at the mirror and pulled away from the kerb. His face was composed, his actions crisp and precise. "Did she say how she found out?" he asked, as though the answer was of only minimal importance to him.

"She said she'd seen us together and followed me back to Priory Lodge. But I think Mick must have told her."

"Have you seen him?"

"Yes. He says he didn't."

He shrugged. It didn't much matter to him how it had happened. Except perhaps for future reference.

He found a bus stop with a shelter, let her out and then accelerated away at an alarming rate. "Tonight," he'd said abruptly before slamming the passenger door. "Oh, and will you promise me one thing? To change out of those wet clothes as soon as you get indoors?"

As solicitous of her as she'd been of Mick. Perhaps only a reflex response. As hers had been: adult to child, doctor to patient. This time a geological age passed before the bus arrived, and the tears ran down her face all the while, but nobody noticed because of the rain.

31

"She had an appointment with her psychiatrist. His consulting-rooms are at that side of the park. She saw my car stood at the corner and she followed that little path through the trees down to the summer-house. Do you remember, that Monday afternoon when we heard the leaves rustling?"

When you told me that the strain was shortening your life, she thought. She moistened her lips. "Were we . . . ?" she said.

"We were, and I quote: 'sitting there looking so abjectly miserable' that it was obvious we were having an affair. She remembered meeting you in a café – you never told me," he said accusingly, "and she waited until you emerged and followed you back."

"She didn't say anything about Mick?"

"No. If he'd told her I'm sure she would have said so."

"Perhaps she'd want to protect him."

"Why on earth would she want to do that? She's a very straightforward person. There's absolutely no reason to doubt what she says."

He sounded rather annoyed as though she was being presumptuous in guessing at the motives of the wife whose psychological processes were an open book to him.

Oh Mick, she thought, Mick, and hoped that her accusations had not been misdirected. Better to suppose that he had betrayed her than to be obliged to accept that she had wrongly accused him. There had already been too many instances of that.

He pushed a glass of beer abstractedly around the table. She drained hers for courage. Studious avoidance of eye-contact was maintained. In the same manner as his wife, earlier in the day, he kept thinking of things to say, and not saying them while Colonel Pritchard, unnoticed at the far side of the room, looked across at them and thought, well, I'll be damned. These quacks must be an oversexed lot, forever getting themselves into the mire over some woman or other. You'd think with all that prodding and poking of the privates, it'd put them off for life.

"What did you tell her?" he asked. "This morning?"

"That I was leaving in a few weeks so there was no reason for her to worry about it anymore."

Between his visit to Merryfields and his appointment at the Health Council, Emlyn had been home. He had closed the door upon his housekeeper who was preparing the evening meal and who, in her time, had been responsible for the circulation of much gossip, and had poured himself a very large whisky from the bottle he had bought that afternoon (ever since Diana's illness had been diagnosed he'd refused to keep drink in the house). Then he had tracked his wife to their bedroom whence she had retired complaining of giddiness.

She'd been lying on the bed. She'd opened her eyes and closed them again and said, "I can see that you've been given the message. That was quick."

"Are you all right?"

"Uxoriousness, at this stage of the game," she had said, "is not the right approach. Unlike most of the women you choose," she had said, "I am at that age when we have to expect to feel rotten most of the time. Or so you tell us."

"Oh, no, we don't," he'd said. But he did, was as guilty as the next of assessing a woman's age and attributing her complaints to the atrophying of her sex hormones. The menopause, like puberty, provided a wonderful excuse for lax diagnoses.

She had kept her eyes closed. "Pretty," she had said. "Little What's-her-name. What *is* her name? The day you make a play for a plain woman I'll believe that vanity isn't involved."

She always said that, as if there was something astonishingly perverted about being attracted by good looks.

"She looks very much as though she could be hurt," she'd said. "You should pick them tougher. Like that one who went and got herself pregnant that time. She was tough, wasn't she? This one doesn't even begin to make the weight."

"Stop it, Diana," he'd said. "This isn't a game we're playing."

"Isn't it? I rather thought it was. I drink, you run after women. Then we blame each other. At least I do. I tell Tom Jenkins that I drink because you're unfaithful to me. By the way, if you want to keep your assignations secret, you really ought not to park your car on the corner of the road where my psychiatrist has his consulting-rooms."

"I didn't think you went there anymore."

"Now and then. That's a game too. I tell him what he wants to hear: about my ambivalent relationship with my father, and meeting you and you being so flattered at my attentions that you upped and married me in haste, and about my barren womb and how unfair that is for you and how you're obliged to impregnate other women to compensate, but how you're always able to arrange for the life you've created to be murdered, because it's one thing to know that you can make babies and quite another to actually be lumbered with offspring."

She'd continued in the same vein. "This is the sort of situation that can precipitate a crisis and lead me back to the bottle," she'd said mockingly. But Diana never turned to the bottle at the time when you expected it. "A bit more guilt for you, darling," she'd said. "You love having guilt, don't you?"

Years ago, once or twice, he'd hit her. Not hard. Never more than a cuff. Just to stop her cruel mocking mouth. But she bruised easily and when he'd realised what was happening – the danger of insidious progress in that direction – he'd thrown things instead: whatever came to hand, at walls, at mirrors. He'd been astonished at the rage within him: a sort of generalised rage that simply used her as a target. Gradually he'd gained control over himself. Nowadays his tongue did the hurting. But it would never be as effective in that capacity as hers.

"You should have screwed more often when you were young," she'd said. "Got it out of your system instead of poring over your books and playing with yourself." And then, suddenly, there was real anger: "I could have you struck off for this, you bastard."

"Really?" he'd said. "And how will you do that?"

"No," she'd said, resuming her mocking tone, "you're too damned cautious for that, aren't you? Your love-affairs are about as spontaneous as military strategy. I hope this poor little bitch realises the way it goes, that once it gets threatening, she gets the brush-off?"

"Shut your damned mouth," he'd said. Unfortunately, during her periods of sobriety, he was unable to say, "Shut your drunken mouth."

"I wonder what will happen when you can't get it up quite so readily." She'd sounded thoughtful. "Still, I suppose you've years yet."

"When I was a student," he'd said, "I did a course in psychosexual medicine. We were told that men complaining of impotence were usually complaining about their wives. Put them into bed with a new woman and they could perform as well as the next. So if ever I can't get it up you'll know why."

More of the same had followed: hackneyed abuse aimed low. The scene had been played before, though not as many times as she pretended it had. And she exaggerated the number and seriousness of his affairs, as she had obviously exaggerated them to Elsa who said, "According to your wife, this is routine: the warning-off of your women. She told me that one of them got pregnant and you arranged an abortion for her."

He picked up his glass and downed its contents. The effect of the beer was made more potent by the whisky that had preceded it. He spread the fingers of his hand on the tabletop, moved each finger in turn to emphasise his points. "*Fact:*" he said, "women – affairs – whatever you like to call them – four. In twenty-two years of marriage."

"Twenty-three," Elsa said. "She said you'd been married twenty-three years."

"Then she's wrong. It's twenty-two years. Diana's wrong about a number of things. *Fact* continued: of those four women, one had reason to believe that she might be pregnant. There was some doubt whether it resulted from marital or extra-marital relations. I pointed her in the direction of a clinic where she was supplied with what is popularly known as a 'morning-after pill' which caused her period to start. Not as dramatic, I'll grant you, as a thorough-going, foetus-practically-born-alive abortion, but the truth, nevertheless. *Fact*: Diana definitely discovered two of them and subjected only one to what you were subjected to this morning. The reason that she did nothing about the other one was that she was having an affair herself at the time. *Fact*: I did not ditch those women when the going got 'sticky' as you call it. They tired of me. With every justification. Not much fun being a married man's mistress. And, as you so rightly said, I don't have an awful lot of spare time to devote to the activity. *Fact*: it always hurt, the end of the affair, but eventually I recovered, even wondered, after I'd recovered, what all the fuss had been about. Perhaps it'll be like that with you, but this time I can't begin to contemplate 'afterwards'. Oh, I know I'll go on going through the motions. I know eventually I'll find someone else. She said, this afternoon, what happens when you're past it? Except she put it more crudely than that. As though, when my virility goes my heart'll die too. I don't think it will. I think I'll be a pathetic old man mooning about over some woman who thinks I'm a joke. I don't want that to happen. I want you to be the last of them and the only way that that can occur is if you're the one who *doesn't* tire of me." He paused and then said, "Excuse me a minute. I've left something in the glove compartment," and went out into the car park and while he was away she caught sight of Colonel Pritchard and had to pretend to be so deep in thought that she could look directly at the space he occupied without recognising him.

"It's entirely the wrong moment, I know. But I never bought you anything other than a drink and the occasional meal. I'd have bought you a raincoat but it'd have been the wrong size or style. I saw this the other day in that antique shop near the market – the owner is a patient of mine. I remembered how little and thin your fingers are and I'd never seen a ring so small, so I bought it. But you don't have to accept . . ."

"You can save it for your next," she said, opening the box. It was an antique ring, turquoise and silver, delicately fashioned, more beautiful than all Mrs Pegler's flashing diamonds put together. "When you're an old pathetic man, mooning," she said, slipping it on to her finger.

"But who's to say she'd have the right-sized fingers?"

For the briefest of moments, despite Colonel Pritchard and anyone else who might know him, his hand closed upon hers, pressing the shaft of the ring into her knuckle, and then he took it away and reached out, automatically, towards his cigarette packet and remembered he'd had his ration and fiddled with his beer mat instead.

She spread *her* hand and admired the ring. Without thinking, she had put it on her wedding-finger. Perhaps she should have refused it, but accepting a souvenir was different from accepting a gift. She had been upset at her lack of a memento. Now she had one. The kiss-off. Or was it? She glanced at him. He too was now staring at Colonel Pritchard as though he were a block of stone or a fading sunset. But his failure to recognise the old gentleman was quite genuine, stemmed from his being so deep in thought that even she had to touch his sleeve twice before he registered the fact that she was speaking to him.

"She said, this morning, that you needed her more than she needs you."

But that wasn't exactly what she'd said. She'd said that he thought he stayed with her for her sake, but actually it was for his sake, because he couldn't manage alone. And that meant something different.

But he didn't answer her and instead looked mournfully into his empty glass.

"Twenty-two years," he said eventually. "Or, according to her reckoning, twenty-three. It would be very surprising if habit hadn't got a grip. Habit's a terrible thing. When people try to give these up" – he touched his cigarette packet – "they talk about nicotine-deprivation and psychological cravings and physical withdrawal symptoms and all sorts of nonsense. What they really mean is the agony involved in getting accustomed to a way of life that doesn't include cigarettes. Anything you do for long enough becomes a crutch, whether it's smoking or sniffing cocaine or being married."

"And has she never wanted to leave you?"

He reached his hand out to the packet, paused for a moment, then took a cigarette and lit it. Acknowledgement of being in thrall. The inhalation restored him somewhat. He spoke quickly, tapping ash agitatedly against the edge of the ashtray. "Yes. About ten – twelve years ago. She met someone who wanted to marry her. He was a reformed alcoholic. Some sort of an engineer. He was going out to Canada and he wanted her to go with him. I expect, as he'd been in the same boat himself, he'd have known how to help her to keep off the booze. I think he genuinely cared for her."

"So why didn't she go?"

"Because I persuaded her not to."

"I persuaded her not to" – how civilised it sounded, what a false picture it suggested. The reality had been abuse, tears and vilification, raving jealousy, pleading – "Please, Diana, oh please!" – promises, assurances, threats – "If you go, I'll kill you and then I'll kill him and then I'll kill myself!" His skin still crawled when he thought about it.

"I don't expect you to understand why."

But she did understand, remembering how fervently she had begged Rob to stay, remembering the tears and the threats and the murderous jealousy. A relationship might be bled dry, totally atrophied, capable of providing nothing in the way of joy or fulfilment, but at the moment of parting one's whole being – the being of the one left behind – cried out in protest at the betrayal, the waste, and finally at the prospect of starting anew.

He had succeeded where she hadn't. Diana had turned, unpacked her case, replaced her clothes in the wardrobe. But then, in her own marriage, life had expired long since; perhaps, in his, there remained a spark that would allow resuscitation.

"I asked her whether she loved you."

"And what did she say?"

Diana had prevaricated, sought for definitions. Like him, she had pleaded the excuse of habit. Custom and practice, she had said, more or less, too long together to think of either him or the marriage dispassionately.

"A lot of red-herring stuff. But I think she does."

He grimaced, as at a bitter taste. He said, "All my life I

believed that 'I love you' meant the same as 'I can make you happy'. Why was that, I wonder?"

"It's a fairly common misconception, I should think. Do you love her?"

"Yes. But I couldn't make her happy if I worked at it for the rest of my life."

"But perhaps by leaving her you'd make her less happy."

What about me? What about me?

He ground out his cigarette. "She's going to London again next week. This gallery is arranging an exhibition of her work. If it wasn't for this she'd be on top of the world. Instead she's drooping round like the Lady of Shalott with dysmenorrhoea."

"What's dysmenorrhoea?"

"Period pains. And that's another thing. She's going through the menopause and it's unpleasant. What happens when she comes down to earth again? Troublesome physical symptoms, rivals, the bottle beckoning . . . If I wasn't there, who would take care of her?"

"Perhaps she'd take of herself. It's possible. I never thought I could until I had to."

"Maybe you're made of stronger stuff."

"I doubt it. But anyway weakness is the most powerful weapon of all."

"You think I should leave her?"

He was holding her gaze now, and looking at her as though she held the definitive answer to the dilemma.

"Oh, Emlyn, I don't know. I think if you've been together for all this time despite infidelity and alcoholism and God knows what else it's unlikely that you'll be *able* to leave. Ever."

"And lose you?"

"Perhaps it's just sex," she said, with a half-hearted smile. It was a joke between them: "just" sex, as though either of them was the sort for whom a relationship could be just that. We should be so lucky, they'd joked.

Then she said, "I'm only going to Manchester."

"As bold as brass," said Mrs Booth-Powell, who was a great one for the appropriate cliché – you waited for it coming, and winced when it came. "Beside his car in the car park."

She will now say: "You could have knocked me down with a feather," Colonel Pritchard thought.

"You could have knocked me down with a feather. I don't know what things are coming to. Practically in broad daylight."

(Sodium light, actually, and a clear night; even so she'd needed to strain her eyes to identify them.)

"I didn't know, Mrs Booth-Powell, that you were an habitué of The Hawk and Bottle," said Mr James, the new resident who had recently moved into Mr Golding's old room, kidding her.

"I was coming back from the Genealogical Society," she said coldly. "I was taking a short cut through the car park, actually. I always do on these light nights. And there they were: embracing by the side of his car. They must have been drinking in that public house," she said, as though that attracted almost as much opprobrium as their adulterous embrace.

Colonel Pritchard spoke up. "Well, so was I," he said, "drinking in that public house. And I never saw them. Are you sure you didn't make a mistake?"

He'd have lied merely to contradict her, the silly woman. But she was a malicious gossip as well, and he liked the girl, Elsa. She was very civil and obliging. And pretty.

"Are you sure you didn't go into the pub before you crossed the car park?" asked Mr James, persisting in his facetiousness.

"I find your tone offensive," she replied.

"Oh, no offence, no offence," he said quickly. As the newest resident he was anxious to retain their goodwill. They could make life hell for you otherwise.

Miss Vyner kept her own counsel. She remembered seeing them, months ago, emerging from the tropical plant house in the park, remembered how obvious it had been that they were involved with each other and how she'd never given it any more thought because such affairs weren't usually worthy of attention: either they petered out or they progressed until a new relationship was established and finally granted society's blessing.

Mrs Pendennis smiled a little wistful smile publicly, hoping that they would recognise it as conveying nostalgia, hoping that they would realise that a woman of her charms would be bound to have had some romantic encounters outside wedlock. Marriage didn't automatically make one attractive only to the marriage partner and, in her case, it had been foolish to suppose that it would. Not that she'd ever have allowed overtures to be made in a situation as sordid as the car park of a public house, of course.

"There's always some woman to threaten a man's position," Mrs Booth-Powell persisted rather defensively. Women had thrown themselves at Basil. Or so she liked to believe. As she'd also liked to believe that Basil, cognisant of the jewel he had for a wife, had rejected them all out of hand.

Miss Johns sorted the post, which today consisted mostly of bank statements. Only a few personal letters. One for Mrs Pendennis from her sister-in-law on the Isle of Wight, one for Miss Vyner from that friend of hers in Chester (you got to recognise the postmarks and the handwriting), the Ambrose Wilson catalogue for Mrs Pegler, the Book of the Month Club for Mrs Grey, nothing for Peggy Johns, not one single solitary birthday card, though how could there be unless she'd sent one to herself? No living close relative to think of her, and no one else knew. Marion Pendennis always announced her birthday at a strategic point in advance so that everyone (except for Mrs Crookthorne who was deaf to all such pronouncements) felt obliged to commemorate the occasion with a card, at least. But Peggy Johns was far too shy and retiring to attempt to emulate those sort of tactics. She sighed. Seventy-two, and all those experiences forfeited, opportunities missed: sex, marriage, children and travel and a career. Though she'd always known, somehow, right from childhood, that her life would be severely circumscribed, that she'd end up alone with no one to send her a birthday card.

Funny how you did know. As though everything already existed and was just waiting to be unfolded like a blossom from a bud.

Only one staff letter. For Elsa: "Ms E. Franklin" (terribly scrawled, scarcely legible – perhaps it was from the doctor, her paramour; the handwriting of members of the medical profession was usually scandalously ill-formed). Miss Johns looked at the postmark for clues, but there wasn't one. Neither was there a stamp. This was a hand-delivered letter, pushed through the letter-box either very late last night (or else Mrs Speakman would have seen it), or early this morning. Perhaps, thought Miss Johns, remembering a recent library book she'd read, the doctor's wife had found out about his infidelity and had roared to the door in her sports car (driving it shoeless) to deliver the letter that warned of retribution. Tearfully, thought Miss Johns, the lovers would renounce each other and years later they would meet up again after the doctor's wife's death (though Mrs Rees was remarkably healthy-looking considering that she drank) and live out, in peace and tranquillity, their true joint destiny.

Back Street, Fanny By Gaslight, Jane Eyre, Rebecca – she might not have any first-hand experience of the pains of love, but she'd read all the relevant literature, seen all the appropriate films. And Miss Johns, on her seventy-second, uncommemorated birthday, was deeply envious. Given the ghost of a chance, she could have loved passionately, cleaved through thick and thin, waited uncomplainingly for her day. But she handed the letter to Elsa without comment, her curiosity having been temporarily displaced by the keen ache of deprivation.

Elsa, who was feeling exceptionally fragile as the result of the previous day's excessive expenditure of emotional energy (not to mention the previous night's excessive consumption of alcohol), laid the letter aside until she'd finished her breakfast duties. Nellie Macpherson's clattering of trays, Marguerita's crashing of cutlery, Rosa's tuneless humming, had her frayed nerves on edge. Like Nora, when threatened with a migraine attack, she pressed a hand to her brow, but *her* headache didn't take fright and depart; it continued to ache and throb remorselessly. She had half a mind to ignore the letter; the way things were going, it could only contain bad news.

But was there ever anyone who could resist opening an unexpected letter? Its hand-delivered nature intrigued her and she ripped open the envelope.

Dear Elsa (she read),

Just to let you know that I *didn't* rat on you, whatever you might think. It doesn't matter much, I suppose, but I'd like you to know that. Sorry if I caused you embarrassment, smashing up the Priory and so on. I was mad. I thought I'd got my head together, but I haven't, I don't think I ever will. It's all just been too much, this summer, what with the police business and then making a tit of myself with you, etc. It was all my fault, thinking that you felt something for me. So don't blame yourself in any way. I've just had enough.

What *is* he on about? she thought crossly. This morning, I just cannot cope with that sort of melodrama.

Wherever I go I bring trouble. It won't happen anymore. I'm going to make sure that it doesn't. Remember me with affection. Please?
      Love,
      Mick.

So *that's* what he's on about, she thought. And then she read it again and she thought, oh no you don't, oh no you bloody don't.

32

Miss Vyner's friend Gertie, who'd carried her years so well, went to bed one night, drank her Ovaltine, read a chapter of *The Stars Look Down*, fell asleep, suffered a cerebral haemorrhage and didn't wake up the next morning. By this time Miss Vyner, increasingly incapacitated by arthritis, had had to leave Priory Lodge. Even with her Civil Service pension she couldn't run to a decent nursing-home, and the cheaper ones were suspect, so she had to consent to a place in the local authority old folks' home. Not quite the geriatric ward, she repeated constantly, to console herself. Not quite but nearly. Never a minute's peace, what with the relentless organisation of unwanted entertainment and the senile tantrums and the petty quarrelling. And not a compatible soul in the place. Imprisoned in her chair by her stiffened joints, flanked by an ancient male with no teeth and fewer brain cells and an old woman whose intelligence quotient made Ivy Pegler seem like the Brain of Britain, she set her face to the wall and concentrated upon dying. Her life had been characterised by meticulous organisation; she'd always called the tunes. Whereas death, she now discovered, was completely beyond her control, and only arrived in its own good time.

Mrs Pegler sent a wreath. Though, since joining the Spiritualists, she appreciated that such symbols of mourning were inappropriate. She awaited another message from Dad; she wanted him to tell her to move from Grey Towers where, although there were no sinister stains on the carpet, her fellow-residents betrayed a greater degree of snobbery than had been the case at Priory Lodge. But Dad, having spoken twice in rapid succession, was now silent. She began to reduce her contributions to the coffers, and had a shrewd idea that when they reached a certain level Dad would come through once again.

Occasionally, on her way to services, she caught sight of Mr Gentile going into Our Lady, Star of the Sea, but she never let on – there was no communication between the residents of Grey Towers and those of Priory Lodge, any more than there used to be between First Class passengers and Steerage.

The reason for Mr Gentile's regular attendance at church was the bankruptcy of the family firm. Although his own assets had been severed from it long since, the shame of seeing the family name brought low was no less keenly felt. In church he prayed to God for its resurrection. He even confessed the bad act that had taken place in Cairo in 1938 in case God was punishing him for this omission. The priest, after imposing a perfunctory penance, advised him to have a medical check-up, just to put his mind at rest. But it would have had the opposite effect and, as he'd lived this long not knowing, he reckoned he might safely continue in ignorance to the grave.

Had he felt the urge to confide, he would have found a willing ear in fellow-sufferer-from-financial-troubles Mrs Crookthorne. As she had feared, her capital was dwindling at a more rapid rate than her physical decay. She was obliged to move from Priory Lodge and into the local authority old folks' home just a few weeks after Miss Vyner was carried out of the same establishment feet first. But before this she had been apprehended by the store detective in a local supermarket attempting to smuggle out two tins of Danish ham in her handbag. In view of her age and the adverse publicity (some old dear, prosecuted for shoplifting only a couple of months before, had topped herself) the store decided to let her off with a warning. Had they known that in her wardrobe she had enough stolen provisions to stock a shop, they might not have been so compassionate. Faced with removal, Mrs Crookthorne realised the impossibility of transferring her hoard; she was loath to dump it, or give it away, so she ate it instead, and though she suffered a bout of that sort of indigestion that is so appallingly painful that death seems not only inevitable but greatly to be welcomed, she survived it and henceforward was subject to fewer and less intense pangs of hunger.

If he had known, Colonel Pritchard would have recognised

this effect as being closely related to a technique of behaviour modification known as flooding. A documentary on this subject was the first programme that he watched on his new portable television set. The programme was on Channel 4 and he watched it perforce because the aerial appeared to be a bit wonky and all he could get on the other three channels was snow and crackle. It was quite fascinating though: all these characters with phobias and obsessions and what-have-you were divided into groups. Some were given no treatment, some were given tranquillising drugs before the panic-inducing agent was introduced, and some, like Mrs Crookthorne, were subjected to the sudden introduction of vast quantities of whatever it was that obsessed their thoughts or gave them the screaming ab-dabs. One poor woman was surrounded by spiders – damn great hairy things; she screamed like a stuck pig, poor soul. He was reminded of Maud who, before he took her out East, had confessed to a horror of crawling insects. He'd never known just what she'd endured. He'd never known because she kept it from him, as she attempted to keep anything of a bothersome nature from him. A good sort. The very best.

He'd fiddled with the aerial, switched the set off and wiped away his tears. The years passed, moss grew upon her headstone, but the ache persisted.

The ache persisted too for Mr Edward Green, married now to Marion Pendennis. And every day that passed he grew more conscious of it. He climbed into his rose-pink sheets and thought longingly of the crisp white linen laundered by the first Mrs Edward Green. He tried frantically to disguise a hair-oil stain on the cornflower chintz chair-cover and remembered the impervious dark moquette and the antimacassars on the three-piece suite that Marion had sent to the tip. He stood miserably, alternately scalded and frozen, beneath the shower – he *couldn't* get the hang of it – and was reminded of soaping the first Mrs Edward Green's back in the big old cast-iron tub; sometimes, if the children were asleep, he'd got in with her. That, of course, was before his prostate trouble. But prostate trouble notwithstanding, he couldn't imagine soaping Marion's back in the bath, never mind getting in with her, even though she spent hour upon hour beautifying herself in there and got very ratty when she had to allow him in. "I can't think how we're supposed to manage in a house with only one lavatory," she'd say, witheringly, as though only persons of the lowest sort inhabited a house with such basic amenities.

He'd not have married her if Esmé Grey had agreed to be his wife. He'd cursed his luck for finding Esmé Grey after he'd met Marion. Otherwise, he told himself, it might have been a different story. A woman of such integrity, it seemed, that she couldn't contemplate stealing another woman's fiancé, her response to his proposal, during their final meeting at the French Circle, was so vehement that anyone might be forgiven for assuming her to be horrified rather than deeply regretful. He knew that she'd be discreet, so he married Marion. And thought longingly of the first Mrs Green.

Marion too began to doubt the wisdom of her decision to be his wife. Once the house was finished to her specification (or as near as his meanness would allow her to get: you'd think replacing a chain-pull lavatory with a low-slung syphonic cistern and bowl was an act of wild profligacy), it became apparent that nothing more exciting lay ahead for her. Quite quickly his admiration for her evaporated. His idea of conjugal bliss was to spend an evening reading the newspapers with his feet stretched out on the hearthrug. When she suggested a holiday he frowned and started counting up his granny bonds. He spat in the mornings in her beautiful lilac-tinted, everything-matching bathroom. He scratched himself. He had a dense fuzz of grey hair like barbed wire on his chest and his thin white legs were knotted with blue veins. Worst of all, he had no *go* about him. Jack, for all his disgusting sexual demands, had had plenty of that. So, all in all, she wasn't unduly upset when, wearing the leather mules she'd bought him, he tripped down the terrace steps in the back garden and fractured his skull on the concrete clothes-post and never regained consciousness. She sold up and went back to the Priory.

Mrs Grey enjoyed the French Circle. Friends that she made there introduced her to the Gramophone Society and the Writers' Club. A short story she'd written was accepted for publication. She didn't delude herself into thinking that she had any prospect of a literary career, but it was an achievement, and so pleasant to be able to present one's poetry for the positive criticism of like minds after all the years of it being subject to Ronald's ridicule. She was very sad when she heard of Edward Green's death; he had seemed a decent-enough fellow, although his caution at keeping Marion Pendennis on ice in case she, Esmé, should turn him down, amused her. Typical male, she thought, and wondered how he could possibly have imagined that she might welcome a proposal of marriage from him. For was it not written upon her face; thanks given for her timely relief from men and all the grief they could cause? She wondered if perhaps she was an undisclosed lesbian. Women who didn't like men were all supposed to be lesbians these days.

Peggy Johns read the same article about lesbianism in *The Observer*. The article featured interviews with established couples who lived together, it seemed, in the same responsible and staid fashion as did heterosexuals, long married. In everything but name and the capacity to impregnate each other, they informed the interviewer, they differed from no other ordinary married couple. Peggy Johns read about them and was deeply envious. Partners. Almost everyone had them. Except Peggy Johns. Her deprivation in this area seemed to affect her more the older she grew. She tried to immerse herself in her scrapbooks, devoted more time to the corner of the garden that she had persuaded Mrs Speakman to allow her to cultivate. (Mrs Speakman had handed it over gladly, wondered if she could divide the whole lot up between the residents; it would certainly save her money.) She visited the library with Mrs Grey, and once she went to the amateur operatics with Mrs Booth-Powell and, generally speaking, managed to fill the unforgiving moment. But every minute of every waking hour the knowledge was borne in upon her that her destiny had been wrong. She had become, she was sure, what she had been destined to become, but it was wrong, and no amount of adjusting and adapting and making do could cancel out the unhappy awareness of that fact.

"A bit fussy," Mrs Booth-Powell said, confidentially, apropos Peggy's garden. Neat rows of lobelia and salvia and alyssum there were, Union Jack colours, rigidly demarcated. Nothing bold or striking. "A bit spinsterish in fact," Mrs Booth-Powell said. Her garden in Old Colwyn had been crammed with sunflowers, hollyhocks, gladioli, flag irises, anything that gave you a show for your money. After all, if your prosperity couldn't be deduced from your living standards, the show you put on for your fellow man, what was the point of being prosperous? "There are no pockets in the shroud," she told Lily Crookthorne, "no rich men in the graveyard." And, after a lifetime devoted to responsible thrift, Mrs Booth-Powell began to spend. And discovered, having begun, how difficult it was to stop: clothes, holidays, hairdos, magazines, comfortable shoes, tickets for shows and chauffeur-driven hired cars to take her there. Life assurance policies were surrendered. Her son tried, unavailingly, to have her committed before his patrimony dwindled to nothing. And so the night he answered the telephone and found himself speaking to the hospital sister, the sigh that he emitted signified relief rather than sorrow. His mother had been coming back from Manchester where she'd been watching a performance of *Barnum* at the Opera House. She'd chatted to the chauffeur for a while and then her eyes had closed. He'd heard what he thought was a snore, but it wasn't a snore, it was the death-rattle.

Hilda Leggat and Muriel Selby took the *Sunday Telegraph*, so missed the article on lesbianism but had they read it it would not have occurred to them that they might be considered to fall within that category. Their relationship was characterised by a scrupulous regard for one another's privacy. Never once in the fifteen years they'd lived together had Muriel entered Hilda's bedroom without knocking, never once had they seen each other unclothed. If ever Muriel gave thought to the matter, it seemed to her, despite their contemporaneousness, that Hilda had taken over where Mother had left off: dominating, decision-making, demanding obedience. "Bullying" was the first word that had sprung to mind before being hurriedly rejected. Though Muriel was not entirely without spirit. At Easter, she expressly flouted Hilda's wishes (which were that they should have a walking holiday in the Lakes) and went off on a coach tour of the West Country. She was seated next to an elderly gentleman, a Mr Walter Wilson, a widower. They got on famously right from the start. In Ilfracombe he took her hand, in Paignton he kissed her, in Newquay (or "Nookie", as he pronounced it) he did the honourable thing and proposed marriage. He was a builder with a small business of his own and a bungalow built of Accrington brick in Accrington. She accepted him, but when she got home and told Hilda the news, Hilda got into her Beetle and drove over to see him. Muriel never knew what passed between them, she knew only that she was to take it that her engagement was no longer valid. She played war for a bit but was secretly rather relieved, the upheaval being too radical to be accomplished without an enormous expenditure of effort. The year after they compromised and went for a boating holiday on the Broads.

Mr Golding never had another holiday. "You," said one of the nurses cheerily, "your life's one long holiday." And although, as far as he could recall, holidays were not supposed to be characterised by dullness, he assumed this to be so. Dullness was not too hard to bear. He'd been accustomed to it most of his life, simply exchanging, at intervals, one routine for another. Only Priory Lodge had provided small diversions: a drink with the Colonel in The Railway Tavern or The Hawk and Bottle. Here in the hospital there was no one he'd want to make a pal of. Either they were a few bricks short of the load or else their bizarre behaviour precluded the development of intimacy. One of them ate the flowers out of the vases and another wept so copiously and so continuously that you wondered how there could be any moisture left in his body. Generally speaking, they were a rum lot. But he couldn't complain, his surroundings were pleasant, his food good and plentiful, his nights characterised by deep and uninterrupted slumber. And the cocktail of medication that they gave him to swallow daily had smothered the stirrings of those old terrible memories in which young female flesh and policemen and white rooms and blood and lavender-scented cachous and military bands all combined to terrify him until he was beyond the call of reason. Sometimes he vaguely remembered taking two old ladies for a drink after a funeral and how he'd felt, then, that a new sort of existence – free and brave and *normal* – was possible for him. But the recollection was only faint and spasmodic and then he swallowed his medicine and realised, with gratitude, how very much better off he was, protected from the anxiety-inducing aspects of living. In here all actions, save for the most fundamental, were performed on his behalf, all decisions were taken for him, all memories suffocated before they could surface and trouble him. He was lucky, really . . .

Rosa was lucky too. She proved to be so adept at looking after incurables and her understanding of English progressed at such a rate that the trustees of the home arranged for her to be trained as a psychiatric nurse at their expense. During her training she met and married a fellow-pupil. They produced two beautiful children, photographs of whom were sent back at intervals to the Portuguese hovel to which Rosa had no intention of ever returning, even for the briefest of visits, because her husband, who was a bit vague concerning geography and national characteristics, cherished pictures of grandees and haciendas and vineyards rolling across the white dusty plain, and would have been desperately disappointed to discover that his in-laws shared their living-quarters with a goat, several hens and a motor-cycle.

Marguerita, however, was not nearly so lucky. A persistent dragging pain in her pelvis, a profuse menstrual flow and a distension that she had attributed to a general condition of overweight proved to be the manifestations of cancer of the womb, and though she was assured that a hysterectomy would provide a complete cure, it was not so and the disease transferred itself to her breast. A radical mastectomy, they said, was the answer. They said it twice, once for each breast. But even after the removal of her entire stock of female organs, the ravening beast was not content and sited itself within her liver where excision and removal were not possible. The medical profession could do little else so very soon afterwards she died.

None of the residents of Priory Lodge knew of her death. Indeed, few of them even remembered Marguerita alive. Fresh preoccupations dominated, new people to gossip about. The same hierarchical nature of the place persisted but different incumbents now occupied positions of authority: from being the newest, lowest of the low member of society, Mr James joined Colonel Pritchard and Mesdames Pendennis and Grey at the forefront of the pecking order, and for a while prompted Mrs Pendennis whenever she regaled newcomers with tales of throat-cutting in the lift, devastation in the

Gloucester Room, a kitchen-hand suspected of criminal activity, adulterous entwining in the car park of The Hawk and Bottle.

Mrs Speakman, passing by, overheard the gossip, remembered briefly the boy, the young woman and the doctor, but rarely gave them any more thought. Nora Speakman lived almost exclusively in the present, occasionally raising her head to see what lay on the horizon. She had to: Rodney's asthmatic attacks were becoming more frequent and less amenable to the medication available. Sometimes he went blue in the face. She recognised that his chronic invalidity was a distinct possibility, remembered John Fox saying something about an aunt of his having died of asthma, recalled the skipping-a-generation nature of the disease and knew that her efforts to provide for him must be redoubled. Money was speculated so that it should accumulate. Refurbishment of Priory Lodge took place. "Your comfort is our aim" became a motto that was adhered to more strictly: rooms were more luxuriously furnished, extra bathrooms provided, recreational facilities introduced, a better class of staff employed. And the speculation paid off eventually; she was even able to poach a few clients from Grey Towers.

Superior staff did not include Nellie Macpherson, however. She finally retired and, driven out of her cramped flat by claustrophobia, spent a great deal of time at her sister's, boring her silly with tales of how she once served King Haakon of Norway and was given a pound by Jack Buchanan. Occasionally, on her way home, she encountered Mrs Randall, cooking still at the Priory (superior or not, her cooking couldn't be surpassed, given the proper ingredients), and they exchanged a word or two. Mrs Randall's Doreen had run off with a rep for office furniture that she'd met at a Scottish dancing-class. The most acrimonious of divorce actions was being fought. (Doreen's husband had sawed all their long-playing records in two: all the Barry Manilows and the Richard Claydermans. Spite, of course.) "Kids," Mrs Randall often said to Nellie Macpherson, with feeling.

Superior staff could not possibly include Mary Reilly, either. Des had gone back inside, fitted up for the Nottingham job. Out of work and no likelihood of being in it, skint, she found herself a new feller. He was the owner of the fairground stall who had donated a set of glasses to Mrs Crookthorne on the strength of her elderly spirit of adventure. He was not short of a few bob and he hit her less than Des had done, plus he owned a car which was very convenient for taking her to visit her boy, Wayne, who had been transferred from the Catholic children's home to an institute for young offenders in Cumbria. Mary wept, for all the lost years of motherhood until Sam, her new feller, told her to shut up for God's sake, if there was one sort he couldn't abide, it was a misery. So she wiped her eyes and pasted on her smile (no one wanted a misery), but there were times when she couldn't help thinking about her shortcomings as a parent and wondering just how much of the blame for her son's antisocial behaviour could be laid at her door.

Mrs Wynn occasionally grieved, too. Though only for herself. She never, consciously, acknowledged that she was in any way to blame for what she considered to be the dreadful waste of her son's life. "He could have been anything," she'd say, to anyone who'd listen; she'd cite the number of his O-levels and A-levels with their respective grades, as if to prove that while under her direct supervision, he had behaved like any normal intelligent young man. And mostly, when she spoke of him, it was as if he were dead.

But he wasn't dead. He was alive. Thanks to Elsa's quick action and persistence: an ambulance, a stomach-pump, a waiting-room vigil. Suicide, Emlyn had said, is more difficult than most people suppose: arteries are hard for the untrained to distinguish, tablets and drink induce vomiting, and so on, Emlyn had said, and quoted the Dorothy Parker poem, which surprised her because she hadn't been aware of his literary tastes, hadn't been aware, indeed, that he had any.

"Nick" she thought Mick had said when first she met him. Nick had died because of her negligence. And somehow, her success in preventing Mick from doing so helped, to a degree, to cancel out the guilt. A good act, she discovered, can be the only antidote to a bad one. "Why did you interfere?" he'd moaned, when he came round, tucked tight into the hospital bed. "Because you wanted me to," she'd replied.

On the last day of August she accompanied him to the

magistrates' court where, despite a demeanour so guilty-looking that it suggested the commission of mass murder, he was bound over to keep the peace. After he'd walked free they celebrated with a cup of coffee in Reece's and then she went into the stationer's next door and bought a packet of envelopes and a quantity of writing-paper and handed them to him. "Make some serious effort," she said. "You've messed about for long enough."

"I'm not sure if I can manage," he'd muttered, chewing the ragged skin around his fingernails, "on my own."

"You won't have to," she'd replied. She found him a room close to hers in Manchester and a job serving behind the bar in the students' union. If she was honest with herself, she had to admit that she was glad of his company during the first alien and confusing weeks of her course. After that she began to settle down, familiar faces started to emerge from the throng of strangers, the routine of her working days established itself, the projects she was expected to tackle seemed less daunting.

In the meantime she encouraged him to try for jobs, jollied him along when the inevitable flood of rejections fell through the letter-box, pressed his suit whenever he was summoned for an interview. Eventually he was taken on as a management trainee with a chain-store – the same chain that was still owned by members of the Golding family, though Mick wasn't aware of that. "I'll give it a month," he told her. At the end of six months they transferred him to Birmingham. He wrote to her, telling her that it was a pain in the arse but the money wasn't bad. From Luton he wrote to say that he'd gained promotion. The following Christmas he returned for a flying visit from Wellingborough and talked a lot about a girl called Alison. He kissed Elsa under the mistletoe in the art school foyer, a fraternal kiss. "I'm in furniture and fittings at the moment," he said. "Following in father's footsteps." And he imitated his father's violent tic, but without rancour, and then looked down at the crown of her head and said, "Christ, Elsie, you've got a grey hair!" And she said, "All right, no need to mock, you won't be that far behind."

But far enough. There was a Boxing Day party to which, she gathered, he was escorting Alison. Alison was a nurse, sounded a decent sort. Postcards arrived from him, irregularly, from Birmingham, Luton and Wellingborough. One day, she supposed, there might be a wedding invitation, a Christmas card maybe, the names at the bottom of it increasing as the years went by.

And she'd feel sad, because good acts might induce a temporary glow but couldn't prevent the sadness of knowing that growing-up meant drifting away.

At the end of the first term all those on Elsa's course were provided with a grant to take them to London to look round the art galleries. She went with another mature student, a woman of around her own age, a divorcee with a couple of small children, called Sarah. Sarah had been obliged to move back to her widowed mother's house in order that the kids could be looked after while she was at college and the arrangement was resulting in four sets of frayed nerves. So for her at least, the trip represented a most welcome break and she was determined to make the most of it and never let up for an instant, dragging Elsa to every affordable attraction that presented itself: to the tour of the major galleries were added films and concerts and exhibitions. Sarah was especially interested in photography. And so it was that at the Galeries Nouveaux, somewhere in W1, Elsa came face to face with the likeness of a startled Rodney Speakman and, although she'd known that Diana's exhibition was scheduled for the end of the year, it still came as something of a shock.

She moved around the room, looking at beaches at sunset and little girls with flowers in their hair and three old ladies sitting stolid in a seafront shelter. "They look just like those three old ladies in that painting of yours," Sarah said. "They do, don't they?" Elsa replied.

That night in the hotel bedroom, while Sarah was in the bath, she took Emlyn's latest letter from her handbag and reread it, though she already knew it by heart.

". . . I am so lonely for you. It seems an age since we were together and the days might be short but the nights are so long . . ."

His handwriting had surprised her, being large and neat and legible. His style too had surprised her, veering as it did towards a fulsomeness that had only rarely been expressed in person. She had been quite seduced by those letters; compared with the thrill of receiving and reading them, their actual encounters seemed a bit of an anticlimax.

". . . Diana is off to London again in the New Year. She'll be staying there for a few weeks, so I thought I might take some time off and come over to see you. If that suits . . ."

A note of humility. No mistaking now who had the upper hand.

". . . things are hectic, what with the whooping cough epidemic and trying to tie up all the ends before I leave. We've had a lot of enquiries about the house but no definite offer as yet . . ."

Diana wanted to move nearer to London. Indeed, Diana intended to move nearer to London, whether he accompanied her or not. Her late-blooming career required her to be closer to the centre of things. Her "hobby" as he had called it had now become her profession and maybe she was no longer in need of his care and protection. On the wagon now for the best part of a year, her life had validity, incentive. She presumed, she told him, that his affair with Elsa was over, but it was less important to her than it had been when she found out about it.

So he had given in his notice at the health centre and put the house up for sale, although his movements depended to a great extent on the decision he would make during the next few months. They depended also, to an extent, on the decision that Elsa would make.

". . . of course, wherever I end up, it doesn't mean that we can't continue to see each other. That is, if she and I decide to stay together. Otherwise . . . I love you, Elsa. I know you don't want to be tied down, but that doesn't stop me wanting to do it . . ."

She took a writing-pad from her bag and replied to the letter. She too wrote "I love you", and that the future without him seemed inconceivable, and these were not simply the conventions of love-letter writing, they were the expression of sentiments that were sincerely felt: in the course of her writing she stopped and closed her eyes and imagined that they were together and for a few minutes she ached, physically, for him, for the touch of his hand and the lilt of his voice and the steady regard of his golden-green eyes.

But, on the other hand, there was the competing attraction of losing herself in work, the equally seductive thrill of achievement, the glow that derived from the favourable criticism of informed opinion, and the easy fluid relationships that prevailed in the art school – and a certain tutor who looked at her with an eye that was far from being wholly professional.

". . . I miss you," she wrote, "not all the time, but some of the time so much that all I want to do is to jump on to a train that will take me back to you and our summer-house and Captain chasing rabbits and the birch trees rustling. And yet sometimes it all seems such a long time ago . . ."

Nothing will be allowed to impinge to the extent that it could impede my progress, she had told herself, quite illogically in view of the fact that she had already acknowledged that the proper experiencing of life demands constant impingement and that true affection is too rare and too precious to be deliberately squandered.

"I suppose," she wrote, "everything there looks so very different in the winter: the sands deserted, the amusements all closed down, only the hardiest of souls taking their constitutionals along the marsh road (and possibly Rodney Speakman with his binoculars) . . ."

A few months later, his future still undecided, Emlyn sent her a cutting from the local paper. Alan Smith, a twenty-seven-year-old commercial traveller from Croydon, it said, had been convicted of aggravated burglary, a crime which had been committed on May 23rd last year. He had pretended to be a house-buyer, gained entrance, and assaulted and robbed an elderly lady. He had been sentenced to three years in jail.

So that seemed to be that. Nora, at least, would be relieved, might be able to relax her constant vigilance. It was love that prompted it: that stifling attention, that stultifying chaperonage, that inability to see things clearly because of fear. Love could be terrible. Unless a mistake had been made. It was so damn difficult to spot the mistakes until long after you'd made them, and sometimes they were impossible to rectify.

"Dear Emlyn," she wrote, "*Cariad*. But I need more time . . ."